Sins
of
Intent

Randy Roeder

Dusty Typewriter Press • Cedar Rapids

Copyright © 2017 Randy Roeder

Cover design by Jenn Roeder

Cover photo courtesy of the History Center, a facility of the Linn County Historical Society.

Dusty Typewriter Press
5001 1st Ave SE
Ste 105 #243
Cedar Rapids, IA 52402
http://dusty.typewriter.press

ISBN 978-1-940509-24-2

First Edition April 2017

Version 1.0.2

For Kristina,

I wish we'd had more time

1

As Nick Thilmany piloted the full-sized Buick Electra through the deserted streets, his hands shook so badly he could barely keep the lumbering gunboat between the lines. Even the radio failed to distract him. George Wallace ripping on Bobby Kennedy usually made for good entertainment, but it would take more than that to calm his nerves tonight. Stealing the car was bad enough, but when that cop followed him for five blocks, he nearly lost it.

What had started as a perfectly good day began to deteriorate when his employer, Midwest Vending & Novelties Company, wanted him to haul a load of cigarette machines to Cedar Rapids. The front part of the delivery truck's cargo compartment included a few items not on the manifest: four slot machines, a dozen color televisions, and a thousand cartons of cigarettes that had disappeared from a Chicago warehouse earlier in the week.

The Des Moines-to-Cedar Rapids route usually went off without a hitch, but whenever the haul involved unscheduled merchandise, the boss assigned Gabby Khoury to ride along. Gabby was a talkative, excitable Syrian and, in Nick's opinion, a bit shy in the mental stability department.

When Nick tried to get Khoury pulled off the assignment, his boss cut him off coldly.

"George Rahbani is a good customer, and Gabby is some kinda cousin to him. Georgie places a lot of machines, he knows how to move merchandise, and he makes his payments on time. We wanna keep him happy. You don't like drivin' for us, just let me know and we'll find somebody else."

Nick knew better than to argue. "No problem. I can handle it."

Khoury had talked non-stop for the entire trip. While Nick found it hard to believe the man's nickname had nothing to do with his endless jabber, Gabby claimed it was short for Gabriel. Nick didn't believe a word of it. Just when he thought his companion had run out of things to say, Gabby launched into a story about getting sent to reform school for stealing hubcaps. The tale hadn't been much the first six times Nick had heard it, and it didn't improve any with age. By the time they reached the warehouse, Nick was ready to run through the streets screaming.

The truck unloaded, he'd been only too happy to walk a few blocks to the C.I.O. Tavern, leaving Georgie and Gabby back at the warehouse swapping stories. George Rahbani gave him the creeps. Permanently angry, the guy reminded him of a volcano ready to blow. If it ever happened, you knew it'd be ugly, and you knew you'd want at least a county between you.

Rahbani had been bad enough, but then the guy's psycho son Habi showed up—after the work was done. A skinny guy in his late twenties, the younger Rahbani imagined he was some kind of rock and roll hoodlum. As lazy as the day is long, with a mouth full of insults and as dumb as a bag of hammers, Habi Rahbani was a punk so full of himself Nick had wanted to beat him to pulp from the first time they met—a case of hate at first sight. The only reward he'd get for creaming the little snot would be a free ride to the six-by-two farm, so Nick left him alone. He didn't think much of raising daisies.

Nick had finished three cigarettes and two beers by the time Gabby rejoined him. If the man had been wound up before, he was flying now. It happened every time Habi showed up. Nick suspected Habi was feeding Gabby uppers.

"Nicky, I got us a job—good money, but we gotta wait until late to make the delivery," Gabby said.

"Sounds good. When's the pick up?"

"After midnight. I thought we could grab some steaks and go watch the dancers out at the Moonglow."

Great, just what Nick needed. "Tell you what," he said, "I'm tired and won't be good company. I'll take the truck and meet you back here at one."

Gabby looked crestfallen. "Your loss, but if that's what you really want, fine with me."

Congratulating himself on his escape from an evening spent with a certifiable looney, Nick drove downtown and checked into a cheap room at the Hotel Magnus. The late pickup meant tonight's load involved hot property. *No biggie*, he thought, *a few hours' sleep will do me good.* He yawned, stretched out on the bed, and conked out like a dead man.

But now, at the wheel of the Buick, heading east on Sixteenth Avenue with his guts quivering, Nick wished he'd abandoned Gabby the minute he showed up with a stolen car. Tonight's cargo was more than he bargained for.

"This is as far as I go," he said. "I never been mixed up in anything like this in my life, and if you think I'm gonna spend another second in this goddamn car, you're outta your tree. One of us coulda brought the truck along, but no, you thought somebody would see it. Now, no matter what route we take, we gotta walk a couple a miles, cross the bridge like sittin' ducks, and cut through Colored Town. I hope they're still not mad about that guy who shot Martin Luther King. We'll stick out like sore thumbs over there and might as well be carryin' a sign that says 'Stupid White Guys.'"

"I told you Nicky, I brought fishin' poles. Anybody sees us on the bridge or close to the river, they'll think we're doin' some night-

3

time catfishin'. You worry too much about the East Side. I grew up in Cedar Rapids. You don't bother nobody in Colored Town, they don't bother you."

Nick grunted. Anxiety roared through his chest like a chainsaw revving at full power.

"Habi will be mad if we don't finish this," said Gabby.

"Screw Habi. This is close enough, and I ain't crazy enough to drive another block in this wagon."

"We're still a few blocks from the river, Nicky."

"You saw that cop behind us. We were lucky. What if somebody reported the car? I'm outta here. Switch off the dome light. We don't want nobody to see us."

Gabby reached for his pocketknife and smashed the light.

"What the hell did you do that for?" asked Nick.

"I don't know nothin' about findin' a switch."

Nick sighed and flicked off the headlights as he pulled up to the J Avenue stop sign. He turned right and eased the Buick into the dark corner of a supermarket parking lot. At this rate, he wouldn't get back to Des Moines until after sunrise, and he hoped he'd never see this stinking burg again. Damn Habi, damn Gabby, and damn this job. The Buick Electra rolled to a stop. Nick put the car in park and opened the door. His wobbly legs almost failed him as he exited. He bent over and vomited.

"Don't slam the goddamn door, Gabby."

"You think I'm stupid, Nicky?"

You don't wanna know, thought Nick. He picked up a tackle box, watched Gabby grab the fishing poles, and set off beside him. They abandoned the car with its engine running and all four doors open.

———————————

In the neighborhood everybody called Bohemie Town, Eddie Brada dribbled a basketball across the asphalt lot of the new Me Too supermarket. His best friend, Billy Rehak, walked beside him. Eddie was in high spirits following a successful escape from his parents' house. It hadn't been easy. He'd had to sneak by his folks' doorway, an entry usually left open to guard against such nocturnal exits.

Luck had smiled on him. Not only were his folks snoring like lumberjacks, he'd managed to pilfer a pack of Pall Malls from a half-full carton on the kitchen counter. The householders' nightly consumption of a six-pack of Grain Belt didn't do much to promote their alertness—a circumstance Eddie counted on.

Eddie bagged groceries and did odd jobs at the Me Too. Earlier in the day, he'd seized the opportunity of a lifetime. The hurried unloading of a late delivery had resulted in a six-pack of Wiedemann's Bohemian Beer left beside a stack of fruit crates. Eddie's boss had been distracted when called out front to deal with an irate customer complaining about some spoiled milk. The exchange grew testy, and the woman's voice could be heard throughout the store—the situation all out of proportion to the perceived outrage. Eventually placated with a replacement container twice the size of the first, the vindicated shopper withdrew, and the boss went out front for a smoke, muttering something along the lines of, "No job is worth this bullshit."

As his shift wore on, Eddie realized the beer was long forgotten. When the opportunity arose, he'd slipped the bottles of amber delight out the back entrance and into a nook behind the trash barrels.

Now the time was ripe for a return visit. A warm, starlit June night, a basketball, twenty cigarettes, and six bottles of beer, it was the stuff his dreams were made of. Realizing the thumping basketball might attract attention, Eddie quit dribbling as he and Billy crossed the empty lot and made for the back of the building. The Me Too's trash barrels bordered on the parking lot of the Safari Lounge, a disreputable gin mill whose customers were exiting due to the state-mandated closing time.

With one eye on the bar's neon-lit jungle foliage, Eddie and his friend slipped into the shadows and waited—listening to slamming car doors and the alcohol-enhanced conversations of the Safari's departing clientele.

"They're gone," Eddie observed as he pulled a church key from his pocket and opened the first of the glossy brown soldiers. "We can relax."

"I don't know about you, but I need a cigarette," Billy replied. "I'm hooked bad on them coffin nails. I got so shook the other day I had to smoke cardboard to keep my nerve up."

Eddie didn't buy it. "Right, and you're a real man who needs pussy, drinks liquor, and gets into fights on Saturday night. You've never drove a car or had a girlfriend. You don't need pussy—you are a pussy."

Billy exhaled, laughed, and responded, "Get bent, butt wipe."

"Jag-off," said Eddie.

The night was glorious, the crickets loud, and the beer warm. Experienced enough to avoid getting smoke sick, Eddie poured his beer down his throat a bit too quickly. Within the hour, between the cigarettes and the beer, he'd reached the state his elders referred to as feeling no pain. All thoughts of nighttime basketball left his mind as he and his partner in crime watched the lights of the Safari flicker into darkness.

After reviewing a litany of dirty jokes, he and Billy moved on to the mysteries of the female anatomy. When Billy expressed disappointment that Playboy showed only the top half, Eddie voiced his agreement. He considered it one of life's great tragedies that the racy magazine left so much detail to the imagination. The discussion of life's pressing biological problems came to an abrupt halt when a car slipped into the Me Too lot with its headlights turned off.

Eddie watched the antics of the exiting driver and his passenger with astonishment. The driver threw up when he got out of the car, and the men began arguing. The strangest part of the entire episode occurred when the men removed fishing equipment from the car and abandoned the vehicle with its doors open and engine running.

"They're eight blocks away from the river," said Billy. "They must not know where it is."

"Maybe they're from out of town, or stupid." Eddie fell silent as he pondered the scene that had taken place. More puzzled than alarmed, he could think of no reason for the men's behavior.

A few minutes later, Billy said, "I wonder when they're coming back."

"Don't know and don't care," replied Eddie.

"Let's go for a ride, Mr. I-Drove-on-the-Farm."

"What if they come back?" Eddie cautioned.

"They've got fishing poles and a tackle box. If they haven't come back yet, it means they're going all the way to the river."

Of one mind, Eddie and Billy broke for the car. Eddie took the wheel and slammed the door shut. Billy took shotgun. Eddie had learned to drive on his aunt's farm, and discovered the Buick—with its power steering and automatic transmission—easier to handle than his Uncle John's Allis-Chalmers tractor.

He drove carefully, heading for the REA dam on the river road. Sensing a distraction on the passenger side, he turned to see Billy reaching under himself, looking as if he'd just been goosed.

"Geez, what am I sitting on?" Billy muttered as he groped the seat beneath him. "Woo hoo! I found a pocketknife." He waved his loot in the air.

"Put the radio on WLS," Eddie ordered as he focused on driving. The voice of Ringo Ron Riley soon filled the car, promising "the hits would keep on happening."

"Think Ringworm Ron's better than Clark Weber?" Billy wondered as the sound of Tommy James and the Shondells' "Mony, Mony" filled the car.

"Don't know, don't care. Look in back, and see if you can find anything good."

Billy turned around. "There's a dip net and some Emil John's Stink Bait and a bunch of blankets stuffed down in front of the back seat."

"No wonder it smells in here, you'd think somebody would know enough to keep stink bait in the trunk."

"Dip net or pocketknife?" asked Eddie.

"I'll take the dip net," said Billy as he handed Eddie the knife.

Eddie pocketed the knife. "Pull up those blankets and see if there's anything else we can use."

Eddie braked for a stop sign and pocketed the knife. Intent on his search, Billy had leaned so far over the back of the seat that his butt stuck in the air. Eddie couldn't resist. He gave his partner's backside a good whack, and grabbing his legs, shoved him over the seat.

"What'd ya do that for?"

Eddie howled with laughter.

"Hey, there's a woman under the blankets back here."

"Right, and my old lady French kisses a carp before breakfast every day."

"Holy shit, Eddie. She's dead."

2

"Another beer, Cletus?"

I nodded. It was Saturday morning, the first day of June, 1968. The Avenue buzzed with reports of a woman's body found in an abandoned car over at the Me Too store. I didn't want to think about it, so I'd taken refuge in one of the back booths at Ernie's Avenue Tavern, a place where a man could drink his breakfast and nobody would raise an eyebrow.

Ernie's opened early to catch the guys coming off the graveyard shift, and though it was almost eleven, a handful of packing plant workers were still at it. Ralph, the resident rummy, sat quietly by himself a little way off from them. His fondness for booze had long ago rotted his brain. When he decided to strike up a conversation, all you got were mumbles, drool, and the stray bit of spit in the face. I'd learned to avoid him.

I'd come to Ernie's to sort through the mess I made of my life, and I didn't want to care about a dead woman in a car. Everybody dies somewhere—at home, the hospital, in a car, or maybe the river—and somehow—heart attack, cancer, a gunshot to the gut, a steering column though the chest. None of it's important to the deceased. Heck, they're not even around to think about it. For those of us left behind, the details provide an endless source of fascination. Throw in a little guilt, speculation, and recrimination, and it's the stuff of the best gossip around.

But I didn't feel like gossip, and I didn't want to socialize. Normally, I wouldn't spend a beautiful day in a Sixteenth Avenue dive watching the rippling waters of a Hamm's clock, but when I do, I don't want to waste my time thinking about bodies in cars. I want to think about how I ended up in Cedar Rapids. I want to brood.

Five years ago, I had a wife, a family, and a business in Bellevue, Iowa, a little town on the banks of the Mississippi River. The third generation of my family to run the local haberdashery, I sold suits to bankers, overalls to farmers, sports shirts to golfers, and underwear and shoes to all of them. I met my wife some twenty-five miles north of town in what passed for a city in our area—Dubuque—a burg thirty times larger than Bellevue with sixty times the glamour.

I'd signed up for lessons at Faber's School of Dance on South Jackson Street. I originally intended to use my budding dance skills to date as many lovely ladies as possible, but something unexpected happened. I discovered I was good. I had rhythm, and I had the moves. Tango, rumba, waltz, or cha-cha, I caught on quickly and discovered the gift of gab I'd mastered as a boy working in a clothing store made me the life of the studio's weekly parties.

Within a few months, Edwin Faber, the headman and owner, offered me a job as a teacher. I couldn't see it as a career, but the owner of a small-town men's shop can always use extra cash. I hired on for four nights a week and arranged for my cousin to help out at the store.

Faber's kept its male instructors on a short leash. No scandal, no off-hours fraternizing with the female customers, and no showing up unless dressed to the nines. The setup didn't square with my reasons for learning to dance, but I didn't care. I was having too much fun. Then one Wednesday evening, Edwin introduced me to

Myra Hinkley, a new student who'd signed up for the four-lesson introductory course. Myra—a pretty brunette—had an average smile, an average bust, and average dancing ability. As bland as a glass of milk, nothing about her impressed me.

By then I was familiar with the routine. No matter if the girl had the grace of a water buffalo and couldn't count to four, I was to charm her into thinking she was the next Ginger Rogers and an unbelievably fulfilling social life awaited her if only she'd contract with us for a series of lessons. One of the seamier sides of the operation, the business depended on it; no matter how good the teacher, continued employment depended on getting names on the dotted line.

"Hey, Ernie." A customer's voice echoed through the bar. "It's time for the noon news. Turn on the TV—KCRG. See if there's anything about the woman at the Me Too."

Ernie put down his towel, reached up, and switched on the set. The newscast led off with a segment on the car at the Me Too. The grainy black and white picture showed a late model car surrounded by policemen. A crowd of onlookers stood in the background, and as far as I could determine, officials had already removed the body. A disappointment from the get go, the story failed to answer the two questions anyone who'd heard of the incident wanted to know. Was it murder, and did I know her?

Though I watched along with the rest of the bar, I resented the distraction. The newscast was anything but newsy. Worse, it interrupted my ruminations on the past. I still missed Myra, and feared I was losing my memory of her a bit at a time. She deserved a fate better than that of a fading image on an old photograph.

From the first second of our first meeting, I'd known Myra was attracted to me. She had an air of vulnerability that brought out my protective instincts. I knew I'd have no trouble pressuring her into signing a contract for a series of dance lessons, but for once my conscience got the better of me. By the end of the third lesson, I still hadn't gone into my sales pitch.

"Cletus?" she asked.

"Clete," I said.

"Cletus, aren't you going to try to sell me a contract?"

I was floored. Things weren't going the way I expected. When Myra looked up at me for an answer, I was tongue-tied. For the first time, I noticed the intelligence behind her brown eyes, and I observed her smile transforming itself into an ever-so-wicked grin. She was playing with me. The thought I ought to get to know her better hit me like a hammer between the eyes. The realization served to increase my paralysis.

"Cletus, everyone knows dance studios try to sell you a contract."

"You can call me Clete."

"Cletus, didn't you ever learn to flirt?"

She signed a six-month contract, but I'd blown the opportunity. She never did call me Clete. The months passed, and I learned almost nothing about her. Myra played me like a fish, letting me run with my fantasies, then reeling me back into the cold light of dashed hopes. By the time of our last lesson, I had no contract extension, no date, and no hope. As we walked off the floor for the last time, I broke into my standard farewell speech.

"Well Myra, that was our last lesson. You've been a wonderful student, and if you ever decide to continue with your dance lessons, be sure to think of us here at Faber's."

"Cletus," she replied, "aren't you going to ask me for a date?"

Hooked, landed, skinned, gutted, and fried. Apparently, her air of vulnerability was matched in equal part by my air of stupidity. Not that I cared, I was smitten.

I suggested a Saturday evening at Timmerman's Supper Club, a swanky venue perched atop a hill overlooking the Mississippi. Located across the river in East Dubuque, the venue was architecturally modern, quiet and cool, and patronized by businessmen, doctors, and lawyers. All in all, an expensive place, but I wanted to impress.

I'd chosen wisely. Her eyes sparkled as I led her through the double doors to the lounge where we awaited the call for our reservation. We took seats at the bar. No noises from the dining area intruded on our conversation as the sound system seduced us with the silky voice of Patti Page and her beautiful *Tennessee Waltz*. Just the set-up to show a younger woman how much I knew about the world, I was getting ready to help her with the drink menu when the bartender came over to us.

"Hi Clarence, I'll have a martini," she said by way of greeting.

"Why hello Myra, how've you been?"

Strike one.

Clarence asked for my order as I picked my shattered illusions off the floor. "I'll have a Wisconsin Old-Fashioned," I replied.

"Oh, you mean where they substitute brandy for the people who don't like the taste of whiskey?" Myra asked.

Strike two.

"Cletus, this is my Uncle Clarence from Maquoketa. I came over here to visit one afternoon, and he made me a martini."

Ball one.

Clarence was busy, so Myra and I exchanged pleasantries as we waited for our reservation. When the hostess called our table, we took our drinks into the dining room, ordered, and had our first real conversation in all the months we'd known each other. I learned Myra had moved to Dubuque from Maquoketa, the seat of government for the county that included my hometown. Away from home for the first time, Myra worked as a sales girl at the cosmetics counter at Roshek's Department Store. Her mother was a nurse, and her father worked for the county.

"So, what does your dad do?" I asked.

"He's the County Sheriff."

"Your dad is Brute Hinkley?"

"Brutus, Cletus."

"What?"

"His name is Brutus."

We ordered the lobster and a bottle of white wine, and as the evening went on, I lost count of my balls and strikes. We chatted easily about what we were looking for in life and enjoyed as pleasant a dinner as two human beings can have. I liked the girl and wanted to play this one carefully. I drove her home, kissed her goodnight, and made a date for the next week. No home run, but at least I didn't strike out.

We enjoyed spending time together and continued to date. Myra's rooming house didn't allow male visitors. Since I lived in Bellevue, we contented ourselves with regular trips to Julien Dubuque's grave, a secluded historical site that served as a lover's lane. It didn't take me long to realize I wanted to make Myra my wife. I figured decency required I'd wait a year before popping the question.

We were in the car going at it hot and heavy one night when Myra sat up and gave me a look I'll never forget.

"Cletus," she said, "aren't you going to ask me to marry you?"

Eddie Brada picked up the phone. Billy was on the line. It had been eight hours since their ill-fated joy ride.

"You make it back home in time?" Billy asked.

"Yeah, you?"

"I wouldn't be on the phone if I didn't. We gotta talk. Jones Park?"

Eddie volunteered an okay, went outside to his bicycle, and pedaled up the hill to the park. He rode hard, but Billy beat him to the rendezvous. As he walked his bike across the grass to their favorite picnic table, Eddie noticed Billy wasn't looking well. Eddie could relate to the situation. He didn't feel well himself.

A full five minutes passed before either spoke.

"Eddie, my mom went to buy groceries this morning. The cops had half the lot blocked off, and everybody in the store was talking about the dead woman in the car. There was blood on that blanket. What if they find out about us and think we killed that woman?"

"They won't. They'll never know we were in the car. We did everything right."

To Eddie, it seemed like they had. At Billy's insistence, he'd pulled over on Mallory Street and parked. A quick look over the back seat convinced him Billy had told the truth. Somehow, they'd managed to swipe a car with a dead woman in it. The shock of the discovery had sobered him immediately. After a few minutes' consideration, he drove a panic-stricken and tearful Billy back to the Me Too parking lot. Eddie parked the car where they found it. They abandoned the vehicle just as they'd discovered it—with the engine running and doors open. The task completed, they went back to their homes.

"Eddie, I left my basketball in the car."

"You what? You dick-brained numb-nuts!"

Eddie knew the history of the basketball he'd dribbled across the Me Too lot. Billy's brother copped it from Wilson Junior High a couple of years earlier. The ball was marked WJH. Given that half the basketballs on the southwest side bore similar markings, he concluded it'd be hard to trace it back to them. Although they'd almost certainly left fingerprints behind, neither he nor Billy had ever been printed, so he believed they were okay.

"Maybe we should go to the police. We didn't murder anybody," said Billy.

"You need to get your head examined. We stole a car. Even if we did bring it back, it's reform school. Don't know about you, but the state home in Eldora isn't my kind of place."

Eddie spent a miserable two hours with Billy at the picnic table. Short of sleep, sick with worry, and scared, no amount of talking could erase the horror of the night before. Having solved nothing, Eddie left his friend sitting at the picnic table and headed off to his job at the supermarket.

———————————

Billy rode his bike over to St. Ludmila Catholic Church, mounted the steps, and slipped inside. He waited in the shadows until a cassocked Father Blazek strode down the aisle and entered the oak confessional. Seeing none of the other would-be penitents were ready, Billy slipped into the darkened box, knelt, and looking at the cloth-covered screen, whispered to an unseen presence.

"In the name of the Father, and of the Son, and of the Holy Ghost. Amen. I confess to Almighty God, and to you, Father, that I have sinned. My last confession was four weeks ago. Since then, I've taken the Lord's name in vain about ten times a day. I used foul language maybe twelve times a day. I drank three stolen beers, even though I was underage, and smoked stolen cigarettes six times. I had impure thoughts daily, and I stole one car. I'm sorry for these sins and the sins of my whole life, especially for the sin of car-stealing."

If Father Blazek recognized Billy's voice, he didn't let on. He spoke. "You've been busy, and it hasn't been the work of the Lord. Before I give you absolution, I need to know more about the situation with the car."

"I didn't drive. We gave it back." Billy could feel butterflies in his stomach. "We put it back where we found it and didn't break anything."

Billy waited in an eternity of silence.

"You took the car for a spin without the owner knowing it. That's a serious matter, even if you didn't break anything. You know what you did is a serious sin and wrong on many levels?"

Downcast, Billy replied, "Yes, Father."

"You know what restitution is?" God's substitute intoned. "It costs money to operate a car. You used some of the owner's gas and oil, there are extra miles on the car, and the owner is likely to experience mental distress if your joy ride is discovered. You need to make up for the financial damage to the owner."

"I can't make a payment, Father. I don't know who the car belongs to. It was in a parking lot."

"Sometimes an individual victim can't be found and restitution can be made to a charitable group or for the improvement of society. For your forgiveness to be complete, you must make restitution equal to the amount of trouble you've caused."

"Yes, father."

"For your penance, say three Our Fathers and three Hail Marys, and for the car, a rosary every night for ten days—on your knees. For your restitution, Mission Sunday is coming up in two weeks. You can put an offering in the special Mission Sunday collection basket. Now, say a good Act of Contrition."

Billy recited his Act of Contrition, was told his sins were forgiven, and advised to go in peace. As he exited the church, he thought through the details of his restitution assignment. Gas cost twenty-nine cents a gallon. He and Eddie probably used a gallon. Of course, the Electra was a big car, so to be on the safe side, he'd better figure two. They couldn't have used more than a nickel's worth of oil. The wear and tear on the car might come to another quarter. The total came to something like eighty-eight cents.

Eddie would be responsible for half that.

Randy Roeder

3

Monday morning. As I folded polo shirts in the menswear department at Killian's Department Store, I looked up to see Pudge Davis skirting a display of Jockey shorts. A police detective and persistent pain in my neck, I'd asked the man not to visit me at work. I didn't know it at the time, but asking Pudge not to do something guaranteed you'd get the opposite behavior. I made eye contact with Pudge and called to my supervisor, "Reg, something's come up. I'll be back in fifteen."

I thought of Pudge as a parting gift from my former father-in-law. Brute Hinkley never forgave me for Myra's death. Not that I couldn't understand, I'd never forgiven myself. I'd have given anything to erase just nineteen hours of my life, but no matter how much armchair philosophers talk about second chances, I could never go back to undo the mess I'd made. My monumental selfishness and stupidity had killed my wife—as surely as if I'd wrapped my fingers around her neck and strangled her.

At Myra's interment service, Brute called me aside for a chat.

"Cletus, the wife and I are getting a court order to keep the kids. No judge in this or any other county is going to give you custody after the stunt you pulled. So listen up, and listen good. If I ever catch you within twenty miles of either of those kids, I'll kill you on the spot. No hello, no chat, no time for you to think. You'll be dead. I see you from the front, you're dead. I see you from the back, you're dead. I see you asleep, you're dead. You're talking to a minister, you're talking to a cop, you're dead. Dead, get it? Dead, dead, dead."

I got it. Dead, dead, dead. Brute Hinkley had a reputation for being good with his fists and quick with his sap. He'd killed two men in the line of duty, one of them with his bare hands. I did not doubt for a minute he was capable of killing me and meant every word he said. At any rate, my kids were better off with the Hinkleys than with a father capable of making such a colossally stupid mess of his life. The one blessing in an otherwise unredeemable situation was also my biggest heartbreak—my little boy and girl were so young they'd never remember me.

"I understand, Brute. I'll be out of the county by the weekend."

Brute Hinkley wasn't quite done with me though. On learning I'd moved to Cedar Rapids, he made a call to the local police department and embroidered on a run-in I had with the police back in Dubuque. The Cedar Rapids cops put me in their sexual deviants file. Although Brute hoped to force me even farther from my home, I kept my word, stayed put, and didn't knuckle under to the pressure. Still, every time anything remotely related to a sex crime came up, I could count on a visit from good old Pudgie.

I headed toward the side door with Pudge at my heels. We were on the street in less than a minute.

"What's it this time?" I folded my arms across my chest.

Pudge looked up at the sky. "When a good-looking woman ends up dead in a car, I go down my list of perverts and ask questions. And you know what? You're on my list."

Crap, the dead woman at the Me Too. "A dead woman and you automatically think of me? The connection's a bit thin."

Having lost interest in the sky, Pudge looked over my shoulder. "Sometimes women get dead when playtime gets too rough," he said. "Maybe you didn't mean to do anything, but maybe you snapped when she wouldn't play your little dungeon games."

He waited for my reaction. Didn't get one. "So, where were you Friday night?"

I told him. "I finished giving dance lessons at ten and then went over to the Golden Key. George Rahbani finally had the sense to schedule Suzanne LaRue on a Friday instead of bringing in some out-of-towner. I went home at midnight."

"Anybody with you the rest of that night, Pervie? Oh, I forgot, maybe you were all tied up." Pudge stepped forward and slapped me on the back, snorting at his attempt at humor.

"I was alone," I said, recoiling from his touch.

Cedar Rapids detectives didn't work with partners, so there was no good cop, bad cop routine. Pudge was working full time on the bad cop side, and come to think of it, I'd never seen any other. After another five minutes of insults, threats, and pointless questions, he tired of his game and turned to walk off. Not bothering to face me, he tossed a parting comment over his shoulder.

"I'll be watching you, Efferding."

"Not very original, Pudgie," I hollered. "You've been watching too many cop shows."

Silently calling for Pudge's eternal damnation, I returned to the store in a foul mood. I needed to humor Pudge. Although department stores are rife with petty scandal, they like to present themselves as bastions of respectability. I'd no doubt Killian's management would kick me through the nearest plate glass window if they discovered the police department had me listed as a sex criminal.

Nailing the position at Killian's had been anything but easy. When Myra died, I left Bellevue with two hundred and fifty dollars in my pocket and three suitcases full of clothes. I settled in Cedar Rapids, but discovered good jobs were hard to come by.

Too depressed to put any effort into selling myself, I took the first thing that came along—a job in the pens at the Wilson & Company meatpacking plant. A job in the pens might seem preferable to working with raw meat in the refrigerated cutting rooms, but it was an unskilled position with no status. I alternated between the pens and the kill floor, spending my days standing in urine-impregnated manure and stunning hogs.

The stench imbedded itself in my clothes, hair, and skin. Although I'd shower before leaving the plant, the smell stayed with me. Even worse, it became part of me. In summer, the stink, heat, and humidity shriveled my brain into a glob of dung the size of a walnut. In winter, I froze right down to my muscles, at times becoming so stiff and clumsy I'd slip on frozen pee and land in six inches of hog-manure slush.

Things went from bad to worse when the payments from the sale of Efferding's Menswear dried up. I'd sold the business to my cousin on contract, but she stiffed me by borrowing lavishly against the store and declaring bankruptcy. The money was supposed to tide me over until I found a better job and set myself up with a house and new car. I had legal claim to some sort of settlement, but I couldn't go back to Jackson County because Brute Hinkley would have made it a one-way trip.

A failure with my business, home, and family, I worked the job I deserved. I spent my nights in the packers' bars on the Sixteenth Avenue strip and slept downtown at the Hotel Magnus in a room illuminated by a single bulb. The Magnus could just as well have been called the Magnet. The facility attracted the lion's share of the vagrants, dead-enders, and winos who frequented the downtown area. The dingy, five-story hotel employed just one cleaning lady. Arthritic and at least sixty years old, she spent much of her day napping in a supply closet.

Drinking heavily, I reached the point where my life had shrunk to two things: the pens and the booze. When the middle-class shopkeeper's clothes I'd brought from Bellevue were stolen by some guy who'd crawled over my door's transom, I didn't care. Where on earth would I ever wear them?

The next summer I realized that while I'd made some big mistakes, there was no reason to continue to abuse myself. I wasn't much of a man, but I knew I could do better than the pens. I applied for, and got, an inside placement boning meat. Considered skilled work by the standards of the plant, the job required intense concentration, manual dexterity, and high-speed acrobatics with a knife sharp enough to remove a thumb with a single slip.

I cleaned up my act. Only a fool would bone meat with a hangover. When I sobered up, I started saving my money and rented an efficiency apartment. Within six months I had some decent clothes again, so I hit the street and snagged the menswear position at Killian's. Now, three years after leaving Bellevue, my new life still felt fragile.

Working as a department store haberdasher might seem glamorous, but the salary and commissions were modest. I didn't earn any more than when I owned the little shop in Bellevue. Since my car was ready to give up the ghost, I decided to look for a second job to get my finances on track. I made a long-distance call to Edwin Faber in Dubuque and couldn't have been more thrilled when he agreed to write a recommendation for me.

Armed with Edwin's letter, I put in an appearance at the Arthur Murray Studio on Third Street. The boss asked me to take a trial whirl with an instructor named Diane. The idea was to show him I knew what I was doing.

"You're pretty good," Diane said as we waltzed through a number. "Nice Cuban motion," she added as we slid into a cha-cha. "Mr. Efferding, where do you get your moves?" she asked as we Lindy-hopped to an up-tempo number.

"I get by," I mumbled.

Out of practice and not at my best, my dance slippers felt as heavy as the rubber boots I had worn to hustle livestock in Wilson's pens. When we finished the Lindy and started a fox trot, I relaxed a bit. Without thinking about it, I led Diane through a fall-away with a syncopated chassé, followed by a triple twinkle and parallel vine, ending in a free turn. Not a particularly difficult sequence, but the owner wouldn't have expected some guy to walk in off the street and pull it off without working it up with a regular partner.

The boss hired me on the spot.

Within a few weeks, Diane Novacek became my friend, something I'd been missing since I moved to Cedar Rapids. I'm talking about a real friend—not a date, not a girlfriend, not a lover, but a deep down, once-in-a lifetime, honest-to-goodness best friend. Diane even introduced me to her family, and they began to invite me to picnics and family dinners. For the first time in a long time, I belonged. I felt blessed.

Damn Pudge Davis. That he expected my involvement with the woman in the car triggered a fresh descent into my unending cycle of blame for the loss of my wife and family. Forget Killian's, forget my new life—maybe the Hotel Magnus and the packing plant were the best I deserved.

Maybe they were more than I had coming to me.

I spent the rest of the morning fretting about Pudge and feeling bad about myself. Our encounter bothered me more than usual, and I needed something to get me out of the dumps. Thank goodness, I'd planned a lunch with Jim Weiss.

Jim sold cars. We'd become acquainted when I was shopping for wheels with the extra money I'd earned as a dance instructor. He sold Buicks and Oldsmobiles for an upscale dealership, and although my circumstances were such that I'd bought a more affordable baby blue Nova at the Chevy shop down the street, we really hit it off. Most people don't realize car salesmen are plugged into the man-about-town gossip network. Yes, men do gossip, and I've generally found those in the business community have the best poop. As we sat down to coffee and turkey sandwiches in the bustling lunchroom of Armstrong's Department store, Jim didn't disappoint.

"Clete, I had a visit from a police detective this morning."

Fearing the worst, I asked, "Pudge Davis?"

"No, Earl Erikson. He wanted to ask me about a white Buick Electra I sold a few months ago. Turns out it was the car they found that dead woman in. I sold it to a dentist, Gordon Cole. I wouldn't want to be in his shoes."

I put my fork down. "Think Cole did it?"

Jim looked down at this coffee, considering his answer. "I don't know. Erikson asked the standard things like if he paid cash, was a woman with him when he bought it, was he concerned about financing. One question didn't fit. He asked me if I knew whether Cole was a fisherman. Turns out they found a dip net and a container of catfish stink bait in the car."

"Ah, the Catfish Caper," I quipped. "A real stinker."

We chuckled a bit. Jim continued in the same vein, "He might be off the hook."

"How's that?" I asked. "You got me interested."

Jim took the bait. "He phoned the police station to report a stolen car at ten o'clock the night before the body was found."

"It all depends on the timing," I said. "Poor sucker could be up Alibi Creek without a paddle. Any ID on the lady yet?"

"Don't know," Jim replied. "When a policeman leaks information like that, you ask a question and he might clam up."

I groaned.

"One more thing," said Jim. "They found a basketball in the car, too."

"It only means something if the stuff they found in the car doesn't belong to the dentist," I replied.

Jim looked at me over the top of his glasses. "Of course, it doesn't belong to him. Otherwise, why would Erikson mention it?"

I wondered whether Erikson was cut from the same cloth as Pudge. "This Erikson guy, what's he like?"

"A real lady killer. I see him around town. Good-looking, nice suits, swanky apartment, women fall all over him. Drives a new Oldsmobile and breaks a heart a month. Half the guys in town would give their right arm to date one of his rejects. All that on a cop's salary—no way. Must be a trust fund baby."

I looked up. The clock on the wall above the lunch counter showed ten minutes to one, time to get back to the herringbone, gabardine, and twills. I bid Jim farewell. If the police had another suspect, maybe Pudge Davis would leave me alone.

At five o'clock, I finished up at Killian's and walked over to my second job at the dance studio. By six, it was apparent Diane wasn't showing up for work, and her appointments weren't covered. Between the boss, an instructor-in-training, and me, we managed to fill in. I felt vaguely uneasy all evening, but at 8:30, I remembered my conversation with Jim Weiss, and a jolt of anxiety hit me like a semi-truck doing ninety on Interstate 80. I excused myself, walked off the dance floor, went into the office, and dialed Diane's number. No answer. I dialed again. Again, no answer. The boss came in.

"I've already tried," he said. "Diane and I planned on lunch Saturday, but she didn't show up. This isn't like her."

I could tell he shared my concern but not if he shared my thinking.

He did. "Clete, there has to be another explanation."

I sat at his desk so shaken I knocked the phone onto the floor. The dial tone screamed up at me from the receiver, the sound the embodiment of all the horror in the world.

"It's not her," I said—denying the possibility because thinking about it might make it true.

I walked back out to our practice area and informed my bewildered students there'd been a family emergency, and I would be unable to complete the night's lesson. I waved to the boss, left the studio, and drove over to Bohemie Town. I parked in front of a dimly lit, shotgun-style house on Eighteenth Avenue, just two blocks away from the strip. The corner window on the first floor of the two-story shop behind it projected its warm light onto the grass. The light meant Lumir Sedlak was in his workshop.

I knocked on the shop window, and Lumir let me in. A widower and retired meatpacker, he spent his time building furniture from hardwood sawn on his family's farm a half century earlier. Lumir was also Diane's grandfather. We'd grown close, a relationship fostered by Diane's inviting this lost sheep to family events and dinners. I'm not a warm fuzzy guy, but Diane, Lumir, and my buddy Jim are the three people in this world I call friend.

"Clete," he smiled warmly, "it is good to see you, and at night when you are mostly working. But why do you look so worried?"

"I'm just winding down after a really long day."

I didn't want to alarm him unnecessarily, but I didn't know how to accomplish my task without getting to a question whose answer had the potential to destroy his world. "Seen Diane lately?" I asked casually.

"No, not since Thursday last. She brought me a birthday cake."

"I didn't know," I replied. "Sixty-eight?"

"Yes, and enough wood upstairs in the loft to last me twenty more years."

"It's the wood downstairs that counts," I teased.

"Oh, you young people, you don't know anything about anything."

My heart wasn't in it. Given the situation, small talk was torture.

"Lumir, I'm worried about Diane. She didn't show up for work today."

Lumir didn't need a road map. The car in the Me Too parking lot had been the talk of the neighborhood since Saturday.

"Let's go to the house," he said. "It is time to make phone calls."

A half dozen calls later and no Diane. Lumir decided to call her parents, Roy and DeeDee. After speaking to him, the distraught couple drove to the police station. By now, a small circle of people knew Diane was missing. Come what may, the phone lines would be busy this evening. Lumir and I settled in for a long night, drinking tea and playing cards.

Randy Roeder

4

Eight o'clock the next morning at the Butterfly Café, I stared at the congealed eggs and cold bacon on my plate. It was Diane. The bad news came in at 3:00 a.m. I'd driven Lumir over to her parent's home on Twenty-First Avenue. I could see by the cars parked out front that Diane's brothers, Stan and Buzz, had beaten us to the house. Though I wanted to be with all of them, I went home. They'd need their privacy.

I didn't cry. I hadn't slept. I felt empty. Facing the dreary prospect of a day spent selling clothing, I tossed my napkin on the counter and walked over to Greene Square where I decided to wait until my shift started.

The day was already hot, and the humidity warned of an approaching thunderstorm. I picked a bench in the shade of an elm tree and watched a squirrel pilfering potato chips from a trash can. I'd have been justified in asking for the day off, but what good would that do? I wouldn't be able to sleep, and I hated the soap operas on daytime television. I'd just spend the time looking at the walls and thinking about Diane. Thinking about Diane would lead to thinking about Myra.

Myra. My sweetheart didn't want to be the pregnant bride at a big church wedding, so we eloped. As happy as two people can be, we doted on each another. We celebrated the arrival of our son six months later. Our little girl greeted us a year and a half after that.

Things went south not long after. For some reason, Myra withdrew into herself, at times not talking to me for days. I took on the nighttime baby bottles, but she rarely slept and developed bags the size of quarters under her eyes. Then one day, I came home from work and found her still in her pajamas, sitting in her favorite chair and looking as if she hadn't moved since morning. A glance at the wet spot on the upholstery confirmed my impression. Our little girl hadn't been changed or fed. Our son clutched his blanket and cried.

"Myra, what's wrong?"

No answer.

I called her mother, and her parents drove over from their home in Maquoketa. She wouldn't speak to them either. It didn't take long to realize we were looking at a full-fledged nervous breakdown. I couldn't run the store, take care of Myra, and look after the kids, so when the Hinkleys agreed to take the children until I got Myra squared around, I was grateful beyond words. Two months passed. Myra showed no improvement; Brute and Velma still had the kids.

The doctors thought Myra should have shock treatments, but I didn't have it in me to do that to her. I desperately needed time for myself. One day when Myra seemed better than usual, I locked the store for the afternoon and escaped to Dubuque. I headed for Rosie's Tap Room on lower Rhomberg Avenue.

An old-fashioned barkeep, Rosie wore a towel for an apron and kept a baseball bat stashed behind the bar in the event trouble broke out. He was a tough man—pretty much a requirement for running a tap in a neighborhood bordering a packing plant. Rosie recognized me from my dancing days when I occasionally stopped in with my old high school friend Dale, who at six-foot-six and 260 pounds spent his days lugging quarters of beef. Like a good barman any-where, Rosie remembered me.

"What'll it be, Clete?"

It was a question easily answered since the options were Blatz, Potosi, or Dubuque Star, all on tap.

"I'll have a Potosi."

Five Potosis and a Blatz later, I called Rosie over.

"I'd like to check in with somebody upstairs."

"Suit yourself," he replied, looking me up and down. He made a quick phone call.

"Just ring the bell and somebody will be down."

I exited, went around to the side door, and rang. Rosie rented the upstairs apartments to some girls who worked as independent contractors. I'd never done this kind of thing before and despite the beers, felt as nervous as a boy with his finger in a light socket. The door opened—a brunette.

"Looking for anybody in particular?" she asked.

"You'll do," I replied.

"Mr. Flattery," she said as she motioned toward the stairs with a turn of her head.

About fifteen minutes later, I heard an infernal racket in the stairway and a loud crash as a pair of uniformed patrolmen forced my companion's door and found us on the couch in a state of com-plete undress. Ordered to the floor, I watched as they handed my companion a bathrobe and herded her out the door. After she left, the uniforms allowed me to put on my shorts and trousers, cuffed me, hustled me out of the room, and led me down the stairway. As I reached fresh air, a light went off. Somebody was taking pictures.

Either Rosie missed one of his payments, or one of the swells in city government was working on his image. Someone had tipped the press. A van pulled up to the front of the bar, and a half-dozen pok-er-faced patrolmen loaded three girls, another gentleman, and me into the back. The drive to the century-old police station took less than five minutes, the booking operation another thirty. The prelim-inaries completed, an ill-tempered officer led me to a holding cell and shoved me in. The filthy enclosure stank, the sheet-metal bed had no mattress, and I couldn't make a call because the telephone was broken. Four, five, or six hours later, a beefy sergeant ambled over to the cell door.

"Cletus Efferding, that you?"

I nodded.

"The Jackson County sheriff bailed you out. You must have some pretty good pull."

News travels fast in law enforcement circles. My father-in-law had arranged my bail. I left the stationhouse and walked back to my car. I couldn't begin to imagine how I'd ever look him in the eye. Shirtless and shoeless, I made the trek back to my car and drove home. It had not been a good day.

Things got worse. The next morning, there I was, above the fold on the front page of the *Telegraph Herald*, cuffed and shirtless, situated squarely beneath the half-inch banner: "Arrested in Prostitution Crackdown." As I read, things got even worse. One of the girls kept a pair of handcuffs and a leather vest in her bedroom closet. The paper's editor had decided to play up the whole sado-masochistic thing, complete with such words as *den*, *bondage*, and *perversion*. I put the paper down. Myra was sitting in her chair, looking out the window with a tear in her eye. The way things were going, she pretty much looked that way every morning. Her sadness had become a routine. She wouldn't talk to me, but the paper had been unfolded. She knew.

I tried talking with her. No response. I poured my heart out, and still no response. When I couldn't think of anything else to say, I kissed her on the forehead and left to open up the shop. I'd have to come up with a plan for dealing with the situation, but for now I was stumped. Not a soul came into the store, so I busied myself with paper work and tidying up the inventory. Not that it made any difference. I was finished. No small-town mother would bring her son into a store run by a sado-masochistic pervert, and no self-respecting local businessman would sully his reputation by putting a foot across the threshold.

About eleven o'clock my cousin came in, looked at me sadly, and said, "Cletus, Myra's dead."

I passed out, taking a rack of sports coats to the floor along with me. I regained consciousness as she removed the hangers and fabric covering my face.

"You're a jerk, Cletus," she said. "A first-class, sleazebag jerk."

After I'd gone to work that morning, Myra left the house, walked over to L & J's Maid-Rite Shop, and purchased an ice cream cone. She crossed the street to sit at one of the benches overlooking the Mississippi to eat it. After she'd finished, she walked down the wooden steps to the rugged beach below, where she took off and carefully folded her sundress and clad in bra and panties, walked out into the river.

———————————

I came back to the present to find sweat seeping through the front of my shirt. When I realized the beads of perspiration running down the front of my face were tears, I picked up my lightweight jacket and Panama hat and walked over to Killian's. In weather like this, succumbing to the allure of the store's air conditioning beat the heck out of watching the antics of a squirrel.

As I approached Killian's, a familiar figure leaned against the plate glass window some twenty feet from the main door. Pudge.

"Hey, Pervie. You and I gotta talk."

Just what I needed. "What's it now, Pudge?"

"Looks like your girlfriend's dead. I gotta ask, she a slut like you?"

I looked at his piggy eyes, realizing I'd never understood how deeply I could hate another human being. I waited for the adrenaline to subside before answering. The delay only made me angrier.

My voice gunflint and cold steel, I let him have it. "Her name is Diane, and she was my friend. The combined brains of a hundred thousand cretins like you couldn't begin to understand that."

"I'm hurt." Pudge appeared unfazed. "Wanna play nicey-nice here or take a trip over to the station?"

My anger and insult had done nothing to penetrate his hardness. I felt powerless, but the prospect of a trip to the station cleared things up for me. So much for manliness, gunflint, and cold steel—I'd play nicey-nice.

"Ya know, Perv, you ain't in the best situation. I ask you about a dead woman in a car, and then it turns out you know her. And don't give me any of that friend crap. It ain't possible for a man and a woman to be friends. There's always some kind of sex attraction at the bottom of it—even if it's all on one side. All you're telling me is you couldn't score. Maybe you got mad and aced her."

The futility of trying to communicate with the man overwhelmed me.

"The two of you been seen all over town together—dancin', havin' drinks, eatin' out. Maybe you been doin' the mattress mambo, maybe not. Maybe you wanted to, but she didn't."

It was useless. The man would never get it through his skull that Diane and I weren't romantic.

"Pudge, the only mambo we've been doing is on the dance floor. We teach dance, remember?"

"Okay, you tell me you weren't datin' each other. What about the dance studio? She fool around with other guys that didn't date her?"

I wanted to bang my head against a wall. Talking to Pudge was as frustrating as trying to communicate with a chunk of concrete. "As far as I know, Diane hasn't dated since her husband died three years ago," I said.

"How'd he die?"

"He was a lineman for the telephone company," I said. "Got struck by lightning."

"So, Efferding, you fish?"

"What?"

He'd changed topic so abruptly I had trouble understanding. Then I remembered Jim's report that fish bait, a landing net, and a basketball were found in the death car. Our joking about the so-called Catfish Caper felt cruel and stupid now that Diane had been identified.

"You used to live in that little town on the Mississippi River. Do you fish?"

"Not since I was a kid," I said.

"Catfish?" he asked.

"No," I answered, "bass, crappies, bluegills—stuff like that."

I'd already guessed a basketball question would be next.

"So," he said, "when you gave up fishing, did you give up basketball?"

"Never played much," I answered. "Didn't care for the game."

"I'm not surprised. Lookin' at you, I'd say you ain't much on the physical side. Maybe that's why the girl didn't want you."

Now that he'd done his best to ruin one of the worst days of my life, Pudge seemed satisfied and turned to go.

"Pudge," I asked, "what happened to Diane?"

Diane's family had been told only that the circumstances of the death were suspicious and an autopsy had yet to be performed.

Pudge turned and faced me. "Efferding, this cretin's got nothin' to say."

Randy Roeder

5

Eddie Brada waited for Billy at Jones Park. His friend had phoned him with some cock-and-bull story about giving fifty cents to the missions to make up for stealing the car. Sometimes he wondered how he'd ever become friends with Billy. The crazy loon seemed more worried about fifty cents than the dead lady in the car.

He'd been wanting to talk to Billy. Seeing the article and picture of the car in the newspaper got him thinking it wasn't right to hold back information about a bad crime. There was blood on the blanket, and the paper didn't say anything about suicide. Stuffed between the seats like that—somebody probably murdered her.

"Eddie," Billy called as he pulled his bike up to the picnic table. "Eddie, I confessed to stealing the car and got a penance of ten rosaries and fifty cents for restitution. You can do the same. Actually, it comes to forty-four cents—I rounded it up to fifty," Billy announced.

"Dick brain." Eddie voiced his frustration. "What about the dead lady in the car?"

"No skin off my nose. We didn't hurt her. Stealing the car—that was bad."

"We didn't hurt anybody, but I'm thinking somebody murdered that lady, and we know something that might help the police."

Billy looked at Eddie with disbelief. "You said yourself we'll go to reform school if the police find out we took that car."

"Yeah, I been thinking about that. The weird thing is somebody probably stole the car before we did. I mean, think about it. If you had a dead body, would you leave it in your own car where the police would find it? That'd be stupid."

"We swiped a stolen car?" Billy appeared relieved. "That doesn't seem as bad as stealing an un-stolen car. I'm not going to say any more rosaries, and screw the restitution. Ain't gonna make restitution because we borrowed a car from a criminal who already stole it."

Eddie felt like he'd stepped into an episode of the *Twilight Zone*—that creepy show he watched on Channel 2. He never realized just how much Billy thought like a kid. Billy's folks still gave him money, so he didn't have a job or spend much time around grown-ups. Come to think of it, his friend spent a lot of time hanging out with younger kids. When this thing was over, he'd find somebody else to hang out with, somebody who didn't act like a seventh grader.

"Billy, the fact somebody else took the car before we did helps us out. It makes it harder for them to catch us. I thought about it a lot. We need to tell what we know."

"I'm not gonna get sent to Eldora." Billy's voice revealed a stubborn streak. "You go."

"Listen, the woman in that car was a real person. Her name's not in the paper yet, but everybody at the grocery store already knows who it was. She married a Novacek, but she was a Sedlak. My mom knows her folks, and they only live two blocks from our house. I cut their grass when they were on vacation last summer."

Billy folded his arms across his chest, looked at Eddie defiantly. "All the more reason to keep quiet. You go, and leave me out of it."

"Won't do it," said Eddie. "We're eyewitnesses, and it means more if two people saw the same thing. If you don't go with me, I'll rat you out. Besides, you're the one who wanted to go to the police right away."

"You're the one who worried about Eldora reform school."

"I got a plan, Billy. We don't say anything about taking a ride in the car. Then we can tell what we know and maybe help catch those guys. No stolen car, no reform school. We can practice our story until we've got it down cold."

"I'll help you practice, but that doesn't mean I'll go to the police with you."

Eddie wasn't about to take no for an answer. "Why do you always wear that t-shirt with those big orange stains on it?" he asked.

"They're not stains. It's tie-dyed. I told you before—my aunt Jane made it for me."

"Too bad she didn't use red-brown."

"What's that got to do with the car?"

"That's the color your shirt's gonna be when I'm done hammerin' on your face because you didn't go to the police with me."

Billy grew pale. "Okay, okay. Jesus, no need to get all shook."

Sensing he'd won, Eddie began grilling his friend about their nighttime adventure, picking at his answers and hammering on inconsistencies. Tears soon rolled down Billy's cheeks.

"You can't cry, Billy. They're gonna give us the third degree. Now it's your turn. Start in on me, and be tough."

Billy surprised Eddie with the intensity of his questioning. The guy tore into him, poking holes into his story every chance he got. When Billy finished, Eddie started in on him again. Eventually satisfied they had their story down pat, he was ready to stop.

Billy, however, still had doubts.

"Eddie, what about the basketball? It's marked WJH, for Wilson Junior High."

"We weren't in the car, so we don't know anything about it. Even if they did figure out we looked in the car, they still won't know we took it for a drive. They can't even blame us for stealing the basketball. Your brother did it. We just gotta stick to our story and hang tough."

"Man, I'm really gonna get in trouble with my parents for being out so late," complained Billy.

"Forget about the rosaries, that's your real penance."

"Eddie, they'll probably take away my allowance."

"That's your restitution."

———

Pudge Davis sat in a plastic chair across from Earl Erikson. They'd commandeered a corner of the Cedar Rapids Police Department's empty squad room. Pudge had chosen the room for its amenities—vending machines. Candy wrappers, overflowing ashtrays, and crumpled paper cups covered every surface.

Pudge pulled the wrapper off a Baby Ruth and added it to the clutter. "I'm glad the captain assigned you to Gordon's side of the case. It's way too close for me to be workin' on it, and I know you'll be fair."

"There's no way you can be expected to investigate your own bother-in-law," Erikson replied. "The fact you're on the case at all shows how much the captain trusts you."

"What do you think so far?"

"I don't think Gordon's mixed up in this," said Erikson. "What guy would leave a body in his own car?"

Pudge pushed the candy bar into his mouth, chewed three times, and downed it in one swallow. He licked his fingers. "Maybe if he got panicked." He shrugged. "So, what's your next move?"

"I need to make a list of Gordon's patients and run it against the records at the dance studio. If any of them know the Novacek girl, things could get interesting in a hurry. In the back of my head, I have an idea whoever stole the car might know your brother-in-law. It's a long shot, but for now, it's all I have. Let's face it; Gordon is clean, but I've got to make an all-out effort. Otherwise, people will think the investigation stinks because he's your relative."

"He's innocent," Pudge replied. "He wouldn't be in this situation if he didn't keep leavin' his keys in the car. I talked to him about it before, but he says he forgets. I've never seen a guy with so many brains act so stupid."

"Well, he's not alone. People just don't understand the town is changing."

"Earl, you find anything—anything at all—run with it. I won't be the first cop who's wrong about a relative. But family is family, and I ain't doin' nothin' different with stuff like dinners and social calls. I know people think it'd look better if I stayed away from him and my sister until this is settled. Screw 'em. I ain't changin' a thing."

"You're doing the right thing. Gordon has a pretty good alibi. He worked at the office until 1:30 Friday afternoon. He was home by six and with his wife all night. Too bad nobody saw him play golf after work. We have a four-hour gap in the timeline, but it could be a lot worse. He likes to golf alone?"

Pudge pulled a box of Milk Duds from his pocket, thought better of the idea, and returned it to its place of origin. "Yeah, he ain't such a good golfer, but it relaxes him. He goes alone and uses a city course because he gets embarrassed. If he joined a country club, he'd have to get to know people." He paused and changed the subject. "What do you make of the dope we got from the Brada and Rehak kids?"

"None of it really helps us much. They saw two guys, but it's generally hard for one man to handle a body, so I already figured on more than one. Efferding and your brother-in-law don't look like they visit the gym. Either one would have needed help putting the body into the car. Since Gordon was home when the girl was dumped, he'd need two accomplices to do the job. From what I've seen of your brother-in-law, I can't imagine he'd know one—much less two—lowlifes like that."

Pudge wadded up his candy bar wrapper, threw it at a wastebasket, missed. "The guys with the car, it don't make no sense. They leave the engine running. And then there's this thing about walkin' away with fishin' poles and not takin' the bait. What the hell is that about? Maybe they was gonna take the car to the river and stopped way before they got there. The poles and stuff coulda been a cover if anybody looked too close. Like, maybe they didn't know how far the river is. Maybe they're out-of-towners? I'll check with some of the

guys who fish the bridge at night. Maybe they noticed somethin.'
How about you lookin' at the places that sell catfish bait?"

Earl studied his fingers and pulled a nail clipper from his pocket. "I can do that. Trust the kids' story?"

"We ain't gettin' all of it," Pudge replied. "Did ya see the looks
on their faces when we wanted to know what they was doin' out at
three in the morning? Like they never expected we'd ask."

Earl turned his attention to an index finger. "God, I hate hang-
nails," he said as he snipped the offending protrusion. Pocketing the
clipper, he returned to the topic at hand. "Well, they did own up to
sneaking out to drink beer when we pressed. After that, they zipped
up."

"Did you see the look on the Rehak woman's face when she
found out what her son was doin'?" Pudge smiled at the recollection.
"I bet she don't let him outta the house again until he's twenty-one.
Somehow that kid ain't quite right."

"Those kids were in that car," Earl observed. "A Wilson Junior
High basketball for Christ's sake. Maybe they were looking inside for
stuff to swipe."

"And found the body," Pudge added. "They think we're stupid?"

"I didn't want to push too hard in front of Mama Rehak," said
Earl. "Did you see the look on the kids' faces when I said we might
have to call them back in so we could get fingerprints?"

"It wasn't half as good as Mama's. I thought she was gonna
jump out of her chair and take you down."

Earl chuckled. "That's one ornery woman, but I have to feel sorry for the Brada kid. He comes to the police station to give evidence,
and nobody from his family comes with him. Mama Rehak would
have sold him down the river in half a second if she thought it'd help
her kid. I think the kids know we didn't buy the story, and they're
scared."

"Scared shitless," said Pudge. Thinking about the boys' discom-
fort brought a warm smile to his face. "I bet they practiced their story
over and over, but never thought about the beer part. Let 'em sit and

worry a couple of days—they'll talk. When they do, I doubt any of it will help much."

"I agree. Think the medical examiner will rule murder?" Erikson asked.

"Sure as hell don't look like suicide. I think some pervert mutilated that woman."

"Think it's Efferding?"

"He's been in sex trouble before—that whips and chains thing with a hooker. Besides, who else we got?"

Randy Roeder

6

Wednesday morning, I bought a copy of the *Cedar Rapids Gazette* and drove over to Tommy's Restaurant for a cup of coffee. The place made the best cheap breakfast in town. It looked like I'd have a ten-minute wait to get a seat at the counter, so I sat on the narrow bench just inside the door. I'd already seen the article but wanted to read it again.

Woman in Car Identified

The body of a woman found in a parked car at a Cedar Rapids supermarket has been identified as Diane Novacek, 27, of Cedar Rapids. Novacek's body was discovered in the parking lot of the Me Too Supermarket, 1624 J St. SW, early Saturday morning. Novacek, a graduate of Jefferson High School, worked as a salesgirl for the Hiltbrunner Music Company and as an instructor for the Arthur Murray Dance Studio. The cause of death remains under investigation.

That was it, short and not so sweet. Disappointed the article contained nothing I didn't already know, I let out a sigh loud enough to attract the attention of the guy seated at the nearest stool. He checked me out. I glared at him, and he returned to his pancakes.

It didn't seem right. My best friend, a woman who'd taught hundreds of people to dance, an amateur singer and a joy to everyone she met, had died under questionable circumstances and rated a single paragraph. A few lines in the paper—as if someone of no real value had quietly passed away. At least Monday's coverage had included a picture of the car. I grew depressed. Unable to stomach the thought of eating breakfast surrounded by people indifferent to the tragedy that had taken place, I left without ordering.

The loss of Diane hit me hard, and I didn't have anyone to talk to about it. Lumir had his own grief to deal with, and although Jim Weiss and I were close, we didn't have a spill-your-guts friendship. I'd been through this kind of thing when Myra had taken her life. It seems the way someone dies has a lot to do with how hard it is for a survivor to handle the situation. Myra's death had been premature and unnatural, and I considered myself responsible. The guilt had never gone away; it fed upon itself, growing into a dark, suffocating cloud, one that would surround me until the day I died.

In one way, Diane's passing was easier. No matter what Pudge Davis thought, I had nothing to do with her demise. In another way, it was much harder. It looked as if someone had deliberately taken her life. I had trouble reconciling myself to a world filled with the sort of evil that allows such a thing to happen. This grief was a different animal. A mixture of sadness and anger, the torment made me want to strike out at everyone and anyone involved with Diane's premature death.

I now understood Brute Hinkley's hatred for me in a way that hadn't been possible before. The combination of my actions and his daughter's suicide must have ratcheted up his grief and anger to a level beyond my comprehension.

Myra's death had taught me that the way to deal with loss was to keep slogging in the hope of reaching the other side. For me, slogging meant work. I'd take my shift at Killian's today, and after that, I'd head back over to the Arthur Murray Studio. My boss there would have given me more time if I needed it. I did appreciate his kindness, but truthfully, he needed me to cover Diane's classes. Being needed felt good.

I'd been at Killian's a half hour when Lumir Sedlak walked in. Although we were friends and had been together when he got the news about Diane, some formality seemed in order.

"Lumir," I said, "I am so sorry for your loss."

"Thank you, Clete." he replied. "It was a comfort that you waited with me and drove me over to the house. I'm here to invite you to stop by Roy and DeeDee's any time you want to over the next few days. You know, you're like part of the family. We'd like you to be with us."

Touched, I struggled with my composure.

"I'll be sure to stop by," I said.

I could see unshed tears in his eyes.

"There's something else," he said. "I'd like you to help me pick out a new suit for the funeral. I should have got one when Klara died, but did not. I want to look nice for Diane."

Never in my life had I so wanted to find the perfect ensemble for someone.

"Lumir, let's start with color. Black is traditional for funerals, but you see quite a bit of navy blue."

Lumir shook his head. "No black, no dark colors. Losing Diane is sad enough without me looking like the undertaker. I don't want gray either."

The selection was becoming limited.

"Brown's a nice color, and I have a couple of nice numbers in your size. Let's go over and look."

Lumir followed me to the rack. I pulled out two suits, one with off-yellow pin stripes and one with steel blue. Lumir slumped, barely looked at them.

"No," he said.

"Lumir, I think we could be running out of options here."

Then it hit me.

"I have an idea, Lumir. Let's go to the rack on the west side."

Reg and I jokingly referred to the west rack as Seersucker Corner, since seventy percent of the summer suits featured there were made of that fabric. I walked to the end of the rack and pulled out an ivory-colored linen suit. Lumir's eyes lit up. He felt the fabric, reached for the price tag, and examined it.

"It costs too much," he said.

I lied. "Not really, I can get a fifty percent discount. While you're here, let's set you up with a new shirt, tie, and a belt. Then we'll go over to the shoe department and have Max fix you up."

Then I lied again. "I get a fifty percent discount on all of it, even the shoes."

I watched Lumir straighten up and smile. "My family needs me right now. I want to make an example for them to be proud of—proud of Diane and proud of the Sedlaks."

"You'll do well, Lumir, and you should be proud of your family. They're good people. Normally we think about the shirt and tie at this point, but with a light-colored linen suit, we'll want to consider the shoes and belt next. Black, gray, or brown?"

Lumir did not hesitate. "Black," he said, "and a shirt with narrow stripes, with a tie to match the color of the stripes."

Now that I knew the color of the accessories, I found a shirt with narrow, dark blue stripes, and a tie that was a gift from the gods —dark navy with abstract cerulean accents. Lumir took the works, went into the dressing room, and came out ten minutes later with a smile that stretched all the way from Second to Third Avenues. I marked and pinned the cuffs of the pants and took him over to the shoe department. Lumir insisted on wearing the shoes he'd selected as we walked back to the dressing room.

"One more thing, Lumir," I said. "Stay right here, and I'll be back in a minute."

I returned holding an ivory-tone straw fedora trimmed with a dark blue band. I placed it on his head. Lumir stepped over to the three-angle mirror and studied the effect. The man looked good. A lifetime of hard manual work had kept him trim, and his snow-white hair and mustache only added to the overall effect. Despite the sadness of the occasion, the shopping spree had done much to lift his spirits. To top it all off, I made a sale I'd cherish for the rest of my life.

"Clete," he whispered, "there's something else I need."

"What is it?" I asked. "Socks? Handkerchiefs?"

"Do you have any of those silk boxer shorts?"

Thursday, 11:00 a.m. I was at my post in the Killian's Menswear Department setting up a new display of neckties when Diane's brothers walked in. Three years older than Diane, Stan and Buzz were non-identical twins. Built like football linemen, with biceps straining at their shirtsleeves, the brothers made an impressive pair. As they approached, I noticed Buzz looked puffy-eyed.

Stan didn't beat around the bush. "The medical examiner released Diane this morning. We got a preliminary report late yesterday afternoon. I expect the newspaper will get hold of it tomorrow."

Grief is a funny thing. A guy can be buzzing right along, when out of nowhere, it grabs him by the throat and squeezes. The image of Diane on a coroner's slab hit me like a line drive to the face. The room dissolved. Fearing collapse, I grabbed the corner of a display table.

Buzz looked at me with concern. "I think we'd better go somewhere to sit down."

I asked Reg to cover for me, and we walked down a flight and into the men's lunchroom. It was a little early for lunch at the Man's Grille, so we had our choice of tables. Although I thought it a little old-fashioned for a department store to have an all-male lunchroom, I welcomed the extra privacy.

"Clete..." Stan began, halted, and started in again. "Clete, Diane wasn't murdered. She died from an abortion that went bad."

I started to sob softly.

Stan continued, "She wasn't pregnant."

Time stopped. I heard the shuffling of feet on the terrazzo floor, the cough of a distant sales clerk, the pulse of the blood in my ears. A phone rang, coffee cups clinked, chairs scraped floors, and surely, surely, I'd lost my grip on reality. I looked at Stan and Buzz without comprehension.

"What?" I said.

Stan repeated himself. "Diane died from an abortion, but she wasn't pregnant."

"No." I shook my head from side to side. "No. It doesn't make sense. It can't be. Diane would see a doctor. She'd want to know."

"Mom and Dad asked a dozen times. The coroner says she wasn't pregnant."

A futile, unnecessary, and senseless death, a heartbreak beyond description—I couldn't begin to imagine how Roy and DeeDee were handling the situation.

"How are your folks taking it?" I asked.

Stan looked at the floor, Buzz answered for him. "Mom keeps crying, and Dad doesn't talk."

"And Lumir?"

Stan looked back up. "Grandpa's mad," Stan said. "He wants to beat somebody to a pulp. Delores and Brenda are holding us all together. They're helping Mom and Dad with the funeral home and church."

Stan and Buzz had married sisters. Delores and Brenda were identical twins and a couple of the finest people on earth. Twins marrying twins. It happens, and if the Sedlak brothers and their wives were any indication, it should happen more often.

I took a couple of breaths to get my composure and leaned forward in my chair. I had something I needed to tell them. "Guys, I'm pretty sure Diane wasn't seeing anybody." I paused a moment. "And she wasn't seeing me."

Stan nodded. "We know you were good friends, and if you were dating, Diane would have talked about it. Thanks, but not to worry."

"None of it makes any difference," Buzz interjected. "No matter how you slice it, some bastard killed Diane, just as sure as if he used a knife or a gun."

I looked from Buzz to Stan and back again. "I'm sure all of you have been asking the same question. If Diane wasn't dating anyone and wasn't pregnant, why would she get an illegal abortion?"

"Right now," said Stan, "the why doesn't make any difference. We've got to find a way to get through the funeral. The time for questions, the time for blame, the time for anger, and the time for the law comes later."

I felt myself getting angry. "No matter what the law says, some butcher killed her. Doing that to somebody when you don't have the training is just plain murder."

"Clete, we need a favor," Stan interjected, changing the subject just in time to keep me from exploding.

"Anything," I replied.

"Buzz and I need new dress shirts and ties. Do you think we can get that fifty percent?"

I lied again, of course. By the time we finished, I'd outfitted Stan and Buzz with new dress shirts, ties, belts, handkerchiefs, socks, boxers, and shoes. I'd have gladly set them up with new suits, but given the size of their arms and torsos, the alterations on the jackets wouldn't have been ready in time for the funeral. Between Lumir, Stan, and Buzz, I'd spend the next two weeks working for free.

Randy Roeder

7

I called into Killian's. My boss bent the rules for me and arranged for up to two days of funeral leave—without pay. Expecting friends and neighbors would be dropping in at the Sedlaks, I picked up a couple dozen kolaches from Sykora's Bakery and drove over to visit Diane's parents. When I arrived, all was pandemonium. The Sedlaks' church had not done well by them.

Things went south when the pastor at St. Wenceslaus Church read about the cause of Diane's death in the Friday *Gazette*. He called Roy and DeeDee early that morning and cancelled the funeral service. According to the venerable Father Kun, Diane had attended a Catholic school and knew right from wrong. That knowledge meant she was automatically excommunicated from her church the moment she decided to have an abortion. Excommunication meant no Catholic funeral Mass.

The announcement devastated Roy and DeeDee. After stewing an hour, they announced they were leaving to look at floral arrangements. Knowing the bereaved couple wanted to be alone, the family went along with the charade.

Diane's sisters-in-law, Brenda and Delores, drove over to the St. Wenceslaus rectory to persuade the old priest to change his mind. They found him in his office. Since Diane had not been pregnant, they argued, no abortion occurred. Father Kun maintained the issue was one of intent, and he'd made his decision on the basis of Canon Law. By saying the funeral Mass, he said, he'd be guilty of supporting a woman's decision to murder a baby.

When Brenda and Delores persisted, the old priest grew angry and pointed out that Diane's abortion attempt was "notorious." Newspapers throughout the state would cover the story, and the publicity might persuade others to take a similar action. Father Kun called the situation open-and-shut, and he wouldn't bother the offices of the Archdiocese for an interpretation. End of discussion.

Appalled by the tale, I asked, "So, you're out in the cold?"

"Maybe, maybe not," Delores replied. "Old Father Kun still lives in the 1920s, and besides, he wants to cover his butt in case someone complains to the bishop. St. Wen's is out. Sad, because even though we live on the west side of the river, the Sedlaks have been members of St. Wenceslaus parish forever. Most of the Czechs on this side of the river go to St. Ludmila, just a few blocks away. I called Father Blazek there and asked him to stop by."

A few minutes later, the doorbell rang, and Stan ushered Blazek into the living room. Buzz rose to give him his chair, but the confident young priest declined. Surveying the situation, Blazek pulled a hassock to a spot in front of the television, sat, and asked the family to fill him in. With Roy and DeeDee absent, the younger set could speak freely without upsetting them. Father Blazek listened to their protests, thought a few moments, and when he was sure he had everyone's attention, he spoke.

"Just between us, I believe Father Kun is wrong—wrong in his understanding of Church doctrine and wrong in his understanding of his responsibility to his parishioners. I think we can work something out."

Blazek paused a moment and continued, "Since I may be putting myself in a pickle, I'd like you to know the thinking behind my decision. First, understand that no abortion took place. Without a fetus, there can be no abortion. Father Kun's reservations center on the issue of intent—in this case, the intent to end the life of an unborn child. The Church has argued for years about sins of intent and has been consistently inconsistent in applying the concept to individual situations. I doubt any two theologians would give you the same answer in a case like this."

"Doesn't sound as clear cut as Father Kun thinks," said Stan.

Blazek rubbed his face. "It's a complex issue. None of us can know the state of Diane's mind when she decided to have the procedure. Under great emotional stress, her thinking may have become irrational. For an automatic excommunication to take place, the decision to abort would have to be made with a cold and clear understanding of the consequences. Since Diane is no longer with us, I can't determine if she was thinking with clarity."

"You'd be willing to give her the benefit of the doubt?" Stan asked.

"I don't feel qualified to make a judgment on Diane's state of mind. Beyond that, I've taken a vow to comfort those who mourn. Denying your family the consolation of religion seems unnecessarily harsh. I'll do the service."

Despite his bravado, Father Blazek did not look comfortable with his decision. Buzz picked up on it. "What's the matter?" he asked. "You look like Father Kun the day he caught me chugging the altar wine."

"If Father Kun takes the matter to the archbishop, I'll get called on the carpet."

Stan's face showed his concern. "What happens to you then?"

"It depends on the archbishop. The least he could do is rip me a new one."

Brenda giggled. Given the occupation of the speaker, Blazek's colorful phrasing seemed incongruous.

"What's the most he could do?" Stan asked.

"I could get transferred or disciplined. No matter. I'm confident enough of my understanding of Church doctrine and my clerical responsibilities that my conscience requires me to see a funeral Mass takes place."

The room fell silent. Apparently, archbishops were not to be trifled with.

Stan broke the quiet. "We'll keep it low key."

The younger Sedlaks' consideration for the well-being of Father Blazek surprised me. As they planned the funeral, the family made compromises to reduce the risk to his career. Then too, they had no interest in a large funeral with the inevitable attention of the press and curious onlookers. Their vision of the ideal service included only family and friends.

I watched as the younger Sedlaks completed arrangements for the funeral. The service would take place at St. Ludmila Church on late Monday afternoon, a time when there would be no other activity in the building. Diane's obituary would include information on the visitation but make no mention of a religious service or interment. Family and friends were to be invited by word of mouth, and care would be taken that the Janeba-Kuba Funeral Home did not leak information during the Sunday visitation.

Everyone hoped the low-key approach to the funeral Mass would avoid a reaction from the church hierarchy. Things were back at square one if Diane's parents did not sign on. They did.

Moved that the family had allowed me into this very private part of their lives, I can't say their church impressed me. I'm not much for robes, incense, and flapdoodle. Blazek seemed like a good man, but the whole affair came across as a bureaucratic obsession with trivialities. Old Father Kun's oddball rationale that Diane's death would encourage others to seek an abortion seemed the strangest of all. Call me unimaginative, but I couldn't picture someone thinking she'd get an abortion so she could end up dead like that Novacek woman.

Diane deserved a beautiful, well-publicized funeral. But then, who was I to judge? My stupidity had caused my wife's suicide and the loss of my children. Catatonic with guilt and grief, I had let the Hinkleys make the arrangements for Myra. In doing so, I'd failed her yet again. A man owes his wife the simple decency of involvement in the preparations for her final journey.

I made my farewell and walked to the car. The Sedlaks' relationship to their church was none of my damn business.

George Rahbani sat at his walnut desk looking at the family photos enshrined on his bookshelf. His office was his refuge, and he'd taken pains to see it was as well-appointed and comfortable as possible. The Rahbani family had come a long way since leaving the Bekaa Valley a half-century earlier. George's office served as testimony to the hard work required to achieve his position in life.

He'd grown up in a crowded, single-story wooden house next to the railroad yards. Blessed with a leaking roof, covered with tarpaper, and retaining little heat during the long Iowa winters, the little home had become for him a symbol of the prejudice his father encountered in trying to make a living for his family. George's sister Miriam died in the house, the victim of a case of pneumonia resulting from the river dampness that penetrated the dwelling each evening. Money was scarce. On more than one occasion, the Rahbani family's evening meal had consisted of potato peelings fried in lard.

George lit a cigar. His father had done everything possible to make a home for his loved ones. He picked through other people's trash looking for items to sell for scrap. He did their yard work only to be shorted when the time came to pay him. His father would speak glowingly of the day when he'd finally saved enough to buy a horse and wagon, allowing him to drive around the town selling tinware to housewives. The wagon represented the family's first step on the road to a better future. The city's boosters might have called Cedar Rapids the Parlor City back then, but no member of the Rahbani family had ever been invited into one of those parlors.

Now the town called itself The City of Five Seasons—the four regular seasons, and a fifth season to enjoy the others. What a joke. The name was only a few months old, and already folks referred to the place as The City of Five Smells. Everyone knew the first four smells: Quaker Oats, Penick & Ford, Wilson meatpacking, and the sewage treatment plant. There was much discussion and no agreement about the fifth odor, but George Rahbani knew it, and knew it well—the smell of money. Legal, illegal, or in-between, the smell was the same, and each greenback he earned put one more step between him and the tarpaper house. With money came respect, with respect came influence, and with influence came more money. With more money came fine cigars, nice clothes for his wife, vacations in Mexico, and swanky Eastern colleges for his daughters. For George Rahbani, the smell of money more than made up for the aromas of cereal, sewage, and hog guts wafting through the city streets.

His only son Habi was a disappointment. A world full of opportunities awaited the boy in the City of Five Seasons, but he had no discipline. Habi wanted money, but he couldn't smell it; because he didn't smell it, he did not work for it. George could only hope that one day Habi would wake from his dream and make something of himself. He couldn't imagine Habi running the motel, the nightclubs, the real estate, and the less-than-legal sidelines. George had structured the legal side of his businesses to provide for his wife and daughters. One day Habi would get the rest. If he didn't change, he'd run that portion into the ground.

George puffed his aromatic, full-bodied cigar and sighed.

"He will be less than I," he said quietly. "For a father to have such a son is a disappointment, but to have no son is worse."

He looked again at yesterday's newspaper and re-read the paragraph on the right of the front page. The brief article updated a story that first appeared almost a week ago.

Woman found dead in C. R.
Victim of Failed Abortion Attempt

The Office of the Linn County Medical Examiner reported Thursday that a woman found dead last Saturday in a supermarket parking lot died of hemorrhaging incurred as a result of an attempted abortion. The body of Diane Novacek, 27, was found in a car parked at the Me Too Super Market, 1624 J St. SW. Novacek was pronounced dead at the scene. The medical examiner reports there is no evidence that Novacek was pregnant. Police officials confirmed the case remains under investigation.

A sharp rap at the door interrupted his thoughts. It opened. Framed in the doorway, he saw his handyman Gus with a slouching Habi standing behind him.

George barked, "In, Habi. Now!" He looked at Gus, mouthed a thank you, and said aloud, "You can close the door, Gus. Habi and I have business."

Habi stood before his father. George let the silence build.

Growing steadily more uncomfortable, Habi straightened up and spoke first. "Good morning, Baba. How's Mama?"

"Take a seat. Mama is fine, but she doesn't see you enough. I don't see you enough. You've stayed away for two weeks."

Habi sat. "I've been busy. The motel, the Moonglow, the dancers, the collections—it all takes time."

"It all takes time? Time for what? At your age, I could take care of that much in a day."

George folded his newspaper so that the Novacek update was on top. He rose and skirted his desk. Positioning the paper twelve inches from his son's face, he pointed to the article.

"A Cedar Rapids woman. A Cedar Rapids woman! You fix a procedure for a Cedar Rapids woman, and when it goes wrong, you leave the body at a grocery store?"

He brought the paper down hard on his son, hitting him again and again on the face, the ears, and the shoulders.

"It wasn't me, Baba. It wasn't me. I only fix procedures for dancers and people from out of town, like you said." Habi raised his hands to protect his face. "It wasn't me."

The blows continued until the newspaper was in tatters. His fury spent, George returned to his chair and sat back down.

"Fool," he spat. "You fix a procedure for a Cedar Rapids woman, and you don't use Mari. I called Mari. She became angry when I thought this was her work. She took insult we used someone else. The Novacek woman wasn't even going to have a baby."

Habi insisted, "It wasn't me."

"It was you!" George roared. "Don't lie to me. If I was that stupid, I'd still be washing dishes."

"Baba, please." Habi simpered. "It wasn't one of ours. We don't make such a mess. Zaineb found the girl in a room at the motel. You can ask her. We can't have the police investigating the motel and the Moonglow. I paid Gabby to take care of things, but it went bad."

"You should have come to me, not that fool Gabby. A Cedar Rapids girl died. People will not forget. They will look for you. If they catch you, how will people treat your mama? Your sisters? Me? I don't know if I have enough money to fix this mess. If they catch you, everything I built for our family will be swept away. Do you like that? Are you proud of yourself?"

Habi sat in silence.

"There could be more trouble, Habi. If our friends in Des Moines hear about this, they may not trust Gabby to work with us anymore. If they think we are stupid, they will not want to work with us at all. The machines, the cigarettes, the televisions, the dancers—all could be gone."

"I'm sorry, Baba."

"You are not sorry Habi, but you will come to church and dinner tomorrow. Don't forget to bring flowers for Mama and candy for your sisters."

Habi stood up to leave.

"One more thing. Don't ever make me send Gus for you again, Habi. You brought me shame. A father should not have to send a handyman to look for his son."

"I understand," Habi said softly as he made for the door. "I'll be home for church and dinner."

8

I picked out my bright green tie for Diane's funeral. Not the sort of thing you'd usually wear to such an event, the tie held special meaning for me. I'd put it on when Diane and I went to the Golden Key, a downtown nightclub featuring the best jazz in the area.

One of the problems with being a dance teacher is that when I'm on the town, students want me to dance with them. Normally the attention is fun, but sometimes I'd rather listen to the music and focus on my tablemate. Diane routinely informed her students that she was unavailable at the Golden Key. The idea of an occasional uninterrupted night out appealed to me, but Diane's method depended on location. I wanted more freedom; I told my students a green tie signaled I wouldn't dance. Diane thought my choice odd and would tease me about it. I'd wear it today in her memory.

I sent flowers but passed on Diane's visitation. I couldn't do it. The funeral and hassle with the church had become so entangled with my wife's suicide that my emotions were running riot. I didn't trust myself to be presentable but managed to pull myself together and take a platter of ham sandwiches to the house before lunch. I stayed long enough to ask Roy and DeeDee to forgive me for skipping the Sunday wake. Their kindness and understanding were phenomenal. I left feeling like a heel.

At five o'clock, I drove to St. Lud's for the funeral service. I picked a spot in the last pew. Either the church was not air-conditioned, or the cooling system was on the fritz. My black suit was winter weight, and though my daily attire included a jacket and tie, I was sweltering. Fans ran full blast and the windows and doors were left open, but blowing hot air around the building did little to improve the climate. Although Diane's funeral had not been publicized, the extended Sedlak family was large and well-connected. As the number of attendees grew, it became obvious the church would be almost full.

I felt a tap on my shoulder. I turned to see Suzanne LaRue, the weeknight singer at the Golden Key, indicating she'd like to join me. I moved over. Suzanne had gotten to know Diane at the dance studio. Although Suzanne could warble like a nightingale, she found dance practice tiresome. She lasted four lessons, but became friends with Diane. Diane looked up to Suzanne, in part because Diane dreamed of becoming a singer. I kept it to myself, but her chances were slim. When it came to singing, Diane had no stage presence. The sparkle and vitality that infused her conversation and animated her dancing evaporated the minute she approached a microphone.

Suzanne and Diane enjoyed each other's company, getting together for lunches and chatting at the Golden Key during Suzanne's breaks. Suzanne was a stunning brunette, Diane a wholesome Czech blonde. When the two shared a table, the sight was enough to derange the thought processes of the average sex-starved male. The women had been the cause for more than one overly persistent customer being ejected from the Key. Unwilling to hire a bouncer, the club's owner, George Rahbani, handled the job himself. Apparently up to the task, he bounced so efficiently no one could remember an ousted customer ever returning.

The service droned on, and I found myself tuning out. I started thinking about my friendship with Diane. Maybe we weren't as close as I thought. I'd assumed when she started dating again, she'd introduce me to her beau. When that day came, I expected we'd be seeing a lot less of each other. Although I'd miss the easy access to her companionship, one thing I was sure of—come hell or high water—our friendship would endure.

I couldn't square what I knew about Diane with her keeping me in the dark about a love interest. Did she think so little of me she feared having a man in her life would strain our friendship? Perhaps she feared our friendship would intimidate her new boyfriend. I couldn't imagine Diane tolerating that sort of man, but love can lead someone to act in unexpected ways.

Diane was my best friend. I owed her the benefit of the doubt when it came to our friendship. Once you're over thirty, a best friend is a treasure not to be taken lightly. Diane had died horribly. I made a promise I would see that the individual who committed this atrocity paid full price for his actions. I owed as much to myself, to Lumir, and the rest of the family. I wouldn't be able to live with myself if I didn't.

I came back to the present as Father Blazek gave the blessing over the casket. The pallbearers exited their pews and lined up alongside the coffin as the soloist sang a song called "May the Angels Lead You into Paradise." When the catafalque started moving down the aisle, Diane's family filed in behind. DeeDee was, of course, crying. Roy looked as if he'd been so badly sucker punched he might collapse. Stan and Buzz stood protectively behind them, looking for all the world like bodyguards on the alert for potential assailants.

Lumir followed his grandchildren, walking tall and proud in his new linen suit, trying his best to be strong for his family. Although he'd been a meatpacker, the man knew the secret of how to dress. It's not what the clothes do for the man; it's what the man does for the clothes. A man who cares about his appearance and carries himself with pride is but a small step away from a man well dressed.

As occupants of the last pew, Suzanne and I were among the last to leave the church. I missed the tolling of the church bell. Since the funeral was supposed to be low key, a ringing bell was not in the cards. It seemed wrong somehow.

As we approached the vestibule, I saw the bell ropes hanging near a staircase in a side corner. They'd been loosely looped up to prevent the younger parishioners from tugging on them. I dropped Suzanne's arm, grabbed one of those long-handled collection baskets, and used it to unloop them. I pulled hard on the thickest of the knotted ropes. A bell pealed. As it swung in the opposite direction, the return almost lifted me off my feet. I waited until the sound had almost faded and pulled again. No one came to stop me. I tolled the bell until the last car of the funeral procession drove past the open door. Suzanne watched with a smile on her face, and when I finished, she took my arm again, and we descended the steps.

Although she'd brought her own car, Suzanne asked to ride with me to the interment at Bohemian National Cemetery. I welcomed the companionship. Suzanne looked stunning in a form-fitting black dress and veiled pillbox hat she'd tilted at an appropriately stylish angle. Although we flirted with one another on occasion, it had remained for both of us an amusing game with nothing more than the mutual enjoyment of a pleasant acquaintance behind it. Because of my bell ringing, we were a bit late to join the funeral procession. I wasn't concerned—we'd have no problem making the interment.

The choice of the Bohemian National Cemetery instead of the consecrated ground of St. John's, the Catholic burial ground on the east side of the river, was another compromise made to keep a low profile. Diane's interment there would raise conservative hackles. The tradition that an excommunicant be denied burial in a Catholic cemetery had an especially heart-wrenching repercussion—Diane would not be laid to rest next to her late husband.

As I pulled onto the street, I asked, "Did Diane have a boyfriend I didn't know about?"

"You never did quite get it, did you Cletus?"

"Get what?" I asked.

"She was stuck on you. You never saw it, and she was afraid if she said anything, she'd scare you away. That's one mighty big torch you're carrying, and she knew you wouldn't put it down. When you consider she still wasn't over the death of her husband, it wasn't in the cards the two of you would get together."

What was, what might have been, what could have been. Given the situation, I never saw us as anything more than friends. On some subconscious level, I'd known what Suzanne was telling me, but if Diane or I had followed up on our mutual attraction, the result would have been disastrous. We were too wounded—I more than she. I handled it by remaining in denial. We enjoyed a deep and genuine friendship. That we might have been in love seemed beside the point.

I sighed. "Maybe you should turn in your microphone for a psychology degree. You'd be good at it."

Suzanne laughed and said, "Getting back to your question, the police detective asked the same thing—did Diane have a boyfriend. I knew what he meant and gave him the same answer I'm giving you, 'I don't know.'"

"Did you catch his name?" I asked.

"The detective? He was a vile little man—Davis, I think."

"Did he ask about me?"

"No, he didn't. Mostly he implied Diane and I were bar flies who spent our free time sleeping around. I get the impression that's his method—keep stirring things up until somebody gets mad and talks too much."

Returning to the original point, I said, "Diane must have been with someone, or she wouldn't have worried about a pregnancy. I can't understand how she found time. She worked two jobs, went out on the town with me a couple of nights a week, sang with those rinky-dink Zmolek brothers, and visited her family on Sundays. She had a full plate."

"Believe me," Suzanne responded, "when a girl is looking for a little something on the side, she can always find the time."

We reached the cemetery with minutes to spare. Blazek did the committal. When he finished, Suzanne and I made our way to the mourner's chairs where Lumir, Roy, DeeDee, and the rest of the family sat. We hugged, shook hands, and said our goodbyes. I got to DeeDee last.

"Well, it looks like the good Father Blazek went out on a limb for you," I said.

"Oh Cletus, you don't understand," she replied.

"Understand what?" I asked.

In spite of her grief, DeeDee managed a smile.

"Why church politics, of course," she replied. "Father Blazek is taking a calculated risk. The only person who might complain is old Father Kun. If he goes to the Archbishop over this and fails to make his point, Father Blazek wins, and Father Kun is on his way to retirement. Since Father Blazek took steps to show respect for Father Kun by making Diane's funeral low key, he has a good chance of coming out of it smelling like a rose. Of course, Father Kun knows this and probably won't press the issue."

DeeDee kissed my cheek patted me on the shoulder. "Don't worry about us. As weird as it is, we love our church."

9

Gabby Khoury paused outside the door of Phil Ruggiero's office at Midwest Vending & Novelties Company. A little over a week had passed since he and Nick Thilmany returned from their ill-fated trip to Cedar Rapids, and as far as he could tell, news of their misadventure hadn't made it back to the workplace. Although he had an appointment, Gabby knocked twice before pushing the door open. He found his boss seated alongside his desk in a heavily upholstered chair, reading the morning paper and looking decidedly unhappy.

Before Gabby had a chance to open his mouth, his boss shot out of his chair, grabbed him by the shirt collar, and slammed him against the wall.

"What's wrong, Phil?"

Phil didn't answer. He made a fist with his free hand, cocked his arm, and rammed a bucket full of knuckles into Gabby's sternum. When Phil let go of his shirt collar, Gabby slumped to the floor, trying to breathe.

As he lay on the floor, unable to comprehend what had just happened, he felt a sharp blow to his testicles. Another followed in quick succession. He passed out, and when he came to, he understood Phil had kicked him. When his eyes focused, he saw Phil back at his desk, sitting quietly, staring at him.

Unruffled, Phil spoke quietly, "Nick Thilmany came in first thing Monday morning and quit. I send you to Cedar Rapids to make a simple delivery, and not only do you screw it up, you get into so much trouble you could end up in the penitentiary."

Realizing he might not survive a second episode, Gabby looked silently at the man who had just given him the beating of his life. He could barely breathe, and his groin howled with pain the like of which he'd never known.

"Lie there and catch your breath," Phil said. "When you're ready, take a chair and tell me all about it."

He did as he was told. The phone rang, and Phil answered it, scheduling a delivery and filling out the paper work. A few minutes later, Gabby got up, struggled into the chair, and sat. He waited for Phil to speak.

Phil looked up and spoke without emotion. "Nick had quite a story for me, and some of it sounded so wild it's hard to believe. Maybe you'd better tell me what happened."

"Phil, it's like this. Georgie's boy Habi needed a favor, so like you always tell Nicky and me, keep Georgie happy." Unsure of what Phil knew, he decided not to go into any details. "Habi wanted us to make a late-night delivery. The money sounded good, so I said yes."

"Habi is not Georgie," Phil observed. "A favor doesn't mean leaving a dead woman in a parking lot. That's cleaning up another guy's dirt. You screwed up big time, and now you've got a problem."

Gabby sat silently, waiting to see what Phil would do next.

"Your problem is the situation with Nick. He's got a lot on you. If he's got a lot on you, it could make trouble for you, and trouble for you could make trouble for the company. I think you and Nick need to work this thing out. He said something about going to drive a feed truck for his brother in Toledo. Look him up, and set things straight."

"Toledo is a long way, Phil. How am I gonna find him?"

"Toledo, Iowa, stupid."

Gabby didn't need the sarcasm, but Phil had a point. The situation with Nick created a problem. Gabby hadn't imagined the delivery would bother the guy so much he'd leave his job. He needed to get straight with Nick. The bad blood between them would only fester and wouldn't do anyone any good. He waited to see if Phil had anything else to say.

"Let me know how things work out." Phil looked down at his paperwork. "Go."

Gabby rose from his chair with difficulty. Walking unsteadily, he made it through the door, closed it, and collapsed in the hallway.

Gabby sat in his recliner with his legs splayed, mentally replaying the beating Phil had given him. You had to hand it to the guy; he knew how to work somebody over. Phil had temporarily disabled him and inflicted maximum pain in a way that created no need for medical care. He'd done it alone, with no help. These Chicago guys knew what they were doing.

Gabby got the message: don't screw up. He liked his drugs. Thank God Phil didn't know about them, but uppers made him erratic. Under the influence, it seemed entirely reasonable to dump a body for somebody he knew. After all, he and Nick didn't kill anybody, and in his altered state, driving a body through town and dumping it in the river didn't seem all that different from taking out the trash.

And now he had to straighten things out with Nick. Hiring Nick was a mistake from the get go. He'd never understand why Phil thought he could make a driver out of that small town nobody. The clod had no nerve. If Nick hadn't chickened out, they'd have dumped the body before they ditched the car. What the hell good is a driver who won't drive?

Too high to drive anyway, Gabby had let Nick get behind the wheel and leave his prints all over the controls of the car. He couldn't believe it when the stupid hick panicked, parked the car, and left behind his share of the fishing gear. Then he had to listen to Nick whine about walking all the way back to the truck. No matter how you cut it, the guy was a loser.

Gabby smiled. Phil needed him, and so did Georgie. The two had never met and, as far as he could see, they wanted to keep it that way. The Cedar Rapids operation earned Phil good money, and the guy would be lucky to find another good go-between. Nick, on the other hand, was a nobody. What Phil wanted is what he'd get.

Gabby was stoic about pain, but he'd never been so badly racked in the nuts in his life. His groin throbbed and his ribcage screamed. Swollen and blue in both locations, he'd need a couple of shots of Canadian Club and another Seconal or two before he could nap.

Gabby woke early. He'd been medicating himself on and off for the last eighteen hours, downing the fifth of Canadian Club and a half dozen Seconals. He stank, had a hangover, and every movement hurt. He'd conked out with the windows closed, and overnight the temperature and humidity had gone through the roof. Sweating like a pig, he made his way across the room and turned on the radio. The weatherman expected a heat wave that would last a week or more. He stumbled to the bathroom, urinated copiously, and examined himself. His equipment looked terrible but didn't hurt so much any-more. His rib cage told another story.

"I hope that son of a bitch didn't break any ribs," he muttered. "Jesus, Phil, what'd I ever do but work for you?"

Well, he had his assignment: get straight with Nick and report back as soon as possible. He'd have to get cleaned up, find some more Seconal, and make the trip to Toledo. With luck, he'd be there late this afternoon or early evening. Oh yeah, and stop by the state-owned liquor store. Nick really liked his Chivas Regal.

By mid-afternoon, Gabby was cruising east on Highway 30 and in good spirits. A couple of Seconals had eased the pain in his rib cage, and he'd cranked the air conditioning on his Oldsmobile. Given the events of the past day and a half, he felt reasonably alert. Iowa's Toledo was a small town, so it wouldn't be hard to find Nick. If he stayed with somebody he knew, it might take a couple of days. If he'd shacked in a motel, a lot less.

As he approached the outskirts from the west, Gabby spotted something called the L-Ranko Motel. Trimmed with so much neon it must have escaped from Las Vegas, the place looked anything but rank. When he pulled into the parking lot to look around, Lady Luck didn't just smile on him, she gave him a big wet kiss on the cheek. Gabby noticed a car parked in front of a solitary freestanding cabin. Nick's car.

Nick Thilmany smiled contentedly as he pulled at his beer. Although he bailed on Des Moines just a week ago, he'd already snagged another job. His brother fired a driver for drinking during work hours and needed a replacement right away. He'd let Nick off early today. The air conditioner on the delivery truck didn't work, and the cab felt like the inside of a blast furnace. Freed from responsibility, Nick sought shelter back in his motel room. Daffy Duck cavorted across the TV screen courtesy of one of those afternoon cartoon shows. The show's hosts, a fake doctor and a grease-painted clown named Mombo, were hard to take, but Nick didn't care. The Looney Tunes shorts made up for it.

Nick considered himself lucky to be out of that nuthouse called Midwest Vending. Since his brother Dommy's weird-o wife precluded a stay at the house, he'd checked into a motel, intending to stay until he got his first paycheck. Dommy's old lady tried to convert everyone she met to her Pentecostal religion, and she didn't know when to back off. Although Dommy didn't seem to notice her one-track mind, holy rollers made Nick crazy. As for the motel, despite the name, it was nice. The manager told him the L-Ranko name had something to do with Rank, the owner's name. Poor guy.

That last trip to Cedar Rapids was the straw that broke the camel's back. Nick wasn't a goody two shoes and didn't mind shagging hot property, but hanging around drugged out crazies and hauling corpses was another thing altogether. He'd been scared shitless.

Chauffeuring a dead woman; Gabby's endless Nicky, Nicky, Nicky; walking around town at three in the morning carrying fishing poles; a partner higher than Mount Everest—where did it end? He had to get out of the car that night, or he'd have gone wacko himself.

Holy Mother of God. The way Phil looked at him when he told the story—like he was the nut. Not that Nick could blame him. How could any person with a normal brain imagine an everyday delivery could turn into something from the *Addams Family*? And the dead woman's face, she looked so spooky he half expected her to sit up and take a bite out of him. Whatever was going on at Midwest Vending & Novelties, he was glad to be out of it.

Somebody knocked on the door. Nick turned and looked through the window. Jesus H. Christ, it was Gabby. Nick rose from his chair, but the Syrian had already stepped inside.

"Hi ya, Nicky."

Nick glared.

"Look, I wanna apologize to you. Phil is mad at me and says I owe you. I know you don't like me, and I know I messed up big time in Cedar Rapids."

"You're right about me not liking you." Nick's mouth straightened into a thin line. "What I'd like is for you to leave."

"Nicky," Gabby whined, "I'm in trouble with Phil big time. I think I might lose my job. I know you like Scotch, and Chivas is your favorite. I'd like to make it up to you, so I brought you a bottle."

Nick's face hardened. "You can make it up to me by leaving."

Gabby looked stricken. "At least take the scotch. Then I can tell Phil I gave it to you."

"Leave." Nick said. "Make like a leaf. Dry up and blow away."

If the guy didn't leave, Nick was ready to paste him one in the kisser. Gabby got the message. He put the bottle on the floor inside the door, got into his Oldsmobile, and drove off.

———

Gabby drove the rest of the way into town and stopped at a diner down the street from the county courthouse. A hand-lettered sign identified the place as the Trojan Inn. With a name like that, a guy might think there'd be a condom dispenser in the men's room. There wasn't, but his pork chop, potatoes, and gravy more than made up for the deficiency. When he tried to joke with his waitress about the name, she rolled her eyes, said she'd heard it all before, and pointed to a note on the menu. Turned out the owner named the joint after the local high school team.

His meal finished, Gabby exited the Trojan and headed around the corner to a place called Pelzer's where he played pinball and lost five dollars at the pool table. When he tired of the games, he headed to the bar, ordered a beer, and stared at the television. Some crazy Arab shot Bobby Kennedy five days ago, and the news still played the story like it happened yesterday. *Big hairy deal, one less rich guy to tell everybody else how to live.* He stared at the tube for an hour, got up, and headed out into the heat.

Nothing stirring, not even mosquitoes. Certain that living in a place like Toledo would turn anyone's brain to applesauce within a week, he walked the downtown, checking out the red-brick courthouse and store windows. It didn't take long to exhaust the sights. He left downtown, walked past the school and over to a nearby graveyard. Hoping to find a bit of a breeze among the tombstones, he walked into the cemetery. Nothing doing. Disappointed and sweating profusely, he returned to Pelzer's. Killing time was part of the job, but his ribs throbbed, his painkillers were gone, and he felt irritable. Settling in over another beer, Gabby reviewed his day.

He'd spent almost two hours working on Nick's bottle of Chivas. He'd purchased an extra—just in case. He steamed the tax stamp and neck label off the first and carefully removed the foil capsule. After unscrewing the cap, he poured the powder from six Seconal capsules into the bottle. He re-screwed the cap and carefully bent the little plastic legs that joined it to the neck ring back into place. Using a pin, he added the tiniest bit of airplane glue to the juncture where each of the separated legs met the ring. Satisfied with his work, he re-wrapped the foil and re-glued the neck seal and tax stamp.

The result didn't look half-bad, and a return to the Chivas presentation box made for the final touch. If Nick didn't examine the bottle for tampering, the effort would do. The first bottle turned out so well Gabby would be able to drink the second.

Proud of his accomplishment, he sipped his beer. They didn't teach him stuff like that in reform school. He'd had to pick it up on his own. If the camouflage didn't work and Nick became suspicious, he'd have to straighten things out some other way. He didn't worry Nick would go to the police. The guy had a visceral dislike of the law.

At three a.m., Gabby quietly approached the door to Nick's cabin. The lock was no problem. A quick shim, fingers slipped inside to undo the chain, and he was ready to enter. He listened, and heard Nick snoring. In the dim light, he could see a third of the bottle was gone. Nick had thoughtfully left his keys on the nightstand—there'd be no need to empty his pockets.

"Thank you, Nicky," he whispered to himself.

Gabby picked up the keys, the Chivas box, and the bottle. He wiped the doorknob, the lock, and the chain, then returned to his car where he'd left gloves and supplies earlier that evening.

Now, if his luck would only hold.

10

Willing to do anything I could to aid in the investigation of Diane's
death, I phoned the Cedar Rapids Police Department the day after
Diane's funeral to arrange for an appointment with Pudge Davis.
When I spoke to the operator, my request was met with an "Excuse
me?"

"Pudge Davis," I repeated.

"Sir," the voice said coldly, "I believe you want to speak with
Detective Florian Davis."

Florian? Who knew?

I had the afternoon off, so I made an appointment for later
that day. Statues of two small lions greeted me as I walked up the
several steps of the tan art-deco building. If the building's architect
had intended the lions to represent the majesty of the law, he'd failed
miserably. Anything but imposing, the diminutive lions looked more
like housecats in starched collars than regal guardians of the law.
When I checked in at the counter, an elderly receptionist escorted
me to a second-floor room with a dozen desks. Pudge Davis, the only
occupant, sat at one of them.

Pudge looked up and, though I'd made an appointment, acted surprised.

"Efferding, imagine seeing you here. You come to confess?"

Good ol' Pudge, you had to hand it to him. He really knew how to win you over.

"Pudge," I suggested, "why don't you call me Cletus, and I'll call you Florian."

"It don't work that way, Pervie. I'm the police detective, and you're the lowlife sex creep."

Well, at least I tried. "I know you and I don't get along the best, but I'm here to give you all the help I can on the Diane Novacek case. Names, addresses of people she knew, all the background I have, help with her family, you name it."

Pudge leaned back in his chair and snorted. "See, the case ain't so important anymore. There ain't any murder. There ain't any abortion."

"But a woman died," I said.

"Some crazy woman, who shoulda known better, decides to break the law, hooks up with some quack, and something goes wrong. Maybe the guy goes down for involuntary manslaughter but probably something a lot less. That means the priority on the abortion side of the case isn't much higher than on the stolen car."

"Pudge, something is wrong here. Doesn't it seem odd a woman who wasn't pregnant would get an abortion?"

"It takes all kinds, Pervie. In this job, I get to see 'em all. Some woman thinks she's knocked up and don't want her doctor to know about it. Most barflies ain't too bright, and if they're dumb enough to get an abortion, they're dumb enough not to get tested. Sometimes it's better if people like that don't add to the population."

I couldn't believe what I was hearing. Surely, Pudge was trying to egg me on.

"Look," I said, "I'm serious. I really want to help with this."

Pudge slapped his desk with his hand. The sharp crack echoed through the deserted room. "Listen, and try to get this through your thick skull. It's over. Nobody is gonna touch this case. It's unsolvable.

There ain't any murder. The so-called victim was a barfly who brought it on herself, and working on it wastes manpower and money. We got orders. I'm off the case; Erikson's off the case. It's over. It don't exist anymore. Go find yourself a new girlfriend—one who likes your little tie-me-up games."

"You're just trying to get to me. I'm willing to help however I can."

"Look on the bright side. There ain't no investigation, so you ain't a suspect anymore. It don't matter you think you can help. The case is dead. Now get out before I have somebody from downstairs throw you out."

Pudge picked up a file from his desk and began to leaf through its contents.

"Efferding, leave," he said.

"I'm going, Florian."

Halfway to the door, I turned and addressed the most disgusting human being I'd ever met. "I never liked you, and I never thought you were a good detective, but I did think there was more to you than this—that somewhere inside, you might have a bit of humanity."

"That really hurt, Pervie. You should go home and write sermons."

Back at my apartment, I stood in front of my dresser. I picked up and folded my green tie and put it in the back corner of the top drawer. I doubted I'd be wearing it again. It brought back too many memories of Diane. If I needed to, I'd find another way to let my students know I didn't want to dance.

My trip to the cop shop left me with a case of the blues. I sighed, walked over to the couch, and sat down in front of the TV. I didn't bother to turn it on.

I couldn't afford to hire an investigator. Even if I did, the pickings would be slim. Anyone plying the trade in Cedar Rapids would have acquired his training by way of one of those correspondence courses advertised in the back of *True Crime Magazine*. I'd have to solve Diane's murder on my own.

Although I'd lived in the place three years, I really didn't know the city. I had no police or military experience. Heck, I didn't even read murder mysteries. All I could think of was to start with what I knew, and the only things I knew I'd read in the newspaper or heard at my lunch with Jim Weiss.

Focusing on the negative wouldn't help me find the person responsible for Diane's death. I needed to get off my butt and act like a man. I slapped myself in the face. It didn't hurt enough, so I let go and hammered myself again. I caught the end of my nose, and it started to bleed, a result I hadn't intended. I walked to the kitchen, grabbed a tissue, and began blotting. I paced back and forth, thinking and blotting, blotting and re-thinking.

Diane grew up in Bohemie Town. I wondered if the grocery's location might prove to be a link between the neighborhood and the crime. It didn't take long to abandon the idea. The notion that Diane would have made an appointment with the friendly neighborhood abortionist seemed so farfetched I nearly slapped myself again. Then too, nobody would steal a car to dispose of a body just to park it on a nearby street.

Why a grocery store? I couldn't think of a reason. Perhaps someone who worked or shopped there might have seen something or have an idea. Hamstrung without a badge, I couldn't very well go into the store and begin questioning employees and customers. I'd be shown the door within two minutes. Frustrated I couldn't think up a plan to con my way into talking with the staff, I continued to pace.

I doubted I'd learn anything interesting from the basketball or fishing equipment found in the car. They were in police custody where I couldn't examine them. Besides, a basketball was a basketball. There'd be one in most of the houses in town. I couldn't imagine a dip net would tell me much about the owner. I might visit bait shops to see who sold stink bait, but it was widely available, and I didn't know the brand name. The contents of the car were of no help, and as for the car itself, I suspected it had been returned to the dentist.

I paced, grabbed a fresh tissue, and went back to the couch. My best option was to check out the police department's other suspect, Gordon Cole—the dentist who owned the car. I picked the phonebook up from the end table, opened to the yellow pages, and almost missed the listing because guy's name started with a K. I made a quick flip to the white pages. Gordon A. Kohl, DDS, had a house on Grande Avenue and an office on Tenth Street. I needed to get my teeth looked at anyway.

Tomorrow, I'd schedule an appointment.

Jim Weiss and I met for breakfast at Tommy's Restaurant. I'd chosen the venue because I liked the food, the strong coffee, and the bustling waitresses shouting orders to the cook manning the grill. Breakfast at Tommy's made for an eye-opener that inspired a man to sit up straight and rip right into the day. A clattering, crowded place, Tommy's was a poor choice if you wanted to sit and think, but a good selection if you wanted to talk without being overheard.

"Jim," I began, "there's so much about this town I don't understand. I went over to the police station yesterday and offered to help with Diane's case. Davis told me to forget it. He said there's no case—they'd been ordered off it. Not only that, he called it low priority, an embarrassment to the city, and something they'd never solve anyway. What the hell is going on?"

Jim lit a Marlboro, sat quietly for a moment, and began thoughtfully. "You need to remember this thing is more important to you and the Sedlaks than to anyone else. You're suffering, but for most people, the details of Diane's death are just grist for the gossip mill. Think about it. How much coverage has there been on TV or in the papers? A lot the first day, less when Diane was identified, and not much more for the release of the medical examiner's report. Now that people know we don't have a homicidal maniac running loose, they're not very interested."

I sighed. "I don't get this town at all. Back home, they'd be chewing it over for the next five years."

"In a little town like Bellevue, they don't have much to talk about. You're not going to like this, but some people in Cedar Rapids think dying from a botched abortion is the sort of thing that happens to the daughter of a Bohemian factory worker. If Diane belonged to one of the country club families, the story would be different."

"We had the same thing in Bellevue," I said. "A doctor's son counted for more than a commercial fisherman's daughter. I guess in the scheme of things, rich people count for more."

I'd lost Jim's attention. "Jim?" I asked.

Jim stubbed his smoke. "The part that interests me, and should interest you, isn't who's rich and who isn't. What's interesting is that Davis and Erikson have been pulled off the case."

"Pudge called the case unsolvable, and a waste of time and money," I said.

"Bullshit, something stinks."

"What do you mean?"

Jim peered over his glasses to ensure he had my attention. "It looks like I'll have to draw you a picture. You know about the state law that requires a mandatory suspension of your driver's license if you get too many moving violations, right?"

"Sure," I said, "the point system. Each violation you get so many points. When you reach the magic number of points—p-f-f-f-t, your license flies away."

"Not true for everyone in town," Jim explained. "It's easy to fix a ticket so you don't go over the top on your points. If you're in the know, you phone a lawyer who does traffic appeals, and he sets up a hearing. On the day you show up in court, you bring an unmarked envelope with a hundred-dollar bill tucked into it and give it to your lawyer. He takes it up to the front of the room, there's a conference, and your ticket goes away."

I picked up my coffee, took a sip, and considered the implication of what Jim was saying. "You mean—"

"Clete, you're a strange guy. One day you surprise me with how much you know, and the next day you come off like a Boy Scout. The reason the investigation is on hold is simple. Somebody has connections—the fix is in."

I didn't want to believe him. "I'm floored. Every city tolerates a certain amount of vice and corruption because they're almost impossible to stamp out. But a fix on a case like this? A death? I can understand it might happen in a place like Milwaukee or Chicago, but Cedar Rapids, Iowa?"

Jim shook his head. A lifelong resident of the city, he understood the ins and outs of the place on a level that'd remain foreign to me if I lived here twenty years.

"Cedar Rapids is a nice place," he said, "but it doesn't have a monopoly on virtue. Like you said, graft happens everywhere. I liked Diane, and I'd like to help you with your investigation."

"I just think somebody should pay for what happened," I said. "I don't know if you could call it an investigation."

"Whatever you want to call it is fine by me. My sister-in-law works as a clerk in the police department. She's a straight shooter, so I doubt she'll bend the rules for us. But it won't hurt to ask. Maybe she'll accidentally leak something."

I drained my coffee and said, "I can't tell you how much this means to me. Right now, I have zero to go on."

"Don't get your hopes too high. She may know nothing at all. Shirley's pretty low on the totem pole."

Someone dropped a tray of dishes. The sound brought me back to the present. I'd eaten an entire Tommy's Shipwreck with no memory of having done so. Considering the size of the dish, no small feat.

———————————

Jim called me on Thursday morning. His sister-in-law Shirley, our potential mole in the police department, wanted to meet me. I asked him to arrange a get-together that evening. He reserved a dinner table at the Elks Lodge.

I showed up at the Elks' five minutes early. I worked the knob furiously, but the door wouldn't open. Hearing voices and music coming from within, I pounded on it. A buzzing sound and clicking lock mechanism rewarded my efforts. I'd missed the button and "Please Ring Bell" sign to the left of the frame.

A smiling greeter directed me to the hat rack and then escorted me to the bar where Jim and Shirley waited. They were drinking Old-Fashioneds, so I ordered one too. When my drink arrived, Jim led us to our table where we made small talk while waiting for our food. I could see Shirley sizing me up.

Before I could launch into my request, she put down her glass and asked, "Do you mind if I call you Cletus, rather than Clete?"

An odd request, people usually asked to use the short form. "Please do," I replied.

"Cletus, give me one good reason why I should betray my colleagues and jeopardize my job to satisfy your curiosity about a young woman's tragic death."

While I searched for a reply, Jim fumbled with a cigarette and said, "You can see Shirley takes her job seriously. I've spoken about you a number of times, and she wanted to meet you."

"I can take care of this, Jim," she said. "Cletus, answer my question."

Shirley was a no-bullshit woman. I'd have one chance to make my case, and even if it was good, the answer might still be no.

"Diane Novacek was my best friend. I've been through enough ups and downs in my life to know real friends are rare. Real friends deserve loyalty. Diane died under circumstances I don't understand, but I do understand her life was cruelly taken from her. She was a remarkable woman, and her family and friends have a hole in their lives that can never be filled. Diane deserved better. I could talk all night, but there's nothing more I can say that will add to that."

Shirley looked at Jim. She looked at me, then nodded to herself. "I really don't know what I can tell you. I move files around. I hear a lot of gossip, but I'm not always sure if it's reliable."

"For a start, you could tell me a little bit about Pudge Davis. I've never met a cruder, more insulting human being. I have doubts about his ability to do anything with the case."

She smiled. "Oh, Florian. He lives with his mother in an older house a couple of blocks from Coe College."

I was incredulous. "His mother? Pudge Davis lives with his mother?"

"As far as I know, he never left home."

"Does he know what he's doing? Is he a good detective?" I asked.

"Well, Florian is old school—a little rough around the edges. They won't let him anywhere near the upper crust. He gets assigned the sex crimes and cases in the poor neighborhoods. As far as I know, he's as good as any of the other detectives."

Our orders arrived, and the conversation turned to the news about town. Not wanting the business at hand to detract from the ambience of our meal, I put a lid on it. I was walking a fine line with Shirley and didn't want to push. When the three of us had finished and were waiting for dessert, I got back to the reason for our meeting.

"Is Pudge Davis in charge of Diane's case?" I asked. "Earl Erikson seems to be working on it too."

"I've seen the file on Florian's desk, so I suppose he's the lead investigator," she replied. "The detectives share their work. Right now, Earl's main concern is that murdered woman they found at Coralville Lake. She was from Cedar Rapids you know."

Jim chimed in. "The ex-husband did it."

Shirley looked as if she didn't buy his explanation. The conversation promised to be interesting, but I wanted to stay on track. "Pudge told me they quit working on Diane's case. I don't know if it's true, or if he's trying to keep me off balance. Do you know anything about the case? Are they still working it?"

"Oh, I haven't heard anything about that," she said.

I continued. "Any chance somebody might have put in a fix? You know, money changes hands, and the case goes away?"

Jim's eyes widened to twice their normal size. He held up both hands, waving them side to side as he shook his head. Too late.

"Shirley, I—" he began.

"Wait one minute, Buster." Shirley glared at me. "I work for the Cedar Rapids Police Department, and no one there has been anything but decent to me. I don't know a good detective from a bad one, but I can tell you Florian Davis is an honest man. I don't think I want any part of you poking your nose into police business."

With that, she folded her napkin and stood so suddenly she overturned her chair. The noise brought the room's activity to a standstill. All eyes turned as Shirley shouldered her purse, made an about-face, and strode to the exit.

"We'll talk another time," Jim said as he rose and rushed to join his sister-in-law.

I had yet to recover when one of our fellow diners detached himself from his table, walked over, looked down at me, and announced, "Guests of the Elks Club are to be accompanied by members at all times."

I could take an unsubtle hint. I asked the waitress for the check and paid up. I had to hand it to myself, when it came to women, I could really read 'em.

11

Phil Ruggiero was sitting in his office at Midwest Vending & Novelties Company when Gabby walked in, tossed a thin newspaper on his desk, and waited. Phil picked up the paper. The masthead announced he was looking at last Thursday's edition of the *Toledo Chronicle*, a publication serving Tama County. Phil chuckled. The *Chronicle* belonged to that class of small town papers known throughout the Mid-West as "Astonishers." Published just once a week, the newspapers had earned the nickname because a reader would have been astonished to learn something he didn't already know. Gabby had circled an article on the front page.

Suspected Suicide at L-Ranko Motel

The Tama County Sheriff's Department is investigating the death of Nicholas Thilmany, 32, of Des Moines, Iowa. Deputy Sheriff Russell Hardinger was called to the motel Tuesday when a maid discovered a body of a man in a freestanding cabin at the side of the main building. One end of a hose, which terminated in the cabin's interior, was taped to the tailpipe of a late model car. The car's engine was left running.

Thilmany had recently taken a job delivering feed for his brother Dominic and was reported to have been despondent after abruptly leaving his previous employer, a Des Moines-based vending machine company.

Phil let out a low whistle. Gabby had straightened things out with Nick and handled it well. There'd be an investigation, but with suicide by carbon monoxide so common, Phil doubted it would be comprehensive. When Gabby was good, he was very good, but when he screwed up, he screwed up royally.

"Gabby," he said, "have a seat."

As Gabby sat, Phil leaned back in his chair, locked his hands behind his head, and looked up at the ceiling.

"Looks like you got things straightened out with Nick. Nice work. Poor guy, taking his own life like that."

Phil watched Gabby swell with pride.

"See Phil, I got this—"

"Good job. Let's leave it at that."

"Thanks Phil," Gabby said. "I try."

No doubt the man wanted to spill the details, but Phil didn't need to know. He put his feet up on the desk. "You know, we've had quite a bit of excitement around here lately, what with that woman in Cedar Rapids and now Nick. If anything goes wrong, it could get hot. Maybe you should leave town for a few weeks."

"Whatever you say, Phil."

"I've just been talking to my cousin in Peoria, Rick Spano. He could use some help right now."

"Don't know him," Gabby responded.

"He's a good guy. He'll treat you right."

Phil leaned forward to tug at his socks, settled back again, and looked at Gabby.

"You know, I been thinking about starting a branch office in Omaha. As far as I'm concerned, you earned a promotion. Can you run it?"

"I know the business, inside and out."

"We'll get started when you come back. Georgie might be a problem. Will he trust any of our guys? The Cedar Rapids business is good for us, but you and Nick are the only ones who ever met him, and Nick ain't here no more."

"Georgie's smart, Phil. But think about it, he needs us worse than we need him. We protect his territory. Without us, he gets no swag. Without us, he has to find his own dancers. Without us, he gets no skim from the machines. Without us, his earnings take a hike to the toilet."

"What about Marco?" Phil asked. "He's not Syrian. Will Rahbani trust him?"

"Marco's a good man," Gabby said. "I'll need to make the introduction. Georgie will be okay, if the financials don't change."

"You and Marco take separate cars to Cedar Rapids—tonight. Put four cases of Canadian Club and a box of those Cuban cigars in Marco's trunk. After you introduce Marco to Georgie, Marco will give them to him."

He handed Gabby a sheet of paper. "When you're done, drive straight to this address in Peoria. Ask for Rick. He'll let you know when I want you back. It should only take a few weeks. Oh yeah, take a box of cigars and a case of Canadian Club for Cousin Rick, and a box and a case for yourself. Celebrate your promotion."

Gabby left. Phil put his hands back behind his head and considered all that had transpired. He had no intention of giving the Syrian a promotion. He'd made the offer to get Gabby's cooperation in giving up the Cedar Rapids business. He called Marco, filled him in on the situation, and hung up.

That couple of weeks with Rick in Peoria would give Phil the opportunity to see how George Rahbani responded to a new representative. Marco had more on the ball than Gabby, and he'd never be happy with Gabby's percentage. Phil was damned if the difference would come out of his own pocket. Georgie would have to swallow it. The body-in-a-car deal meant Gabby was dangerously unfit for any job. Phil had no intention of opening an office in Omaha and no intention of promoting anybody.

Instead, Gabby would get a horizontal transfer—to a dead-end position.

Dr. Gordon Kohl's receptionist greeted me with a cheery smile. She was a pleasant woman of about forty who'd have looked younger but for the curse of old lady's hair. The frizzy, tight little curls that characterized her short locks added a good fifteen years to her appearance. I found it hard to believe the woman paid someone for the privilege of making her look so bad. Gentleman that I am, I refrained from giving her the advice she obviously needed—especially since I hoped to pump her for information. I tried to strike up a conversation, but the phone rang and a drawn-out conversation about impacted wisdom teeth ensued.

I filled out some paperwork, sat back, and took in the surroundings. A cheerful, well-lit waiting room furnished back when Danish modern was all the rage met my eye. The setup spoke of a small, well-managed operation—one that wasn't going gangbusters but one that didn't lack for clients. I waited for the sufferer with the impacted wisdom teeth to get off the phone so I could return my completed forms and chat with the receptionist. The interminable phone call ended, and I was about to start a conversation, when someone called my name.

The voice belonged to a pretty young redhead who escorted me back to a patient's chair. Apparently, Dr. Kohl had joined the ranks of dentists who hired young women to clean their customers' teeth. Kohl's assistant introduced herself, tilted me back in the chair, and made small talk about the weather while I considered how to begin a conversation about the theft of her boss's car. I waited a bit too long and encountered an unexpected difficulty. My mouth was occupied.

"I eah Doctah Koe cah wah stola," I said.

A jolt of pain shot through me. I saw stars as my nerves crackled from the back of my jaw to the roots of my toenails. The young lady cleaning my teeth had jabbed her pointed instrument between my gum and last molar. She'd done it deliberately, and she'd done it hard. I tasted blood.

"Okay," she demanded, "what's this all about?"

I exhaled, unglued my fingers from the arms of the chair, and pushed in on the outside of my throbbing jaw.

"I hear Dr. Kohl's car was stolen."

"Listen," she said, "Dr. Kohl is a good man, a happily married man, a fine dentist, and my uncle. He doesn't need nosey first-time customers who come here to satisfy some kind of sick curiosity about a woman's death. What kind of loser are you anyway?"

"My friend was in that car," I said.

"I don't care if God's own mother was in that car. One more question like that, and this instrument goes straight into your eye. Do you hear me?"

I contemplated getting out of the chair and leaving, but I needed the checkup. It made sense to stick it out. Maybe I'd still learn something.

"I hear," I replied.

The rest of the cleaning proceeded in silence, although I can't say I found it very relaxing. When my cleaning lady finished, she called Dr. Kohl into the room.

"What do we have?" he asked.

"Some bleeding on number thirty-one, but otherwise everything looks okay."

Gordon Kohl turned out to be a short, pear-shaped man with coke-bottle glasses and well-oiled hair. As his examination of my mouth progressed, it became apparent his pleasant manner and light touch had much to do with the odd-looking man's ability to maintain a successful practice. If nothing else, my visit today made one thing abundantly clear. There was no way the homely Dr. Kohl could have been Diane's secret lover.

That didn't let him off the hook. A dentist would have a good knowledge of anatomy and ready access to instruments and drugs. Though I didn't peg him for it, Gordon Kohl would have made a good abortionist. With his dental training and professional manner, women would have trusted him.

My examination over, Dr. Kohl left the room. His comely assistant removed my bib, stepped back, and glared at me with her arms crossed, eyes spitting fire, and the instrument of my recent torture grasped firmly in her hand.

"Do come back, Mr. Efferding," she said, waving her stainless-steel weapon just enough for me to notice. "And don't forget to floss. You know it's standard hygiene these days. Would you like to make another appointment? By the way, I'd be doing your cleaning."

I passed. Investigating Diane's death was turning out to be harder than I'd expected.

The next day, I found Pudge Davis waiting for me as I exited Killian's on my way to the dance studio.

"Okay, Pervie," he said, "we gotta talk."

"What's wrong, Flo?" I asked.

Pudge turned red with anger, the color contrasting nicely with the sandy tone of his flattop haircut. "One of these days, you're gonna regret that big fat mouth of yours."

"Florian," I replied, "you can call me Cletus."

Pudge's eyes narrowed, his nostrils flared, his hands balled themselves into fists.

"Listen Creepus, I come here to warn you. I got a complaint from a dentist's office about you nosin' around. Stay the hell out of police business."

"You told me yourself, the department can't make the case," I said. "No leads, too expensive, Diane was worthless. I got the message. Diane is no longer police business."

"Get over it," he said. "Your girlfriend is gone. You playin' detective won't bring her back. Find a new chippie to beat you up. You're dirt, Efferding. I can put you in the hospital, and nobody will believe your story. Nobody's gonna care if you end up in a wheelchair."

I let go of my anger. Did I want to risk a beating from a man who could break me in half? I'd pushed Pudge to the edge of violence several times. I'd gain nothing from it, so I held my tongue.

"Where'd you find out about the dentist?" he demanded.

"A friend of mine recognized the car from the picture in the newspaper. He thought he'd sold it to a Dr. Kohl. I went to check it out, and it turns out he was right."

"Stay out of this," he warned. "We ever pick this case back up, you'll have everything so balled up no one will ever solve it."

"Sure thing," I said without conviction.

"Don't 'sure thing' me. You leave that dentist's office and the people who work there alone. Remember, I can hurt you, Creepus. Back off."

"On second thought, Florian, only women call me Cletus. Maybe you should stick with Clete."

"I'll be sure to remember, Efferding. No Creepus, just plain Creep."

Randy Roeder

12

Almost every dance studio plays host to a group of students who take lessons on a long-term basis. A cross section of the studio's clientele, they may be young or old, single or coupled, talented or untalented. People drift in and out of the group as their interest in dance waxes and wanes. Some may take lessons for decades yet seldom appear at a public dance. Others frequent all the dance venues in town. The studio where I worked was no exception, but our group of regulars was different. They'd given themselves a name—the Studio Rats.

When one of the Rats discovered my upcoming thirty-fifth birthday, the group decided to organize an outing in my honor. Armar Ballroom, the home of the largest dance floor in the area, had scheduled a first-class big band for the weekend. The Rats decided to reserve tables for the event so we could sit together, eat cake, and dance the night away.

The idea didn't thrill me—Diane had been dead less than two weeks. I couldn't think of a gracious way to refuse the offer, so agreed to the outing. As I thought about it later, I was happy I did. The Rats and I shared a history, and that history included Diane. Wrapped up in my own grief, I could easily forget she played a part in other lives as well. The Rats were hurting. An evening out would do us all some good.

That night I drove the Nova over to Armar, a remodeled aircraft hangar on the border of Cedar Rapids and the neighboring town of Marion. I parked in the spacious lot, locked the car, and presented myself at the ticket window. I can't say I was surprised to learn no one had ordered a ticket for me, so I paid my way into my own birthday celebration. The Studio Rats were nothing if not thrifty. I took my ticket and entered. As soon as one of the female Rats spotted me, she waved me over to our designated area and directed me to the folding chair of honor. A hearty exchange of huzzahs, handshakes, and busses on the cheek followed. I was happy to see Dr. Willy Schreiber and his wife joining the Rats tonight; I had some medical questions I wanted to ask him.

The initial greetings over, I sat down, laced on my dance shoes, found an available Rat, and slid out onto the dance floor. I knew by the time the evening was over, I'd have danced with every woman in our group. Whether young or old, thick or thin, talented or untalented, it made no difference. My role for the evening was to serve as Mr. Smooth, ensuring everyone had fun. I didn't mind. At an event like this, it's all about the group dynamic—and sharing dances increases everyone's enjoyment.

When the band took a break, I went over to speak to the Schreibers. I managed to pry Willy away from the group he and his wife were talking to.

"Willy," I said, "I'd like to ask you a question. It's about Diane."

Willy raised his eyebrows. "Let's go somewhere where we can talk."

We headed for the snack window, bought cokes, and picked an empty table. Diane's death was on his mind too.

"The poor girl," Willy said, "so young and to die that way. It's sad for me and Gertrude, sad for everyone at the studio."

"That's what I want to talk about. I need to know more about how she died. I want to know how an abortion can go wrong."

"Are you sure you want to know about this? Will it make you happy? Will your pain go away?"

"No, it won't make me happy. Yes, the pain will still be there—but knowing will help me understand."

"If it's what you want, I will tell you, but not here at your party. Come to my office on Monday."

The band was still on break when we re-joined the Studio Rats. My absence had been a cause for concern, since they planned to serve my birthday cake during the interlude. Rather than have my tardiness put a damper on the event, the Rats decided to go ahead without me.

Willy's wife had successfully rescued a piece of cake for him. Someone saved a piece for me, but when a late arrival turned up, it had been cut in half so no one would do without. Be that as it may, the Rats serenaded me with a hearty rendition of "Happy Birthday" as I put a fork to my half-piece of cake. I suspected my piece had presented too much of a temptation for someone—most of its frosting was missing.

Despite our shared tragedy, the evening turned out be a success. The Studio Rats, warts and all, I couldn't help but love 'em.

———————————

On Monday morning, I called Willy's office and set up a fifteen-minute appointment during my lunch break. On the way, I stopped long enough to wolf a quick sandwich plate at the Armstrong's lunch room. Willy's digs were located on the upper floors of a bank building a couple of blocks away. I entered through a side door, took an elevator to six, and found Willy's suite. His receptionist showed me to his office, where I discovered Willy seated at his desk, studying a colored illustration of the female reproductive system.

Willy looked up and smiled. "I've been getting ready for you. Pull up a chair."

"Will do. Remember my knowledge of all this is zero. The frogs we cut up in high school biology class didn't teach me much. My college biology class was all about cells."

Willy placed his chart—a frontal view—atop the cluttered workspace. "It's not that hard. The common method of inducing an illegal abortion involves the insertion of a foreign object into the uterus." He pointed to the organ with the tip of a pencil. "The abortionist gains access to the uterus through the vagina. You can see here the vagina terminates in a narrow passage called the cervix. The cervix provides access to the uterus. The common risks associated with an illegal abortion are hemorrhaging, the creation of an embolism, and infection."

He looked at me to see if I understood. I nodded my head.

Willy continued, "Around here, most abortionists use a catheterization procedure. A catheter—essentially a flexible hollow tube—is inserted in the uterus with the intent to induce contractions and cause a miscarriage. The catheter is gently manipulated in order to irritate the uterus. If successful, a miscarriage takes place within a day or two. A simple catheterization has the advantage of being the safest of the back-alley variations, but it is less successful in creating contractions strong enough to expel the embryo. Are you following me, Clete?"

"So far, so good."

"Some abortionists insert a small wire into the catheter and use the end of the wire to irritate the uterus or pierce the amniotic sac containing the embryo. This second step increases the odds for success but greatly increases the risks of excessive bleeding, embolism, or infection. If something goes wrong, death may occur hours or even days after the procedure."

Although the Merchants' Bank building was air conditioned, Willy's office felt warm and stuffy. I could feel beads of sweat breaking out on my upper lip and forehead. My palms felt clammy. I hoped I didn't look as green around the gills as I felt.

Willy noticed. "Are you sure you want to continue? This cannot be an easy thing for someone who has had a recent loss."

"Willy, I want to know it all," I said. "In the long term, it will help me come to grips with Diane's death."

"I will continue. The most dangerous way to create a miscarriage involves the insertion of a rigid object into the reproductive organs, the coat-hanger technique people joke about. But it's no joke; it's pure butchery. Back in Indiana, I treated several women who had this done to them. I will never forget. Their pain was incredible. One —a fifteen-year-old girl—I could not save."

Although he covered his emotions well, I could see Willy still took the loss personally. He soldiered on.

"With all these methods, there is a danger of piercing the walls of the vagina or the uterus. If the bleeding becomes serious enough, death can occur within a half hour. At other times, the injuries can become infected and fester to the point the woman's private parts begin to emit a putrid odor. In this case, death may happen within a day or two."

I blanched. This time, Willy didn't notice.

"Let's move on to Diane. While there is no reason for someone not pregnant to undergo an abortion, the procedure poses less risk than for a woman with child. When an embryo begins to form, the blood vessels in the uterus enlarge to provide nourishment to the fetus. This blood-rich environment increases the risk of accidental death from hemorrhage. Since Diane was not pregnant, death may have taken hours because the uterine blood vessels were not engorged. I suspect a grossly incompetent abortionist used the coat-hanger method and then prevented her from seeking medical care when problems developed."

Willy reached for another colored illustration of the female reproductive system. A side view with the organs colored coral pink, greenish blue, and mustard yellow swam into my field of vision.

"These procedures are dangerous because of a woman's basic anatomy. The cervix and uterus lie at an angle to the vagina making it difficult to navigate the curve without injury. I am sorry if I sound like a professor. I will miss Diane too, but it is hard to break the habits of years of teaching. Is there anything else I can do for you?"

"Thanks Willy. I can't tell you how much I appreciate the information."

Willy leaned back in his chair. "I hope our little chat helps you understand more about the way Diane died. Most people do not want so much detail, especially about the death of someone dear to them."

"I'd better get going," I said. "I need to be back at the store in ten minutes."

We said goodbye. I left the office, barely made it to a men's room, and said goodbye to my lunch. The Armstrong's Double-L Special—a lettuce and liverwurst sandwich topped with dill pickles—no longer seemed like a good idea.

My first dance student had canceled her lesson—I used the unexpected free time to explore the stacks of the Cedar Rapids Public Library. I put my books on the counter and smiled at the bespectacled woman behind the counter.

"I'd like to get a library card," I announced.

Looking somewhat surprised, the woman squinted up at me, silently studying my face. I don't know what she expected to find there, her long lost brother perhaps, or maybe a future leader for the local Friends of the Library group. Eventually satisfied I'd met some sort of criteria known only to her and the Good Lord Almighty, she spoke.

"Are you a resident of Cedar Rapids?"

"I am."

She handed me a form. "Please fill this out at the counter over there. I'll type up your card and stamp your books when you come back."

The librarian was touching up her lipstick when I returned with my application. She returned the tube to her purse, typed up my card, and handed it to me. My books were still on her side of the desk.

"Do you go by Cletus?" she asked.

"None other."

She touched a pencil to her re-conditioned lips and studied my face again. "Cletus, the books you picked out, *Murder at the Vic-*

arage, *Easy to Kill*, *Find a Victim*, are all light reading. Murder mysteries won't improve your mind. I'd be happy to recommend some classics, something like *Lady Chatterley's Lover* or *Fanny Hill*. They make for stimulating reading."

"Not me," I said. "I like 'em easy, short, and sweet."

She pushed a stray lock of hair behind her ear. "Not everyone likes short and sweet." She looked at me over the top of her glasses, and smiled. "Some of us like things long, stimulating, and hard."

We were holding up the checkout line, a situation that made me uncomfortable. I wished she'd get on with it and give me my books. I could feel the people behind me getting impatient.

"Miss," I said, "it's been nice talking with you, but I need to get to work."

Still looking disappointed at my choice in literature, she squinted again, and handed over my books. "You don't know what you're missing out on, Cletus."

"Bye now," I said.

What a strange creature. She needed to get some new eyeglasses, and besides, what possible interest could she have in my reading hard books?

I needed to focus on learning about the detective business.

I got home from the studio earlier than usual. The dance business falls off in summer, and while I enjoyed the extra free time, I was paid on percentage. My finances were taking a hit.

I poured a glass of lemonade and settled onto the couch with one of my library books. The story wasn't too bad, but more importantly, my reading gave me some confidence. If an old busybody like Jane Marple could solve crimes without training, a man about town like me wouldn't have any problems. About the time I hit the halfway point, the phone rang. I picked up.

A woman's voice. "Cletus Efferding?" she asked.

"Speaking."

"This is Shirley Weiss. I think the least you can do for me after last Thursday night is to take me to the Dragon for dinner."

"How about tomorrow night at eight o'clock?"

"I'll see you there," she said and hung up.

I settled back into the couch, puzzling over the motivation behind Shirley's unexpected call. She'd left the Elks in a snit and had now invited herself to dinner at my expense. The woman didn't beat around the bush. I doubted her call had lasted more than ten seconds.

I hadn't spoken with Jim since the incident at the Elks. What a great guy. I couldn't wait to learn how he persuaded her to talk to me, so I phoned him—first to apologize for the incident, then to learn what had transpired. Jim was as mystified as I. When he'd last spoken to Shirley, she was still angry with both of us.

13

Chinese food doesn't excite me, but the Dragon Restaurant had great décor and made for a quiet place to chat. Shirley and I reached the entrance at the same time. I held the door for her while we greeted one another and exchanged pleasantries.

A young woman who looked like she'd just stepped off the boat from Sweden led us to a quiet corner where Shirley ordered sweet and sour pork and I the egg foo young. Hoping I'd learned something from our last encounter, I waited to see where Shirley wanted to take the conversation. It didn't take long.

"I've seen your police file," she said. "Quite the place you visited there in Dubuque."

My heart sank. "I made a mistake. I went there for all the wrong reasons, but there weren't any whips and certainly no chains."

"The file had a lot about you in it," she said. "I know about Myra's suicide."

Neither of us spoke for what seemed like an eternity. Shirley looked me full in the face without rancor, judgment, or curiosity. She reached for the oversized handbag she'd set down and removed a large manila envelope. She placed it on her lap.

"I've decided to help you. Late yesterday afternoon the detectives' room was empty. I found the Novacek file at the bottom of a pile on Florian's desk. We have a Xerox machine for making copies. I didn't include anything about you. I figure what the police department knows about you is none of your business. I skipped the crime scene photos too. Your friend deserves privacy in death, and you don't need to see them."

She paused while our blonde waitress poured our tea and then picked up as if there'd been no interruption.

"There isn't much, a dozen or so sheets. There was an unopened envelope addressed to Florian from the Linn County Medical Examiner's office. Of course, I couldn't open it, but I photocopied the outside."

Shirley reached across the table and handed the manila envelope to me. "If anyone finds out about this, I'll lose my job. I could even end up in jail."

"Thank you. I never expected you to do anything like this—even before we talked at the Elks. I don't know what to say."

"I don't want Jim to know I helped you. I don't want anyone to know."

"I won't say a word, but Jim does know we're having dinner tonight."

"Tell him I wanted to smooth things over after the Elks."

When our orders arrived, Shirley dug into her sweet and sour pork with gusto. I picked at my egg foo young and asked for a beer. Shirley had finished by the time my bottle of Schlitz arrived. I took a sip and asked, "Mind if I ask why you changed your mind?"

"Cletus," she said, "you made a big mistake you'll carry with you for the rest of your life, but that hasn't stopped you from trying to do right by your friend Diane."

I nodded, and Shirley continued.

"Dan and I don't have any children. We both love kids, but it's not in the cards. Just after I graduated from high school—before I met Dan—there was somebody else. I got pregnant, and he bailed on me. I was scared, broke, and didn't want to raise a baby alone. One of my friends knew somebody in Des Moines who could help me out. I borrowed money and took a bus out there to see that man. After it was over, things went bad. I got sick, and now I can never have a baby. Dan doesn't know because I never told him. He's always wanted kids. I live with that every day."

The woman knew a thing or two about guilt. "I am so sorry, Shirley," I said. "I am so very sorry."

Shirley looked at her watch and rose. She hoisted her bag onto her shoulder and left with a parting comment.

"You find that bastard. Find that dirty bastard who killed your friend."

———————————

Back home from my meeting with Shirley, I opened the packet. As she'd said, the contents were slim. I found copies of the medical examiner's initial report with the Xerox of the unopened envelope, four reports written by Pudge, and two by Erikson.

The placement of the folder at the bottom of Pudge's stack and the unopened envelope from the medical examiner squared with his statement that the investigation was over. Pudge had given me a laundry list of reasons for the case going inactive. I ticked them off in my head: no murder, no abortion, bad publicity for the city, no leads, Diane brought it on herself, the case wasn't important enough to justify the effort.

He'd given too many reasons for abandoning the case. As I sat replaying our conversation, I kept coming back to three short words, "We got orders." I'd thought it had been a question of departmental resources, but now I knew better. Jim Weiss was right—someone had quashed the investigation.

"It's over, Pervie," Pudge had told me.

Not on your life, Pudgie, I thought. *Not on your life.*

I looked through the medical examiner's report. Death caused by "exsanguination, likely over a period of several hours." There was no sign of pregnancy.

In plain English, Diane bled to death as the result of injuries from an unnecessary abortion. Damage to the tissues of the upper vagina, cervical walls and the uterus had been "severe and extreme." The damage sounded as if it might have been the result of the coat hanger method Willy had mentioned. Diane's abortionist allowed her to bleed to death rather than seeking professional help when things went south.

Not pregnant and unlucky enough to meet up with a butcher. If Diane had been anaesthetized, someone with access to sedative drugs—such as a dentist—would make an ideal suspect. If sedatives were involved, the report would have mentioned it. The medical examiner enjoyed a good reputation. Linn County, home to the second biggest city in the state, had the resources to do things right.

Apparently, Diane had been conscious as she slowly bled to death. Surely, she'd complained of pain and begged for help. Perhaps she moaned or screamed. Only a depraved, hard-hearted, ball of slime would allow another human being to suffer like that. Shaking with anger, I got up, walked outside, and took deep breaths in an attempt to compose myself. I paced back and forth in the parking lot and then turned down the block.

When my rage subsided, I found myself downtown, striding west along First Avenue, the town's main drag. I did a quick reckoning—I'd traveled almost a mile and a half from my apartment. I turned around and headed back, forcing myself to walk at a deliberate pace. The medical examiner's report on my coffee table demanded my undivided attention, and I needed to slow down so I could think clearly.

When I got back to the report, I discovered the examiner had found it difficult to fix the time of death. His initial examination took place at the Me Too lot at 6:40 on Saturday morning. By that time, Diane had been dead for somewhere between fifteen to twenty hours. Diane had not eaten on the day of her death, so some of the common digestive evidence wasn't available. Her body had been moved at least once. Since changes in location can result in changes in temperature and affect the onset and dissipation of rigor mortis and other markers of decomposition, the examiner was hesitant to pin things down too closely.

I stood, went to the kitchen cupboard, and poured myself a large brandy. The contents of the report were hard to take. The cold, clinical details ate at me. The part about the weight of Diane's internal organs left me rocking back and forth on the sofa whimpering like a sick puppy. I didn't know if I'd ever be able to look at the document again.

I sipped my drink and went to work on the police reports. Pudge Davis caught the call. His first report included an identification of the car and its owner. Diane had been found between the front and rear seats partially wrapped in a blood-soaked, blue acrylic blanket. The trunk was empty save for the jack and a spare tire.

Given the difficulty of carrying a body, Pudge believed more than one person was involved in transporting the victim. He asked that technicians dust the vehicle for prints and compare the results against the department's fingerprint cards. They came up with several sets of prints. When none matched those in the local files, the department sent copies to the FBI lab in Washington.

The ashtray of the car contained the butts of several Pall Mall cigarettes, and the vehicle's radio was tuned to the WLS station from Chicago. An aluminum-handled dip net and a container of Uncle Emil's Catfish Stink Bait sat on the backseat. A basketball initialed 'WJH' lay on the floor of the front passenger's side. The initials and proximity of the grocery to Wilson Junior High suggested the ball may have been the property of the school. School officials confirmed they marked athletic equipment in this manner to discourage theft, but much of it still went missing.

Gordon Kohl's car was found with the doors left open, the keys in the ignition, and the switch in the 'on' position. A dead battery and empty gas tank indicated the vehicle had been abandoned with its engine running. The passenger compartment's overhead light was broken, and the presence of plastic and glass shards on the floor indicated the damage was recent. Pudge believed the light was deliberately broken so it would not shine on the occupants as they left the car.

Three days later, Pudge had added a second report to the file. Two adolescent boys reported they'd been on the premises of the Me Too Supermarket drinking beer at approximately 3:00 a.m. and saw two men exiting the car. They noted the men had taken fishing poles and a tackle box from the vehicle. Reluctant to go to the police because of the beer, the young men waited several days to come forward. Pudge identified the boys as Edward Brada and William Rehak.

The report noted the owner of the Riverside APCO had called the department on the morning the *Gazette* identified Diane Novacek as the woman in the car. On the morning of her death, Diane had taken her car to the APCO for an oil change and requested a ride out to the K-Mart on Sixteenth Avenue. The owner asked his son to drop Diane at the store. When she didn't stop back for her vehicle, he asked the boy to park the car farther on up the block. Business was brisk on Saturday, the station closed on Sunday, and things were hectic again on Monday. No one gave the car much thought. The owner wasn't worried about payment—he'd known the Sedlaks for years.

I stretched, got up, fixed myself another drink and a sandwich. I knew the APCO station. A neighborhood institution, the owner and his customers were well acquainted. Located on a v-shaped lot across from the Penick & Ford plant, the operation consisted of two gas pumps, a building the size of a one-stall garage, and an exterior hoist. The guy who ran the place had my vote for the toughest man in Cedar Rapids. I'd once seen him standing under the hoist, surrounded by snow and greasing a car on a five-degree morning.

Taking my brandy and ham salad on rye with me, I headed back to the couch and polished the sandwich off in seconds. I tossed down my brandy and made another trip to the kitchen. Armed with another drink and large size bag of potato chips, I got back to work.

Pudge followed up on the call from the APCO station by checking with the manager of the west side K-Mart and speaking to staff who'd worked that day. He hit pay dirt when he located a cosmetics clerk who'd gone to school with Diane. Expecting additional singing opportunities were coming her way, Diane had come in looking for makeup colorful enough to hold up under stage lights. The two had spent some time catching up, and Diane left the cosmetics counter with a remark about having lunch in the store. When Pudge showed Diane's photo to staff working the cafeteria, no one remembered seeing her. He checked with the local cab company, but they'd had no requests for a mid-day K-Mart pickup. The bus driver who worked the K-Mart route that day didn't recall seeing anyone who looked like Diane.

Davis wrote the report on the search of Diane's car and apartment. The effort failed to turn up anything useful. Diane kept a tidy apartment, but no diary or appointment calendar, and she corresponded with no one but members of her family. She did keep a file where she tossed receipts, and with that information, the police had been able to identify her doctor and dentist. The file included a handwritten note to the effect that Diane's physician indicated she hadn't requested a pregnancy test. A check on her dentist revealed she was six months overdue for an appointment. The missed appointment had not been scheduled with Gordon Kohl.

I needed a break to let things sink in, so I poured myself another three fingers and caught the tail end of the *Tonight Show*. I had to hand it to Johnny Carson, the guy wore great suits. I prefer a looser cut, but Carson's tailoring was impeccable. When Johnny and Ed signed off, I went back to work, this time on the Earl Erikson reports.

Erikson made the rounds of the bait shops and sporting goods suppliers. A half dozen local merchants sold Emil John's Stink Bait. The proprietor of Walt's Bait Shop reported an obvious greenhorn had come in the weekend of Diane's death and purchased poles, a landing net, tackle, and stink bait. Since he'd paid cash, there was no way to follow up on the transaction. The owner described a customer of average height and weight, with a dark complexion and well-oiled hair. Though the man had no accent, the shop owner thought he might have been Spanish, Greek, or Italian.

Pudge had stapled a note to Earl's report. He spent several evenings questioning guys who fished off the Sixteenth Avenue Bridge. He spoke with a total of nine anglers. Two of them were fishing in the early morning when the car with Diane's body was abandoned. They recalled others had fished from the bridge that night, but they hadn't spoken to them or noticed anything unusual.

I rubbed my face and yawned. One more report to go, and thankfully, a short one. The dentist Gordon Kohl gave Erikson access to his records. Erikson confirmed Kohl had never looked at Diane's teeth. Since Lucinda Kohl didn't drive, the family had just one car. The dentist reported it stolen at 11:00 p.m. Friday night, and his wife had been with him from 7:00 that evening until 7:30 the next morning. Unless Mrs. Kohl was a liar or an extraordinarily sound sleeper, the dentist was off the hook for dumping the body. That didn't clear him on the abortion itself, just the aftermath. A cross check of Kohl's patients showed no overlap with Diane's dance students.

That was it. I'd consumed two sandwiches, an entire bag of chips, and four glasses of brandy. Too tired to make sense of what I'd just read, I leaned back, and drifted into an uneasy sleep. I dreamed Pudge Davis arrested me in Dubuque for consorting with a prostitute. Stranger still, my late wife Myra was having an affair with him and left me.

Killian's didn't expect me until noon the next day. I decided to try to locate the boys who saw the men abandon the car. Rehak and Brada were Czech names, so I started with Lumir.

Suspecting he would be in his workshop, I drove over and walked on back to his shed where I knocked perfunctorily on the door and opened it. Inside I found Lumir engaged in an animated conversation with Joe Nemec. I'd met Joe on an earlier visit. He was ninety-two years old, as sharp as a razor blade, and enjoyed stopping by the shop to pass the time of day. Although he had little occasion to use the language, Lumir was still comfortable speaking Czech. Joe, while comfortable with English, was mentally and spiritually at home with the Czech language. Although I didn't understand a word, the conversation seemed to revolve around a coffee mug lying on its side on Lumir's workbench. The mug's handle had broken off.

Lumir and Joe brought their conversation to a close, and Lumir greeted me.

"Good morning, Clete."

"Morning, Lumir," I replied. "Morning, Joe."

"Joe brought this mug over to see if I could repair it," Lumir said. "I was just telling him about this new super glue they have come out with. Bonds instantly and is the strongest glue around."

"Never heard of it," I said.

"Joe hasn't either. We are ready to make a repair, but you must be careful or you can glue your fingers together or the cup to your hand. You will lose skin if you try to pull your fingers apart."

I wasn't about to let Lumir pull one over on me. "Yeah, and the next thing you'll show me is a can of checkered paint."

"You think I'm joking? Here, read the warning."

Lumir handed me the warning sheet that came with the glue. I read through it. "What'll they think of next?" I said.

I looked up to see Lumir pressing the handle to the mug. He held it in place for a couple of seconds, stopped to admire his handiwork and handed the repaired mug to Joe. Joe looked at it for a moment, put his finger through the handle, and gave it a shake. The glue held, resulting in laughter and much prattling in Czech. Satisfied, Joe waved his mug back and forth above his head, bidding us goodbye as he walked into the beautiful June morning.

After Joe left, Lumir pointed in the direction of a coffee pot perched atop a hotplate on the table next to his roll top desk. Lumir made his coffee the old-fashioned way—a couple of scoops in the bottom of the pot, pour water over the top, and heat. Your mug would always contain coffee grounds, but it was the sort of coffee that made a man of you.

I nodded, pulled up a pressed-back chair, and mulled over how best to approach the business at hand. I elected to remain silent about my belief that something was amiss in our fair city's police department. Lumir handed me a steaming mug and sat down in his captain's chair. Seeing Lumir in his shop, sitting in his chair with one hand on his desk and a mug in the other was a sight so comforting it was hard to believe the events of the past weeks had taken place. Still, I had an agenda and got down to it.

"Lumir, I found out two boys—Edward Brada and William Rehak—saw a pair of men abandoning the car in the Me Too parking lot. They didn't get a good look at them, because it was almost three o'clock in the morning and still dark. They didn't go to the police right away because they were drinking beer."

"Two men. How did you find out?"

"I've given my word I won't reveal the source of my information. The person who helped me would be in trouble if anything I've learned gets out. I'd like you to keep what we talk about to yourself. Roy and DeeDee don't need to know."

"Clete, what you ask is little. Roy and DeeDee are too hurt to know. What about Stan and Buzz?"

"They might be able to help out somewhere along the line. Just ask them to keep it under their hats."

I summarized what I knew about the discovery of the car and its contents. I included the details of what the police had learned from their inquiry of the local bait shops and anglers on the Sixteenth Avenue Bridge. Lumir would have been dense not to realize my information came from within the police department. He wisely chose to ignore the fact. Although he must have had questions about the department's lack of success, he kept them to himself.

Lumir said, "I think the boys know more about the car than they admit. The basketball, the teenager radio station. I think they looked in the car—maybe even sat in it. Did they look under the blanket and see Diane? There is more to this."

"I think so, too," I replied. "I'd like to talk to the boys, but a guy just can't walk up to the front door of a house and start asking questions—especially without a badge. I'd be lucky if they didn't call the cops on me. I wonder if you have any neighborhood connections that might help out."

"I know of one Brada family. It's an unusual name. A Bob Brada used to work for me when I was foreman at Wilson's. There are many Rehaks. I do not know where a man would begin."

"I have the addresses and telephone numbers, Lumir. What I don't have is a way to get the families to let me talk to the boys. I'm hoping you have an in."

Lumir and I walked to the house and checked the phone book. Bob Brada lived at the same address as the Eddie Brada listed in the police report. They were almost certainly father and son.

"I'll talk to Bob," Lumir said. "Maybe we can work something out so that you can talk with this Eddie. I don't know the family of the Rehak boy. I will talk to them, but in this, I have no more influence than you."

When I got up to leave for Killian's, Lumir's parting remark demonstrated his grasp of the situation.

"I think the police will fail Diane—almost four weeks and nothing happens."

Lumir had picked up on it. I'd said nothing about the department's malfeasance, but he hadn't missed the detectives' failure to follow up on the investigation.

I didn't want to discourage my friend. "Let's see what you turn up. One way or another, we'll get to the bottom of this."

I spent a good chunk of the afternoon outfitting a father and five sons for a wedding. Time flew by, and halfway to the studio, I realized I'd forgotten to eat lunch. Just as well, I'd put on a few pounds in the last month.

When I got to the studio, I walked into a minor kerfuffle—one that involved me. A group of Studio Rats had requested I do a month-long series of special lessons so they could bone up on their polka for an event at the CSPS Hall. Two Rats—Dottie and Velma—were going at it hammer and tongs.

"Velma, you set up the special lessons, and you never asked him? What were you thinking?"

"I can't help it if you can't get a date. You need to be thinking for yourself."

I immediately understood the issue. The polka group was un-balanced. Not mentally by any means, but more women than men had signed on, and most of them had regular partners. Since I taught the class, the Rats assumed I'd be attending, but no one had checked. My absence would mean less opportunities for the single women to dance. Though tempted to stand back and enjoy the show, it was my job to ensure lessons ran smoothly.

Feigning ignorance of the dust up, I walked onto the floor and asked, "How many here are going to see Leo Greco at CSPS Saturday night?"

Of course, everyone taking the special lessons raised a hand.

"Let's see," I said, "it looks like seventeen, and with me that will be eighteen. Are there any volunteers to get there early and save us some tables?"

Several hands went up, and order was restored. Of course, that meant I'd be going to the CSPS hall Saturday night, but I had no problem with that. Most dance teachers like to dance socially, and I was no exception. The rest of the lesson passed without incident.

I drove home and made a peanut butter sandwich, but before I took my first bite, Lumir phoned. He'd met Bob Brada for drinks at Spryncl's Tavern, an eastside bar popular with guys who worked at the packing plant. Lumir bought Bob four rounds to his one. They arranged for the two of us to speak with Eddie about his night at the Me Too parking lot. We were on for one o'clock Sunday afternoon in Lumir's shop. Sunday afternoon being the Bradas' regular pinochle game, neither Bob nor his wife would be present when we talked to their son. Lumir also had a job for Eddie. He'd be paying him five dol-lars to re-stack lumber in the workshop's loft.

Lumir struck out with the Rehaks. Distressed to learn their fourteen-year-old had been out drinking beer at 3:00 a.m., they no longer allowed their son to associate with Eddie Brada and sent him to spend the rest of the summer with an aunt in Wisconsin. The Re-haks informed Lumir they resented his intrusion into family matters and asked he not call on them again.

I put down the phone and reviewed the events of the day. I hadn't made much headway on Diane's case but felt a surge of satisfaction when I considered the way I'd handled the dust up between Dottie and Velma. When it comes to the life of a dance studio, I—Cletus Efferding—am a smooth operator.

Randy Roeder

14

Smoking a cigarette and seated in his small office at the back of the Moonglow Lounge, Habi Rahbani considered his future. If he followed in the path laid out by his father, he'd be older than the pyramids before he'd amount to more than he was now. Twenty-eight years old, and the sum total of his life amounted to a two-bedroom house with a one-stall garage, a BMW motorcycle, and a new Chevy Camaro. Habi owned them free and clear, but he wasn't going anywhere he wanted to be.

Habi wanted out of Iowa, but out of Iowa on his terms. He'd learned one thing from his father, and he'd learned it well. The key to prosperity lay in running a legitimate business and growing it by investing the proceeds from illegitimate sidelines. His father was masterful, but he thought small—skimming from slot and vending machines, running girls, selling hot property, arranging illegal abortions, working the margin on untaxed booze and cigarettes. An old-fashioned, labor intensive setup, too much of the proceeds went to Des Moines. Sure, Baba and Mama had a nice house, a pair of nightclubs, a motel, and a dozen rental properties, but he had to live on their table scraps.

His father had created G & HR Enterprises as an umbrella for his businesses and divided his time between his cushy office on the east side of the river and the Golden Key. Habi's office was a dingy storeroom at the Moonglow Lounge, a stripper bar adjoining the family's motel on the west end of Sixteenth Avenue. The Ultimate Motel catered to truckers and traveling salesmen. It also housed the lounge's visiting dancers and served as a convenient place for them to conduct private sessions with their admirers.

The Rahbani Booking Agency was a subsidiary of G & HR Enterprises. Habi's father had set up the agency to book the entertainment for the Moonglow and Golden Key. The booking operation served as a tax dodge. The elder Rahbani cared so little about the agency he allowed Habi a free hand in operating it. Habi had worked hard over the last six months recruiting entertainers and developing a portfolio of venues into which he could book them.

Rahbani Booking contracted for exotic dancers from an agency in Des Moines. A non-exclusive arrangement, it provided quality talent at a price better than Habi could get elsewhere. Unfortunately, a series of informal, but very real, agreements made it impossible to grow the stripper side of the business. Although the Rahbanis held the exclusive right to book dancers in Eastern Iowa, the reality was less than met the eye. The Dubuque and Quad City territories belonged to a businessman from Illinois, effectively limiting Habi's exotic dancer operation to Waterloo, Cedar Rapids, and Iowa City. If Habi were to book strippers outside of this territory, he'd likely be beaten. If he persisted, he could end up having an accident.

No one cared about bookings outside the exotic dancer business. Through his own initiative and Gabby's connections, Habi had access to clubs and hotel lounges in a three-state area. He'd booked a dozen lounge acts into Italian and Syrian venues in Des Moines, the Quad Cities, Peoria, Rockford, Madison, and Milwaukee. His contacts were less useful in booking the real money acts—rock music. The big rock acts and good venues wanted big money up front. So far, he had bankrolled one event—an all-day rock festival on a rural property north of Iowa City. He'd created a fictional entity named Flying Toad Productions to promote the concert. He'd barely broken even. For Flying Toad Productions to become airborne, Habi needed capital. If things went according to plan, that capital would come from the drugs.

A cough at his open door disturbed Habi's musing. He looked to see Suzanne LaRue framed in the opening. She cut a striking figure with her dark brown locks and fire engine red dress. With matching shoes, lipstick, and nail polish, the singer looked like something out of a magazine. She sat down in a chair facing Habi's desk, and crossed her legs. She looked him straight in the eye. Disoriented by her sex appeal, Habi took a moment to collect himself. He spoke first.

"I was sorry to hear of the death of your friend Diane," he said. "She had a nice voice. She asked me to book her with those two Bohemie cowboys, but she never would have made it as an entertainer. I had to turn her down. I have a reputation to protect."

Suzanne let her claws show. "Some reputation," she snorted. "Let's get down to the booking business."

Habi smiled, happy to be in adversarial mode as he leered at her torso.

"Business, Habi," she said. "Earl and Tony are ready to go on the road. Merle is out. So, it's a bass, piano, and me."

"I can use you. Of course, you won't have a horn, and booking out of town is expensive. With the smaller group, you'll be harder to book, so the agency's percentage goes up."

Suzanne smiled. "We gave your dad a good deal because it's a local gig and regular work. The three of us should be easier to place because our travel expenses—just two rooms—will be modest. That means we're looking at the same minimum for the three of us, plus the expenses. Your percentage stays the same, and you figure it before adding the travel. I get a copy of the contract for each and every venue. When I sing without the guys at the Flame Room, there's no percentage for you, but you don't have to worry, there's not enough money there to keep me from booking with you every chance I get."

"This is a good opportunity for you," Habi replied. "I can book you in three states. You'll get exposure. With the Golden Key closing in August, you're going to need work. If you don't keep performing, you can kiss your career goodbye."

"We'll be an easy sell. You're trying to get your booking business going. Some of your acts aren't so hot. You need us as much as we need you."

Habi looked at Suzanne. The woman could put a song across, and her group would be popular, but he wanted a bit more.

"I think we can work something out. If you're nice to me once in a while, I might be willing to meet your terms."

"Listen," Suzanne said, "My real name may be Susan Rooney, and I may have grown up in the Time Check neighborhood, but I'm not too stupid to realize the terms of the contract will be the same whether you get your jollies or not."

"What, growing up across from the cereal factory made you so smart? Where will you find an agent who can get you into the sort of clubs I can arrange for you?"

"Davenport or Des Moines," replied Suzanne.

Habi sighed. Suzanne's group would have little difficulty finding an agent. The woman was being all business, but if that was so, why had she come to his office looking like an ice cream sundae? He had the looks, and women liked him. He could see the interest in the singer's eyes—maybe she wanted a strongman approach. If that's the way she wanted it, business first.

"I'm a businessman, and you've been around long enough to understand I have to try to get the best deal for the agency. I can meet your terms. We'll use our standard twelve-month contract. I'll fill in the blanks. Are you authorized to sign for the others members of the group?"

"They work for me, Habi. It's Suzanne LaRue, a keyboard player, and a bassist. If the venue wants a horn, I can provide a union sax or trumpet for an additional twenty-five percent plus travel. You can either ink it in or add it to the venue contract with a rider."

Habi began filling in the blanks. When he finished, he passed pen and paperwork across the desk. "It's my habit to celebrate a new contract with drinks. Can I fix you something while you read the papers?"

"Bourbon and water," she said.

Already thinking about his next move, Habi opened a cabinet behind his desk, retrieved the essentials, and mixed the drinks. When he'd finished, he looked up to find Suzanne signing the paper. He walked around his government-surplus desk and offered Suzanne her Jim Beam.

"To business," he said as they clinked their glasses.

"To business," she replied and downed the first two fingers of his overly generous pour in a single swallow. She put the remainder of the drink on the desk, shouldered her purse, and was about to exit when Habi stepped in front of her, blocking access to the door. Facing her, he reached back and closed it.

"Don't fight it. I know what you need," he said, pulling on her hair to force her against the side wall. He began kneading her breasts and grinding against her.

"Give a girl a little air," she said, "I don't want to wreck my dress."

Sensing he was about to get what he wanted, Habi stepped back a few inches. Suzanne rewarded him with a light touch to his groin and then pulled him forward toward her. Suddenly, something was wrong. Suzanne's caress had transformed itself into a hard prod to the gonads. Habi looked down to see a small pistol jammed into his privates. When he tried to step back, Suzanne moved forward with him.

"It's a lady's gun, Habi. A .25 caliber Colt semi-automatic that fires a shot every time I twitch my finger. It's cocked. I can shred your goodies with three shots in a second and a half and still have three to go if that doesn't convince you."

Habi's eyes bulged to the size of fifty-cent pieces.

"Okay, you can step back now Habi."

He did, and Suzanne held up the gun for him to see.

"My uncle's. I begged and begged until he gave it to me. From the first time I saw it, I just had to have it. It's such a cute little thing with the shiny plating, pearl handles, and all. It's cocked and loaded, but not to worry, I had the safety on when I jabbed you."

"Are you crazy?"

"No, I'm smart. A girl working the club circuit needs all the help she can get. You know, you really need to improve your pickup technique. The caveman approach might work with your dancers, but only because they need the job. You should try being nice to them sometime. I guarantee you'll have more fun. I have an early dinner date, so I've got to go. You can start booking the boys and me whenever we're not scheduled for the Key."

Suzanne put the pistol back in her purse, pulled out a compact, and checked her face in the mirror.

"Pulling my hair hurt, you dope. I hope I can get it straightened up before my date. That handsome police detective Earl Erikson asked me out, and I want to look good."

After she left, Habi finished the rest of Suzanne's drink and then his own. He lit a cigarette and settled back into his chair. He really needed to get out of Cedar Rapids.

Suzanne LaRue giggled as she sat across the table from Earl Erikson at Ced-Rel.

"You didn't," Earl said.

"Yup, I stuck my little automatic right in his rocks."

"I wish I could have seen the surprise on his face."

"Surprise doesn't quite cover it. It was more of a 'holy crap this can't be happening to me' look. I'd like to think the entirety of his misspent life passed before him."

Earl leaned back and looked at his date. "Suzanne, you'd better be careful. There's more to the Rahbanis than meets the eye. You might think Habi is a horny little jerk, but his dad, George, is dangerous, and George has friends who are even worse. If you get on

George's list, you can kiss your singing career good-bye, and then count yourself lucky if that's all you lose."

"I know more about George than you think. I didn't last three years at the Golden Key by being stupid. If Habi lives long enough, he might rise to the level of a little punk. George knows it and has to keep fixing his son's messes. Habi won't say a word about what happened today. The abuse he'd have to take if George found out would be worse than if I'd shot him in the privates."

"Do yourself a favor, and don't tell a soul about what happened. If George thinks you humiliated his son, you'll pay for it. He'll see Habi's humiliation as his own, and with George, pride and reputation are everything."

"Uh-oh," said Suzanne, "I wasn't looking at it that way. When Habi pulled that ape-man thing on me, I couldn't help myself. I wanted to see him sweat and didn't think about the consequences."

"Keep your lip zipped. If you play it cool, no one's going to know."

Suzanne pushed Earl's warning to the back of her mind and surveyed the room. She'd lived in Cedar Rapids her entire life and had never been to Ced-Rel. The popular dining spot five miles outside town enjoyed a storied history. Its location in rural Linn County allowed the owners to wink at state liquor and gambling laws. The club's racy reputation lent the place an air of sophistication, and the venue had become a popular destination.

In the 1950s, the owners built a motel on the property. This development, rather than the establishment's storied reputation, gave Suzanne pause. The proximity of the club to the motel called up visions of a swanky dinner followed by a roll in the hay. Those images had persuaded her Ced-Rel might not be the ideal location for a date. That said, a rendezvous with Earl Erikson was incentive enough to throw caution to the winds as a roll in the hay might well be in order. The man was so good-looking he'd put a Greek god to shame.

Earl placed his hand on Suzanne's, a move that brought her back to the present.

"Did you notice the porthole window in the door when you came in?"

"Can't say I did."

"One-way glass left over from the time the place was a key club. You can look out from inside, but you can't see in from the outside. The porthole let the staff keep the riff raff out and gave them early warning of a raid."

"Leave it to the handsome detective to have an in on all the historical details. I suppose you're going to ask if I know the Lighthouse Inn has a bullet hole in the wall from John Dillinger's gun."

"Oh, you heard."

"I also hear you're a popular guy. Tell me what happens after you impress your dates with all your secret cop history?"

"They ask me about the cases I'm working on."

Suzanne smiled. "Not your gun?"

"Most of them don't seem to like guns."

"That's no fun." Suzanne licked her lips. "Do you have a big gun?"

"A .38 Police Special."

"Oh, a special gun. I bet you really know how to use it."

"I qualified my first time at the range."

Suzanne leaned in toward Earl. "It's good to know you and your special gun are so well-qualified."

"I've always been a good shot. I started with a long gun, hunting with my dad."

"You're a good shot with a long gun—sounds deadly."

"I like every part of the hunt—the anticipation, selecting your quarry, the buildup, the release you feel when you shoot."

"Hmm," Suzanne purred, "tell me more."

"I've never met a woman so interested in guns. The two of us should do some shooting."

"If you let me have that long gun."

"I can't. I traded it for a superposed Browning. The short barrel gives a better follow through on upland game."

Suzanne almost choked on her drink. The double entendre had gone over Earl's head. The guy had about as much imagination as that Joe Friday guy on the *Dragnet* show. All those good looks—wasted. As far as romance was concerned, Earl had just gone down in flames. Suzanne changed the direction of the conversation—not that her dinner partner would catch on.

"So, Earl," she asked, "you guys making any progress on the Novacek case?"

"That investigation belongs to Pudge Davis. I helped on it some, but I've been putting most of my energy into the Maggert case. The Novacek investigation has petered out. It might not be solvable. Just between us, the captain put it on the back burner. He's taking a lot of heat on property crimes right now and wants his detectives to concentrate on robberies and break-ins."

Suzanne nodded sadly. Diane was already old news. Her death belonged to a part of the life of the city most people chose to ignore. Suzanne had been looking forward to a fun evening, but Earl's inability to engage her mentally and the news about Diane's case had taken the bloom off the rose. She pleaded a headache, and they left the restaurant. Earl seemed genuinely surprised she was in no mood to get physical.

Desultory conversation marked the ride home. After a flat, uninspiring goodnight kiss, Suzanne made her way up the stairs to her apartment. She changed into her robe, took her place at the bathroom mirror, and began removing the makeup she had so artfully applied earlier in the day. First Habi the Beast and then Earl the Dense—ugh. She sighed and brushed out her hair.

Still, one bright spot had marked her day. She'd gotten the contract she hoped for. If she played her cards right at Habi's regional venues, she might get a crack at Chicago.

Randy Roeder

15

Saturday night, and I was getting dressed for the much-anticipated dance at CSPS Hall. I picked a light gray pinstripe suit and pastel blue tie for the evening. My choice of attire would put me solidly into the minority of those attending. I like dressing up, and I've always been convinced that the better I look, the better I dance. There'd be no air conditioning, but the early June heat wave had broken, leaving the nights unseasonably cool. I suspected the hall's doors and windows would be open, and pole fans would make the building comfortable.

Although the neighborhood was well past its prime, I encountered unexpected difficulty in finding a parking space. The discovery was less than welcome—a crowded floor can take some of the fun out of dancing. I circled the block looking for an opening, and realized I needn't have worried. The nearby ZCBJ Hall had scheduled a popular country and western band so the streets and sidewalks hummed. Crowded dance floor or not, the alcohol would be flowing in old Bohemie Town tonight.

I parked, and climbed a flight of stairs to the main floor where I bought my ticket and entered. As I'd predicted, my sartorial splendor put me a couple of notches above the average. While I looked good, many in the down-home crowd would have given the best-dressed honor to the band leader, Leo Greco. At ease and handsome, he made his claim for the title in a cream-colored jacket embroidered with crimson roses and black wagon wheels. He accessorized with a crimson neckerchief and topped the whole thing off with an ivory Stetson. I had to give the guy credit, from the gleaming mother-of-pearl panels of his accordion to the crimson accents on his cowboy boots, Greco looked every bit the star.

Anticipating a crowd, the organizers had leveraged the available square footage by stacking tables in the corners and moving the chairs to the outside walls. I found the Studio Rats clustered in one of the corners. Since Leo Greco was quite the personality, they were primed and ready for action. One thing I had to give him, he played a wide variety of music—pop standards, country, waltzes, and polkas. Tonight's performance would include a special treat. After the first break, Czechoslovakia's reigning national polka champions, Pavel and Zora Rohner, would be putting on an exhibition.

I danced my way through the first set, found a good vantage point, and took in the polka champions' showcase. Thank God, they dressed like human beings—I hated the corny lederhosen getups seen at American polka competitions. Pavel wore understated black pinstripe pants with a matching vest and Zora a strapless blue gown. They danced the obligatory polka, followed with a fast European waltz, and ended with a comic two-step routine. Despite their flawless performance, I'd have been astonished to learn they'd earned anything for their gig. At best, a state-sponsored cultural exchange translated into a free vacation to the American Midwest.

The exhibition over, I noticed a well-dressed man waving at me and heading in my direction. Clad in an off-white linen suit with a matching hat and dark blue tie, Lumir Sedlak wanted to chat. I recognized the companion on his arm as Betty Drahozel, the cheerful clerk who worked the counter at Sykora's Bakery and sold me kolaches when my sweet tooth got the best of me.

The band broke into a polka. Lumir waved me off, turned, and squired his date onto the floor. It took all of thirty seconds for me to realize Diane had inherited her dancing ability from her grandfather. Despite his grace and obvious skill, I knew he hadn't been on a dance floor since his wife died. It made no difference. The man was in great physical condition.

Lumir led his partner through turns, windmills, back steps, and moves the like of which I'd never seen. I never suspected it, but Lumir was a polka god. When his dance with Betty ended, I walked over to express my admiration. I shook his hand and congratulated him on the best polka I'd ever witnessed.

"You should have seen Djeddo Kosek," Lumir said. "Now there was a man who could dance."

I greeted Betty, but after the three of us had chatted a bit, I left the budding romantics to their own devices and rejoined the Studio Rats. I'd no sooner reached my chair than I felt a hand on my shoulder. Zora Rohner asked me to dance. Flattered someone of her caliber had chosen me for a partner, I led her onto the floor where we waltzed to a lovely tune. Dancing with a national champion can be intimidating, but I was in good form and certain I'd make an impression. As we waltzed, she looked up at me with parted lips and the eyes of an angel.

"You know the man with white mustache?" she asked.

"Sure, his name is Lumir Sedlak. He's a friend of mine."

"Please," she pleaded, "please, I must be dancing with him. He has soul of polka. I do not see polka before with so much spiritness. We have war and revolution—forgetting so much dancing in my country. You introduce to me—please?"

"Lumir has a big date tonight, but I'll see what I can do."

"Please," she insisted, "he is sexiest man alive."

At the end of the waltz, the twenty-fourth runner-up for sexiest man alive introduced Zora Rohner to Lumir and Betty.

The introduction complete, Zora asked Betty. "Do you mind if I dance with your man? He is excellent dancer."

Betty glanced at Lumir, who nodded his assent. Good manners dictated I'd dance with Betty. Lumir hadn't seen the exhibition and had no idea the woman was a national champion. The band played another a polka. Lumir, knowing only that Zora wanted to dance, was taking it easy with her. Betty and I danced up to them.

"Lumir," I said, "you can let 'er rip. She can handle it."

Lumir's eyes lit up, he paused for a beat, and away he went, twirling his partner madly.

From the microphone, Leo Greco let out a "Hoo hoo hoo! We've got a live one out there tonight folks."

He turned around, gave his band a thumb's up, and they picked up the tempo. Lumir and Zora twirled across the room as here and there guests took up the call of the male polka dancer. Cries of "Hoo hoo hoo!" echoed throughout the room.

As the tempo quickened, many couples began leaving the floor. Betty tugged my sleeve and pointed to some vacant chairs. I was only too happy to oblige.

Greco leaned in to the microphone, twirled his finger in the air, and said, "Okay, boys, let's get the lead out and show 'em what it's all about."

The music raced. Only four couples remained when Greco kicked it up yet another notch. The couples broke, formed a circle around Lumir, and began clapping as he executed solo moves in a style that hadn't seen the light of day in half a century. He was magnificent—back stepping, twirling, and leaping into the air as he folded and unfolded his arms. I realized I'd begun crying. The reality that Diane couldn't share her grandfather's moment of glory hit me so hard I almost dropped to the floor.

I nodded to Betty, excused myself, and walked outside to pull myself together. I didn't want to be seen weeping outside the hall, so I headed back to the Nova for some privacy. When I got to the car, I discovered someone had put a note under the passenger-side windshield wiper. I unfolded it.

Mind your own business Danceman or get hurt

Who knew what I was up to? I got into the car, and sank into the seat. It took ten minutes for my brain to engage. Lumir, of course, Stan and Buzz, Jim Weiss and Shirley, Pudge, and Kohl's nasty dental assistant. I could assume Pudge talked with Earl and word of my interest had spread through some portion of the police department. Kohl's nasty little hygienist or Pudge may have said something to the dentist. People blab, so a number of friends and spouses could have heard. The worst case: thirty to forty people might know I was following up on my friend's death.

I'd been careful, but not careful enough. I considered calling it a night, but after spending a half hour in the car, I realized I wouldn't solve any of my problems sitting at home. When a quick check in the rearview mirror showed that my eyes were no longer red, I walked back to the dancehall.

When I returned, I discovered Lumir and Betty had gone, as had the Rohners. One of the Rats grabbed my hand and led me back to the group. "I found him," she announced. Some of the group considered me derelict in my dancing duties.

After the Rats passed me around for a couple of dances, I joined a schottische. In a schottische, participants arrange themselves—couple by couple—into a large circle on the floor. Each couple does a pre-set sequence of moves that ends with them separating and moving on to new partners. By the end of the dance, each man will have danced with each woman in the circle and each woman with each man.

As I worked my way through the circle, I looked up to see my next partner, the young woman who cleaned teeth for Gordon Kohl. I shuddered as I recalled the pain she'd delivered with her pointed dental pick. She smiled as we began our pattern.

"Mr. Efferding," Her voice dripped with venom. "I asked my Uncle Florian to speak to you about harassing his brother-in-law."

Ignoring her comment, I asked, "Does your Uncle Gordon like to fish?"

"You don't learn, do you?" she said.

As we separated to move on to our next partners, I felt a jolt of pain so intense I nearly lost my balance. Gordon Kohl's niece had driven her spiked heel into my instep with as much force as she could muster and then ground down on it. She slapped me in the face, called me "fresh," and moved on to her next dance partner. The thin leather upper of my dance shoe offered little protection from injury.

"Damn, what'd you do that for?" I cried.

No answer.

"Serves you right for pawing that girl!" my next-up partner snarled as she indignantly by-passed me.

"Lady," I said, "I'd rather kiss a porcupine than lay a hand on that nutcake."

"Pervert," she replied, "you shouldn't be allowed around decent people."

That was it. Unjustly accused of copping a feel from the nastiest piece of femininity in the city, I left the line of dance, picked up my street shoes, and to the dismay of the Studio Rats, limped out of the building. As I drove home, I turned the air inside my car first blue—and then purple—with bitter invective.

The next morning, I couldn't put weight on my foot. Since it was a Sunday, I went to the emergency room at Mercy Hospital. The doctor ordered an x-ray, and reported that though my foot had extensive bruising and swelling, no bones were broken.

"Unfortunately, an x-ray isn't very helpful in revealing tendon damage," he informed me. "You'll want to ice your foot three or four times a day and stay off it as much as possible for two weeks. If it's not better by then, come back, and we'll determine if something more extensive is warranted. If a tendon detaches or breaks, you'll need surgery. In the case of surgery, we don't want to delay or the tendons may not heal properly. In that case, your toes may never again function as intended. Pain after two weeks of rest is a negative sign."

I asked about a return to dancing, and he said I'd need to be pain-free for two full weeks before I could even consider it.

The vindictive little witch was costing me money. The order to stay off my foot for two weeks meant no work at Killian's. If my foot still hurt, I'd be unable to work at the studio for even longer. Severe tendon damage could compromise my ability to dance. The doctor ordered me to use crutches during my convalescence.

I can't say I was surprised to learn the nasty little psychotic was related to Pudge Davis. She'd obviously spoken to her uncle Pudge prior to the day he threatened to put me in the hospital. I wondered if mental illness ran in the family. If Pudge's sister—Mrs. Gordon Kohl—was as strange as Pudge and his niece, she'd never marry someone normal. Her bug-eyed, toad-like husband Gordon looked better and better as Diane's abortionist.

Rather than abandoning the investigation due to a fix from above, Pudge may have sandbagged it to protect his brother-in-law. Even scarier, Pudge might have another sibling—gender unknown—twisted enough to raise the vicious little brat who'd stabbed me in the mouth with a dental tool, threatened to take my eye out, and damaged my foot so severely I might never dance again.

Randy Roeder

16

Sunday, about noon. I'd just returned from the hospital when Lumir phoned. Eddie Brada had helped him sort the lumber in the loft of his shed. The two got on well. Now off the clock, Eddie was sharpening the blades of Lumir's hand planes in exchange for lessons in using them.

"This is a good boy," Lumir told me. "I do not want to scare him. I think you should stay home today."

I did my best to hide my disappointment. I'd intended to disobey doctor's orders and drive over to the shop. Since Lumir arranged for the boy's appearance, the show belonged to him.

"I have to get back to the shop now. I will call you." With that, he rang off.

Lumir didn't want to see me and was in a hurry to get back to his shop. I wondered what I'd done to cause his remoteness. I let out a sigh—it cleared my head. I don't know how I missed it. Lumir's great-grandchildren were too young to be good shop companions. Eddie, on the other hand, was older and interested in woodworking.

Lumir would enjoy his company. My probing questions would have put a damper on his afternoon.

Doctor's orders or not, I itched to do something. I picked up the *Gazette* to check the afternoon movies—the sports section lay atop the pile. The city's minor league team was playing at Veteran's Stadium. Since the Cedar Rapids Cardinals were on a streak and second in Midwestern League standings, planning for the afternoon became a no-brainer.

I picked up my crutches, wobbled out of the house, and drove to the ballpark. I thanked my lucky stars Pudge's despicable excuse for a niece injured my left foot rather than my right—at least I could operate my car's foot pedals.

The game was a corker, filled with bunts and a butt load of stolen bases. The scoreboard showed a 3-3 tie when I made my way over to the food stands at the seventh inning stretch. As I got in line at one of the windows, I felt a tap on my back. Sam Olds and his wife Helene had moved into line behind me. Expressing concern about my physical condition, Sam offered to pick up my popcorn and buy me a beer while I sat at a nearby picnic table. I happily took him up on his offer—my foot throbbed.

Sam and Helene had been part of Diane's circle of friends. Sam worked as an accountant and represented an interesting mix of spendthrift and penny pincher. One of his recent splurges had been a full-sized, turquoise-blue convertible—an Oldsmobile, of course. Helene, intelligent, slender, and good-looking, worked as a reference librarian at Coe College.

"So, Sam," I asked, "how's the big project coming?"

"On schedule," he replied. "Still, we need a day off now and then, and today's the day."

"Oh, brother," Helene rolled her eyes, "we'll be back to the shovels and wheelbarrows a half hour after we get home."

Sam and Helene's unusual project reflected Sam's thrifty side. They were digging a hole in their back yard for a swimming pool. They started when the ground thawed in March and expected to be pouring concrete in August. Though they'd become more tanned and fit, I found it hard to imagine them capable of such sustained discipline.

"I don't know how you stick with it," I said. "I wouldn't have the patience."

"Mind over matter," Sam replied. "Every night when we're done, I take a shower and pour myself three fingers of bourbon. I sit in my recliner and think about the word 'smooth.' Smooth, like the bourbon in my glass. Smooth—the way my yard's gonna be when we get the low spot in the back filled in. Smooth—the way life's gonna be when I'm floating on my back, looking up at the stars."

Helene changed the subject. "How are things at the studio? I cried and cried when I heard about Diane, and I'm still not over it. It's been such a shock we haven't been able to go back."

"It'll be a long time before things seem normal again," I said. "Diane was the best partner I ever danced with. Not only that, she was a first-rate teacher."

"The poor kid," said Sam. "So excited about a singing career, but she didn't have the knack for it. And then those guys she was singing with—an accordion player and a drummer. Those two thought they hit the big time when they booked the American Legion in Springville. Singing 1940s country songs with Curly and Red Zmolek isn't the way to get anywhere."

After discussing the ballgame and gossiping about life at the studio, I pulled myself up on my crutches, wished them luck with their project, and started for my seat. I'd barely gone ten feet when my foot insisted I go home. I should have paid attention to the doctor. I barely made it to the car and struggled to get back out when I got home.

When I got my foot up and on ice, I settled back on the couch and reviewed the events of last night. The warning under the windshield wiper made it clear I was onto something. My investigation into Diane's failed abortion had provoked a reaction. Though I'd been threatened with violence and deliberately injured, I didn't see a link between the two events. Kohl's sadistic niece couldn't have planned to stomp on my foot. Her action was a spontaneous response to my asking about her uncle.

The warning note represented something more sinister. It didn't take a genius to figure a dance teacher would be at most of the big dances in town, but whoever left the threat on my windshield knew my car, and I didn't think a sore foot was what the writer had in mind.

The phone rang.

"Come on over," Lumir said. "I have something to show you."

"Sorry, Lumir. I injured my foot last night, and the doctor told me to stay off it. Instead, I went to a ballgame this afternoon, and now the thing is killing me. I'm not supposed to go to work tomorrow because an eight-hour shift will only make it worse. What say I drive on over around ten tomorrow morning, and we bring each other up to date?"

"You will need to tell me all about your foot, and I will tell you about Eddie."

When I got to Lumir's, I didn't bother checking the house. My friend spent most of his time in the shop. I knocked, juggled my crutches, and let myself in. The sight of a smiling Lumir sweeping a pile of wood shavings into the corner greeted me. Polka music blared from the radio, and for a moment, it almost seemed as if he was dancing with his broom. I didn't know whether to attribute his good humor to his big date on Saturday night or the time he'd spent with Eddie.

"Why Clete," he said, "look at you. What happened?"

I related my tale of woe, describing the behavior of Gordon Kohl's twisted niece and detailing the conditions for my recovery. Not wanting to alarm my friend, I didn't mention the warning note.

Lumir clucked appreciatively.

"But what about you?" I said. "No two ways about it. You tore up the floor Saturday night. You're in better physical condition than most young men."

"You don't know because you work so much, but I like to get out during the daytime. The old people in this neighborhood need yard work and house repairs. I mow six lawns with a hand-powered mower, and I shovel snow for those same six houses. I do repairs. Last year I painted one house and shingled another one with the widow's grandson. Most of them, I don't charge. I keep my own place up, and deliver groceries for the shut-ins from Saint Wenceslaus. Where's the work in a little dancing?"

I knew Lumir was old school, but the extent of his generosity surprised me. "But sorting lumber is a two-man job?"

Lumir leaned his broom against the wall and motioned to the chairs by his desk. We sat. "I asked for Eddie's help to sort lumber so he would get something out of coming over to answer our questions. Eddie has a sad story—his parents drink too much. Their card parties and tavern friends are more important to them than their son. The boy is welcome in my shop whenever he wants to come. He is a good boy, already working for his money. If he wants to help me on my lawns or home repairs, I will pay him even if I do not get anything myself."

Lumir seemed defensive. Unsure of where he was taking the conversation, I left him in the driver's seat.

"My father drank too much," he said. "We almost lost the farm. A boy should not grow up with a father who ignores him."

I didn't know what to say. Lumir often spoke fondly of his parents. Apparently, he'd long ago forgiven his father's flaws. A good Midwesterner, I changed the subject.

"Did Eddie say anything that might help us?" I asked.

"I have learned much from Eddie. As we thought, the boys were inside the car. What we did not guess is they took it for a little drive. They did not realize Diane was in back until they were on the road. Eddie was the driver. He drove the car back to the Me Too store and left it like they found it—except for two things. They left their basketball inside."

Lumir paused, waiting for me to ask the obvious question. Just as obvious, he was enjoying the wait.

"And the second thing?" I asked.

Lumir reached into his pocket and handed me a folding knife. "Eddie found this on the front seat of the car."

The knife was a standard three-blade pocketknife a bit over average size. Bone-handled and nicely shaped, the knife's construction was a cut above the norm. Judging by the wear to its surfaces, it had spent much of its life in someone's pants pocket along with the typical assortment of coins and keys. The knife seemed to fit with the fishing equipment found in the car, but for one discrepancy. The police report indicated that the fishing equipment in the car looked to have been recently purchased. The pocketknife was well-worn and, from the look of it, had never spent time in a tackle box.

"It doesn't look like a fishing knife, Lumir. It has carbon steel blades, and none of them have seen a trace of rust. These blades never spent much time around water."

"I know that, forget the fish—look at the shields."

One of the nickel-silver escutcheons on the knife's panels featured a coat of arms with a sort of three-armed cross on it. The ends of the cross's arms were worn, but looked like they once terminated in tiny clovers. The other shield was worn smooth. I could make out the letter "G." By holding it at an angle to an incandescent bulb, I could see the faint outline of the letter "K." The letters probably represented the owner's initials. If anything else had been inscribed on the escutcheon, years of jostling against the contents of a pocket had obliterated it.

My initial reaction was one of excitement—at last, a real clue. Reality soon set in, and my excitement waned. "Lumir, could you make out the letters on the shield?"

"I could see a 'G,'" he said, "and maybe an 'H.'"

"I think it's a 'K.' Finding Gordon Kohl's pocketknife in his own car doesn't do much for us."

I watched as my friend's eagerness evaporated. I could understand the feeling. It mirrored mine.

"I don't know how much farther I'm going to be able to take this," I said. "All I can think to do now is start following Kohl around to see if he does anything suspicious. Now that I'm on crutches, I have the time. I won't be able to do it for long—he'll start recognizing my car."

If he hadn't already.

"You could use the Falcon, and my pickup."

"Great. I'll take you up on the offer."

Lumir had purchased Diane's Falcon from Roy and DeeDee, so now owned two vehicles. Between my Nova, Diane's car, and Lumir's pickup, I'd have a small fleet of vehicles available for a stakeout. The odds I'd learn anything were long, but I'm nothing if not stubborn.

Despite offering his vehicles, Lumir did not seem optimistic. "The police are sitting on their hands, and we are no closer to finding Diane's killer. I feel discouraged."

"But we know so much more than a few weeks ago. Everywhere we turn, it seems we keep coming back to the dentist. I have to ask why his niece is so protective of him. Stranger still, why did Pudge threaten to put me in the hospital—or even worse, a wheelchair—if I didn't stay away from Kohl's office? Maybe the police investigation is going nowhere because Pudge is protecting his brother-in-law."

"That's two whys and a maybe, Clete."

"There's another maybe." I said. "Maybe Kohl gave his keys to somebody. You'd think a stolen car would have been hot-wired."

Lumir leaned back and stretched. "Why bother to hot-wire a car when you can walk a few blocks and find one with the keys still in it? Besides, a dentist would be a smart man—too smart to leave Diane in his car."

"Maybe not all that smart. What if he hired the wrong people to get rid of the evidence?"

Randy Roeder

17

Gordon Kohl lived in the 1800 block of Grande Avenue. As an amateur at the surveillance game, I considered that a blessing. The street saw a fair amount of traffic. Still, I couldn't spend much time in the neighborhood without drawing attention. The safest place for me to begin monitoring the dentist's activities would be at his workplace. I phoned Kohl's office under the pretext of needing a late afternoon appointment and learned I could book as late as 4:30, Monday through Thursday, and 12:30 on Fridays.

I decided to watch the office from a small parking lot bordering on a vacant storefront a half block away. I took up my position at 4:45, equipped with a pair of sunglasses and a plaid driving cap worn low so the bill covered most of my eyes. Outside of the car, the getup wasn't much of a disguise. Inside, it concealed my face without looking too conspicuous. A pair of field glasses I'd picked up at the Army Surplus Store lay on the seat beside me. I'd have to be careful when I used them—binoculars could easily draw unwanted attention.

A few minutes after five, a bright yellow Mustang pulled out of the office's lot and headed in my direction. As the vehicle passed, I recognized the dental assistant from hell behind the wheel. Since she didn't try to ram my car, she obviously didn't recognize me. A white, full-sized sedan pulled out, Kohl in his Electra. I started my engine.

He turned onto Tenth Street, heading away from me. I pulled out. Although I was a little too far back to catch the first traffic light, I could see he'd turned left. Driving a little faster than I wanted, I managed to catch up with him and soon realized Dr. Kohl was heading home. When he pulled into an empty space in front of his house, I parked across the street, a bit down the block, and waited. Picking up a book, I pretended to read. I didn't know how long I could stay in the spot without attracting too much attention—maybe a half hour, tops.

Thirty minutes later, I started the car and pulled out. I drove through the neighborhood, circling back onto Grande every twenty minutes or so. After an hour and a half, I parked again—on the other side of the street from my first stop. I tapped my fingers on the steering wheel. The reality of the boredom inherent in a stakeout began to dawn on me. I consoled myself with the thought that Pudge Davis did it for a living.

At a quarter to eight, Dr. Kohl and a woman exited his house, entered his car, and drove off. I followed at a discreet distance as the dentist piloted his vehicle over to a neighborhood of older homes on the northeast side of town. When his turn signal indicated he was pulling up to the curb, I kept my distance, parked, and waited.

I'd no sooner maneuvered into position than Kohl pulled out again. I did the same. As I passed the house where he'd stopped, his passenger was standing on the porch, in the process of being welcomed into the front door. When the dentist returned home, he pulled into the alley behind his house. Since it looked like rain, I assumed he'd decided to park in his garage rather than out front.

Time to get out of the neighborhood. Surveillance sounds simple—a guy just waits and follows someone around until something happens. That won't work in a small Midwestern City. I could see no way to keep the operation alive on an extended basis without someone noticing me—even with access to three different vehicles.

I decided to swing by the two-story home where Kohl had dropped his passenger. As I passed, I noted the house number. I couldn't miss the long wooden ramp leading up to the front porch— someone who lived there used a wheelchair.

The next day, I had a lunch appointment with Jim Weiss. I left early so I could stop by the Coe College Library to do some research. I parked as close to campus as possible, grabbed my crutches, and headed for the building. When I got to my destination, I found a new reason to curse Gordon Kohl's psychotic little assistant. Eight massive limestone steps stood between my crutches and the entrance to the building. I slowly worked my way to the top. As I limped into the building's vaulted, wood-paneled lobby, I saw Helene Olds standing at a small table with her back to the massive oak card catalog, busily riffling through a drawer full of cards. She looked up as I approached.

"Cletus Efferding," she said, "I never expected to see you here, especially with your crutches. Why on Sunday, I didn't think you'd make it back to your car. Feeling better?"

"No, but I'd go crazy sitting around the apartment."

Helene shuddered. "Ugh, every dancer's nightmare—an injury. You didn't say, how long will you be laid up?"

"Two weeks, minimum. More if it doesn't heal."

"I feel for you. But hey, I doubt you braved the library steps just to say hello. What can I do for you?"

"Can you show me your Cedar Rapids crisscross directory? You know, the one where you look up an address, and it tells you who lives there."

"Of course."

Helene led me to the shelf that housed the city directories. She pulled the most recent volume and carried it to a table for me.

"I'll leave you to your work," she said. "Let me know if you need anything."

I thanked her, eased into a chair, and began working my way through the weighty volume's address and personal name sections. A Margaret Davis lived in the house that Kohl's passenger visited last night. The book listed the same address as the residence of Florian Davis. Since Lucinda Kohl didn't drive, I concluded the dentist had driven his wife to visit her mother and perhaps her brother. Since only two adults lived in the house, the ramp in front indicated Margaret Davis needed a wheelchair.

I felt dirty. I'd inadvertently spied on a woman whose only crime was visiting her invalid mother. Then too, I'd misjudged Pudge Davis as some sort of twisted Mama's boy when he likely lived at home to care for her. The whole experience was a letdown. I had to remind myself I had no other leads, and if I was going to solve the mystery of Diane's passing, I'd have to bulldog it.

Sick mother or not, Davis still took the prize for the most disagreeable human being I'd ever encountered. Heck, even Nazis loved their mothers. As I pondered what I'd learned, I found myself revising my opinion. Pudge was only the second most disagreeable person I'd ever encountered. His niece, Gordon Kohl's assistant, took the cake.

My business at the library concluded, I found Helene, thanked her for her assistance, and worked my way back to the Nova. None of what I'd learned had changed anything—Kohl could still be an abortionist.

Right on time, I limped into Killian's Man's Grille for my lunch with Jim Weiss. Jim ordered the Cobb salad, and I a BLT. I answered the inevitable questions about my foot and filled him in on what I'd learned so far. Mindful of my promise of confidentiality to his sister-in-law, I chose my words carefully. I needn't have worried; Jim didn't ask about the source of my information. When I got to the details of my surveillance of Gordon Kohl, he put down his fork and looked at me. I knew the look well. Jim had a particularly good piece of information.

"If you're tailing Gordon Kohl, I have news for you. He's taking delivery on a new red Electra tomorrow. I can't say but I'd do the same. Who wants to drive a car with a history like that? Last week, he had us tear out the carpet and the lower part of the back seat. Uh, we couldn't get the stains out . . ."

I didn't need the mental image so held up my hands, palms out. "I get the picture. I appreciate the information on Kohl's car. By tomorrow night, I'd have been out in the cold. A red Electra will be so easy to spot it's like a gift."

Jim said, "I asked the guys in the shop to let me know what they found when they rehabbed the vehicle. They didn't come up with a thing, not even a scrap of paper or a broken pencil. The police were pretty thorough."

"You didn't tell them why you were interested, did you?"

"I just mentioned a friend of mind was unhappy with the police work on the case and would want to know if anything turned up."

My chest tightened. "Did you mention my name?"

Jim looked at me quizzically. "No. What's up?"

I filled him in on the threat I found on my windshield.

Jim pulled out his lighter and fired up a cig. "This isn't good. You're making enemies. Other than Pudge Davis and his family, I can't think of who it might be."

"If I knew who it was, I'd have the abortionist."

"You better be careful," Jim said. "Davis has you down for a murder suspect. That means he knows your car. Do you know what he drives?"

"No, but I wish I did."

"Wish no more," replied Jim. "When he's not on duty, Pudge drives a ten-year-old Studebaker Commander. It's copper-tone and has big fins on the back. I doubt there's another one like it in town. We took it on trade about five years ago and sold it to Pudge dirt cheap, just to get it off the lot. That was one ugly automobile."

I grimaced. "I never expected to come anywhere near Pudge when I started looking into Kohl. I've got two other vehicles I can drive: Diane's car and Lumir's pickup truck. I'd better start using them."

"Make that three other vehicles," Jim said, "you can borrow my sixty-two Impala. We're about the same size, so I have a camouflage hunting cap you can borrow, some bibbed overalls, and a pinstripe Oshkosh farmer's cap. You can use those with Lumir's pickup. You should buy some of those non-prescription window glasses. Get thick frames. They'll help disguise you when you don't want to wear sunglasses."

"Window glasses are a good idea. I very well can't wear sunglasses at night, and I'll take you up on the Chevy and old clothes."

"Don't forget, Davis knows what Diane's car looks like. He might even have been part of the team that searched it."

His lunch break over, Jim went back to work. I stayed behind for a third cup of coffee. Jim was a good friend. I'd trust him with my money, and I'd trust him with my life. But, like most guys working in sales, he liked to gossip. I'd lay even odds he let my name slip.

I drove back to the apartment, iced my foot, and settled back on the couch. A leisurely browse of the *Gazette* beckoned, but my weary eyes demurred, asking instead for a catnap. I folded the paper and tossed it at the multi-story stack in the corner. Not only did my missile fail to land at the top of the heap, it destabilized the entire structure, resulting in a collapse that sent its constituent pieces cascading across the floor.

I didn't bother with my crutches but lowered myself off the couch and scooted across the floor. Spewing bitter invective as I made my way to the site of the disaster, I hooked my bad foot on the coffee table—an action that resulted in imprecations that dwarfed my previous efforts and did nothing to quell the pain. Punctuating the outburst with a final request to send the world and everyone in it to a god-forsaken stinking hell, I began to reassemble the devastated tower.

I was about to add the last paper to the pile when the familiar face of a young woman holding a trophy looked up at me from last week's women's section. Suppressing a shudder, I read the caption beneath the picture.

Local Woman Wins at Drag Strip

Sally Davis, daughter of Milton and Mary Davis, proudly displays the trophy she won at the Women's Semi-Finals at the Quad Cities' Cordova Dragway. Miss Davis noted that more women are taking up the sport—adding proudly that she'd "smoked" her competition with her 1968 Ford Mustang.

So, the vile little dental assistant was Pudge's blood niece. Maybe there was something to my inherited mental illness theory. Now that I knew her name, I looked her up in the phone book. She lived in Carriage Hills Apartments. Considering her Mustang and the nice address, Sally didn't seem to lack for money. Her uncle by marriage, Gordon Kohl, had just traded for his second new Electra in a year. Was it possible they earned extra money from an illegal abortion business? That could explain why she protected her uncle's privacy so aggressively.

I couldn't follow everyone who might have a connection to Gordon Kohl. The extra cars I'd arranged for would only extend my surveillance a few more days. I had to prioritize, and Sally Davis represented an unnecessary diversion. Then too, a run-in with the obnoxious little snot would likely leave me in a full body cast.

Randy Roeder

18

Roy and DeeDee Sedlak invited me to their Fourth of July picnic. A family tradition, I'd attended with Diane last summer and doubted the particulars varied from year to year. Roy would fire up his charcoal rotisserie and make his fabulous salty-skin chicken. His method was simple, the result sublime. He'd rub the chickens inside and out with a mix of black pepper, hickory smoke salt, and garlic powder and then roast at high heat. Roy loved his baster. He'd cover the birds again and again with the contents of the roaster's dripping pan. Their skins would glaze to a crispy golden brown while the meat inside stayed moist and tender. DeeDee would bake homemade bread and whip up her secret-recipe potato salad. I'd been looking forward to the event all week.

I appreciated the way the family handled the situation with Diane. They acknowledged her absence at the prayer before the meal, but no one felt a need to turn the event into a second funeral. Roy—struggling with his emotions—left the table after the grace, but returned five minutes later, to all appearances no worse for the experience. No matter how you cut it, the Sedlaks had class.

After eating, the women retired to the kitchen to gossip and play cards while the men stayed behind in the yard, drinking beer and playing horseshoes. Stan took the afternoon's honors, Lumir came in second, the next-door neighbor third. For all his physical strength, Buzz was not good at the game. He threw too hard and either missed the stake entirely or bounced the shoe off it. I watched with envy, cursing my crutches and wishing evil on Pudge's demented niece. When the game wound down and the yard began to empty, Buzz took me aside for a private conversation. We sat at the now-empty picnic table.

"Clete," he asked, "How's it going? Learn anything new about the abortion?"

"Not much. The cops are sitting on their hands. Has Lumir been keeping you up to date?"

"Yeah, and I'm madder than hell. I want to go downtown and raise a big stink at the police station, but I don't want to make waves if it won't do any good. Mom and Dad want us all to settle down and get on with our lives. They say stirring things up will just make it harder for them and nothing we do can bring Diane back. If going to the station won't help, Stan and I are going to stay clear."

"I think that's a good idea. I promised myself I'd pursue this until I found the person who did it, but your family's peace of mind comes first. Do you want me to lay off?"

"Stan, Grandpa, and I are pullin' for you all the way. So are the guys at work. Give it everything you've got."

"The guys at work?"

"You bet. They know we don't wanna take this lyin' down."

Another leak. Between Buzz and Jim, I could figure another twenty-five people knew about my investigation. "Do me a favor," I said. "These things work out best when they're done quietly. People gossip, and it might get back to your folks. Worse yet, it could somehow get back to the abortionist."

And get me hurt.

Buzz looked me in the eye. There was no mistaking his feelings. "I'll keep quiet. It'll be hard because I'm pissed. And you wouldn't believe about Grandpa. Before this started, I never heard him swear. Those days are over. When I went to see him, he kept calling the guy who killed her 'a counterfeit' and 'a goddamn, dirty, hound-dog, sonofabitch.' Nearly blew the windows out of his shop."

Until he got to the part about the shop, I thought Buzz meant his other grandpa. I couldn't picture it. I'd never heard Lumir curse—and I'd been on the scene when he'd taken a three-inch gash from a protruding nail.

Buzz continued winding himself up. "I want to see that dirtball suffer, and if there's anything I can do to make that happen, you better believe I'll do it. That sucker's gonna hurt so bad he'll beg me to kill him."

It happened so quickly I almost didn't see it. Buzz shifted in his seat and brought his fist down on the picnic table for emphasis. I heard a crack and saw a hunk of two-by four detach itself from the end of the table. The guy was as strong as anybody I'd ever seen.

"We'll keep what you're doing away from the folks," he said as if nothing had happened. "They don't need to know, and if nothing turns up, they won't be disappointed."

"You read my mind," I said, still recovering from his violent outburst. "Right now, I can't think of anything you can do."

"If you need us, Stan and I are ready."

"Believe me, Buzz. I don't doubt it for a minute."

What with it being a holiday, I wasn't sure if there was much to learn by tailing Gordon Kohl but decided to give it a go. Given that he might recognize my car, I had no business doing it, but I felt edgy and wanted to keep things moving. Since parking the Nova on Grande Avenue two days in a row was risky, I contented myself with periodic drives by the Kohl house.

I spent the downtime parked in the lot of a medical office perusing a popular best seller, *Rosemary's Baby*. Intended as a break from the detective stories I'd been reading, the book didn't do anything for me. The lead character was a ditzy housewife who moved into an apartment building where her elderly neighbors belonged to a satanic cult. She got pregnant, and her baby turned out to be the spawn of the devil.

I lost interest and tossed the book into the back seat. It was too improbable. The Anti-Christ was already alive and living in Cedar Rapids. Her name was Sally Davis. I suspected she was the result of Satan's second attempt at procreation. He tried a generation earlier when her uncle Pudge was conceived, and although he'd come close, he hadn't yet perfected the formula. With Sally, he hit the jackpot.

As I flipped the ignition switch preparatory to making another drive by Kohl's, I looked up and saw his new red Electra heading west on First Avenue. Mouthing a "thank you" to the gods, I pulled out and followed. Just before he reached the river, he turned left and drove into a parking ramp. I parked illegally a half block farther on and watched the pedestrian exits. Kohl and the woman I now took to be his wife came out the exit nearest me and walked over to the Paramount Theater.

I looked up the street, took in the marquee, and discovered my luck was still with me. *Planet of the Apes* was showing. Since I wanted to see the movie, I crutched my way over, bought a ticket, and hobbled inside. I'd no sooner settled into my seat than I saw Gordon Kohl heading up the aisle in my direction.

My window glasses did the trick. He walked on past with no hint of recognition. To some extent, I felt sorry for the bespectacled, pear-shaped little fellow. A homely man, Kohl's life would not have been an easy one. His preference in clothing wouldn't have helped matters any. Tonight, the man wore a purple Nehru jacket, a garment all the rage last season and one that looks best on tall, skinny men. To put it kindly, the short, wide-bottomed dentist made an unforgettable impression. He had so little going for him and good fashion advice would have done so much. My kindly haberdasher instincts aside, I knew my concern for his appearance would turn to deep, unmitigated hatred if he were involved with Diane's abortion.

Planet of the Apes more than beat my expectations. The critics didn't get it, but it was a corny-good flick in the way that *King Kong* and the Frankenstein films were. I'd no doubt but that people would talk about it for years. Poor Charlton Heston. One day he's the apple of the Lord God's eye—the prince of a chosen people, parting the seas and bringing the Ten Commandments down from the mountain; a dozen years later, he's on a strange planet running away from a bunch of monkeys so he doesn't get castrated by a cranky orangutan. I'd take the staid life of a well-dressed dance teacher to that of a bad actor any day.

Randy Roeder

19

White light streamed through the curtains as Gabby Khoury opened his eyes in a non-descript motel room. Nothing unusual about strange motels, but he wasn't quite sure where he was. Chicago? Maybe Peoria? His body felt like a team of horses had trampled it, and he had trouble organizing his thoughts. He lit a cigarette. When the nicotine hit his blood stream, his brain kicked in.

He'd crashed at the Rahbanis' motel in Cedar Rapids. Last night he joined Habi in sampling some of that LSD that was all the rage in California. He'd picked up a small quantity of the drug during his stay in Peoria. The stuff really screwed up his brain. "I swear on my grandmother's grave," he muttered, "I'll never touch that crap again."

He and Habi had spent a good part of last night on the roof of the motel watching distant fireworks and, later on, shouting obscenities at the moon. The decision to climb onto the roof represented a prime example of less-than-stellar thinking. He had to talk Habi out of an ill-considered desire to pee over the edge of the roof. The goofus kept talking about wanting to see his pee drops fly off into the air like spaceships. When Gabby finally convinced him to urinate on the roof rather than off it, the idiot kept yelling "I'm peeing stars, Gabby. I'm peeing stars." The sun was up by the time they felt steady enough to climb back down the maintenance ladder. Still flying like a kite at 5:00 a.m., he'd accepted Habi's offer of a room key, taken two Seconals, and nodded off into an unrestful sleep marked by vivid and troubling dreams.

He needed to find Habi. Yesterday had been the Fourth of July, a day to celebrate. Today was a day for business. Squinting against a light so bright it brought him to the point of tears, Gabby walked into the sunshine and took in his surroundings. He put his hand to his forehead to shade his face and saw Habi's Camaro still parked alongside the Moonglow. More than likely, he'd grabbed a hotel room or crashed in his office. Gabby sauntered over to his Chrysler, unlocked the trunk, and removed two duffle bags. Hoisting them onto his shoulders, he walked to the lounge and entered the door nearest Habi's office.

Gabby looked at Habi through the open doorway of the Moonglow's office. In yesterday's clothes, wearing sunglasses, and cradling a cup of coffee, Habi looked every inch the bedraggled drug user coming off a bender. Gabby spoke first.

"Hey Big Boy, what'd ya think of the merchandise?"

"I feel like a washing machine."

"A washing machine?"

"Maybe a clothes dryer. One's as bad as the other."

"Your head is still fried," said Gabby, re-shouldering his duffle. "I'll be back to talk later this afternoon."

Gabby picked up his car and drove downtown. He wanted to grab a pizza and check in with friends. For all the excitement of places like Des Moines and Peoria, he missed his home town. He definitely wouldn't check in with Georgie. To tell the truth, after the events of the last month, he didn't want to be alone with him. Gabby had Marco with him the last time he'd seen the man, so Georgie had been in no position to retaliate for the blunder with the woman's carcass. He knew the guy blamed him for the mess. The anger in his eyes was hard to miss. All because of that worthless piece of crap Nicky. Well, at least he'd had the chance help that chicken shit into the next life.

The promotion to Omaha would give Gabby some much-needed distance from the Rahbani patriarch. Now that Marco served as Midwest Vending's connection to Cedar Rapids, Georgie didn't need him anymore, and the elder Rahbani would be free to punish him for putting Habi in a bad spot. Talk about injustice—all he did was to try to help Habi out of a bind. The kid had no clue about how life in the rackets worked. Habi seemed truly surprised when Gabby had asked him not to tell Georgie he was back in town.

Until Georgie cooled off, Gabby's trips back to Cedar Rapids would need to be low key.

———

When Gabby returned to the Moonglow later that afternoon, he found Habi—disheveled and still wearing his sunglasses—asleep in his office. Gabby slammed the door as he entered, laughing as Habi woke with a start.

"Rise and shine, Big Boy. I gotta get back to Des Moines, and we got business."

"Des Moines is screwing us," Habi complained. "That new guy Marco raised everything ten percent, and my old man's on his high horse. I have to make up the difference out of my cut because he blames me for getting you transferred."

Gabby put his duffel bags down and took a seat. "I got promoted, not transferred. Your old man's got no cause. I told Phil you guys were supposed to get the same rate." Gabby silently cursed himself for not negotiating a better cut as the representative to Cedar Rapids.

"I had to sell my motorcycle to get the cash to do our deal," said Habi. "Even with the discount, ten thousand hits of speed aren't cheap. I didn't have the greens for the rest of the order. My guy in Davenport isn't happy. He says he went out on a limb for me and now he's stuck with those I didn't buy."

"Ya gotta learn, kid. These guys always got some kind of sob story. If he'd fronted you the stuff, he'd have more risk. You paid cash—that makes you a number one customer. Once you come back to him with another order and cash in hand, he'll be your best friend. I just wish you had the dough for all of it."

"I held up my end and got your speed. I took a beating on my bike because you needed the stuff right away."

"Don't think small." Gabby smiled at his protégée. "Once we're up and running, you can buy another bike—something even better."

"What's up with the acid? I want some."

Gabby held up a large sandwich bag stuffed with purple tablets. "It's called Purple Haze. I found a supplier in Peoria."

"I can lay off half that in Iowa City and Cedar Falls," Habi said. "If the college kids think it's cool, I'm good for the rest."

"Small potatoes." Gabby shook his head. "Take it all and pay me later. I can sell a lot more speed than you're getting. With my trucking and bar connections, I can move double that every month."

"I've gotta keep some back for my business," Habi replied. "I could sell even more, but all I have is Cedar Rapids and Iowa City. You've got Waterloo and most of the state sewed up."

Gabby wasn't about to ignore Habi's complaint. Technically, Waterloo was Georgie's territory, so Habi had claim to the city. Since Georgie wanted nothing to do with the drug business, he never realized Gabby was poaching.

"Waterloo is mine. You can sell whatever else you want there, but no speed."

"No problem," said Habi.

Gabby sat down and began unpacking his duffel, pulling out bag after bag of bright red capsules. "My guy in Peoria has so much Seconal he doesn't know what to do with it. He agreed to front it to me for less than the Des Moines cash price. I'll front you what you need."

Habi's eyes widened. "That's a lotta reds. My guys in Colored Town and East Waterloo will love me. The white-guy bar trade won't be so hot."

Gabby pointed to a second, larger duffel bag. "I've got something that'll make you happy. Weed—fifteen pounds. I know you're short on the bucks right now. I'll front you all of it—just like the reds."

"How's the quality?"

Gabby drew a joint out of his pocket, and threw it on the desk. Habi picked it up, lit the end, and inhaled.

"It's the same stuff as in the pounds?" he asked, his voice labored as he'd yet to exhale.

"What, you don't trust me?" complained Gabby.

Habi exhaled. "Just keeping you on your toes."

"I'm doing you a big favor, Big Boy. I owe my sister Leila a grand, and here I am fronting this stuff to you."

"Gabby, my big toe bleeds for you." Habi took several hits while Gabby waited in silence. "Good pot. Let's deal."

The merchandise divided and prices agreed on, Gabby shouldered his bag to head back to Des Moines.

"One more thing," he said. "You keep your mouth shut. You think your old man doesn't like dope—I'll be wearing a dirt suit if Des Moines finds out."

No matter what I might say about Gordon Kohl, I couldn't complain about his work ethic. The Fourth of July took place on a Thursday. The next day Kohl was at his office, working his regularly scheduled hours. How he'd resisted the temptation to cancel his half day in the office remained a mystery to me—four-day weekends are hard to come by. I waited in my spot next to the vacant store. As expected, Sally Davis left the office first. She tore out of the driveway as if escaping the burning fires of hell. The screech of her protesting tires had barely dissipated when she powershifted her Mustang into second and tore down the street, running the first red light she encountered. I couldn't understand why the little lunatic still had a driver's license. It'd be gone in a week if she didn't slow down.

Kohl left the office a few minutes later. He headed downtown, crossed the river, and turned right. His unexpected entry into the Time Check neighborhood gave rise to a hope something worthy of note might be happening. Some parts of the area didn't see much traffic, and the clannish families living in them enjoyed a reputation for being distrustful of outsiders. The folks on those blocks would as soon have walked through the streets in their birthday suits as talk to the police. I couldn't imagine a better location for an abortion operation. My anticipation turned to disappointment when Kohl headed for Ellis Boulevard, the neighborhood's main thoroughfare. I halted at a stop sign long enough to let a car get between us and continued up the boulevard. When he pulled into the entrance to Ellis Park, I overshot the turn.

I waited a few minutes, turned around, and entered. The big red Electra would be easy to spot, and sure enough, I soon found it parked in the lot of the Ellis Golf Course. Watching Gordy play golf wasn't high on my list of priorities, but it wouldn't hurt to learn something about his golfing buddies.

I'd made up a surveillance kit that I took with me when I tailed my man. It contained my caps, sunglasses, binoculars, thermos, and books. I decided to pose as some sort of a goofy birdwatcher. I hung the binoculars around my neck and turned up the bill on my cap. While there was no earthly reason for a bird enthusiast to be hobbling around a golf course on crutches, I'd no option but to make do with what I had on hand.

I found Kohl without much trouble. Golfing by himself and halfway to the first pin, the guy stuck out like a sore thumb—swinging his club wildly, churning up divots the size of pie plates. I watched through my field glasses with wonder. While golfers are known for colorful attire, the dentist took the idea to new heights. I'd never seen a man unafraid to wear a tam o' shanter in public. Kohl's was a beauty—a plaid in purple, yellow, and orange. If I'd ever imagined a guy wearing a bonnet like that would could get away with almost anything, I'd have been wrong. The dentist wore a red-checked shirt, green-striped walking shorts, and black socks with white golf shoes. My eyes ached.

With Gordy golfing solo, I wasn't about to discover anything about his associates. I slowly made my way back to Diane's Falcon.

Exhausted by the time I returned to the car, I discovered I'd leaned too hard on the crutches and bruised my armpits. Happy to be off my feet, I exited the lot, and drove down the lane to the first turnout, where I parked and pulled a detective paperback out of my surveillance kit.

This one was about a fat guy who grew orchids, wore yellow pajamas, and solved crimes without ever leaving his apartment. Nice work if you can get it, but the far-fetched setup didn't get me going. I put the book down and began checking out the view.

I noticed a couple of guys leaning against a car in a turnout a couple of hundred feet from me. I reached for my binoculars to see what they were up to. To all appearances, they were sharing a cigarette. I watched as they passed it back and forth between them. Huge clouds of smoke billowed from their mouths each time they exhaled. The cigarette finished, the men shook hands, and exchanged a package. The shorter of the two returned to a car he'd parked farther on down the road and drove off. I'd heard marijuana had become popular with the younger set. I suspected what I'd seen was testament to that fact.

The guy who stayed behind got into his car, a dark blue Pontiac GTO, a beauty. He'd customized it by painting the name *Sonny* in ornate lettering on the front fender. Sonny sported a Beatle haircut, turned-down mustache, and fringed leather vest. The guy didn't seem to have a whole lot to do with his time. He sat in his car with his arms behind his head and the radio cranked up. I smiled as the familiar strains of "Lovely Rita, Meter Maid" drifted toward me. Ten minutes later, a Volkswagen bug full of college kids pulled up. The driver got out, spoke with Sonny for a few minutes, returned to his car, and left. A quarter of an hour later another car pulled up, the driver exited, and got into Sonny's car. He left ten minutes later.

Call me stupid, but it didn't take long to figure out Sonny sold drugs. The brazen openness of his operation amazed me. The man dressed like a hippy and drove a flashy car with his name painted on it. He conducted business in broad daylight, in a public park with his radio blaring, selling his illegal wares to people who expected to find him in that spot. If I were a law-and-order type, I'd have driven directly to the cop shop and turned him in. Being a live-and-let-live kind of guy, I couldn't get all that excited about a little reefer changing hands. Besides, who'd want to live in a city without any hipsters in it?

20

On a perfect Saturday morning, I stood on the dewy grass looking at sky the color of a robin's egg. Raucous blackbirds cackled in nearby evergreens. Ground squirrels dashed about between the shrubs. The beautiful day didn't match my mood, I was standing at Diane's grave.

The caretakers sodded over the excavation during the heat wave and neglected to water it, leaving the grass curled and yellow brown. A temporary metallic marker stood at the head of the plot. Someone put a flower arrangement on the ground in front of it, but the petals had already shriveled and detached from their stems; the foliage had withered to faded husks.

I never could wrap my mind around the idea that people find consolation in visiting the grave of someone they love. The truth be told, I didn't feel any better than I had for the last month. If anything, I felt worse. My friend was gone, and if I lived a thousand years, I'd never know the joy of her presence again. Looking at a dried-out patch of grass didn't do anything to change that reality. I felt no closer to Diane, and certainly didn't experience anything akin to peace.

In the movies, I'd see someone sitting at a grave, speaking to their loved one, finding comfort in the one-sided conversation. But films are just illusions; the mourners, actors who practice their lines by talking to themselves. My trip to Diane's grave felt as fulfilling as a visit to an empty room. The deserted cemetery, filled with hundreds of empty rooms left me desolate. I thought of that well-known verse from the King James Bible.

> *In my Father's house are many mansions: if it were not so, I would have told you.*

If I wasn't getting much consolation from my visit to the cemetery, I got even less from King James. The joke was on me. There were many mansions indeed—all of them vacant.

And if that cheerful thought wasn't enough, I pictured my wife's final resting place back in Maquoketa. I hadn't been back since the funeral. By now, the Hinkleys would have arranged for a beautiful stone marker, and the grass around it would be well-established and green. I imagined them visiting Myra's grave a few times a year, bringing flowers. Maybe they took my son and daughter along with them.

What could they tell them about their mother and father? They wouldn't be able to say much. Learning your parents were a lout and a suicide isn't conducive to a carefree childhood. No matter how the Hinkleys handled it, I was sure of one thing—my kids would never hear mention of my name.

Despite her lengthy depression and the absence of physical intimacy, I'd loved my wife. I had no plan other than to stick with her, pursue a cure for her illness, and raise our family together. I still cursed myself every day for my reluctance to consent to the shock treatments her doctors recommended. If the treatments had taken, things might have gone better at home and the stress not gotten to me. Maybe I wouldn't have made that ill-fated trip to Dubuque.

I'd lost the two women I'd cared for, my wife and my best friend. Worse, I'd lost my children. As I thought through my losses, I decided visiting cemeteries might be conducive to yet another loss—

that of my mental health. On that cheery note, I reached into my jacket pocket and removed the green necktie I'd worn on so many happy evenings with Diane. I unfolded it, laid my crutches on the ground, and knelt. After knotting the tie to the temporary marker identifying her gravesite, I lowered my head.

"I'll find him, Diane," I said. "If it's the last thing I do, I'll find him."

And with that, I bid my friend farewell, knowing I'd never return.

I stopped by Lumir's to pick up one of the vehicles he'd offered me. There must have been twenty chairs in the room, and Lumir was working like he was killing snakes.

"I don't have time to talk right now." he said. "This yellow glue sets up fast, and I need to get these chairs glued up for the Knights of Columbus. They are having a euchre tournament tomorrow. Take Diane's car. I will need the truck to haul chairs. The keys are on the nail by the door."

"Will do, and thanks," I said.

As I limped to Diane's car, I passed Lumir's pickup. I stopped and looked inside. A typical pickup owner, Lumir had chosen a truck with a manual transmission. I hadn't thought about it until I imagined myself in the driver's seat—my bad foot would keep me from using the clutch pedal. So much for using the truck for surveillance.

Although she hadn't been in her car for a month, Diane's Falcon still smelled like her. She had worn a fragrance called Chantilly. I hadn't paid much attention to her perfume when she was alive, but I caught an echo of the scent when I got inside. The effect was so strong I caught a glimpse of her in the passenger's seat out of the corner of my eye. Of course, she wasn't there. I exhaled, my chest collapsing back in on itself, my eyes watering. Blinking hard, I suppressed the sob rising in my chest.

I began to doubt I'd be able to use the car to snoop on Gordon Kohl. I started the engine and drove unsteadily back to the apartment where I fixed myself a strong lemonade and iced my foot. An hour later, I forced myself to go back outside and look through the vehicle. The police hadn't subjected Diane's Falcon to the down-to-the-frame search they'd given Kohl's Electra.

I could see Lumir hadn't been able to face the task of tidying his granddaughter's car. Although the ashtrays and glove box had been emptied, used tissues and empty fast food containers lay scattered about the passenger compartment. Normally a tidy person, Diane was anything but when it came to her vehicle.

Someone had gathered the owner's manual and a scattering of receipts and papers into a pile on the back seat. I found handbills promoting a gig for Diane and the Zmolek Brothers at a bar in Central City. The text above the photo identified the group as the Corn Fed Clan. Diane stood between the brothers, dressed in a cowgirl outfit, holding a microphone. Curly and Red wore matching cowboy shirts, bolo ties, and feed caps emblazoned with the DeKalb trademark—a flying ear of corn. Beaming from ear-to-ear, a relaxed Red sat at his trap set while Curly gripped his accordion tightly, looking as if he feared a horde of screaming Bohemian teenyboppers might rip it from his hands. The stack of papers included a half dozen unused musician's contracts and a card for the Rahbani Booking Agency.

Diane had put a lot of energy into promoting the group. The effort must have felt like an uphill slog. She told me, in the weeks before her death, she'd come to realize performing with the brothers might not advance her singing career. I had difficulty responding to her revelation. I wasn't sure how a good friend should react. I didn't want to dishearten her but, Zmoleks or not, I couldn't see she had much chance for success. In the end, I simply listened and offered no opinion or advice. I was happy I'd chosen this course. It would have killed me if I'd said anything to cast a shadow on the little time remaining to her.

———————————

Jim Weiss waved me in and led me back to his den. Parked between the two leather recliners facing the television was a small table holding a tray of ham salad sandwiches and a bowl of mixed nuts.

"I was just making us some lunch," he said. "I don't get many Saturdays off, and when I do, I like to fix a mid-day drink. Can I get you something, an Old Fashioned maybe?"

Jim knew my weaknesses well. "Thanks. No whiskey, brandy."

"Sweet, sour, seltzer, or press?"

"Sour."

"Cherries or olive?"

"Cherries," I replied.

"I'm going to be slicing an orange."

"You read my mind, oh Great One."

Ah, the wonderful ritual of negotiating a Wisconsin Old Fashioned with a friend. While Jim mixed our drinks, I browsed the dozens of model cars lining the shelves of his den. Jim worked off the stresses of a day on the sales floor by assembling those kits you find in toy departments and hobby shops. He was good at it.

When Jim returned with our drinks, I had a question. "You've put together a lot of cars. How do you decide which kits to buy?"

"I try to find an example of every model I've sold— whether new or used. If the design changes between the model years are minor, I don't add a new one. Finding some of the kits isn't easy. They don't make kits for cars that don't sell well. I doubt I'll ever find a 1955 Nash Rambler station wagon."

"I suppose the same holds true for Studebakers."

"I can see where you're going with this one," Jim said. "Actually, Studebaker kits are popular. And yes, I have a Commander like the one I sold Pudge. It was such a memorable sale I painted it the same color."

Jim went to the shelf, picked up the car, and showed it to me. I couldn't recall having seen one before, but Jim was right—it was really ugly. We sat down to enjoy our sandwiches and drinks. When we finished, I showed Jim the window glasses he suggested I add to my disguises kit.

"Not bad," said Jim, "but they make you look like a real goober."

"Thanks Jim," I replied. "When you're as good looking as I am, you need something extreme to cover it up."

"Don't worry," he said. "When you're starting at zero, making it all the way to goober is a big step in itself."

I couldn't let that one go by. "Don't get me started. You're an easy target."

Jim grew serious. "All kidding aside, maybe you should reconsider your investigation. You've upset somebody, and they've threatened you. The police aren't going to help. For all you know, somebody on the force could be behind the warning. I know you think this town is quiet, but people do get hurt."

I paused before replying. "I appreciate your concern, Jim. I don't want to go into it, but finding the person who killed Diane is important because of something that happened before I moved here. I need to see this thing through."

Jim raised his brows. "I can't say I understand, but if you have to do it—well, I guess you have to do it. Let's see if we can find a ballgame on TV."

Jim turned on the tube, but couldn't find a game. We watched a thrilling round of golf instead, ate sandwiches, and discussed our car swap. I'd driven Diane's Falcon over and would drive his Impala home. He'd bring her car over to the apartment the next day.

Jim's comfortable recliners, another Old-Fashioned, and the hushed tones of the know-it-all announcer soon had us nodding in our chairs. I awoke during a commercial for life insurance to discover Jim snoring like a longshoreman. I rose quietly and limped to an adjacent table where I picked up a three-inch thick Sears catalog. Positioning myself next to Jim's chair, I raised it over my head and dropped it on the floor. Jim woke with a start.

"A real goober, eh?" I said.

"Clete, only a goober would wake a fellow like that."

I woke up Sunday thoroughly out of sorts. I'd spent six hours on my park-and-drive routine last night and hadn't caught so much as a glimpse of Gordon Kohl. Frustrated by my failure, I vowed to skip breakfast and spend the entire day looking for him. I got into Diane's car and went back to my surveillance routine. The temperature already in the low nineties, a long, miserable day lay ahead.

Kohl continued to elude me, but on a 9:30 pass by the Davis residence, I spotted Pudge a few blocks away from his house pushing an elderly lady in a wheelchair toward Central Park Presbyterian Church. I still found it hard to believe the animal who'd tormented me for the last five years and threatened to break me into pieces would have a mother—much less that he'd wheel her to church. Good ol' Pudge had to have an angle. I wouldn't have been surprised to learn he planned to swindle his siblings out of their inheritance by sucking up to the old lady.

Bored beyond belief and filled with an urge to spy on my nemesis, I decided to go to church. I didn't expect to learn anything, but I was in a bad mood and wanted to go in and hate him for a while. A sign outside indicated services began at ten, so I parked and waited until the show was underway. I planned to slip in and remain in back. I'd leave early so Pudge wouldn't spot me.

At five past ten, I grabbed my crutches and made for the door. I shook my head at the usher who offered to escort me to a pew and stood in the rear of the nave. Although a quick scan of the crowd failed to reveal either Pudge or his mother, I discovered Gordon and Lucinda Kohl seated on the center aisle, about halfway back. Wearing a bright orange sport coat, the dentist was hard to miss.

As my eyes grew accustomed to the dim light, I looked to my left and saw Pudge's mother seated in her wheelchair behind the last row of pews, about twenty feet from me. Talk about dumb. When I get a vengeful, stupid idea, I should learn to run in the opposite direction.

I sidled toward the door, thinking it was just like Pudge to take his mother to church and duck out on the service. I'd almost reached my goal when the men's choir at the front of the church cut loose with "Our God, Our Help in Ages Past." A powerful organ accompaniment filled the building from floor to rafters, rattling the windows in their casements. As I reached for the handle, I looked up and spotted Pudge, standing in the choir, hymnbook in hand, belting it out with the rest of them. I made my escape.

God must have a soft spot for human stupidity. Following Pudge into church was the dumbest thing I'd done in some time. On the flip side, I'd blundered into Gordon Kohl. If I was a religious guy, I might think God was rewarding me for showing up in a house of worship. Then again, the Big Guy had just condemned me to wasting an entire Sunday following Gordy around. Thinking about God confuses me. I try not to do it too often.

21

I looked at the calendar. Thirty-eight days since Diane died, and my surveillance had yet to uncover anything significant. I hobbled out to Jim's car. Though I doubted an abortionist would ply his trade before going to his regular job, I'd neglected Kohl's early morning routine. With a bandanna around my neck, wearing Jim's farmer cap and threadbare bibbed overalls, I drove to the dentist's house. An hour and a quarter before his office opened, my suspect pulled out. Though I hoped something interesting might be breaking, Gordy drove over to the Davis house, picked up his wife, and took her home.

There didn't seem to be much point in following the guy to his office, so I opted for breakfast at Tommy's. I couldn't find a parking place and ended up two blocks away. Another hot day, I was puffing and sweating by the time I got there. I paused, leaned on my crutches, and turning my back to the wall, prepared to struggle with the door. I noticed an attractive young woman in a miniskirt walking down the sidewalk in my direction. I could see her giving me the eye.

I smiled back. As she was about to pass, she paused, turned to me, and took my hand.

"Please," she said looking down at the sidewalk, "take it."

"What?" I said.

"Please, there's no shame in being laid up. Get yourself a good meal or a place to rest. God bless you."

As she pulled her hand away, I saw she'd slipped me a dollar. She was on her way before I could think of anything to say. Not wanting to appear ungrateful, I called after her, "Thank you, Miss."

I rubbed my face and realized I hadn't shaved in forty-eight hours. I needed to go home. I propelled myself in the direction of Jim's car as fast as my crutches could carry me. No matter how desperate, I would never, ever, wear Jim's disguise again.

When I got to the apartment, I pulled in next to the Nova. I hadn't noticed when I left home this morning, but all four tires were flat. Somebody had slashed the valve stems and left a note on the windshield. I opened it.

Mind your own business Danceman. I can get you any time.

I looked around, didn't see anyone. Frustrated and cursing, I made my way into the apartment, drank a pint of chocolate milk from the carton, and thought things over. I doubted the person who wrote the note knew about the surveillance part of my operation. If he did, things would already have gotten rough. The guy must have thought his original warning needed a little reinforcement. This second attempt to scare me could work to my advantage. I wouldn't repair the Nova's tires for a few days and would leave the lights on in the apartment around the clock.

I wanted to give the impression I was staying inside, scared out of my wits. In the meantime, I'd move the Impala and Falcon farther from the apartment and exit through the back door. At a minimum, my plan would buy me a few days. With luck, the guy behind the threats would think I'd given up on my project.

———————

On patrol that night, around 10:30, I sighted a copper-toned Studebaker Commander heading west on Mount Vernon Road. Pudge's car, of course, and though I had no business doing so, I began following at a discreet distance. The little model on Jim's shelf didn't begin to capture the putrid reality. The oversized fins and eyebrows over the headlights were bad enough, but somebody had added fender skirts and a continental kit, a misguided customization my friend's miniature lacked. My delight in the unmitigated ugliness of Pudgie's wheels knew no bounds. There could be no doubt; the guy was a loser.

Pudge turned left on 10th Street Southeast, a neighborhood too quiet for surveillance. Concerned he'd notice me, I turned off my lights as I rounded the corner. I followed him down 10th for something like three blocks before he turned left into a narrow alley. There was no safe way to follow him down the graveled path, so I overshot the entrance, took the next left, and tracked his headlights as he turned into a backyard one house down from where I'd pulled up. I could think of no reason why an off-duty Pudge would be parking behind a house in Colored Town.

I eased the car forward to get a better view and noticed a light burning above the side door. A car door slammed, and I watched Pudge carry two bags of what looked to be groceries up to the door. Moving both bags to one arm, he knocked. A Negro woman stepped out, took one of the bags, grabbed Pudge with her free arm, and pulled herself up on her tiptoes to give him a long kiss. A little boy darted out from behind the woman. He wrapped his arms around the detective's legs and gave him a pint-sized bear hug. The woman let go of Davis and pried the boy off him with her free hand. She turned and led both boy and detective back into the house. As the light over the door winked out, I put Jim's car back in drive and continued down the street.

I circled back to the Mercy Hospital parking lot, pulled in, and thought about what I'd just seen. Pudge was driving his personal car, and the woman and boy were happy to see him. He brought groceries to the house. He'd been expected. The late hour and warmth of Pudge's welcome precluded the possibility of a police department community relations effort. Either the woman was a prostitute, or Pudge was enjoying a fling with a colored lover.

I wondered if the colored woman and Pudge were somehow involved in Gordon Kohl's abortion business. I couldn't rule it out, but the idea seemed far-fetched. The hooker or love affair explanations—while lurid—made more sense. It didn't make much difference to me. In one case, Pudge was a minor offender, in the other, simply a man hiding a colored paramour.

Whether business or personal, disclosure of the relationship had the potential for scandal. If business, a police detective caught visiting a prostitute might face discipline but would be unlikely to lose his job. If personal, there'd be no discipline, but Pudge could expect a wink-wink elbow to the ribs, and the inevitable "once you go black, you never come back" teasing. Unpleasant, but he'd survive.

A serious long-term relationship with a Negro woman would be worse. Few of the good citizens of Cedar Rapids took kindly to the idea of serious mixed-race relationships. I knew enough about my adopted city to understand black and white kept to themselves and liked it that way. In the white community, Rastus and Liza jokes circulated freely, and unlike the ubiquitous Bohemie jokes making the rounds, the race-based humor exhibited a hard edge. On the other side of the divide, the city's black citizenry was predisposed to view mixed race pairings as "trashy."

My discovery meant I had something on Pudge, but I didn't know if I would use it. Basic human decency aside, a carelessly played race card could get me beaten, hospitalized, or crippled. I doubted he'd go that far, but since Pudge was a cop, I could find myself charged with extortion.

Despite the difficulty of exploiting the information, I wanted to know more about Pudge's private life. I might find a way to pressure him back into the search for Diane's killer. It wouldn't hurt to know if Pudge spent the entire night at the mystery house, so I went back to my apartment, carried the alarm clock to the living room, and set it. I flopped down on the couch. When the buzzer went off at four a.m., I roused myself, got into Jim's car, and drove the few blocks over to Colored Town. Pudge's Studebaker was still at the house—he'd spent the night.

Randy Roeder

22

Tuesday morning, while icing my foot, I picked Gordon Kohl's pocketknife from the ashtray where I'd tossed it when I brought it home from Lumir's shop. Lumir had taken it hard when he realized the knife wasn't a clue to the identity of the person responsible for Diane's death. I'd known him long enough to understand his granddaughter's demise hit him harder than he let on. Though he'd taken the dance floor by storm a week and a half ago, the evening had been an anomaly. My friend had been unusually quiet, and much of the bounce had gone from his step.

Lumir still helped his neighbors with their lawns and repairs, but I worried his grief might get the better of him, so I decided to spend a few mornings at his place. One of the few things I'd brought with me from Bellevue was a photo of my grandfather standing proudly in front of the family business. Dressed in his Sunday finest, he stood to the side of a neatly lettered store window bearing the inscription "August Efferding, Haberdasher." The picture had escaped damage when the burglar ransacked my room at the Hotel Magnus and remained one of the few links to a life I could never return to. I'd ask Lumir to make a cherrywood frame for it.

I fiddled with the knife—feeling its weight in my hand, opening and closing the blades, checking on its construction. So far, tailing Gordon Kohl had done nothing to solve the riddle of Diane's final moments. I wondered what—if anything—his choice of a pocketknife might tell me. I'd never thought much about pocketknives before, so I decided to talk to someone who knew something about them.

Not wanting to be seen in one of my alternative vehicles, I took a cab downtown and had the driver drop me on Third Avenue, near the entrance to Kubia's Hardware. The place had been around forever and prided itself on a first-class inventory and knowledgeable staff. After assaulting the door with my crutches, I hobbled to the back where I found the store's display of pocketknives in a wall-mounted case. An elderly salesman dressed in a cardigan embroidered with the name "Ted" soon joined me. By the time he arrived, I'd determined none of the knives in the store's wall-mounted case matched the one in my pocket, so I pulled it out and handed it to him.

"I'm interested in what you can tell me about a knife like this," I said.

Ted took the knife, opened the blades, snapped them closed, and felt its heft. From the way he handled the tool, I could see he belonged to the subset of males who seldom left home without a pocketknife in his pants.

"This is a good knife," Ted replied. "Probably twenty years old, and the blades are as tight as when it was new. Look at how thick the bolsters are—that's why. The springs haven't lost any of their resilience. It's a common setup—two cutting blades and a screwdriver. I can show you two models with the same arrangement and quality. Our handles are high impact plastic, but I can order bone if you'd like."

"Can you tell me anything about this company—Siegley?"

"Siegley doesn't make its own knives and doesn't sell through the regular hardware trade. It rebrands trade items for promotional purposes. Most of what they sell is cheap—Boy Scout merchandise, free steak knives for opening a bank account, prizes for kids selling newspaper subscriptions—stuff like that."

"Oh," I said, "I thought this was a good knife."

"It is. I've never seen a Siegley anything like it. Good quality, and fancy. Those caps are German silver, and the shields are embossed and engraved. The blades are good carbon steel—most are stainless nowadays. Stainless blades don't rust, but they're hard to sharpen on a whetstone, and some of that cheap stainless—let me tell you—it's just junk. This knife was monogrammed and given away as a prize for something."

Ted returned the knife to me. "I don't think you're looking to buy a knife."

"I'm not, but I'd like three of your very best hog bristle brushes—three-quarters, inch, and inch and a half."

The brushes were to be a gift for Lumir. I hoped he'd be able to use them on my picture frame. Ted found them for me, and I went to the front of the store to check out. A girl of about fifteen stood at the register. She greeted me with a smile.

"Hello, Mr. Efferding. You won't remember me, but you came to Franklin Junior High to teach us to fox trot for our eighth-grade dance. I really liked the lesson."

"I'm glad to hear that," I replied.

She frowned. "Do you remember you told us that when a girl gets her foot stepped on in the fox trot, it's her fault?"

I set my brushes on the counter. "I tell most of my beginning dancers that."

"Well, it's a lie. If the guy starts on the wrong foot, you get stepped on."

"Do tell," I said, "then why do you think I said that?"

"Because you're a guy and always take the guy's side."

"Wrong, I'm on the girl's side."

She shook her head. "It doesn't seem like it, Mr. Efferding."

"It's like this," I said as she handed me my bag of brushes. "If a guy is worried about stepping on a girl's feet, you'll never get him out on the dance floor."

"So, we girls have to suffer?"

"Yup. When your foot gets stepped on, you're taking one for the team."

"It doesn't seem fair."

"See these crutches?" I asked.

"Sure," she said.

"Sometimes things don't work out so well for the guy either."

Her eyes grew to the size of saucers. "She must have been a big woman."

"Not big, just mean," I said and turned to hobble on out the door.

I chose Jim's Impala for my surveillance. Once again, Gordon Kohl drove Lucinda over to the Davis house. Gordy's evening activities revealed a distinct lack of imagination. When he drove home and parked in front of his house, I threw my hands up in despair.

I'd hoped Kohl might leave again. He didn't. I needed to find a better hobby, like watching paint dry. I stuck with it until 10:30 and went home. At least I could catch the *Late Show*.

After the TV stations signed off for the night, I drove back to the house where Pudge had spent last night. Bingo! His Studebaker sat in the back yard, an affront to the eyes of anyone who glanced down the alley. Bringing groceries, staying two nights in a row, a little boy happy to see him, the hooker scenario didn't fit. Pudge had something serious going. There's no explaining human nature. No matter how reprehensible, depraved, and twisted the guy, there's always a woman out there who thinks he's the best thing since air conditioning.

My stomach rumbled. Craving for sustenance at irregular hours is one of the hallmarks of an erratic schedule. I'd learned long ago, when a late-night urge strikes, quality is unimportant. At 2:45 a.m., the options were limited. The city's restaurants had shuttered for the night, and since I'd missed closing time, bar food was out. The best I could come up with was the Hamburg Inn, an all-night diner across Center Point Road from Coe College. The Hamburg put out a man-sized bowl of chili, just what I needed before heading home and getting horizontal.

One of those railroad dining cars converted into a hamburger joint, the Hamburg Inn deserved its reputation as a greasy spoon, but I'd been there often enough to know I wouldn't get ptomaine. Customers could get breakfast around the clock, as well as burgers, fries, and a soup or two. I'd never been to the Hamburg at this hour, and although the neon "Open" sign glowed, I found the door locked. A scruffy-looking waitress waved to me through the glass, gesturing that she'd come around the counter to unlock and let me in. I realized the locked door was standard operating procedure at this hour.

"You can never be too careful," she said as she opened the door for me and locked it again after I passed through.

I took a stool and leaned my crutches against the counter. Glancing up at the board, I noted the Burg still sold chili, and ordered. Instead of the students and businessmen who frequented the place for lunch, a lone couple, obviously drunk, sat at one the diner's few tables. The female half of the duo leaned forward in her chair, resting her head on the tiny table. She perked up from time to time to drag on her cigarette. A buxom woman, she had her raven hair done up in a beehive with a spit curl on the side. The lady met my definition of a cheap date. With a bird's nest on her head, dark eye makeup, and a striped sweater three sizes too small, she exuded all the charm of a derby-wearing raccoon staggering home from a raid on the neighborhood trash cans.

Her companion, a side-burned Mediterranean-type in a black leather jacket, slouched in the chair opposite. The Burg's fluorescent lights reflected off his hair, a ducktail dressed with enough oil to fill the reservoir of a small lawn mower. Glassy-eyed, and with arms folded, he sat staring out the window, enjoying the view of the empty street. There not being much else to see, I turned my head and looked down to mind my own business.

The late-night shift had a pace of its own. Gone were the balls of hamburger, lined up along the back of the grill, ready to be tossed onto the hot top and mashed into patties. Gone too was the energetic waitress who helped the fry cook keep the orders moving. They'd been replaced by an overweight, listless cook/waitress. Sweating profusely, her wispy gray locks escaping her hairnet, the diner's sole employee belched as she ladled my chili from a stainless-steel pot. As she approached with my order, I noticed her name tag read "Bertie."

Bertie extended her arm to set my bowl on the counter, I couldn't help but notice the seam of her uniform, ripped from armpit to waist and held together by two small safety pins. The pins weren't exactly up to the job, and through the gap, a generous portion of her not so well-laundered brassiere made its unwelcome appearance. The late shift at the Hamburg was not for the faint of heart, but what the heck—the place was open, the price was right, and I was hungry.

As I pondered how the implications of Pudge's love life might play to my advantage, a woman's full-throated curse brought me back to the present. The dark-haired beehive had come to life.

"Gabriel Khoury, you sonofabitch, you don't have my money? The whole thousand—my life savings?" I turned to see her pick up a heavy glass ashtray and slam it into the side of her partner's head. "You moron. That was a loan. You'd steal from your own sister? How am I gonna pay my rent?"

She looked ready to bop him again, but he grabbed her arm and yelled, "Shut up, skag. You're so damn stupid; you'd just spend it on yourself. I'll pay you back when I have it." Bleeding profusely, the guy would need more than a few stitches.

"Out, out, get out!" Listless Bertie had found a new source of energy and rounded the counter with piece of inch-thick pipe in hand.

"Stay out of this, old lady!" the Gabriel guy warned.

"Out," the cook lady demanded, bringing the pipe down hard on the table an inch from his hand. The violence of the blow proved too much for the safety pins restraining the rip in her uniform. Pin and fabric parted company revealing a world most of us don't ever want to see. Bertie raised the pipe again, prepared to follow up.

"We're going, we're going," the guy said, holding up his hands.

Facing her guests and ready to swing again, the cook lady moved toward the door, unlocked it, and motioned for the pair to pass. Their egress complete, Bertie re-locked the door and returned to her position behind the counter.

"What a pussy," she declared. "I had three husbands who wouldn't let a thing like a little pipe get in the way of a good fight."

"They don't make 'em like they used to," I allowed and went back to my chili.

Ignoring the blood on the table and floor, Bertie hummed to herself as she replaced two of the flypaper coils hanging from the ceiling. If she was concerned about the cracked Formica table, she didn't show it. Finished with her flypaper, she lit a cigarette, let out a sigh, and leaned back against a cabinet. Silhouetted against the pale mustard-colored walls of the diner, a re-invigorated Bertie smoked her unfiltered cigarette with the pride of a champion. Exhilarated by the fracas, oblivious to the view she presented, Bertie made no attempt to repair the tear in her garment. Wise man that I am, I resisted the urge to mention the need for replacement safety pins.

Randy Roeder

23

My stomach full of chili, I slept like a baby. Lumir had invited me over for breakfast or I'd have slept in. I gathered up the photo of my grandfather and the brushes I'd picked up at Kubia's, exited via the back door, and got into the Falcon. By the time I arrived at Lumir's, it was almost ten. I went to the back porch and knocked. Eddie Brada came to the door.

"Morning," he greeted me. "Lumir said to ask if it's okay to call you Clete."

"That'd be a lot shorter than Mr. Efferding," I replied. "What's for breakfast?"

Lumir called out from the kitchen. "Scrambled eggs, *jaternice*, and good, strong coffee."

"*Jaternice*?" I asked.

"Czech sausage." Eddie smiled as we entered the kitchen. "Ears, snouts, the floor, and more."

"Eddie, such talk," said Lumir. "Pohlena's is the best butcher shop in the city."

"Don't worry, Clete," said Eddie. "If you can't hack it, I'll take it off your hands."

The eggs were fluffy and the *jaternice* grand. After we'd finished and transported the dishes to the sink, Eddie and Lumir led the way out to the shop. I crutched along behind them. For the umpteenth time, I wondered why the shed behind Lumir's house was nearly twice the size of his modest home. For the first time, I thought to ask.

"Did you ever wonder why your shed is twice the size of your house?" I said.

"No," Lumir replied.

"It's so unusual, I thought you'd be curious," I said.

"Judas Priest," Eddie sputtered, "haven't you ever noticed the loft?"

"What about it?"

"It's a hay loft."

"So?" I asked."

Lumir cut in, most likely to save me further embarrassment. "I never wondered why the shed is bigger than the house because the man who lived here built it as a livery stable. I ripped out the stalls, stabilized the foundation, and poured the concrete floor. A man's shop should be bigger than his house."

Lumir settled into his captain's chair, and I pulled the photo of my grandfather's store out of the box. "Lumir," I said, "do you think you could make a cherrywood frame for this picture?"

"Your grandfather?" Lumir asked as he surveyed the picture.

"August Efferding," I replied, "the first haberdasher in the family."

"I can make the frame, but I thought your grandfather sold men's clothes," Lumir replied.

"That's what a haberdasher does," I said.

Lumir snorted. "Such a fancy name for selling underwear."

"First-class underwear, Lumir. Nothing but the best." I turned to Eddie. "Never wear cheap underwear, Eddie," I said. "Whatever goes next to your skin should be as good as what you show to the world."

Eddie appeared unimpressed. "Sure thing," he said. "If I get into an accident, I'd hate to have the nurses talking about my skivvies."

I gave up. Trying to impress my companions of the importance of regular consultations with a knowledgeable haberdasher appeared a lost cause. "I have a present for you, Lumir," I said and handed him the wrapped packet of brushes.

Lumir unwrapped the brushes, raised his eyebrows, and let out a whistle of approval. "Where'd you find these?" he asked.

"Kubia's," I replied. "An old guy named Ted said they were the best in the store."

"Ted Kadlec is not an old man! Why he's not even seventy yet!"

I noticed Eddie's eyeballs roll skyward. Whatever the thought that crossed his mind, he chose to keep it to himself. Smart boy.

I thought it best to redirect the conversation. "What's that?" I inquired, pointing to what looked like the world's largest chisel lying atop Lumir's workbench. It must have been three and a half feet long.

"It's called a slick," said Lumir. "Eddie sharpened it yesterday. I gave it to him as a test. A slick is hard to sharpen, and Eddie passed. When he learns to sharpen a saw, he will know everything there is to caring for hand tools."

"Looks more like a weapon than a tool," I said. "What on earth is it for?"

Eddie smiled at me, walked over to the bench, and picked up the slick. Putting one hand atop the wooden handle and the other where the wood met the metal socket, he braced the handle just above his crotch and pushed the blade along a section of the wooden floor. He stooped to pick up the foot-long shaving and handed it to me. It was thinner than a piece of paper. Eddie sat back down without a word.

"Oh," I said, "sure would come in handy in a fight. You could gut somebody with one swipe."

Lumir snorted. "Don't listen to him, Eddie."

I tapped my fingers impatiently on the arm of the chair. I didn't have an appointment and had already waited an hour and a half for Marcus Grainger to call me into his office. I hadn't expected the man would be so busy when I snagged one of the better chairs lining the walls of the room, but I'd chosen well. Most of the terminally bored occupants of what I now thought of as the anteroom to Hell squirmed uncomfortably on folding chairs as they waited to be called into the room next door. Babies cried, old men coughed, tough-looking delinquents scowled, and a pair of noisy kids fought over a broken toy.

I'd come to the Linn County Department of Public Welfare to see if Grainger could help me solve the riddle of what had happened to Diane. Like many dance teachers, my friend had a day job. She worked as one of the department's social workers. She quit last February when one of her charges, an overgrown juvenile delinquent named Curtis, assaulted her as she left her apartment building. Already facing a rap for a string of burglaries, Curtis—high on amphetamine—forced Diane back into the hallway of the building, tore off her blouse, and forced his hand between her legs. Although an off-duty policeman who lived a few doors away ended the perpetrator's idea of a good time, Diane had difficulty putting the incident behind her.

Concerned about gossip and the effect of the incident on her reputation, she refused to press charges. Unfortunately for Curtis, he pulled off an armed robbery two days after he assaulted Diane. His timing couldn't have been worse. The robbery took place the day after his eighteenth birthday, and the state tried him as an adult. At the time of Diane's death, Curtis awaited sentencing in the Linn County Jail. Those in the know predicted he'd do three-to-five at the men's reformatory in Anamosa.

"Buzz Sedlak." A hatchet-faced woman called the name from a half-open door. "Mr. Grainger is waiting for you in Room 106."

Answering to the name Buzz, I struggled out of my chair and made my way to Marcus Grainger's office. When I entered, Grainger didn't look up from his paperwork. Diane's former boss didn't seem interested in making a good impression.

"I'd like to talk to you about Diane Novacek," I said.

Grainger, tipped his head slightly and looked at me over his glasses. "And you are?" he asked.

"Buzz Sedlak, her brother." Lying to the man proved an unexpected pleasure.

My not-so-little and not-so-white lie turned night into day. "Please sit down, Buzz. Those crutches can't be comfortable. Diane was the best advocate for young people I've had the pleasure to work with. You have my sympathy. She was a real gem."

"Thank you," I said. "Our family has been having quite a time. Diane went through so much in the past few years. Almost through college, and her husband gets killed on the job. Then she pulls herself together, graduates, gets started in social work, and gets assaulted by a client. After that, she can't face the job anymore, so she quits and has to start all over. Diane died in a way that doesn't make sense. We don't know enough about what happened, and that makes her death hard to accept."

"I don't know that I can help you."

"I'd like to ask you some questions," I said. "I expect the police have already asked them, but they haven't been willing to share very much with us."

"The police haven't spoken with us about Diane's death," Grainger replied. His response confirmed my belief someone in the department had killed the investigation. There'd have been no way they wouldn't have gotten around to her former employer.

"The police have abandoned Diane's case, and my family and I would like to find the abortionist who killed her. If we bring the information to them wrapped up in a bow, they'll be forced to act. Do you know if Diane dated anyone while she worked here?"

"I wouldn't know, Buzz. I've never made the private lives of our employees a concern of mine."

"Do you know if any of Diane's former clients might have reason to harm her?"

Grainger's eyes narrowed. "While I am sympathetic, I'm afraid I have nothing for you. Beyond that, it sounds to me you've come to believe someone—perhaps someone who has used our services—deliberately killed Diane. It would be unethical for me to share information about any of the department's clients. I find it offensive you believe we wouldn't have spoken with the police if anyone in the department had a suspicion that might be the case. I realize you are working through your grief, but at some point, you need to understand the cause of Diane's tragic death was an illegal abortion. Nothing more."

"Even if she wasn't pregnant?" I asked.

Marcus Grainger looked down to his paper work. "I'm afraid I can't help you."

Hating the man for his callousness, I said nothing more and left. The emotional turmoil that followed Diane's job-related assault caused her to abandon a career she'd loved. She'd been so shaken she took a dead-end job at Hiltbrunner's music store that bored her to tears. Unfulfilled and frightened, she sought refuge in dreams of a singing career for which she had no talent. All that, and Marcus Grainger didn't care.

I found Helene Olds seated at a massive oak table in the Reference Room of the Coe College Library. At least fifty volumes were scattered across the well-worn work surface. An organized clutter, it could only have been the result of numerous trips to the book stacks. Seated in the middle of the conglomeration, concentrating intently, Helene tapped away on a Royal typewriter looking as if the accumulated history of Western thought would fly out the window if she paused for a break. Fearing my sudden presence would startle her, I walked around to the other side of the table so she could catch a glimpse of me.

"Hi, Cletus," she said, typing as she talked. "I'm helping Professor Callaghan assemble a bibliography of works on the topic of blood law. It's his specialty, and he's in the middle of writing a book about it."

"Blood law? Never heard of it."

Helene quit typing. "It's an idea as old as recorded history. When a society doesn't have a legal system, or has a poor one, families who want justice take the law into their own hands."

"Sort of like a lynch mob?" I asked.

"Well, a lynch mob is generally considered to be a group that wants to shortcut an effective legal system. A lynch mob might not include members of the affected family. With blood law, the family has the right, or sometimes even the obligation, to spill blood for blood."

"Like a feud," I said.

"Not quite. It could lead to a feud if both parties feel they have been unjustly wronged. Ideally, when a family in a blood law culture feels shamed by the actions of one of its members, it doesn't strike back."

I shook my head with wonder. "The things you librarians have to know. Say, how's the swimming pool coming?"

"Sam thinks we'll be finished in a week and half. If we are, he plans to have the forms put in the next morning and the concrete trucks driving through the yard late that afternoon. The man has everything mapped out, right down to a pool party the first weekend in August. Consider yourself invited."

"Just let me know when you're ready. Say, I have a reference problem for you. I need to find out more about the cross on the side of this knife."

I handed Helene the knife. She looked carefully at the cross. "That's an easy one. I get the question about once a year; it's an orthodox cross. Let me grab a volume of the *Catholic Encyclopedia* for you."

I selected a nearby table, leaned my crutches against it, and sat down. Helene brought the volume over to me, opened to the proper page. As I began reading, she went back to her work. The article contained a handful of illustrations of Orthodox crosses and a lot more information than I needed. I learned the Orthodox wing of the

Catholic Church had become attached to the symbolism of the three-armed cross, while the Roman wing adopted a more literal version shaped like a lower case "t." The short top bar of the orthodox cross symbolized the inscription over Christ's head; the short lower bar, the block of wood to which his feet were nailed. Clovers decorating the ends symbolized the Christian Trinity.

A newly minted expert on Orthodox crosses, I found Helene, and thanked her for her assistance. Limping down the steps on my way toward Diane's Falcon, I thought about what I'd learned. It didn't add up. Gordon Kohl was a Presbyterian. Why did he carry a personalized pocketknife engraved with an Orthodox cross?

When I'd begun tailing Kohl, the radio had been my friend. But now, as the hours in the car piled up, I discovered cracks had developed in our relationship. I hadn't counted on the downside inherent in the repetition of songs on radio station playlists. I swore to God if I ever met that Bobby Goldsboro who kept singing about his dead wife Honey, her damn puppy, and that scrawny tree, I'd pop him one in the nose. Not only was the syrupy piece of drivel the worst song ever written, the local disc jockeys seemed intent on driving me crazy by playing it every fifteen minutes.

I'd have sold my soul to use my buddy Jim's new car for my project. His latest set of wheels featured an eight-track tape sound system which would have solved the Bobby Goldsboro problem. The setup wouldn't have answered all my prayers, but hey, a little Sinatra doing "You Make Me Feel So Young" does chase the blues.

Tonight's stakeout didn't excite. Gordy took Lucinda to Bishop's Cafeteria. I thought it best to eat something so as not to draw attention to myself, so I picked out a piece of chocolate pie and asked the line attendant to bring it to my table. I might have been able to handle the pie and crutches at the same time, but a dropped plate would have made me the center of attention. By the time I'd finished a forkful, I knew I'd made a wise decision.

Afterward he accompanied her as she shopped for lingerie at Armstrong's. No wonder I'd become cranky. Not only did I have to look inconspicuous while bumbling around on crutches, I was tailing the most boring guy in the city.

On my way home, I spotted Sonny, the drug dealer. He'd stationed himself on First Avenue, in the lot of a drive-through bank that had closed for the night. Slouching against his car, on the busiest street in the city, Sonny looked every inch the drug purveyor. If the man was trying to keep a low profile, he certainly flunked the test.

Randy Roeder

24

Last night's chocolate pie was so good I didn't think I could make it through the day without another piece, so I called Jim Weiss and arranged to meet him at Bishop's for lunch. Jim arrived with his usual full quota of gossip. There'd been some sort of a coup at the Rotary Club, and a prominent lawyer had assaulted a college student he'd caught in bed with his wife. Although she'd been the guilty party, he ended up buying her a new car to keep her happy. What a sap.

After a full five minutes deriding the lawyer and congratulating ourselves on our superior masculinity, I opened up on the inconsistency of a Presbyterian carrying an Orthodox pocketknife.

"You know," he said, "more than one person can have the initials G. K. Maybe Lumir's first inclination was right, and the knife belongs to someone mixed up in Diane's death. If that's the case, that person could be Orthodox."

"It'd be a long shot, Jim. The odds of the coincidence ... I don't think so."

"There are a lot of Orthodox in town. Most are Syrian, but we have some Europeans too. The Europeans go to St. John's; the Syrians are big at St. George."

"I thought the Syrians were Moslems," I said.

"It's a mixed bag—the city has both. They've been here forever, and new ones come in from time to time. The F.O.B.s call themselves Lebanese."

"The F.O.B.s?"

"Fresh off the Boat. The older families came here when Lebanon was part of Syria."

I took a man-sized bite of pie. "I'd hear somebody was Syrian or Lebanese, but didn't pay much attention."

"The older folks in town call them all Syrians. The younger set uses Lebanese."

Jim reached for an ashtray. "You know George Rahbani. He's Syrian, and his family is Orthodox Christian."

"George Rahbani is a strange guy," I said. "I've said hello to him a time or two. He's gracious and perfectly polite, but for some reason, he scares the hell out of me."

"You and half the town," said Jim, "and that half includes me."

"Why?" I asked.

"We hired a new salesman at the dealership last year. He'd only been with us a couple of months when he comes in on a Friday morning looking like he slept in his clothes. He walks straight over to me and wants to borrow enough money to move everything he's got out of town before Monday morning. So, I ask him, 'What's the rush?' and he says, 'George Rahbani.' Turns out he was down at the Golden Key, chatting up George at the bar, and he mentions wanting a color TV. George tells him he could get him a good deal and had one in the basement. Well, the guy goes into the basement, and there's a dozen of them down there, new in the boxes."

"They must have been hot," I said.

"Sure they were. So, he says to George, 'You know, you don't have to do this. You've have a night club, property, money. What more do you need?' The next thing he knows, George tells him he

196

won't put up with any of his insults, and he'll kill him if he isn't out of town by Monday."

"He must have believed him. What happened?" I asked.

Jim reached for his lighter. "A couple of us gave him money. He moved out the next day."

"You think George Rahbani is that dangerous?"

"I wouldn't want to be the one to find out."

I spent the better part of Saturday morning calling around for somebody cheap to come over and replace the stems on my tires. Any advantage gained by pretending the notes on my windshield had scared me into staying home wouldn't last much longer. The estimates for repairing the damage set me back on my heels. I finally phoned the guy at the Riverside APCO. The owner planned to send his son over to jack up one side of the car, take two wheels back to the shop for repair, and then repeat the process for the other side.

The call completed, I realized I'd failed to speak to one of the last persons to have seen Diane alive. My interest in tailing Gordon Kohl bordered on an obsession, a fixation that blinded me to other possibilities. Whoever slashed my valve stems had inadvertently done me a favor. With no planning on my part, the guy who'd driven Diane out to K-Mart on the day she died was coming to my apartment. While I waited, I started in on another crime story—a whodunit by Ed McBain.

The bell rang sometime after noon, and I opened the door to find a big guy in an APCO uniform. A single eyebrow stretched its way across his forehead, shadowing a pair of slow-moving, dull gray eyes. Based on what I'd read in Pudge's report, I'd expected someone still in high school. This guy looked closer to thirty.

"My name's Arthur. I'm here about your tires," he announced. "Where's your car?"

Given that he'd just walked by the only car in the lot with four flat tires, the question seemed unnecessary. I could see Arthur wasn't the sharpest hoe in the shed.

"Out front, the Nova," I said pointing to my car just thirty feet away.

There didn't seem to be any need to be subtle with Arthur, so I came right out with it. "I hear you were the guy who drove that Novacek woman out to K-Mart."

Arthur didn't seem at all disturbed by my question—in fact, he seemed flattered by the attention. "Yeah, I recognized her right away because she'd be down at Ernie's to sing and drink too much."

Drink too much? I wanted to slug him. If anything, Diane believed in moderation. The guy's loose talk about someone who wasn't around to defend herself grated on my nerves. Still, I wouldn't get another opportunity to question the guy like this, so I held my emotions in check. "Kind of interesting thing, one day you're talking to somebody, and the next day they're dead."

Unsure of what to say next, Arthur furrowed his brow.

"Ernie's is quite the place," I continued, watching him fold and unfold his eyebrow. "I go there now and again, to catch a ballgame on TV."

"My Dad doesn't like me to go there because of all the drinking. He's always telling me about how the church doesn't like it. But a guy like me has gotta live a little, and the people there are friendly."

"So, Arthur, the Novacek woman, what was she like? Friendly?"

"Pretty, really pretty. I never talked to her. Girls like that, they make me nervous."

"You never talked to her?" I asked.

"Nope."

"Not even when you gave her a ride out to K-Mart?"

"I couldn't think of anything to say. She talked to me a little."

Finally, we were getting somewhere. "What did she talk about?"

"She said she wanted to go to K-Mart, and she'd call the station if she needed a ride home."

I wanted to bang my head against the door frame. "What else?" I asked.

"Nothing. Girls like that, they make me nervous. I better go work on your tires."

With that, he turned and left. Arthur was a man of few words.

Arthur went to work on the Nova, and I stuck my nose back in my book. This one featured some Jewish cop saddled with the name Meyer Meyer—a double-barreled moniker if there ever was one. I'd just picked it up again when the phone rang.

"Clete!" Lumir sounded frantic. "The police have arrested Eddie. They found him standing in the intersection of J Street and Wilson Avenue, singing and directing traffic in his underwear. They took him to St. Luke's Hospital, and locked him up in Two East."

I didn't know what to say. Two East was the psych ward, and while I hated the idea, it sounded like Eddie belonged there. My friend had become so attached to the boy he'd begun sobbing, an unexpected display of emotion given the strength he'd displayed at Diane's funeral.

"Hang in there," I said. "I'll be over in ten minutes."

"Something's not right. I know Eddie. The boy is not crazy."

"I'll be right over."

―――――――――――――

Lumir paced the floor of his shop. "I told you everything I know. I think we should go over to visit him."

"Sit down for a minute," I said, "I doubt Eddie has visiting hours yet. I know somebody who works at the police department. Her name's Shirley. Let me call, and see if I can find anything out. You can make us some of your he-man coffee."

While Lumir busied himself at his hot plate, I hobbled over to the house and phoned the number I had for Shirley. Someone picked up on the second ring. I recognized the voice of Jim's sister-in-law.

"Shirley," I said, "Cletus Efferding here. I heard the department picked up a kid directing traffic in his underwear over on Wilson Avenue. The boy works for a friend of mine, and he's worried about him. Are you allowed to say anything?"

"Naked as a jaybird except for his white J. C. Penny briefs. Police reports and investigations may be confidential, but loose talk is fair game. Let me fill you in."

And she did, doting on every juicy detail. When Shirley finished, she asked how things were going with my search for Diane's abortionist. The question stung. She'd done so much for me, and to say she was disappointed in my lack of news would be an understatement. Aware of the declining value of my stock on the gossip market, I promised to keep her up to date.

After we signed off, I returned to the shop to fill Lumir in. "Eddie went to work this morning stocking shelves. For some reason, he started rolling canned goods down the aisles. When they asked him what he was doing, he said, 'I'm rolling the beer barrels out of heaven.' That's when he started knocking the cans off the shelves. He kept saying, 'It's thundering. It's thundering.'"

Lumir looked thoughtful. "That comes from an old saying. I did not think a youngster like Eddie would have heard it. When I was young and thunder would shake the house, my grandfather would say, 'Lumir, do not be afraid of the thunder. Thunder is the sound of old Saint Peter rolling the beer barrels out of heaven.'"

I continued. "The store manager, Ted Kral, tried to grab Eddie, but he got away. That's when Kral called the police. By the time they caught up with Eddie, he was in the intersection singing a Beatles' song about a yellow submarine. He went with the police when they asked him. They took him straight to St. Luke's Hospital."

"What happens now?" Lumir asked.

"Shirley doesn't know for sure but she guesses they'll hold him for observation for a few days. He'll be examined by a psychiatrist who will talk to his parents to see if he can be released or if he needs in-patient care."

"In-patient care? Lock Eddie up in the looney bin? Locking the boy up, now that would be crazy."

"It will be the Brada family's decision, Lumir. Even though his folks aren't the best, I'm sure they'll do the right thing."

My statement seemed to calm Lumir down.

"The Bradas don't pay enough attention to Eddie, but they are not stupid people," he said. "I will call them and offer to mow their lawn or do some chores for them—even if they spend the time with their friends instead of Eddie, they will need distraction from worry."

"And so do you," I said, "and I know just what you need. Let's go downtown to Bishop's and get some chocolate pie and coffee. I'll tell you what I learned about the knife Eddie found in Kohl's car. When we're done, we'll go over to Kubia's Hardware and look at the tools."

"Okay," said Lumir.

Sometimes I think I'm a genius. I'd gotten Lumir calmed down and lured him out of his routine with the promise of dessert and a tale about Kohl's pocketknife. Best of all, I'd created a situation where I could enjoy my third piece of chocolate pie in as many days.

Randy Roeder

25

Gabby Khoury entered the Moonglow through the front entrance. The curving hallway leading to the lounge never failed to impress. From floor to ceiling, pieces of translucent purple quartz protruded from the plaster walls. Habi once told him the decorator wanted customers who entered the place to feel like they were immersed in a new adventure. That's why the hallway curved. Somebody coming in from outside would pass through the hallway, turn the corner, and see a whole new world pop open. Habi claimed every time the decorator used a three-dollar word like "immersed," it cost his old man extra money.

When Georgie wanted class, he got it. The place had more golden railings and ornate gilt-frame mirrors than all the nicest strip clubs in Chicago combined. From its red and black patterned carpet to its candy apple booths and black-tufted Naugahyde walls trimmed with gilt buttons, the Moonglow made an impression.

Eager to protect his investment, Georgie ordered Habi to maintain the club in good order and keep the place immaculate. Unruly patrons were bounced long before things got out of hand, so Gabby was surprised to find Habi directing the replacement of one of the large, gilt-framed mirrors at the rear of the stage.

"Hey, Big Boy, what happened to the mirror?" Gabby asked.

"Somebody tossed a beer bottle into it last night."

"Guess he really hated the dancer."

"Nobody on stage. He pitched it during the 11:30 break. The guy was sitting there minding his own business when all of a sudden, he stands up, screams 'Revolution now!' and heaves a bottle through the mirror. Musta' been one of those radical nutcases. Anyway, they had to take him to the emergency room after Leo broke the guy's arm."

Gabby shook his head in commiseration. "Some people are worse than animals. Can you get away right now? A lot of stuff's come up."

"Sure," said Habi, "let's go to the office."

"What the hell happened to you?" asked Habi as they walked past the bar. "That's one nasty cut on your face. Come out on the wrong side of a fight with a twelve-year-old?"

"It happened at the Hamburg Inn."

"The Hamburg Inn?"

"I was sitting there with my sister Leila, minding my own business, when this big guy who looks like a Hell's Angel walks up and says I been messin' with his woman, Next thing I know, he slams a glass ashtray into the side of my head. I hit him with a chair, and he went down hard. If my sister hadn't been there, I'da fixed him good, but I had to get her out safe. Had so much blood in my eyes I could hardly see. It took twenty stitches."

"You're lucky you got out before the cops came."

"Yeah, but they showed up at the hospital. I said my sister hit me, and I didn't want to press charges."

Gabby followed Habi into his office and flopped into a chair opposite the desk. "Things are moving so fast I don't know where to start. The boss wants all my business tied up so I can set up the office in Omaha. He thinks it should be easy because he doesn't know about all the goodies I move on the side. It's a bitch. I'm makin' more on dope than at Midwest Vending, but the connections I make working there are the key to the whole thing. I was happy about the promotion, but now I wish I could tell Phil to screw it. When I'm not at Midwest, I'm on the road. I put over eleven hundred miles on my car and haven't slept for two days. Without those little white cross pills, I wouldn't be able to keep up."

Habi sat down, put a leg on his desk. "Whiner. You're getting a promotion and making dough hand over fist."

"And I wanna keep it that way. It won't be easy to take care of this side of the state from Nebraska—much less get to Illinois for pickups. I gotta change the way I do business. You know, make fewer but bigger buys and have Peoria make deliveries to a central location. I'm thinking something like ten to fifteen grand a pop. There aren't many I can trust with that much merchandise. I'd like you to handle it."

"No way." Habi shook his head. "No way I'm crazy enough to get involved with the kind of guys who carry guns. You can forget that song and dance right now. Ain't gonna happen."

"Listen, Habi. My guys in Peoria got so much supply they've got trouble moving it. They just fronted me ten thousand in product. All you gotta do is take deliveries and store 'em until I come pick up. You'd be my warehouse. I'll take care of all the payments, so you won't be on the hook for anything."

"Yeah, but what's in it for me?"

"I give you all of Waterloo, you never have to pay up front for your merchandise. I'll sell to you so cheap, you'll double your money on everything you lay off."

"Sweet deal," said Habi.

"Just one thing, the Peoria boys got no sense of humor. Anything goes wrong, they kinda get excited. If that happens, don't try to fix things or get all buddy-buddy. Just have 'em call me. Any problem, I'll straighten it out."

"So, you want me to be the connection between you and some bad asses who walk around with guns under their arms? Do I look that damn dumb?"

Gabby leaned forward and rested his elbows on Habi's desk. "The way I figure it, you'll be pulling down thirty big ones a year and not workin' any harder than now. You won't be anything more to the guys from Peoria than a warehouse clerk."

Habi fidgeted in his chair. "Not interested. But I gotta talk to you. There hasn't been enough time to turn over the stuff from your last visit. I've only got half of what I owe you."

"Half ain't whole, Big Boy. I don't make a payment and one of my body parts get broken. You think this is some kind of game where I get hurt, and you get the money? You think I'm a fool or what?"

When Habi looked shocked, Gabby knew he had him where he wanted him—uncertain whether he'd just heard a complaint or a threat. Time for a little more doubt. "Here I am ready to cut you in on the deal of a life time, and you pull a cheap stunt on me?"

"I ... I didn't have enough time to get my guys moving," Habi stammered.

"Just tell me, you in or out? You throw in with me on this, you won't have this kind of problem because you don't pay until all of it gets sold."

Gabby could see the wheels turning in Habi's head. He'd made the sale.

"I'm in," said Habi. "Let's have a drink on it."

The deal sealed with a drink, Gabby left for Des Moines. As he walked to the car he congratulated himself on the bargain he'd just made. No way Habi was in the same league as his old man. He'd been overcharging Habi for the past year. The new price would be identical to what he charged the rest of his customers. He almost felt guilty about the way he'd reamed the guy.

Almost, not quite.

26

Sunday night, I pulled Jim's Impala up to the apartment and picked up my surveillance kit. Since nobody had hurt me and I hadn't received another warning, the guy behind the threats must not have picked up on my Gordon Kohl stakeout. Unless my foot flared up again, my days and nights of driving around town had come to an end. I'd be at Killian's tomorrow.

Once inside, I collapsed on the couch. If the six weeks since Diane's death felt like an eternity, two weeks with Kohl felt like a lifetime. A hen-pecked husband, a nerd in clown's clothing, and a lousy golfer, his life was so desperately dull I worried it might be contagious. If the toad-like little dentist ever did kill somebody, it'd be his wife. I could see it. A social misfit, a woman bullying him into impotence, no social outlets, one day he snaps and gasses his wife. Unsure of what to do with the body, he cuts her into pieces. A week later, leaking and undeliverable packages begin showing up at obscure post offices in Appalachia.

I chuckled. Strange as the little man appeared to be, my surveillance confirmed what I'd thought all along. Diane wouldn't have touched him with a ten-foot pole—he'd have given her the creeps.

I'd learned more about Pudge than about his brother-in-law. The detective kept a black lover and spent the night when he visited. His visits to Colored Town seemed to coincide with Kohl's wife spending the night with her mother. It followed that Pudge's inter-racial romance enjoyed the support of his sister and her husband. The affectionate little boy, the grocery bags, the arrangements for the care of his mother—Pudge's involvement with this colored woman was definitely more than a fling.

The only useful information I'd gained from two weeks of surveillance would be valuable only if I were willing to blackmail Pudge Davis into re-opening the investigation. Although some citizens of Cedar Rapids might preach the gospel of racial equality, the idea of a mixed-race couple remained more acceptable in the abstract than in reality. I believed exposure would turn Pudge's life at the police station into a living hell. While I was ready to do almost anything to get the dirt bag responsible for the death of my friend, I didn't want to cross that line. As much as I hated him, Pudge did not kill Diane.

Time to shift gears. I hummed as I looked in the mirror and knotted my tie. I was wearing a suit again, going back to work, and happy about it. The summer day promised to be unseasonably cool, so I tossed convention to the winds and chose a dark brown suit without a trace of pattern. In the mood for cufflinks, I picked a white shirt with double cuffs and topped the whole thing off with a gold-flecked cranberry tie and coordinating pocket square. I accessorized with a new cordovan belt, and my matching wingtips shined with lovingly applied gloss.

After settling with Killian's for the Sedlaks' funeral outfits, getting my tires fixed, and the paydays lost to foot recovery, my wallet had shrunk to a point beyond thin. The pain in my foot had subsided, and if it could survive a day on the sales floor, I'd be able to return my crutches and begin dancing again next week.

Dressed to impress, I stepped out into the sunshine of a glorious Monday morning with a new attitude of optimism. Humming to myself, I got into the Nova, switched off the radio, and headed downtown. I wasn't taking any chances—my good cheer might not survive another replay of Bobby Goldsboro's dreaded "Honey."

The old routine looked pretty good, until I rounded the corner and saw Pudge leaning against the plate glass a few feet from Killian's main door. I couldn't believe it, my first day back and there he was, waiting for me.

"Well, look who's here. I'll be damned if it ain't Pervie."

"Good morning, Florian," I replied with all the cheer I could muster. Although I had something on Pudge, I felt guilty for spying on the man. As a result, the balance of power in our relationship hadn't changed.

"What is it this time?" I asked.

"You gettin' so you like 'em a little younger now?"

"What do you want?" I asked, relieved Pudge was on another fishing expedition and unaware I'd been spying on his clandestine activities.

"Mostly I wanna handcuff sickos like you and throw 'em in the river. The only trouble is, handcuffs are expensive."

"Imagine that," I said, determined not to let him get to me. "But after a while we'd all float up to the top, and you could get your cuffs back. A little oil, and—presto, they'd be good as new."

"You're a laugh a minute, Efferding. I got a girl who didn't make it home from school Friday. I need to know where you been after three o'clock Friday afternoon, and I need to know it now. I'm here to take you back to the station."

"Am I under arrest?" I asked. "I've been on crutches for two weeks and have a job to go to. Today is my first day back. I can stop by at lunch."

"Don't get cute, Pervie. A kid is missing. Cooperate, or I can fix it so you won't get back to work for the next two days."

"Okay, let me run in and square it with my boss."

"You're coming now. You can make it easy, or you can go in cuffs."

Whether Pudge's actions were legal or not, I couldn't run the risk of Killian's management discovering I'd been escorted down the street in handcuffs.

"Lead the way," I said.

We rounded the corner, got into Pudge's unmarked car, and rode in silence. Though I fumed the whole way, I had the good sense not to bring up Pudge's girlfriend. When we entered the station, Pudge directed a patrolman to lead me to an interrogation room. I waited alone in the airless closet, my morning enthusiasm wilting like an overheated flower and the razor-sharp crease in my pants losing its resolve. Two hours later, another officer opened the door.

"Efferding, you can go," he said.

"What, I wait for two hours, and now you just tell me I can leave?"

"You wanna stay?" he asked.

I swallowed my indignation and left. Priority one was getting back to Killian's ASAP to see if I still had a job. As I walked back over the bridge, I made up a story about having one last doctor's appointment that morning—one I'd failed to mention but could hardly ignore. I gave the explanation to Reg, the head of menswear. He gave me the benefit of the doubt.

Despite the incident at the police station, I'd recovered my good spirits by the time I got off work. I'd been pain free the entire day. Though I yearned to go for a walk in Ellis Park, I thought it best to go home and put my foot up. I had a pizza delivered and drank a beer from the refrigerator while I waited for it to arrive. I ate the whole thing and settled in for a quiet night reading *Time* magazine and watching the Smothers Brothers on TV. Tommy and Dick delivered a hilarious putdown of Bobby Goldsboro's hit song. On my second beer and overjoyed to discover someone shared my disgust for the banal piece of trash, I laughed until my sides hurt.

At ten o'clock, I switched over to KCRG to catch the news. The anchorman led off with a story about an eleven-year-old girl who'd been lured into a car the previous Friday and transported to a run-down cabin on the Cedar River. As he spoke, a shot of a weed-covered, dilapidated structure appeared on the screen. I couldn't place the location, but it could have been along the river road somewhere below the REA damn. The girl managed to escape her sleeping captor early Monday morning and made her way to a neighboring household where the owner phoned the police. Officers arrested the suspect without incident and identified him as an unemployed steel worker who'd done time for felonious assault and a narcotics violation.

Now that I knew what Pudge had run me in for, I had trouble getting a handle on how I felt. On one hand, I felt relieved to be in the clear. Having spent the weekend driving around in the hope of locating Gordon Kohl, I had no alibi. On the other hand, I felt angry, very angry. I'd had grown used to Pudge's ongoing harassment, but the idea he suspected me of kidnapping a child nearly drove me to distraction. God knows what the poor girl had been through.

Five years ago, I made a mistake, and the Dubuque police arrested me for visiting a hooker. Was there no end to the consequences? To top the whole thing off, the Dubuque police arrived before I'd had sex with the lady. Pudge Davis branded me as the worst kind of pervert, when in fact the only person I'd ever slept with was my wife.

I thought back to old Father Kun, Father Blazek, and the whole idea of sins of intent. Some butcher kills Diane, and she gets condemned to burn forever in hell and can't be buried next to her husband because she chose to abort a fetus that didn't exist. I get branded a sexual deviant when I was accidentally faithful to my wife. Right or wrong, this sin-of-intent business was powerful stuff. With all the temptation and real crime in the world, someone who just comes close to messing up should get a pass. But no, they get clobbered anyway—as bad as, or worse than, the person who actually does something despicable.

Ruminating on Pudge's ham-fisted tactics left me tossing and turning all night. I woke groggy and still angry. The more I stewed, the madder I got. The harassment had to end. I decided to go nuclear. I phoned the police department and made an appointment to visit Pudge over the lunch hour. I intended to play my trump card—not only to blackmail him into re-opening Diane's case, but to get the dirtball off my back once and for all.

The clock over the reception desk read ten after twelve when I entered the lobby of the cop shop. Shirley Weiss was passing through the room and looked as if she was about to greet me. As she got closer, her eyes widened. Averting her gaze, she passed by without comment. I'd come to the station with blood in my eye, an anger so obvious a simple glance at my face unsettled a woman who knew how to hold her own.

Close to out of control, I needed to cool down to deal effectively with Pudge. I made a side trip to the gent's room, stopped at the water cooler, took some deep breaths, and collected myself. My nerves steady, I approached the reception desk and stated my business. A uniform escorted me to the detectives' office. Davis, the room's only occupant, sat in his shirtsleeves, a snub-nose revolver visible in his shoulder holster. A worn hounds-tooth jacket hung on the coatrack behind him

Pudge looked up with a frown. "What can I do for ya?"

"I didn't care for the way you rousted me yesterday. This sort of harassment has got to stop."

"Pervie, when I got a missing kid, I don't worry too much about makin' a dirtball feel bad."

"Not only does the harassment need to stop," I continued quietly, "but I want you to do your job and take up Diane's case again."

"You want. You want. Wantin' ain't gettin'."

Time to get louder. "I don't think you heard me." Even Louder. "Lay off, and go to work on Diane's case."

Pudge looked at me with genuine puzzlement. As his befuddled expression passed, his face began to redden. My demands weren't doing anything good for the detective's blood pressure. I got my first inkling of impending success.

"Calm down, Florian," I said. "You'll have a stroke."

He stood up and pointed his finger at me. "You're telling me to calm down? You're telling me what to do? A sleazebucket like you? Number one, the Novacek case is closed. Number two—and you better understand this one Creepus—I gotta job to do, and when I gotta job to do, nobody gets in my way. And Creepus, you're nobody."

"That cuts it. I didn't want to do this, but it looks like I have to. I know all about you, Davis. I know about your nighttime trips to visit your colored girlfriend, and I know it's a regular thing. You bring groceries. How do you think that'll go over? Play ball with me, or a whole lot of other people are going to know about her too."

Pudge sat back down. He leaned back in his chair, was quiet a few seconds, and leaned forward again. Without warning, he began slapping his desk and laughing so hard I thought he'd burst a blood vessel. I stared at the detective in amazement. Pudgie was cracking up.

Some people laugh when they're in a tight spot, but I wasn't about to let up on Pudge. "I mean what I say. I'll do it. The news will be all over town."

Pudge pulled out a handkerchief and began wiping his eyes. "All over town," he chuckled, shaking his head from side to side. "All over town."

At last, after three long years, I had Davis where I wanted him.

Pudge grinned up at me. "Creepus, I don't give a rat's ass about your 'all over town,' and I sure as hell don't give a rat's ass about you. I'm outta here. I gave notice today. This is my last week. I got a job in Joliet."

Anger and resentment began leaking out of me.

"Better sit down, you don't look so good. Florian Davis is sayin' goodbye to the City of Five Stinks and movin' on to a place that's not livin' in the last century."

I stood there stunned, speechless.

"Pervert, you got nothin.' Me—I got a little boy who thinks I'm some kind of hero and a woman that loves me. My family don't give a crap about Layelle's color. We're getting married this weekend. You can go to hell and rot—you racist son of a bitch."

Three inches tall, I left without a word.

Pudge Davis had never been a clock watcher, but since he'd given notice, his cases were reassigned. Some loose ends needed tidying up, but not enough to put in extra hours. He checked his watch, then stared up at the ceiling. A few minutes later, he walked to a row of olive-green cabinets lining a wall, opened a drawer, and bent over to remove a file. He sighed as he straightened up and went back to his desk, where he shuffled through its contents.

The folder contained an unopened envelope. The detective removed a letter opener from his desk, slit the envelope, extracted and unfolded the single sheet of paper inside. Tossing the envelope in the trash, he put the sheet into the file and closed it. Whistling to himself, he rose, walked downstairs to the secretarial pool, and asked that the contents be Xeroxed on the department's new machine.

The beefy detective picked up his copies a half hour later and carried them back to his desk. After consulting the phone book, he wrote Cletus Efferding's address on the back of a new manila envelope and stuffed the photocopies inside. The task complete, he plastered the upper right hand corner with stamps, and still whistling, made his way to his car, pausing only to drop the envelope in a mailbox. Florian Davis looked for all the world as if he'd received news of a large inheritance. The detective fired up his copper-colored Studebaker, and in broad daylight, drove over to a little house in Colored Town. Smiling for ear-to-ear, he pulled up to the front of the structure, put his hand on the horn, and held it down. He honked again and again and, grinning merrily, leaned out the car window and shouted, "I'm home, Layelle! I'm home."

27

Given the progress I made with my foot, I expected I'd be back at the dance studio next week. I kept in touch with the boss. He enjoyed owning the studio more than teaching and looked forward to my return. As much as I liked my dance instructor job, I was going to miss the free evenings. I decided to make an after supper visit to Lumir.

When I got there, the door to the shop was propped open. Inside, Lumir and Eddie bent over a vise with a saw clamped in it. They looked up from their project to acknowledge me. Considering his recent breakdown, Eddie appeared bright-eyed.

"Now Eddie," said Lumir, "every tooth must have the same size and shape. Be sure to count your passes with the file. Three even strokes on each side of the tooth. You will have maybe two hundred fifty teeth to do. At six strokes per tooth, that is fifteen hundred passes with the file. It's best to get it right the first time, but don't worry if you make a mistake. I will file the tips back down, and you can start over."

Lumir unwrapped a new file for Eddie and gave one last bit of advice. "You're cutting two angles with every pass, and you've got to hold the file the same way each time. Don't forget—two angles."

I thought about the assignment Lumir had given the boy. If Eddie wasn't crazy at the beginning of the project, he might well be by the end of it.

"Eddie will be working on your picture frame, Clete. Once he learns how to file the saw, I will teach him how to set the teeth—every other tooth must be bent in the opposite direction. When he's finished, I will tilt the saw, set a needle between the bent tips and let it go. If it slides from the handle to the toe, I'll teach Eddie how to use the miter box. If it doesn't, he'll need to start over."

"Sounds a little rough for a beginner," I said. "Don't you think —"

"The boy will thank me for the rest of his life. Only one man in fifty knows how to sharpen a crosscut saw. The other forty-nine do poor work with saws that don't cut."

Absorbed in his project, Eddie never looked up. Lumir and I chatted for an hour, he at his desk in his captain's chair, and I in one of his pressed-back guest chairs. When Eddie finished the job, he brought the saw over to Lumir. Lumir gave the saw a going over and said, "It is good for the first time, Eddie—very good. Tomorrow I will teach you to set the teeth. Now it is time for you to go home."

When Eddie left, Lumir filled me in.

"It is as I thought. Eddie is not crazy. He got hold of some of that LSD."

"LSD? A fourteen-year old? How on earth did he manage to find something like that?"

"He told the police he did not remember. I don't know if they believed him or not. The drug came from a friend of his who is a little older."

"You have to wonder what the world is coming to," I said.

"His friend bought it right here in the neighborhood, at Jones Park, from some guy named Sonny."

I shook my head in disbelief. "I know what's going on. I can't believe it."

"Clete?"

"When I followed Gordon Kohl to the Ellis golf course, I parked down the road, so I could pick him up and tail him again when he finished. While I waited, I saw a car parked nearby. I didn't have anything better to do, so I watched the driver for a while. It didn't take long to see the guy was selling drugs. People would stop by for a few minutes, sometimes they'd stand around smoking, sometimes they'd go into the car. Nobody stayed very long."

"This is drug dealing?" asked Lumir. "Why don't the police do something about it?"

"I don't know," I said. "The police probably drive through the park and never stop. Unless they watched for a while, they'd think everything was okay. I only saw the pattern after an hour or so. Here's the strange part, the guy looked like a Beatle and had his name—Sonny—painted on his car. I thought he sold pot, I never imagined it would be anything dangerous. It was so out in the open—so obvious."

Thursday morning, I phoned the Cedar Rapids Police Department. Given what I'd learned about Sonny, I considered it my civic duty to turn him in. Anonymous tips and phone calls are easy to ignore. I wanted to speak with somebody face to face. Since Pudge was out of the question, I asked to speak with Earl Erikson.

"Erikson," he said.

I gave him the *spiel* I'd rehearsed. "My name is Cletus Efferding. I have information about an individual selling drugs in our public parks. I'd like to speak with you about it, but I don't want to come to the station."

"Efferding," he replied, "I've heard quite a bit about you, none of it good. I can see why you might be station shy. What've you got?"

"I'd like to do this in person. I work at Killian's and thought we might have lunch in the Man's Grille. It's hard for me to make it to the station and back on my lunch hour. I'll buy."

"Noon?" he asked.

"Works for me," I replied and hung up.

I got to the grille before Erikson did. He showed up right on time and began scanning the room. I caught his attention with a wave. He nodded, and started over to the table. The man knew how to wear a suit. He'd selected a tan linen jacket with matching slacks, a pale salmon-colored shirt, and a brown silk tie held in place with an understated gold chain. The buttons on his coat sleeves told me the suit had been tailored—they were functional, rather than decorative. Earl liked his jackets long and loose, his pants un-cuffed and un-pleated, and his loafers tasseled. The man didn't just wear his suit—he allowed it to drape over his radiant magnificence. If the absence of female admirers within the confines of The Man's Grille disappointed him, Earl didn't let on.

"Efferding?" he asked.

I nodded.

"Erikson," he said as he sat down without shaking hands. "Well, tell me about it."

I gave the man a description of Sonny, his car, and my observations of the activity at Ellis Park. I went on to tell him about Eddie Brada's LSD experience.

"Hmm," he said as he lightly touched the tips of his right-hand thumb and forefinger to his lips. Inclining his head ever so slightly, he used the lightly moistened digits to stroke his eyebrows. He must have hated it when an eyebrow hair was out of place.

"The guy sells the crap in broad daylight," I said. "It shouldn't be hard to make an arrest."

"Hmm," he said again. "What you've given me is hearsay. It's enough to start an investigation, but we'll need to collect evidence and build a case. We'll also want to determine if we can get a line on this Sonny's supplier. You know, get the big guy. It takes some time."

"How long?" I asked.

"If everything goes right, it shouldn't be long—six months."

"Six months?" I sputtered. "Six months? And in the meantime, the guy keeps selling that poison to kids?"

"Efferding, you don't understand police work. Taking out these low-level operators doesn't make a dent in the problem. The only way to make progress is to get the suppliers."

"I can't believe what you're telling me. Something's not right at the department. First you guys bail on the Diane Novacek case. Then you want to take six months to shut down a dealer selling LSD to kids. I won't stand for it. I'm going to go talk to somebody from the newspaper and blow this thing sky high."

"Cut the rant, and think for a minute. You need to understand you're not a reliable source of information. You've got sex problems coming out your ears. You were a suspect in a child abduction case. What would the good folks at Killian's think if they found out they had somebody like you selling clothes to boys? And Cletus, think about how much the lovely women at that dance studio would enjoy dancing with a pervert."

"First of all," I said, "only women and old men get to call me Cletus. Second, I can't believe you'd sink so low as to blackmail me with some two-bit issue from my personal life. It's reprehensible. It's dirty. It's beneath contempt."

Erikson rubbed his chin. "You're right, Cletus. It's beneath contempt. A guy has to wonder what kind of a rancid slime ball would pull something like that. You know Cletus, maybe I should ask Pudge Davis. He's been the victim of this sort of thing—you know, somebody threatening exposure if he didn't get his way?"

The stench of my self-righteous hypocrisy filled the air.

"You do know the penalties for extortion, don't you Cletus?"

I put my brain in park after my meeting with Earl Erikson. I had clothing to sell, and although I wasn't a gung-ho company man, I was a third-generation haberdasher who took pride in his work. Anyone can sell clothes, but only a few understand how to make a man look really good. Take Erikson, for example, he dressed beautifully, but given his innate vanity, he'd have made a better impression if he'd gone for a classic look and a traditional fit. I'd give the opposite advice to a salt-of-the-earth type. I'd have him go for confidence-enhancing elegance, stylish fabric, and a relaxed look.

We were unexpectedly busy that afternoon. When I got off work, I headed over to Spryncl's Tavern to unwind. I planned on a couple of beers, but ended up drinking Seven and Sevens with some acquaintances from my days at the packing plant. Although they'd seen me on the Avenue now and again, I had to endure a fair amount of razzing for the suit I wore. I made up for it by trying to be one of the guys and imbibed more than my share.

I couldn't remember where I'd parked my car and decided to walk home. About halfway there, I remembered Buzz Sedlak planned to come over to the apartment to talk about my investigation. I paused to look at my watch. When my eyes focused, I realized I'd missed our appointment by over an hour. Not much I could do about it. I'd have to apologize tomorrow.

I resumed my stroll. A little guilt would have been in order, but the mild weather, buzzing cicadas, and delicious alcoholic haze left little room for it. Ambling along, loose as a goose, I could just see my apartment building when two guys materialized out of nowhere and blocked the sidewalk. Despite my condition, I understood they had no interest in my continued well-being.

I greeted them. "Evening, gents. You look upset. Something wrong?"

The smaller of the two, a pimple-faced guy of maybe twenty, answered. "Something wrong? You're what's wrong. You didn't listen, and now you're gonna get hurt."

"Nobody talked to me, so I couldn't listen. You guys wrote a note, remember?"

No response. As my words floated off into the night air, I realized I'd just dug myself deeper. I took a step back and turned to walk away. The bigger of the two caught me by the shoulder and spun me around. As I turned, his other hand caught me in the solar plexus. I went down, my head bouncing off the ground. Somebody kicked me in the ribs. I heard feet thumping the concrete.

"This is over right now!" somebody yelled.

I looked up to see an airborne Buzz landing on the bigger guy's knee. It made a cracking sound, and the goon went down like a sack of wet cement, screaming all the way. I faded out.

"Clete, are you okay?" Buzz looked down at me with a face filled with concern.

"Pimple face ... don't know. Hurt."

I heard the goon man moan. "You broke my knee. What'd you do that for?"

"I hurt bad, Buzz. Kick him."

Buzz obliged. I saw him land one in the goon's gut. My head swam. I think the guy puked. Maybe not, but I did.

"Talk," Buzz yelled.

I heard the goon crying. Somewhere between the bawling and moaning, I blacked out. Sirens and flashing lights brought me back. A cop led Buzz away in handcuffs. Some guy strapped me to a stretcher. I hurt like hell.

My body hated me. Nothing else could explain the misery. I tried to move and instantly understood the stupidity of the idea. I opened my eyes, closed them again. Crap, a jail. I wracked my brain —nothing. Wracked it again. Goons, Buzz flying through the air, cops, stretchers. Then, a grey wall of nothing. Zero, nada, zilch.

I raised my head to take in my surroundings—solid steel walls with a row of bars on one side, a bunk above me, no sink, a toilet without a lid. The effort nearly did me in. Not the Hilton, but better than the holding cell back in Dubuque. At least something resembling a mattress lay between me and my sheet-of-steel bed. The sink and a toilet without a lid told me I wasn't in a holding cell. No doubt about it, I'd landed in a real jail. I closed my eyes, trying to make sense of how it happened but lost consciousness instead.

Somebody screamed, waking me. No one came to shut him up. When I opened my eyes, I was still in the cell. I pinched the back of my hand—hard. It hurt, so I pinched myself again. The all-too-real pain convinced me I wasn't dreaming. Try as I might, I couldn't re-member what had taken place. I had a fragment or two of what happened after my head hit the sidewalk, but the rest was gone. The hole in my life frightened the hell out of me. I'd had a lot to drink, and my head had hit the ground hard. I worried about brain damage.

After what seemed like forever, the screaming stopped. I closed my eyes and listened to the sounds around me. I didn't pick up any breathing from the top bunk and didn't sense any movement, so doubted I had a cellmate. I heard a sigh and shuffling footsteps in the box next to me. I listened as the guy paced back and forth. A big fan ran somewhere, with a constant whoosh that nearly drowned out the sound of a distant radio. I tried to focus on what had happened but still couldn't remember.

I heard some rattling, followed by a rolling sound and a loud metallic clank. The sandy scratch of advancing footsteps told me someone was walking toward the area outside my cell. Somebody rattled at the bars. I opened my eyes and raised my head. Two men in sheriff's uniforms waited outside my cell.

"Let's go Efferding," said one. "You're due in court."

Looking over my shoulder, I said goodbye to the Linn County Jail. Buzz, Stan, and I headed in the direction of Stan's Dodge Polara. They walked; I struggled to keep up. I must have had an interesting night. I remembered almost nothing, but could say with certainty it wasn't one I cared to repeat. Apparently, I'd been taken to the emergency room with two cracked ribs and then run through the jail's booking procedure.

Stan arranged for a lawyer to represent me. I spoke with my attorney before the hearing and learned the police didn't buy my story. They got the part about me not remembering just fine but didn't believe the attack was random. My lawyer told me not to answer any questions at the hearing unless he nodded at me. He never did.

The same guy represented Buzz, and I found out later he'd given him the same advice he gave me. We'd been looking at charges for assault and battery, but the hospitalized goon refused to cooperate with the police. When the bailiff called my case, my attorney went up to the bench where he talked to the judge and somebody else. The same thing happened when they called for Buzz.

Buzz had to plead guilty to disturbing the peace and disorderly conduct, while I copped to a drunk and disorderly and disturbing the peace. My fine came to thirty-five dollars with court costs suspended. Grand total for the experience: a thirty-five-dollar debt to Stan, a share of the lawyer's fees, a bill for a hospital visit I couldn't remember, and a sixty-dollar suit ruined.

After we got in the car, Buzz looked back at me from the front seat. "I didn't tell them anything. I said I drove by, saw two guys ganging up on you, and went to help. The cops didn't even ask if I knew you, but they claimed I used excessive force to break up the fight. The guy isn't going to walk so good after this. His knee might not bend right anymore."

"Good," I said. "Those guys wanted to put me in the hospital. What with two of them and me on the ground, you had to come in hard. I don't know how you managed to do it—you flew in like some sort of superman."

"I took a couple of years of karate."

"And I'm happy you did. What were the chances of you passing by like that? Talk about luck."

"Not luck." Buzz looked at me straight on. "When you didn't show at your apartment, I got worried and started cruising the neighborhood. That's what I wanted to talk to you about. Grandpa, Stan, and I know something is wrong. Grandpa told us you lost weight, you look worried all the time, and you've kept stuff from him. Looks like he was right."

Stan still hadn't started the car. He turned to me and said, "That's not all. The guy at the APCO station told me about your car. Somebody cut your tires. That had to have something to do with what happened last night. We said we're in this with you, and we meant it." He reached over the seat and handed me a hundred-dollar bill. "Your suit is ruined, and you got beat up for our family. Clete, you've gotta take care of yourself and not drink so much."

I'd just been called on the carpet for getting drunk and going it alone when the Sedlaks would have been happy to help me. No two ways about it, Stan's rebuke stung. That's the difference between normal people and an outcast. Once you've been utterly, completely alone, it no longer occurs to you to ask other people for help. Worse yet, you get to like it that way.

"I hear you, Stan. I got so wrapped up in this thing I wasn't thinking straight. Why don't we get together with Lumir next week and strategize? We'll come up with something. After what Buzz did last night, I don't think anybody's going to bother me for a while."

"Now you're talking sense, and remember, if anything even a little out of the ordinary comes up, you have two bodyguards. Now where's your car?"

We drove over to Spryncl's and found the Nova where I'd left it —in a lot across the street. I thanked Stan and Buzz, said my good-byes, and got into the car. My head felt like somebody had dropped an anvil on it. My ribs hurt.

When I got back to the apartment, I called Killian's to say my foot had taken a turn for the worse, and I needed another day off. After that, I crawled into bed where I went out like a light. I woke up around six and watched TV for a couple of hours. Realizing I hadn't checked the mail in a couple of days, I went out to the box and found a large manila envelope inside. I couldn't imagine what it might be. The envelope had no return address.

Curious, I picked Kohl's pocketknife off the end table, slit the package, and removed the contents. Inside, I discovered a second copy of Diane's case file. Jim's sister-in-law Shirley must have wanted to keep me up to date. I riffled through the papers and copies of photographs. It looked as if she'd copied the entire file this time. In addition to the reports she'd sent earlier, Shirley included Xerox copies of the crime scene photos of Diane and copies of my police file. The pictures of Diane ripped my guts and left me whimpering like a drowning puppy.

I put the package down, went to the kitchen, and threw down four shots of hundred-proof Old Grand-Dad in quick succession. I settled back onto the couch and stared at the ceiling. The bourbon hit ten minutes later. I cried until I had nothing left and drifted off into a troubled sleep. Diane haunted my dreams.

They were nightmares of the worst type, the kind where I had no defense mechanism, because I dreamed I was lying on my couch fast asleep. The package with the police file lay on the end table next to a shot glass smelling of Old Grand-Dad. Someone touched my shoulder, and I looked up to see Diane standing over me, shaking her head sadly. With one hand, she pointed to the file on the table, then to the glass. Variations on the scene repeated themselves until I awoke, shaking like a leaf.

I sat up and rubbed my face, unable to escape the haunting reality of the dream. The scent of the shot glass, the hum of the air conditioner, the nubby fabric of the couch pressing against my cheek—the lifelike details had convinced me I'd been awake. I shook my head from side to side to clear my senses, looked up, and saw Diane again. I realized then I was still asleep.

A few hours later, I got up, had a puker, and returned to the couch where I sorted through the contents of the envelope. I removed the Xeroxes of the crime scene photos. Trying my best not to look at them, I gathered them up and rolled them into a cylinder. I carried it to the kitchen counter where I found matches, lit the paper, and held it until the heat scorched my fingertips. I let go and dropped the burning roll into the sink. The flames sputtered, consuming all but the tiniest scrap of paper. The fire spent and the ashes cold, I turned my attention to the bottle of Old Grand-Dad and poured the contents into the sink, watching as the swirling liquid carried the ashes into the drain.

Randy Roeder

28

The only good thing about last night's misadventure—Myra hadn't joined Diane in haunting my dreams. Had that been the case, I'd have gotten into the Nova and driven full speed into a bridge abutment. I was drinking too much, something I'd left behind with the packing plant. I vowed I'd never touch liquor again—not neat, not mixed. I said good-bye to the works: brandy, bourbon, rum, vodka, Wisconsin Old-Fashioneds, Daiquiris, the whole kit and caboodle. Although temperance was the order of the day, I had no intention of taking the abstinence pledge. Beer and wine were still on the menu, but if every distillery on the face of God's good green earth were to disappear, I'd care not a whit.

Too hung over for breakfast out, I fried up a couple of eggs and made a pot of coffee. As I carried my cup to the table, my hands shook so badly that half the contents ended up on the floor. My nerves were shot. Threatening notes were one thing; getting jumped was another. When I realized my fried eggs were likely to return the way they went down, I scraped them into the trash.

I resolved to take a couple of days to stabilize before looking at the new copy of the police file. Shirley must have sent the all-inclusive version after I reported so little progress on my investigation. I hesitated to phone my thanks because she'd want to know what I'd learned, and I'd have found it awkward to admit I still hadn't examined the packet. Instead, I penned a brief thank-you note, a missive that would serve the purpose and buy me some time. I'd drop it off at the post office before work. Since it was an in-city delivery, she'd get it by tomorrow afternoon. Thankful the United States had the best postal service in the world, I walked out to the car, ready to begin the struggle to get though the next twenty-four hours.

As the day progressed, my alcohol consumption, the cracked ribs, and the poor quality of my sleep began to wear on me. By the end of my shift, only the pride and professionalism of a third-generation haberdasher kept me from selling a chubby teen a Kelly-green corduroy vest two sizes too small. The lad liked the color and believed if he didn't button the garment, all would be well. I'd about exhausted my professional bag of tricks trying to dissuade him from the regrettable purchase and had come to the last arrow in my quiver.

"You'll look like an egg in a green halter top."

"I guess you're right," he replied. His wistful voice gave new meaning to the word crestfallen.

"No matter what size a man is, he'll look good if he focuses on fit first and color second. A good fit gives you confidence; color sets the mood."

I sold him a gray waistcoat that didn't call attention to his size and gave him the standard instruction to follow in the tradition of Prince Albert and leave the bottom button undone. He left the store a sadder, but wiser, young man, and if he remembered my advice, he'd make the best of what he had to work with. My shift over, I picked up my car and drove over to Ernie's for a beer and sandwich.

As I walked through the door, a poster for the Corn Fed Brothers caught my eye. The black and white placard depicted Curly and Red Zmolek, each looking a good fifteen years younger than they did now. Since Diane no longer sang for them, they'd gone back to the original name for their duet. The switch allowed them to use their older promotional material. I'd seen Diane sing with the brothers at the American Legion last spring. She hadn't been expecting me to show up for the performance and asked me not to come to see the group again until she'd had a chance to work up her material. It seemed a reasonable request—Diane hadn't sung well.

A waitress I hadn't seen before detached herself from the bar and took my order for a beer, hamburger, and bag of peanuts with all the enthusiasm of a queasy maid cleaning a chamber pot. Wondering where Ernie had managed to find this paragon of good cheer, I turned to watch as the late afternoon crowd filed in. A less-than-slender bottle blonde in her late forties came into view and walked up to a gray-haired gent in pinstripe bibbed overalls sitting at the bar. She wrapped her arms around him from the back and kissed him on the ear. Her initial greeting complete, she unwrapped herself, ran her fingers through his stubbly hair, and kissed him on the cheek. He turned his head, smiled, and responded with an affectionate squeeze of her behind. Their obvious affection reminded me it was time to return to my neglected search for Diane's boyfriend.

The people closest to Diane—her family, Suzanne, and I—were in the dark with regard to a possible boyfriend. I'd asked around the dance studio, and neither the boss nor any of Diane's regular students knew of a love interest. I'd gone through the records looking at the private lessons Diane had given in the last six months and discovered only three single males. None of them stayed active with the studio. I recognized two of the names: one an awkward widower in his late sixties, the other a retired minister a decade older than that. An inquiry with the boss eliminated the third possibility when he revealed the customer in question "walked on the other side of the street."

I sipped my beer. A secret boyfriend would not necessarily have involved Diane's life at the studio. I'd been so blinded by my fixation on Gordon Kohl I neglected to consider that her desire to become a professional singer might be related to her death. I decided to rearrange my work schedule next Friday night to catch the Corn Fed Boys in action. Curly and Red could be aware of an admirer unknown to me.

I'd hoped the beer and sandwich would give me a second wind. They didn't. My head still hurt, and I found myself nodding off despite the pain in my ribs. Though it was barely six o'clock, my body insisted on bedtime. I decided to listen and put enough on the table to cover my purchases and tip.

Ernie, the barkeep, nodded to me as I left. A taciturn man, Ernie acknowledged his customers as they exited rather than as they arrived. Contrary to stereotype, he wasn't a good listener and had developed his system as a means of avoiding unnecessary conversation. He once broke down and informed me I was the only customer who regularly wore a suit when visiting his establishment. Two and a half years later, I remained uncertain if the remark was a compliment, a criticism, or simply an observation.

On my Saturday lunch break in the Man's Grille with coffee and a club sandwich for company, I chewed on the problem of Diane's phantom boyfriend. I still hadn't checked on Hiltbrunner's, the place she'd worked after leaving the Department of Public Welfare. The situation was easy enough to remedy, I got off work at three, and the place was just a few blocks away.

Diane had hired on at Hiltbrunner's Music Company, a downtown purveyor of sheet music, records, and musical instruments, hopeful the job would put her in contact with the local music scene. Things didn't work out as planned. The bulk of the company's customer base consisted of school musicians and adenoidal teens with dreams of becoming rock and roll stars. When working musicians stopped by to purchase music, or occasionally an instrument, they showed no interest in advancing the career of the pretty young woman behind the sales counter.

A buzzer rang as I entered the store. A half dozen teenagers sorted through racks of LPs, an elderly gent browsed the sheet music section, and a couple of young men talked to a salesman, a half dozen microphones spread out on the counter between them. I hadn't been in the store before, but Diane had told me the business extended to the upper floors where the instrument displays and rooms for music lessons were located. When I went to the counter and asked for the manager, a sales clerk returned with a stick of a man, at least six and a half feet tall with an Adam's apple the size of a grapefruit.

The manager, Oscar Krivanek, was helpful enough—introducing me to his staff and offering to call others, but as I talked with the employees, I realized Diane hadn't worked at the place long enough to bond with her co-workers. I found it easy to see why. Most of them were a good twenty years older than she. I didn't learn much, but I eliminated Oscar as a potential lover. With his cadaverous face, magnificent comb over, and sepulchral speech, the man possessed the charm of a walking corpse.

I drove the Nova home. One of these days, I'd have to start going out on the town again, but it certainly wouldn't be tonight. I was still sore from the beating, and just as bad, flat broke. Rummaging through the cupboards for something to eat, I came up with a can of shoestring potatoes. The phone rang just as I was about to dig in.

"We did it," Lumir announced. "We got the man who sold drugs to Eddie."

"How on earth did you ever convince the police department to do something? I couldn't get anywhere with Erikson."

"We didn't need the police." Pride filled Lumir's voice. "Bob Brada, a couple of other guys from the packing plant, and me—we got him."

I didn't like the way the conversation was heading. God only knows what had happened, but I didn't want to hear Lumir's news over the phone.

"I'll be right over," I said and slammed the receiver into its cradle.

Filled with foreboding, I sped over to Lumir's place. What had my friend done? For some reason, I fixated on the conversation I'd had with Helene Olds at the Coe College Library. Blood law—the last resort for those who find the legal system has failed them. Lumir and his friends—surely they didn't kill Sonny? Concern gave way to panic, and I started running stop signs.

I found Lumir in his shop, sitting in his captain's chair, his hands folded across his midsection, smiling contentedly.

"Lumir, what happened?" Wild with fear for my friend, I didn't wait for his answer. "Quick, tell me."

"This Sonny will not be selling drugs in our neighborhood anymore," he replied.

"You didn't—"

"What is wrong with you, Clete?"

"What'd you do?" I nearly shouted.

"We went to Jones Park and had a little talk with the man. He will not be back."

I took a deep breath and exhaled. "What happened?"

"Bob Brada and I introduced ourselves, told him about what happened to Eddie, and asked him not to come into the neighborhood again."

"That's it?"

"At first, this Sonny did not like the idea that we do not want him in our part of town. After we started talking with him, he came around and realized he wanted to leave the park. But our trucks were parked too close to his car, so he could not drive out. He began cursing and telling us to move our vehicles. Since there were four of us, I thought it foolish for the young man to act in such a way."

"You asked him not to come back, and he agreed?"

"No, he did not agree. I thought our baseball bats would convince him we did not want him here, but as I said, he was foolish."

"Baseball bats?" I felt my anxiety return.

Lumir must have read the look on my face. "We did not harm him, Clete. We took his keys away from him. When Sonny saw he could not drive away, he got into his car and pushed the door locks."

"You guys must have really scared him."

"I think so. Sonny's car has no lights or windows. Somehow the trunk and hood have big dents in them, and the fenders are wrinkled. That's when we learned they do not make baseball bats like they did in the old days."

"You introduced yourselves, and then you trashed his car? While he sat in it?"

"If the young man had been polite and listened, he would still have a nice shiny car."

"You used your real names?" I asked.

"Of course. We are not ashamed to protect our neighborhood. A drug dealer cannot go to the police. I do not think he will sell drugs in Jones Park again."

"You could be in danger. Sonny knows who you are. You're in the phone book. Some of these drug dealers can be pretty rough."

"You sound like an old woman. This is Cedar Rapids, not Chicago."

Randy Roeder

29

I lucked into a seat at the counter at Tommy's—no small feat at 7:30 on a Monday morning. My foot had healed completely, with no lingering problems. I needed money, so I'd be back at the studio tomorrow night. I planned to phone the boss to tell him I needed to take it easy and stick with beginners for a few days. He'd think it was because of my foot. I didn't plan to mention my ribs.

I'd done some reading about police procedure and discovered the odds of solving a crime decreased by the day. Diane died fifty-two days ago. I'd done everything I could think of, but so far nothing had shaken loose. Defeat clung to me like a jilted lover in the throes of denial.

I ordered a donut and a cup of coffee, and settled in for a few minutes with a copy of the day's *Gazette*. About halfway down the front page, I caught a short article about a murder in Des Moines.

Former Cedar Rapids Man Victim of Foul Play

Police in Des Moines have identified the partially clothed body of a man found floating in the Des Moines River last week as that of Gabriel Khoury, age 37. A trio of young fishermen found the body entangled in flood debris, lodged against an abutment of the University Avenue Bridge.

Detectives identified the victim on the basis of documents found in his wallet and have ruled out robbery as a motive. The Polk County Medical Examiner reports Khoury did not drown but died of a brain injury resulting from a blow to the head. Noting an investigation is under way, a spokesman for the police department had no further comment. Khoury is the son of Cedar Rapids residents, Basil and Roda Khoury. A spokesman for the family reports funeral arrangements have yet to be made.

Gabriel Khoury. The name sounded familiar, but I couldn't place it. I had to hand it to the *Gazette*, when it came to the first report of an unnatural death, they didn't waste words. The guy got about as much ink as Diane. At least she rated a small picture of what I'd come to think of as the "death car." Khoury didn't rate that. I shook my head in disbelief. My peccadillo in Dubuque had made the front page—above the fold—and rated two columns with an oversize picture. I could only guess why the press considered it more newsworthy to embarrass the living than to report an unnatural death.

I had already turned the page when it came to me. Gabriel Khoury was the guy who got bopped by his sister because he didn't pay the thousand dollars he owed her. It figured. Somebody like that would have a lot of enemies. I put down the paper and chuckled. Maybe his sister did him in. After all, a thousand bucks wasn't chump change.

When I reported in to Killian's, I had to put up with some kidding from my boss, Reg. A brief mention of my drunk and disorderly charges had made the newspaper's court report. Normally a peach of a guy, Reggie had a job to do and warned me management would not take it kindly if something like this were to happen again. Grateful the paper gave no details other than my name, age, address, and disposition of the case, I assured him it wouldn't be happening again.

———————

I ran into Suzanne LaRue outside the Butterfly Café. I was going in for lunch; she'd just finished hers. Since we hadn't seen each other since Diane's funeral, I invited her back inside for a cup of coffee. I knew I'd done the right thing when she rewarded me with a smile that nearly buckled my knees. When Suzanne made eye contact and flashed those ivories, a guy would happily drop to the ground and do a hundred pushups to see her do it again. We went inside where a plump but cheerful waitress directed us to a booth. I ordered our coffees and a ham salad sandwich for myself. Cheerful and talkative, Suzanne believed her career was about to take off. Her company made for a much-needed antidote to the frustrations I'd encountered in my search for Diane's abortionist.

"George Rahbani's decision to close the Golden Key could be the best thing that ever happened to me," she said. "I was way too comfortable there."

"I think the city pretty much closed it for him when they picked the block for urban renewal. I'm surprised he didn't reopen in a new location."

"I heard George got tired of working six nights a week. I have a contract with his son Habi's booking agency now. I already have gigs lined up in Des Moines, Madison, the Quad Cities, and Peoria."

"Congratulations, they'll love you."

"Condolences or congratulations, they both fit," she replied. "Habi Rahbani has a rep as one of the nastiest men in the business. He paws every woman he can get his hands on and gets downright mean if he doesn't get his way. I can take care of myself, but the sooner I can lose that little slime bucket, the better. He's a one-man rape epidemic who must have every social disease in the book."

I didn't know what to say. If someone as tough and savvy as Suzanne had to deal with situations like that for the sake of her career, Diane would have been a sheep to the slaughter. For the first time, I was truly happy my best friend didn't have a talent for singing. The predators involved with the nightclub scene would have eaten her alive.

"Hello, Cletus. Are you still there?" Suzanne asked.

"Sorry, I got sidetracked thinking about how tough a singer's life can be. Say, do you have anything booked at the Key? I ought to go there one more time before it closes."

"Nope, I'm done. George has been unwinding the business and cutting back on the entertainment. He's got a jazz quintet coming in from Kansas City to mark the closing. The doors shut in two weeks."

"Too bad, I wanted to see you there one last time."

"You can see me at the Fox and Hounds. Willard Evans, their regular piano player, invited me to join him when I'm available. As a matter of fact, I'll be there next week Tuesday. You'd think it'd be an off night, but for some reason, it's one of the best in their week."

"I'll be there, but I'm going to miss the Key," I said. "I hope working with George Rahbani wasn't as bad as working with Habi."

Suzanne smiled at me over her coffee cup. "Georgie has never been anything but a gentleman around me. He may be a crook and have a boat load of rage inside him, but he knows how to act around a woman."

"Georgie?"

"Some of the guys call him that when he's not around. Nobody's dumb enough to use it to his face."

"I want to ask him about a pocketknife with an Orthodox cross on it. Since George is Syrian Orthodox, I thought I'd go over some night and talk to him."

Suzanne chuckled. "Good luck. He's not a chatty guy. Making small talk about a pocketknife—that'll be a new one for him. Maybe you should try a Greek Orthodox priest."

I fiddled with the menu card. "George may not be easy to talk to, but Orthodox priests really weird me out. What with those robes, the big Smith Brothers beards, the funny hats? No way. At any rate, I'd like to go to the Key one last time before it closes."

"Cletus, open your mind. Shave the beard, and Orthodox clergy have a lot in common with regular Catholic priests."

"After the hassle with Diane's funeral, I intend to avoid them too. Same goes for nuns. Women who go around wearing crosses weird me out."

Suzanne cleared her throat and smiled wickedly. "Do I weird you out?"

"No, why?"

She touched an ear lobe and giggled. I noticed the small gold cross and felt my face grow red.

"Sorry, I didn't know you were Catholic."

"Not anymore, but I still like crosses." She ran a finger along her collarbone and touched her other ear. "So, me and my little earrings weird you out?"

I needed a recovery line. "Uh, no ... only people who wear crosses with dead people on 'em weird me out."

"I have one of those too. I don't wear it very often, but it belonged to my mom and looks nice with a scoop-necked top like I have on today. It comes to about here." She touched a spot about two inches below her neck.

I worked to keep my eyes from doing the telltale drop but failed. Time to change the topic. "You think George will help me out?"

Suzanne chuckled. "He'll probably bite your head off."

"Not much of a loss," I said.

The Hercule Poirot novel resting on my face dropped to the floor as I popped up to get the phone.

"Clete!" Stan nearly shouted at me. "All hell's broke loose. Somebody fired three shots into Grandpa's house."

"He okay?" I should have seen it coming. Sonny wanted payback.

"He was out in the shop when he heard the shots and waited an hour before he went into the house and called me. Mom, Dad, and Buzz don't know."

A voice in the background—Lumir. "And they aren't going to know, either."

"The police just left. I think Grandpa should move out for a few weeks until we know what's going on in the neighborhood. Maybe you can help. Would you talk to him?"

Did Lumir's family know about his involvement in destroying a car? I wasn't about to rat him out.

"Sure," I said. I could hear mumbling and suspected Stan had his hand over the receiver as he tried to convince Lumir to talk to me.

"Hello Clete. Stan won't give me any peace until I talk to you. I did not call the police—he did."

"Lumir," I said, "getting away for a while sounds good to me. You could take a little vacation."

"I am retired—every day is vacation. Nobody is going to scare me out of my own house. Three shots at an empty house. What kind of man is afraid of that? I crawled into machine gun fire for Black Jack Pershing. I did not fight a war so some coward could drive me from my home. I will not go."

Lumir had a point. Crime flourishes when people give in to fear, and Sonny or one of his friends hoped to intimidate Lumir. Although I didn't expect a return visit, I didn't want my friend to take chances.

"Do it for me, Lumir. I lost my wife, I lost Diane, I don't want to lose you."

Lumir took his time answering. "I must be the man Klara married. That man fought for his home, his family, and his country. I am not like Bob Brada who runs away from his house at the first sign of trouble and takes his family out into the country to hide."

"Bob Brada left town?" I asked.

"Someone shot at his house too. He let them scare him because he is weak. He should have sent Eddie and the rest of the family away and stayed to protect his home."

"Do the police know you guys destroyed a car?"

"I did not say." Lumir didn't say because Stan was listening. "I do not know what other reports were made. I think the police will do nothing about it."

"You can help them do nothing about it by leaving town for a few weeks. Eventually they'll get busy with other things and forget about Sonny's car."

"I will not go."

"Does your family know about your raid in Jones Park?"

"I do not know. I have said nothing to anyone but you. Stan wants to talk to you some more. Good-bye."

I talked with Stan again. He and I agreed the only way to get Lumir out of his house would be to bulldoze it down around him. Even then, we expected to see him standing in the wreckage with his arms crossed, telling all and sundry, "I will not go."

"You know, Stan," I said, "there's no way Roy, DeeDee, and Buzz won't find out about the gunshots. News travels fast on the Avenue's grapevine. I think you should tell them yourself rather than have them hear about it. Then you might ask them not to make a big deal out of it. The more they talk to Lumir about leaving town, the more stubborn he'll get. I'll visit him tomorrow morning. I don't start at Killian's until after lunch. Maybe I'll think of a way to convince him to leave town for a bit."

Not that it'd be easy.

Randy Roeder

30

Lumir looked up as I entered his shop. He was varnishing the pistol grip of a sawed-off shotgun. What had been the back piece of the stock and the front piece of the barrel lay on a table beside him. An ancient box of shells with the words *smokeless powder* emblazoned on the side sat next to them.

"Lumir, what are you up to?"

"I am modifying my father's twelve gauge to make it easier to carry. The short barrel will allow the shot to spread out more. That makes it harder to miss."

"Sawed off shotguns are illegal," I explained. "Owning one is a federal offense."

"Selling drugs to kids and shooting into my house are illegal too. Is my crime worse than these?"

"You have a point, but you need to be careful with a sawed-off. A lot of people shoot themselves trying to get them out."

He pointed to a button next to the trigger guard. "The safety works fine. Besides, I will not hide this gun under a coat like a criminal. If somebody comes for me, I want him to see the gun. I will not need to fire. Only a fool would make a move on a man holding a sawed-off shotgun."

I didn't approve of Lumir's course of action in any way, shape, or form. Knowing his stubbornness, I made one final attempt to dissuade him.

"Think about it. The situation is so bad right now you feel it's necessary to arm yourself. Someone fired a weapon into your house. The police are investigating. Why not rent a cabin on the Mississippi and fish for a few weeks? What could be nicer?"

"What good is a police investigation to a dead man? I cannot go to the police about this Sonny because we destroyed his car. I already know they think this is a random shooting by some drunk who took a drive past the Brada house the same night."

I'd given it my best effort, but I had to admit Lumir's logic was as inescapable as his work on the gun was beautiful. Growing up in a river town, I'd seen a couple of sawed-offs. Commercial fisherman kept them in their johnboats for dispatching snapping turtles and beaver. They were typically rusty, single-shot cobble jobs with hacked–off barrels and stocks. I remembered one with a pistol grip wrapped in black electrician's tape so the shooter wouldn't get splinters when firing the weapon. Ugly stuff.

Lumir got up to clean his brush. I recognized it as one of those I'd purchased at Kubia's Hardware. "How'd the brush work?" I asked.

"That is nicest brush I have ever used. Thank you."

"Glad you like it. Say, this is the first time I've seen a sawed-off corn sheller. Most guys wouldn't alter a gun this nice. Why, it's a Winchester Model Twelve."

"A corn sheller, what's that?" asked Lumir.

"A pump-action shotgun. You've done some nice work re-shaping the pistol grip where you cut off the stock. The wood looks as nice as if it just came out of the factory."

Lumir snorted. "The finish looks better than when it came out of the factory. I cannot butcher my father's gun. Change it, yes, but ruin it, no. I have too much respect for it. See, I smoothed the hacksaw cut on the barrel and touched it up with cold blue."

"Maybe you should get some new ammo, Lumir. These shells must be fifty years old."

"They are magnum shells and will do the job. They are loaded with No. 1 buckshot. Why my father had shells for a riot gun, I will never know, but I do not need to buy new."

"Your life might depend on it."

"I do not expect to use the gun, but if a shell misfires, I will rack the slide and shoot again."

"If you have time for a second shot."

"You worry too much, Clete."

Except for a little flak about my arrest for disturbing the peace, the first night back at the studio went well. I taught the Tuesday night introductory class to a group of eleven. I talked more than I demonstrated, and though my ribs were tender, I'd loaded up on aspirin and faked it pretty well. When I left the studio at ten o'clock, I couldn't shake the feeling that someone was watching me. I was so jumpy by the time I got to the car I could barely get my key in the lock. I thought about buying a gun but couldn't picture myself carrying it into Killian's or the studio. It was just as well since I couldn't afford one anyway.

When I got home, I forced myself to go through Diane's police file again. It had been four days since I last looked at it. Happy I'd destroyed the copies of the crime scene photos, I cleared the coffee table, set the contents of the two packages on it, and began a comparison. As I worked, I made a stack for documents from Shirley's most recent packet that were not in the first. When I finished, I had a document left over in the original stack—a page from the first packet that wasn't in the second.

Most of the unique documents in the new batch had to do with me—Pudge's notes for the times he'd questioned me over the years. They made for interesting reading but shed no light on the case. The handwritten notes recording Pudge's first impressions of our encounters were fascinating, his typed reports less so. Reading the detective's hen scratch made for an odd experience. Given his in-person abuse of me, I expected an abundance of words like pervert, dirt bag, suspect, and creep, but Pudge had consistently referred to me either as E or as Efferding. I'd become so accustomed to his insults that in some strange way his notes left me feeling almost respected.

The last of the unique items proved the most interesting. One was the photocopy of the unopened envelope from the Linn County Medical examiner, the other, a copy of a toxicology report from the University of Iowa's Medical Laboratories. Since the unopened envelope had been part of the first packet, and not the second, I concluded it had once housed the toxicology report. As likely as not, someone had opened the envelope, discarded it, and filed the report.

The medical examiner may not have had access to sophisticated labs in Cedar Rapids, but the University of Iowa, thirty miles away, offered first class facilities. Chemistry isn't my thing, but I could tell the university's labs had analyzed a sample of Diane's blood. I couldn't make much out of it, but it looked like she had .21 mg/dL of alcohol and 7 mcg/mL of something called secobarbital sodium in her blood. The alcohol meant she'd been drinking before her death. I didn't know secobarbital from sugar, but I did know the barbital didn't have anything to do with shaving crème. Call me suspicious, but the word sounded a lot like barbiturate.

———————

The next day, I skipped lunch to make phone calls. I couldn't reach Shirley Weiss. I caught a break, however, when I called Helene Olds.

"Stewart Memorial Library, Reference Department, may I help you?"

I recognized Helene's voice immediately. "Helene, Cletus Efferding here. How are you doing?"

"Oh hi, Cletus. You caught me at lunch."

"Sorry. I need a favor. I'm hoping you can look something up for me, and I can call back for an answer later today."

"I'm here until 4:30," she replied.

"Great, I need to know about a drug called secobarbital sodium. What it is, how it's used, that sort of thing."

"You know Cletus, one of these days, you're going to have to ask me something hard. It's a sedative. If all the reference questions that came my way were as easy as yours, I'd be as fat as a hippo because I'd never leave my desk to look something up."

The image brought me up short. Helene's long legs and willowy figure precluded any comparison to the ponderous African river dweller. As for hips, the gentle sway of Helene's hindquarters in a flowing skirt answered all the questions a guy might have about why the garment was invented. I wondered if Helene's grace and elegance were innate or a product of her years of dancing. No matter, Sam Olds was a lucky man.

"Cletus? Cletus?"

"Sorry Helene," I said as I shifted the phone to the other ear, "my mind just took a little detour. You'll be happy to know I do have something harder for you. What does it mean if someone has 7 mcg-slash-ml of this secobarbital in their blood? And what if they've got .21 mg-slash-dl of alcohol in their blood at the same time? Are they looped, sedated, or what?"

"You'd need a pharmacist or biochemist to answer that. I can look through our reference books to see what I can find, but you need to realize that if I draw any conclusion from it, you're getting a strictly amateur opinion. If you weren't a friend, I'd need to consider if I was ethically bound to refer you to someone with real expertise."

"Thanks, and relax, nobody's life depends on it. I'll call back later this afternoon."

I returned from lunch to a sales floor so devoid of customers, I could have laid down between the polo shirt tables and taken a nap. When I couldn't take boredom any longer, I had Reg cover for me and headed downstairs to the pay phones. I called Helene. She'd done my research.

"Well Cletus, you gave me quite a work out. I struck out in the Reference Collection, but I managed to get hold of Professor Cook over in the Chemistry Department. He just called back. A lot would depend on the person's weight and their tolerance for the drug and the alcohol. The alcohol alone would make the average person tipsy. The Seconal would compound the effect. Professor Cook is a bio-chemist, but this sort of work is outside his area of expertise. His best guess is an average person would have serious problems with motor control and be lapsing in and out of consciousness. He believes most people would survive the experience if they didn't get sick and choke on their own vomit."

Helene chatted a bit more. I held up my end of the conversation as skillfully as a talking robot with a rundown battery. Diane had been drunk and loaded on Seconal at the time of her fatal abortion. The whole scene didn't add up—getting an abortion when she wasn't pregnant, getting drunk before the procedure, using drugs—this was not the woman I knew.

Thank goodness we were slow, I spent the rest of the afternoon so distracted I had trouble using a folding board, something I'd been doing since I was tall enough to look down at a countertop. My shift finally over, I left the store.

I found Jim Weiss in the Driftwood Room, the bar of the Montrose Hotel. He'd been wanting to get together for a couple of days, but our schedules hadn't meshed. I took a seat and nearly cried when he ordered a Wisconsin Old-Fashioned. Faithful to my pledge, I requested a beer.

"Did you see the paper on Monday?" he asked. "A Cedar Rapids man got himself murdered in Des Moines."

"Gabriel Khoury," I said. "Talk about coincidence. I ate at the Hamburg Inn in the middle of the night a few weeks ago, and this guy and woman are sitting there drunk as lords. All of a sudden, she beans him in the head with a glass ashtray and yells 'Gabriel Khoury, you sonofabitch, you don't have my money? My life savings?' Turns out he borrowed a thousand dollars from her and didn't pay it back. They get in a fight and the cook chases them out of the place with a steel pipe. You should have seen it. That old lady was a real hellcat, just the kind of woman you'd want on your side in a fight."

Jim raised his eyebrows. "You've been holding out on me. And all the good stuff I have for you. I have more, but now I don't know—"

"Don't cut me off, Jim. I can't live without gossip." Not that I had to worry. Jim would have found it easier to quit breathing than to pass on the chance to spill the poop.

"Gabriel Khoury," he said, "now there's a punk the car dealers in Cedar Rapids won't forget. He swiped over a hundred sets of hubcaps from dealership lots in something like ten days. Turned out he was selling them to a guy in Des Moines. They'd have never caught him, but he had such a big mouth it didn't take long before it was all over town. After that everybody starts calling him Gabby."

"What happened?" I asked.

"He got sent to the reformatory. Didn't do much time before he was out again. Rumor has it he came out anything but reformed."

"Small world," I offered. I'd been eyeing Jim's Old Fashioned so intently, I couldn't think of anything else to say.

Jim lit up and took a sip of the drink. "Maybe smaller than you think."

He paused, the signal there was more to come.

"Now you're holding out on me," I said.

"Khoury is a Syrian name."

"And?"

"Clete, Clete, Clete. Think—G. K., as in an Orthodox pocketknife with initials on it. As in Gabby Khoury."

"Or G. K., as in Gordon Kohl, the owner of the car," I countered. "The simplest explanation is almost always the best."

"As in Gabby Khoury, an unreformed punk who wouldn't think twice about stealing a car. The mysterious G. K., a slime ball so low he'd steal from his sister."

I still wasn't convinced. "For all we know, the guy could be a Moslem."

Jim leaned back and laughed. "You better work on your detective skills. If you'd read the obituary the next day, you'd know the funeral is scheduled for St. George's."

—————————

When I arrived at the studio, I used the boss's phone and tried Shirley Weiss again. I caught her at home.

"Shirley, Cletus Efferding here. Do you have a minute?"

"Why hello Cletus, I do. You didn't need to send a thank you note, but it was nice. Your mama must have raised you right."

"The note isn't enough. That's why I called. You went above and beyond the call when you re-copied Diane's file and re-sent it. I caught something I missed the first time around. A little note doesn't begin to say how much I appreciate the help."

"I didn't."

"Didn't what?"

"Didn't send another copy."

"It came in the mail last week. The whole file, copies of the photos, Pudge's notes on me—everything."

"I didn't send it. I don't know anything about it."

"This is really weird. Can you think of anybody who might have sent it?"

"I can't. You know, this is kind of scary for me. I took a big risk sending you that file, and now somebody else does the same thing."

"I don't know what to say. This is so strange. I'm stunned."

"Cletus, don't get me wrong, but I don't think you should call me at work anymore."

"I think you're right."

31

Habi Rahbani sat at the bar in a deserted Moonglow Lounge. Though a bit early in the day, he poured himself a double Jim Beam on the rocks. He'd just returned from Gabby's funeral service and felt miserable. Other than family, the only people who showed up were friends of Gabby's parents. None of them really knew the guy. It figured. Gabby spent most of his time in Des Moines, and the guys he worked with most likely had offed him. He doubted they'd be interested in attending the funeral.

The wake had turned into a three-ring circus. They'd closed the coffin to hide the poor condition of Gabby's body. As Habi stepped to the front to pay his respects, Gabby's creepy sister Leila cut in front of him. Drunk and crying, she flung herself onto the casket. When her father tried to pull her off, she went ballistic.

"Why did he treat me so bad, Baba?" she wailed. "Why did my little brother treat me so bad?"

After resisting her father long enough to make a big production out of it, she allowed him to remove her from the coffin and buried her head in his shoulder. As he prepared to lead her away, she began pounding on him with her fists.

"You always took his side, Baba. You know what he did? He took my money. When I needed it back, he called me a stupid skag. My own little brother called me a skag!"

Inclined to agree with the sentiment, Habi enjoyed the show, but his father George decided the spectacle had gone on long enough. He separated himself from the other menfolk, walked over, and tapped Leila on the shoulder.

"That's enough," he said.

Leila unwrapped herself from her father and stifling her sobs, joined her mother who led her from the room.

Between the wake and today's funeral, Habi felt like he'd earned his double bourbon. In fact, the entire week had been a hassle. His folks never liked Gabby. Worried their pride and joy had been spending too much time with his now-dead cousin, they'd felt compelled to invite their son to the house for dinner. A relaxing family dinner it was not. His father kept giving him the third degree, grilling him, wanting to know what Gabby had been up to. Though Habi suspected the Des Moines operation killed Gabby for running an unauthorized drug business, he kept his mouth shut.

The family dinner over, Habi had gone to pick out a new suit for the funeral. Even that had gone poorly. Some screwy salesman at Killian's kept trying to put him into a dark-colored suit with a black tie. The place didn't have a decent set of threads in it. He finally found an iridescent green jacket, paisley shirt, and burgundy bellbottoms at Lindale Plaza. The experience just proved people in Cedar Rapids didn't know how to dress.

He stared at his drink as he lit a cigarette. Des Moines must have done it. The guys in Peoria had no reason to off Gabby. With the new drug operation off to a flying start, Gabby would have earned big money for them. The Peoria boys made their first delivery to the Moonglow a week ago, dropping off ten grand in merchandise. Irv and Herman didn't seem half as bad as Gabby made them out to be.

Funny how the poor guy worried about Peoria when the real danger came from the Italians he worked with every day.

Pounding at the back door disturbed his reverie. He got up to check on the situation and discovered Irv peering through the small window. Habi opened the door to let Irv in. Herman pushed through behind him. The men followed him back into the bar where Irv took the stool next to him. Herman remained standing.

Irv reached into his shirt pocket and pulled out a monogrammed cigarette case. When he opened it, the container was empty.

"I can comp you some cigarettes," Habi offered.

Irv shook his head. "Herman keeps my spares for me. You probably don't have Benson & Hedges anyway."

"Never heard of 'em," said Habi.

"I don't smoke crap, son. Hey Herman, I'm ready for some more cigs."

Herman produced a thin square box and handed it to Irv. It contained just enough cigarettes to fill Irv's case. Irv filled it, selected a cigarette, and lit up.

"I'm just having a bourbon," Habi lifted his glass. "I went to Gabby's funeral this morning. Like a drink on the house? I can fix one."

Irv took a healthy drag, set his cigarette on the bar. "Na, we gotta get back home this afternoon. Too bad about the guy, we coulda made a lot of money together. Your old man do him?"

Habi pushed an ashtray in Irv's direction. "Are you crazy? Gabby worked for a bunch of Italians in Des Moines. A couple of them come from Chicago. You know that outfit. They probably found out about his side business."

Irv swiveled on his stool and stared at Habi with pupils the size of pencil points. "Maybe your old man ratted him out."

Habi chuckled. He picked up Irv's cigarette and placed it in the ashtray. "My old man is so out of it he didn't have a clue about Gabby's dope business."

"I hear your old man didn't like Gabby dumping a body in his town. Touch my cigarette again, and I'll kill you."

"Sorry," squeaked Habi.

Irv's lips drew tighter. "Maybe you guys wanted Gabby's business for yourselves."

"Don't need it." Habi took a sip from his drink. He was beginning to feel uncomfortable.

"Hey, Herman," Irv said, "he wanted the drugs, but he don't need our business."

Habi watched Irv's cigarette scorch the surface of the bar. Herman took the stool next to him, opposite Irv. Feeling like a piece of salami crammed into a sandwich, Habi understood why his father made it a rule to meet with associates at a table.

Herman sighed. "Seems to me somethin' ain't right. We deliver ten grand in merchandise—on credit—to this guy sittin' here, and Gabby gets dead. That leaves us holdin' the short end of the stick."

Habi turned on his stool to face Herman and held up his hands. "It's cool, man. He never picked it up. It's all here, you can take it when you go back. We're square."

"Hear that, Irv? We're square."

Irv grunted. "Except for the interest."

"Interest?" said Habi, turning to face Irv.

"We don't front merchandise without charging interest." Irv moved his face closer to Habi. "You're his partner, and the interest is a grand a week."

Habi knew they were shaking him down. "No problem," he said. "I've got it. You can have it today."

Getting out of the situation for a thousand bucks sounded cheap, but Habi wanted to clarify the situation. "One thing you should know, Gabby and I weren't partners."

By now, Irv was twelve inches from Habi's face. "No way that *schlemiel* was smart enough to run a setup like this. You let him do all work while the Rahbani operation sat back and counted the money."

His hand shaking, Habi lit another cigarette. "Really, Gabby ran everything. He cut me a deal to warehouse his stuff until he picked it up. It's all water over the dam anyway, when you pick up the goods and the interest, we're square."

Irv leaned back, his face a display of amazement. "You hear that Herm? Again, he thinks we're square."

Herm faked innocence. "You mean we're not square with Habi?"

"We're not square, Herm."

Irv exhaled, filling the air around Habi's face with smoke. "You and your late associate still owe for the first order. With interest, that comes to eleven thousand."

Sweat began to soak through Habi's shirt. *The idiot hadn't paid these guys.* "Gabby made the deal," he said. "I just bought from him. My distribution isn't that big. I don't deal with that kind of money."

Irv stubbed out his smoke. "That's why we have collateral," said Herman. "Gabby put the motel and lounge up against the merchandise."

Habi protested. "They weren't his. They never belonged to him."

"They belong to his partner, or boss, whatever you are," said Irv.

"I don't own it. It belongs to G & HR Enterprises."

"Habi boy," said Irv, "It's time you shut up and listen. What I gotta tell you ain't hard. Me and Herm here don't care who owns what. We gave you guys credit, and if it turns out you lied about how you could back it up, that makes you the collateral. We'll be back next week. By then, it'll come to twelve big ones. You don't have it, you're gonna end up in a world of hurt. You'll still owe, and we keep adding the interest. It don't end until we get paid, or Herm gets tired of hurting you. Herm gets tired, you'll wish we were Italian. See, we don't stop with the deadbeat. After Herm puts you in a wheelchair, we go after your family—women first. Herm likes doing women. You'll go to a lot of funerals."

Habi turned on his stool to make an appeal to Herman. Herman looked as if he hoped Habi would fail.

Irv rose from his stool, patted Habi on the back, and said, "See you next time, Habi boy."

"Herm, have Habi here get the money and the goods. I'll start the car and get the air conditioning going."

Irv said nothing more and started for the door.

"This way Herm," said Habi, nodding in the direction of the office.

"It's Herman to you, deadbeat."

Habi led him to the office and opened his wall safe. He made good on the interest and returned the drugs. When Herman left, he walked to the men's room, threw up, and went back to his barstool. He lit another cigarette, took a drag. Blowing smoke rings, he thought about his future. The smoke rings rose and disappeared into the air, taking his dreams of becoming a rock and roll impresario with them.

Thursday, I sat at the counter at Tommy's having a breakfast for lunch, wishing I'd been able to attend Gabby Khoury's funeral. My excuses had worn thin at Killian's. Reg had cut me as much slack as possible, but time off for attending Gabby Khoury's funeral wasn't in the cards. I couldn't complain, Killian's had bent over backwards for me the past few weeks.

My brain felt like someone wrapped it in a blanket, and the coffee didn't seem to help. I wondered if I should start smoking. People claim tobacco sharpens their thought processes, and my thinking needed all the help it could get.

"Oh Miss," I said as my waitress passed by, "a pack of Camels."

"Straights or filter?" she asked.

"Uh, filter." I didn't want to be seen picking stray tobacco pieces off my lips.

The waitress tossed my pack on the counter. I picked up a complimentary book of matches from the container next to the sugar shaker and lit up.

Diane ate lunch at K-Mart—in good spirits and apparently sober—on the Friday she died. Sometime between lunch and supper-time, she got drunk, took Seconal, and had an abortion she didn't need. Diane hated drugs, and after Curtis's drug-fueled attack on her, the mere mention of them would set her off on a rant. The Seconal couldn't have been recreational. Diane had been sedated for the abortion procedure.

I puffed on my cigarette, trying not to inhale. K-mart was out on the edge of the city, too far to walk back to town. Pudge's preliminary investigation had been thorough. Diane had parked at the APCO station and didn't take a taxi back to town. The guy who drove the Sixteenth Avenue bus route didn't remember seeing her. There's no way someone with Diane's looks could have boarded a bus and escaped the attention of a male driver. Either someone picked her up at K-Mart, or she'd walked to another location.

And then the crime file. I stuffed out my cigarette. Someone other than Shirley mailed me a copy of a file for a crime no one was investigating. Any number of people at the cop shop could have known I was following up on Diane's death. Pudge wouldn't have sent it. He hated me and had moved to Joliet. Erikson wouldn't have done it, either. He'd threatened to go to my employers and expose me as a deviant if I didn't quit investigating. I didn't know who it might be, but somebody in the department was upset about the situation and wanted to help me.

When I started in on my second cup of coffee, I realized I was onto something. I'd rattled enough cages that someone sent a couple of thugs to thump me. The goons attacked the same day I told Earl Erikson I'd make waves with the newspaper. I doubted the attack was a coincidence. My activities posed a threat to Erikson. What I didn't know was how.

I attempted to pour sugar into the dregs of my coffee and spilled most of it. My shakes had started again. I didn't mind the trembling hands as much as the buzzing solar plexus that accompanied it. Nine days since the beating, I still hadn't figured out what would set it off. I prayed it wouldn't happen to me when I gave dance lessons. Maybe the cigarettes would help.

I'd taken a hard tumble onto the concrete, and those thugs could have killed me. I had to look no farther than Gabby Khoury for an example. He died of a brain injury acquired during a beating. If Jim was right, and Khoury had stolen the dentist's car and dumped Diane's body, he deserved it. I didn't.

Although I had some of the puzzle's big pieces, there weren't enough of them to understand how they fit together. At any rate, my shift at Killian's would start soon. I pocketed my cigarettes and got up to leave.

After working my shift in menswear, I went straight to the dance studio. They had me scheduled until ten. After that, I'd go over to the Golden Key and talk with George Rahbani. I'd be spending money I didn't have, but I needed to put my fears aside before they got the best of me. My absence from the town's night life wasn't entirely the goons' fault—I hadn't gone out since that twisted little snot Sally Davis put me on crutches.

———————

A half dozen customers, four of them solitary drinkers, made for the Thursday night clientele at the Golden Key. The deserted bandstand and empty seats called attention to the important role live music had played in the club's success. The shelves behind the bar held a third of the bottles that once made up an inventory sure to impress even the most demanding cocktail aficionado. A single bartender and a waitress in the club's signature costume—fishnet stockings and a French maid's get up—were on duty. I knew the girl in the fishnets from my many nights at the Key. Her name was Anne. Divorced from a man who liked to hit, she lived with a two-year-old son in the home of her mother. She came to the table to get my order.

"Hello, Cletus, I haven't seen you in a long time. What'll it be?"

"Pabst Blue Ribbon." Anne looked like death warmed over. She worked nights and took daytime business classes out at the Area Ten community college.

"Long night?" I asked.

"We did the lingerie fashion show again last night. We were busy. George didn't show, and the guy at the door didn't feel like bouncing anybody. I got pinched so hard I have a bruise, and then some guy felt my boobs. When I got home, my kid and Mom were throwing up. I'm running on three hours' sleep."

"Hang in there, Annie," I commiserated. "Maybe tomorrow you can catch up on your sleep."

Anne was a sweetheart, and I felt for her. On lingerie nights, the club's waitresses modeled colorful underwear on stage and paraded through the club serving drinks while dressed in baby doll pajamas. Once an occasional feature, I heard the shows had become more frequent as George booked fewer bands and wound the business down. Anne dreaded lingerie nights, but the tips were good. She, her mom, and the boy needed all the money Anne could get her hands on. She'd be looking for another job when the club closed in a few weeks.

Anne returned with a bottle and a glass. "Here you go, Cletus."

"Thanks, keep the change," I said, handing her a generous tip. "I see George is here tonight, how is he?"

"Grouchier than ever. He's never happy, but it's been worse lately. Something must be eating him. Maybe it's the club closing."

Across the room, George Rahbani presided over the scene from his customary perch, a tall table on a raised platform that allowed him to keep an eye on the operation. Save for employees, few people talked to the man. Fingering the folding knife in my pocket, I walked over to talk to him.

I was about a dozen feet from his table when he looked up from his paper work. He watched without expression as I approached. The raised platform and tall stool served to put his face at my level. Perfectly still, his eyes, face, and hands betrayed no trace of movement. Hostility seeped from his very pores.

"George, I'd like to ask your opinion of something. A boy I know found a pocketknife, I think the designs on it have something to do with the Orthodox Church. I'm starting a knife collection and would like to know more about it."

"Maybe I can help you. Put it on the table, and I will look at it."

I removed the knife from my pocket and set it on the table. Rahbani picked it up, turned it over in his hands, opened and closed the blades. A full minute passed before he spoke.

"I know this knife," he said. "It belongs to the family of my cousin Gabriel. He won it in an archery contest at our Orthodox church camp when he was a teenager. Gabriel is recently deceased. How did this boy find the knife?"

"I didn't ask. I gave him three dollars for it."

"Then you made a bad deal. My cousin was very proud of this knife and would not have lost it. The boy must have stolen it. Gabriel's parents are heartbroken by his death, and the return of their son's knife may bring them some happiness."

George slid the knife into his pants pocket, picked up a pencil, and looked back down at his paperwork. Our conversation was over.

Feeling like the dumbest stick in the woodpile, I couldn't think of a response. George Rahbani had maneuvered me out of my only piece of evidence connecting Gabby Khoury to the car that held Diane's body. He did so knowing I'd be too intimidated to ask for its return. Stunned, I walked away without another word and made for the exit.

32

"Just a minute," I said. "I can't hear a thing. Let me turn down the air conditioner." Noisy and not up to the task, my room-sized air conditioner struggled valiantly to keep up with the humidity on a night so oppressive the city's mosquito population had broken out in a sweat. Lumir was on the line.

"Clete, I am staying with Roy and DeeDee for a while. They don't want me at home right now, and I think I will listen to them. If you try to catch me at the house, I will not be there."

"Well, they worry when someone shoots into your house. You have to expect that. I didn't think they'd convince you to move out, but I'm glad they did. Not just for you, but for them. They'll rest easier knowing you're safe at home with them."

"I thought about that in the emergency room. I can stay here a few days while I recover, enjoy DeeDee's good cooking, and everyone will be happy."

"Emergency room? Recover? What happened Lumir?"

"I was out in the shop Wednesday night building a miter jack so I could true up the pieces for your picture frame. That's when it all happened. I ended up with a couple of dozen stitches."

I exhaled and relaxed. I'd been worried my friend had a stroke or a heart attack. A shop accident with hand tools might require patching up, but fingers and limbs usually remain attached. Lumir had mentioned many times the most frequent cause of accident in a woodshop is a wood chisel. It sounded like he'd gotten quite a gash.

"That's a lot of stitches. Any damage to your tendons?" I asked.

"No tendons, I got cut across the chest."

I couldn't imagine how he'd done it. "Was it a chisel? How in the world did you ever cut manage to cut yourself in the chest? I can't picture it."

"A knife, Clete. I lost a lot of blood but didn't have much muscle damage."

"Lumir, please tell me you were holding the knife."

"No, that was our friend Sonny."

The bullet holes in his home had persuaded Lumir to take precautions unusual for him. In addition to the sawed-off shotgun he kept in the house, he'd installed deadbolts and had begun locking his workshop when he worked in it at night. The preparations had proven inadequate.

"Clete, are you still there?" Lumir asked.

"I'm still here. What happened?"

"I heard a big thud and turned around. Sonny kicked the door so hard the deadbolt broke through the frame. You know, that three-quarter-inch pine they use on doorframes can't take much abuse. The bolt really ought to go through a two-by-four or a piece of oak."

Ever the problem solver, Lumir might have spent the next ten minutes talking about the various ways to strengthen a doorframe if I didn't bring him back on topic. I suggested we get back to Sonny.

"He looked crazy, Clete. His eyes were all bloodshot, his face was red, and his hair looked like the wild man from Borneo. He was shouting, 'You can't f . . .' Well, let me put it this way, he said something like, 'You can't eff with me, you motherfather.' He kept waving this big hunting knife around. I tried to talk to him."

"You tried to talk to him?"

"With my gun in the house, what else could I do? I asked him to pull up a chair so we could talk about it. I offered to pay for his car and asked him if he wanted any coffee. He said yes, pulled up a chair, and sat down."

"It sounds like you almost had it under control," I said.

"I did not think so. The man was on drugs, I think he wanted to get me closer to him, but I wanted to get over to my workbench. The slick Eddie sharpened was lying on top of it. I pretended to go to the coffee pot, but when I got there, Sonny jumped out of his chair and swung his knife at me. It went through my shirt and cut me across the chest. I grabbed the slick. He was too close for me to swing it at him, and it was turned the wrong way. The sharp end was pointed at me. All I could do was ram it forward and poke the wooden handle into his chest. I got lucky. He fell down."

"You should have taken the shotgun to the shop with you," I said.

"Do you want to know what happened, or do you want to give me a lecture?" Lumir didn't want to be interrupted. "I knew he was crazy, and sure enough, he picked up the knife and jumped up to come at me again. This time I had the sharp end of the slick pointed toward him. I swung it sideways and sliced him across the belly. I did not do much more than graze him. Sonny is a weakling. When he saw blood on his shirt, he dropped the knife, and ran for the door."

A three-foot chisel with a four-inch, razor sharp tip—once he picked up the slick, Lumir had the advantage. I didn't want to make the mistake of interrupting again, but Lumir had finished his story.

"Did you chase him?"

"I did not chase him. I could see he was more scared than hurt. I did the smart thing. He might have had his gun in his car. I went into the house and waited with the shotgun. When I heard his car drive away, I called Stan to drive me to the hospital. He wanted to call the police, but I would not let him. I told him if he called the police, I would stay in my own house. I told the hospital I had lost control of a chisel on my wood lathe."

"Why on earth didn't you just tell the police?"

"I have an illegal sawed-off shotgun in my house. I helped to destroy this Sonny's car. I cannot go to the police. When Roy and DeeDee found out a group of us destroyed a drug dealer's car in Jones Park, they lectured me like a child for almost an hour. The only way I could get them to stop was to agree to come stay with them for a few days. We made a mistake when we destroyed the car, but it cannot be undone."

I walked into Ernie's in time to see the Corn Fed Boys set up their microphones. I found it hard to believe just a week had passed since I'd seen the poster for their gig. So much had happened. Lumir and his friends trashed Sonny's car, and Sonny retaliated by shooting up Lumir's house. Lumir had armed himself with a sawed-off shotgun but didn't have it with him when Sonny cut him with a knife. Then to top it off, I discovered Diane had consumed enough alcohol and barbiturate to tranquilize an elephant before she died. A night out with a little music would make for a much-needed distraction.

The Zmolek brothers played at Ernie's often enough to be considered regulars, and though the bar didn't want for customers, I could see the boys wouldn't be filling the house. I had a table to myself and lit up a cig while waiting for the show to begin. So far, smoking had done nothing to improve my thinking, and my suits and apartment were starting to stink. I looked at the cigarette in my hand. Whatever attraction cigarettes had for others, they held no glamour for me. I stubbed out the butt, and when my waitress brought my beer, I asked her to take the cigarettes and throw them away for me. I was feeling smug about my decision when an arm insinuated itself around my neck.

"You lie lissnem zoo Corefed Boice musey?"

The fetid aroma of stale beer, rotting teeth, and lousy personal hygiene assaulted me. As I turned my head, the face of Ralph the Rummy obscured my vision.

"Get out of my face," I said in the hardest tone I could muster. "You stink, Ralph. Get the hell away from me. Go bother somebody else."

Mistaking my show of dislike for the warm hand of friendship, Ralph pulled my face closer and started slobbering as he babbled into my ear. His saliva began running down my cheek. I couldn't take it.

"Go away!" I shouted as I knocked him away from me, standing so rapidly I jostled the table and spilled my beer onto the floor. "Get away from me."

Ernie yelled, "Go home Ralph. One more time and you're out for good. Vera, get the customer another round."

Unconcerned he might be barred, Ralph haltingly made his way to the door. He must have made the rounds already—several people clapped as he exited. I fully expected he'd be back the next time I came in. Ernie used the "you're out for good" warning whenever he wanted Ralph to go home.

Order restored and the excitement over, Ernie turned off the TV set, and Curly and Red began to play. What they lacked in talent they made up for with their easygoing back and forth with the regulars. I planned to approach Red during one of their breaks.

The first set dragged. Ernest Tubb and Tex Ritter weren't my cup of tea, and it didn't take long for the accordion and trap set accompaniment to wear thin. When Red announced the break, I made my move.

"Red, I don't know if you remember me. I'm Clete Efferding, a friend of Diane Novacek."

Red patted me on the back. "She was such a nice girl. A tragedy, a real tragedy."

"I'd like to buy you a beer and talk with you about Diane for a few minutes."

Red tipped his feed cap back on his head. "I heard one of Diane's friends didn't like the way the police were handling things and decided to look into it on his own. I guess that must be you."

"How'd you know?" I asked.

Red looked at me with wonder. "Why, once something hits the Avenue, you might as well put it on TV."

So much for a discreet investigation. I invited Red to have a seat and ordered him a beer. As we chatted, I realized he knew nothing about a love interest on Diane's part.

Red took a long pull on his beer. "A pretty little gal like that, lots of guys was interested, but she wasn't havin' any of it. She was a nice one. Too bad we were gonna have to let her go."

I nodded. "She really wanted to be a singer, but she just didn't have the talent."

"Talent didn't have nothin' to do with it. When your friend started drinking, she forgot the words, missed her cues, and would get to giggling. Curly and I ain't God's gift to music, but we couldn't have that."

"Drinking?" I was incredulous.

"Started last February and kept getting' worse. Sometimes I wondered if she liked singing. I think she drank to calm her nerves."

Red's revelation hit me like a ton of bricks. I don't remember the rest of our conversation, but I think I held my end up. When Red returned to his trap set, I left. As I exited, I met Arthur, the guy who fixed my tires, at the door.

"Hello, Arthur," I said.

Arthur paused and looked at me. "Somebody doesn't like you. Your tires, that wasn't an accident."

"What?"

"Your tires, they didn't get flat by accident. I could tell."

"Thanks for letting me know," I said.

"Okay," said Arthur as he brushed by me and went inside.

Somewhere, deep inside me, I had an inkling Arthur would be living at home for a long, long time.

33

The smell of the meatpacking plant settled in over Bohemie Town like a pillow coming to rest on a dying man's face. Ignoring the neighborhood's familiar fragrance, I stood in the darkness on a rickety stepladder outside Lumir's kitchen window. Lumir had stashed the half-rotten deathtrap under his back porch to hedge against the possibility he "might need it for something someday." I'd warned him the ladder might be used in a break in, but the one-in-five-hundred chance he'd find a use for the ladder had won out. After the potshots at his house, I'd encouraged him to fix the broken lock on his kitchen window. He didn't have a spare on hand and didn't want to buy one because "they'd need a ladder to get up to the window anyway." Armed with those two bits of knowledge, I had an advantage over the average burglar.

I pushed the window open and started to crawl through. The wiggling movement made my cracked ribs howl. I paused to consider the situation. Going in head first, over the faucet and kitchen counter, would likely result in a hard landing on the floor. "Okay ribs, thanks for the warning," I said as I wiggled back out. They protested anyway.

I re-entered feet first. Anything but graceful, I knocked a plate and cup to the floor—a minor incident that could have been worse. I'd just missed a stack of dinnerware a foot and a half high.

Thankful I'd avoided a major incident, I stood, waiting for the pain in my ribs to subside. It didn't. I somehow managed to reclose the window, and took a penlight from my pocket. A quick survey of the room revealed Lumir's shotgun still leaning against the wall next to the back door. His father's box of shells rested on the floor alongside. I picked up the gun and racked the slide. No shell in the chamber and an empty magazine tube. I picked up a handful of shells and filled the magazine, leaving the chamber empty.

Lumir was right about most things, and even more right than usual when he said only a fool would make a move on a man holding a sawed-off shotgun. Tonight, I intended to scare Sonny so badly he'd never bother Lumir again. Staring at the business end of a sawed-off shotgun should be enough to educate the guy. With no real need for even the six shells in the gun, I left the rest of the ammo. I didn't have a key to lock the backdoor, so I left it open.

I wanted to track Sonny down before he could locate Lumir. It wouldn't be easy. Lumir and friends had destroyed his GTO, so I didn't know what kind of vehicle he'd be driving. I did know something about his habits. He'd be parked in one of his regular spots, waiting for customers. The city's parks and the First Avenue strip were my best bets. Since the parks would soon close for the night, I chose the Avenue. I cut the gut for almost three hours and had nearly called it a night when I spotted Sonny in an empty parking lot near the Blue Moon Tavern. He stood in front of a beat-up Volkswagen van, smoking a cigarette, and chatting with a couple of long-haired girls wearing headbands. He looked relaxed and stood easily. His run-in with Lumir's slick hadn't done much damage.

I pulled into the Blue Moon parking lot, turned around, and made another pass by my quarry. The guy was still chatting. I'd try again in ten minutes. There didn't seem to be any need for an elaborate plan. When Sonny was alone, I'd park in the lot, pull out the shotgun, and put the fear of the Lord into him. I pictured him on his knees, begging for his miserable life, the muzzle of the gun six inches from his head. Maybe I'd jab him in the teeth with it, just to watch his mouth bleed. I had to be the scariest thing he ever imagined if I were to convince him to leave town.

I reached for the gun and chambered a shell. It didn't hurt to be careful. The guy had cut Lumir across the chest and shot into his house. He might even have a gun. I needed to be ready for it. Waiting, preparing mentally, getting angrier by the moment, sweat began pouring through my shirt—first at the armpits, then at the back. I looked at my watch. Two minutes to go. The hell with it, I put the Nova in gear and started in Sonny's direction.

The girls gone, I saw an unaccompanied Sonny leaning against the side of his van with his arms folded. I turned into the lot, grabbed the gun, and pushed off the safety. Seventy feet separated our vehicles. A surge of adrenalin hit, and the world began to move in slow motion.

I don't remember exiting the Nova. One moment, I was in the car, and the next, I was walking toward Sonny, shotgun at my side. I heard passing traffic, the sound of my footsteps on the asphalt, the closing of a distant car door, a blaring horn. My eyes took in the particulars of the scene with a clarity that hurt. I picked up every detail of the rusty van that had replaced his beautiful blue car—right on down to the name 'Sonny' spelled out in black electrician's tape on the fender.

I can't tell you when it happened, but sometime between my entry into the lot and my first step outside the door, I decided to kill Sonny. I watched as Sonny, frozen in time and place, looked at me with eyes wide and mouth open. I raised the gun.

"This is for Lumir Sedlak," I said, and squeezed the trigger.

Back in my apartment, shaking like a leaf, I replayed how I'd gotten myself into this situation. I wouldn't have gone after the man if the police had done their job. While they played games with a directionless drug investigation, Lumir was in danger. He couldn't go to the police for protection because he'd been involved in an assault and the destruction of a motor vehicle. If Sonny had found out Lumir moved in with his children, Roy and DeeDee would have been in danger as well.

The threat to Lumir and his family had unhinged me. I'd never believed myself capable of killing someone, but the verdict was in. I intended to kill Sonny, and now he was dead.

I'd pulled the trigger. The firing pin clicked, but nothing happened. The antiquated shell had been a dud. Racking the slide, I chambered another shell.

The sound of someone slamming a round into a pump shotgun is as threatening as it gets—the promise of an impending explosion from one of the deadliest close-range weapons on the planet. The ka-chick of the moving slide unfroze Sonny. He made a break for First Avenue, running as if Satan and all the hounds of hell nipped at his heels.

I was about to fire when I discovered the better angels of my nature wouldn't let me shoot a fleeing man in the back. Sonny burst onto the concrete roadway in front of a speeding car. The driver, doing at least fifty, didn't have time to brake. Sonny flew over the hood, hit the windshield, rolled onto the car top, and bounced off the trunk. The vehicle behind the first hit him again, running over his head and torso as the driver lost control of his car, veered off the road, and ran into a light pole. I didn't think it wise to stick around to make an eyewitness report. I picked up the ejected dud and left the scene.

I didn't shoot Sonny, but I'd caused his death. I'd never know if the implied threat to my friends justified my action, but I knew I didn't feel good about it. The responsibility for the death of another human being would weigh on me for the rest of my life, and I didn't know if I'd be able to handle it. I doubted I'd be able to sleep, so I took Lumir's gun back to his house.

The back door was still unlocked. I entered, ejected the shells, and put them back in the box with the dud at the bottom. The sawed-off went back against the wall. Not wanting to leave a mess, I swept up the broken dishes, bagged them, and set them out back. After locking up from the inside, I climbed back out the kitchen window, in the process tipping the stepladder and falling to the ground.

I landed on my back. The fall played hell with my already cracked ribs. I lay on the ground groaning, the pain so intense I was unable to form thoughts. I had no idea how much time passed. When my brain engaged, I knew what I had to do. Somehow, I managed to get the unreliable ladder back under the porch, pick up the bag of broken dinnerware, and drive home.

After the Rahbani Sunday dinner, Habi drove his Camaro across town to see Elie Abdo. Elie was a wheeler-dealer, the only one who'd pay cash for something as big as a house. When dealing with Elie, he'd need to keep his wits about him. When it came to finding ways to screw somebody out of a penny, the old man was a master.

He parked the Camaro in the driveway of Elie's house, an older two-story, and rang the bell. Elie answered. Still in his Sunday suit, he smiled and waved Habi inside.

"Habi, I never expected you to make a Sunday afternoon social call. Would you like some coffee?"

"Actually, I'm here with a business proposition," Habi replied.

"Then let's go into the dining room. Ramza and Marilyn are in back watching television."

He followed Elie into the room and sat at the table. He'd never been to the house before. The room, with its dark oak furniture, heavy curtains, and icon corner, felt foreign and uncomfortable. The Rahbanis hadn't kept an icon corner since Habi started high school. Elie's old-fashioned shrine featured a half-dozen icons, a couple of candles and a prayer book.

Habi had trouble associating the distinguished looking, suit-clad Elie with his alter ego, the grizzled old grouch in a worn-out sweater who ran the surplus store downtown. Elie took a seat at the head of the table. Habi sat to his right.

Scenting a deal in the air, Elie wasted no time. Habi realized there'd be no coffee. "So, what do you have for me?"

Habi relaxed. This was more like it. Elie's phony politeness had unnerved him. "I can get you a good deal on a house. The catch is I need cash for it and don't have time for a real estate agent and paperwork."

Elie smiled, showing his yellowed teeth. "You got a house, and you need cash, why don't you go to Baba?"

Pushing a handful of Polaroids across the table, Habi ignored the question. "I got a deal on it and only paid sixteen. I'll sell it to you for thirteen thousand."

"Not much of a house," Elie said as he looked through the photos.

"It's in a great location on Johnson Avenue. You should be able to get eighteen."

"I should be able to get eighteen. I should be able to get a disease too. You think I'm born yesterday?"

"It's in good shape," said Habi. "Eleven."

Elie looked at Habi like a shark who'd scented blood in the water. "You in some kind of trouble?"

Habi started. He felt like the old man had reached into his chest and jammed a finger in his diaphragm.

Elie showed his teeth again. "I should buy a house from George Rahbani's kid instead of sending him home to Baba? Your old man finds out I'm mixed up in deal with you, I could be in big trouble."

"My dad has no idea what I paid for the house or that I don't have a mortgage. He's not gonna care anyway. I'm leaving town."

"You gotta get out of town, you must be in trouble."

"Ten," said Habi. The smirk on Elie's face was getting to him.

"You might need the money real bad," Elie replied, "but I take all the risk. There's no time for anything but a quit claim, and if I run into a title problem, you'll be gone."

Habi leaned forward. "You've known me all my life. Our families go to the same church."

"Kid, I don't trust nobody."

"Nine," said Habi, "and I'll be out in two weeks."

Elie shook his head. "I don't think so. I can't cross your old man —too much risk."

Habi was down to his last chip. "I'll throw in the furniture, everything. There's a new color TV. You can sell the stuff in your store."

A spark of greed flashed through Elie's eyes. "Okay. I'll help you out because I like you. We got a deal if the house is as nice as you say. I'll come by tomorrow afternoon with the paperwork. What's the address?"

Habi gave him the address and, the negotiations over, didn't stick around. Making small talk with a guy who had just given him the shaft wasn't high on his list of priorities. Nine thousand was barely enough to go somewhere and get into the music business, but Sonny owed him a grand, and he had a good-sized stash of dope in the house. He could sell that and live on the proceeds for a few months. It would be tight, but he should be able to hustle his way into something within a year.

Unhappy with the way Elie had treated him, Habi started the Camaro. The greedy old coot could smell his desperation and had broken his bones. He'd fix the old fart. The night he left town, he'd stop up the bathtub and sinks and turn the faucets on full blast. By the time the old rip-off found out about it, the place would be ruined.

Randy Roeder

34

As I walked down Third Avenue to see Suzanne sing at the Fox and Hounds, I considered my options. Three days had passed since I re-injured my ribs falling out of Lumir's window. Although I'd managed to make it through my shifts at Killian's, I wouldn't be dancing for a while. When I asked for time off to recover, my boss at Arthur Murray sacked me for missing too much work. I took it like a man and told him I understood. The guy was temperamental. I planned to wait a few weeks, drop by the studio, and mention I was thinking about going independent. He'd be worried about the competition and hire me back.

As I entered the club, I could see Suzanne LaRue resting one hand on the baby grand as Willard Evans deftly fingered his way through the break on Eddie Cooley's "Fever." Suzanne had chosen a form fitting, spaghetti-strap gown for her appearance. Swathed in the misty smoke of a roomful of cigarettes, blue sequins twinkling on her dress and bare shoulders glowing softly in the lights, Suzanne made for a vision so lovely my rib cage quivered.

And then she sang.

Male or female—it made no difference. Not a person in the place looked anywhere but at the woman putting the song across as if she'd written it. Suzanne smoldered, turning men into besotted fourteen-year-olds and women into vixens hot enough to devastate their guileless lovers. As her friend, I liked to think of myself as immune to Suzanne's charms; but, God forgive me, I wasn't made of granite and lusted unashamed and unrepentant. When she finished her number, I took a deep breath and struggled to recover. I've always had woman friends and can generally keep my wolfish desires at bay, but caging the internal beast isn't always easy.

A professional all the way, Suzanne ended her set with a number guaranteed to leave them wanting more. Her audience saluted her with whistles and generous applause as she nodded, blew a few two-handed kisses, and left the stage to greet friends and well-wishers. I found a table near the back of the room, ordered a bottle of Budweiser, and wished for a cigarette. Given the venue and the entertainment, a cocktail seemed appropriate to the occasion, but having taken the pledge, I stuck with beer.

I'd caught Suzanne's eye when I walked in, and she began working my way as she exchanged pleasantries with the clientele. It took her a while. The club scene in Cedar Rapids isn't all that large, and most of the customers frequenting the Fox and Hounds knew Suzanne well enough to chat. When she got to my table, she gave me a warm smile. I stood and pulled out a chair for her.

"That's one thing I like about you, Cletus. You're polite in the old-fashioned way. Pulling out a chair for me makes it feel like you're happy to see me."

"Well, I am happy to see you."

Suzanne tilted her head and smiled. "Mae West gun-in-your-pants happy?"

"A real bazooka," I said, "loaded for bear."

"Sounds dangerous, your bazooka might discharge."

"It might, if you were bare."

"Cletus, how you lead a poor girl on."

"Indeed I do. Care for a drink?"

Suzanne dropped her eyes, then looked back up. "You always ask, and I always say no. Ever wonder why?" she asked.

"I ask to be polite," I replied, "and I assume you say no because you don't want one."

"When you're a woman working in clubs, almost everyone you meet offers to buy you a drink. If I took them up on it, I'd end up a fat alcoholic who doesn't sing very well."

"Do you want me to quit asking?"

"That would be nice. I still have a drink now and then, when there's something to celebrate, but I've learned my lesson and need to be careful."

"Sounds like a hard lesson."

"Diane didn't tell you?"

"I'm so sorry, Suzanne. I didn't know you had a problem with alcohol."

"I don't, but I have an addictive personality. I had a little issue a few years ago. I'd get wound up when I performed and have problems getting to sleep when I got off. On nights I'd sing, I wouldn't be able to sleep until noon the next day, so my doctor prescribed sleeping pills—Nembutal. At first, they did what they were supposed to do. I'd be a little groggy when I woke up, but I'd be able to sleep when I got home from work. After a few months, it took more pills to get me to sleep, and then I'd feel like I had a hangover in the morning. When I went to my doctor to see if there was anything else I could do, he told me scientists were learning the pills were addictive, and I needed to get off them."

"You're lucky you did. You could have had a real problem," I said.

"Not so lucky," Suzanne sighed. "I quit the pills, but I slept even less than I did before I started taking them. It got so I never slept more than an hour or two at a time. It went on for half a year, and then I ran into Gabby Khoury."

"The Gabriel Khoury who got killed," I said.

"Yeah, he used to come into the Golden Key when he was in town. One night, he told me Nembutal was old-fashioned, and I should try hundred-milligram Seconal. He gave me a couple. I took one that night, and for the first time in months, I got some real sleep. After the way my doctor lectured me about misusing my sleeping pills, I didn't want to ask him for a prescription. I knew Habi Rahbani was Gabby's friend, so I asked him if he could get some for me. Habi told me he could get as many as I needed whenever I wanted them."

"The Rahbani's are mixed up in the drug business?"

"Habi is, but if Georgie found out about it, he'd get so mad he'd probably beat him to death. Habi made me swear I'd never say anything around his old man. To tell the truth, I wanted those pills too much to say anything to anybody. Besides, if George knew I had some dirt on Habi, he might try to hurt my singing career—or maybe even me."

I didn't know what to say. Diane, Suzanne, and I had been friends, but all this was news to me. "I had no idea. Diane never said anything to me."

Suzanne continued. "Anyway, one night I went home, had a few drinks, and took some Seconals. They didn't seem to be working, so I took some more. What with the alcohol and all, I lost count of how many I took. The next thing I knew, I was in Mercy Hospital with an overdose. I went away to a residential program, gave them all my money, and got clean. Getting back to my old self was hard to do."

My heart went out to her. I touched her hand. "Suzanne, whenever things get bad, you can give me a call—anytime. You want to talk, you want to grab a bite, whatever. It'll be okay with me."

"Thank you, Cletus. That's really kind, but those days are behind me. Still, who knows? I might take you up on the offer sometime."

"I'm glad to hear things are going better now," I said.

Suzanne nodded. "At least now I know why they call those pills red devils. I'm careful these days. The doctors didn't tell me not to drink, but they said with my personality, it would be easy to get in trouble with alcohol. I have a couple of drinks a year. I had my last one when I signed my contract with that feel-happy bastard Habi out at Rahbani Booking. He likes to celebrate all his contracts with a drink, and I went along just to stay in his good graces. I don't trust him, so I made him fix my drink in front of me. I wanted to see what he put into it."

"Out at Rahbani Booking?" I asked. "He doesn't run it from the Key?"

"No, Habi uses the office at the Moon Glow, the lounge next to the Ultimate Motel. It's across from K-Mart."

I was still trying to take this all in when the piano player walked back to the small stage, seated himself, and broke into an instrumental version of "Witchcraft." When he finished, Suzanne pushed her chair back, rose, and leaned over to give me a kiss on the cheek.

"Thanks for putting up with my tale of woe, Cletus. What would you like to hear?"

"How about 'I've Got You Under My Skin?'"

Suzanne raised her eyebrows but said nothing. She knew. When Diane and I met at the Key, we enjoyed dancing to Suzanne's cover of the song. In fact, we preferred it to any of the other numbers in her extensive book. Gliding across the floor with an accomplished partner while Suzanne delivered her rendition of "Skin" was an experience not to be missed. Halfway through the song, I rose, and headed for the door. I turned my head and looked back at Suzanne. Unsurprised by my exit, she nodded.

The tears in my eyes were making a break for my cheeks.

I'd promised to keep Stan and Buzz up to date on my investigation, but the attack on Lumir sidetracked me. I needed to remedy the oversight, so I phoned Stan the day after visiting Suzanne at the Fox and Hounds. Eager to get a progress report, he offered to locate Buzz and come over to the apartment that evening. They knocked on the door at 10:30, and I invited them in. Since I was out of beer, I offered a choice of cola or ginger ale. As I got their drinks, Buzz gave Stan the latest news.

"You see KCRG tonight? They did an update on Sonny Sontag. When the police searched his van, it was full of drugs. Hit by two cars —couldn't have happened to a nicer guy. I bet the sucker was so high he thought the cars would bounce off him."

I watched as Stan shook his head. "Sounds like Mother Nature is thinning the herd again. Too bad the dirt bag didn't suffer, but at least Grandpa gets to sleep in his own bed again."

I pulled a kitchen chair over and sat. I hadn't slept more than two hours at a stretch since I'd seen Sonny die and was having trouble keeping food down. Time to change the topic.

"Remember the knife Lumir told you about?" I asked. "The one Eddie Brada found in the dentist's car?"

"Sure," said Buzz.

Stan nodded.

"Well, I know who it belonged to, and it wasn't Gordon Kohl. The knife belonged to a guy named Gabriel Khoury. Somebody murdered him in Des Moines the week before last. Ever heard of him?"

"He was a few years older than me," Stan said. "Everybody called him Gabby. Never amounted to much and always in trouble. Went to reformatory over stealing hubcaps, came back, and hung around town for a few years. Never heard anything more about him until I read about 'em fishing him out of the drink. Just the kind of guy to be mixed up in something like this."

"How did you find out the knife belonged to him?" Buzz asked.

"I found out the three-armed cross on the knife is Greek Orthodox. That seemed odd because Kohl is Presbyterian. I didn't think it was that big a deal, but it bothered Jim Weiss. When Khoury bought the farm, Jim just wouldn't let it go. He knew Khoury was a punk, and when he found out the guy was Orthodox, it settled it for him."

Stan's didn't look convinced. "There could be a connection," he said, "but there's no getting over the fact that Kohl's initials are G. K."

"I thought the same thing, so I showed the knife to George Rahbani. A guy at Kubia's Hardware told me it's an award knife, and since Rahbani's Orthodox, I thought he might know something about it. He recognized the knife right away. He said his cousin Gabriel Khoury won it as an archery prize at church camp."

Buzz's face lit up. "Now we've got something. We can take it to the police department. With that kind of evidence, they'll have a hard time ignoring us."

I felt my face grow red. "Uh, we've got a problem. I don't have the knife any more. George Rahbani has it."

"You gave away the only piece of evidence we have?" His eyes ablaze, Buzz looked at me angrily. "What were you thinking?"

Stan stepped in. "Slow down, Buzz. It's just as likely the police department would use the knife to put the blame on Khoury and close the case without really knowing if he did it."

Buzz's rebuke stung. I felt the need to defend myself. "George Rahbani wasn't about to give the knife back. Jim told me the man is big-time bad news and can make people disappear, so I didn't push it."

Stan ignored me. He stood up and started pacing.

"Guys," I said, "I had no idea he'd keep the knife. He's second cousin to Gabby Khoury and plans to give it to the guy's parents. Even if I wasn't scared shitless, how could I hold out on a murdered man's parents?"

Stan continued walking. "Nobody can touch Khoury anymore. A punk like that might be involved, but he wouldn't be doing the abortions. The police said it takes two men to move a body, so there'd be at least one other person, maybe more. We're no closer to whoever did it than before."

"I've got more," I said. "Stan, why don't you sit down? I think we should talk about the results of the blood tests the Medical Examiner ran on Diane. Sound good?"

Stan sat and rubbed his face. "As good as anything right now."

"The report was technical, so I called a friend at the Coe College Library. She wrote down the blood analysis numbers and asked a chemistry professor about the results. He says Diane was drunk and stoned on barbiturates when she died. She'd have been out of it, barely able to walk, if at all, and possibly unconsciousness."

With this bit of information, the mood in the room began to change. My defensiveness and Stan and Buzz's frustrations faded into insignificance. I looked at Diane's brothers. Although she'd died almost two months ago, the reality of her passing nearly sucked the air out the room. Our eyes met; no one talked. The quiet hum of the kitchen refrigerator grew to a roar.

At last, Buzz broke the silence. "An abortion probably hurts, so you'd probably want to be out of it. Maybe she had to get drunk beforehand to get the courage to go through with it."

"Diane wouldn't do that," I said. "If she was going to take sedatives, she wouldn't drink. It's too dangerous."

Buzz looked over at Stan. "Maybe you should say something."

Stan looked at the floor and back up again. I don't think he expected our conversation to be so hard. None of us did.

"Clete, when Buzz and I cleaned out Diane's apartment, we found three half-gallon vodka bottles. One was nearly empty. We think Diane was on her way to becoming an alcoholic. Something's been wrong with her since late last winter. We'd ask her about it, but she kept telling us everything was just fine."

Last winter—Diane's run-in with Curtis. I couldn't say anything. I promised her I'd take the incident to my grave, and I would.

Stan continued. "Buzz went to Ernie's to see her sing one night. Diane had been drinking. She sang off the beat and couldn't remember the words to her songs. Anyone can slip up, so he thought it was just the one night. Then the bottles ... we didn't know."

A dog barked outside. I leaned forward, rested my forearms on my knees, and looked up. "I heard about it, but didn't want to believe it. She never drank very much around me. Then one night, I went over to Ernie's to talk to the Zmoleks to see if they knew about a boyfriend. They said Diane had started drinking."

I didn't say anything about the Zmoleks' decision to fire her. More silence, more refrigerator.

"What else did you find out?" Thank goodness for Buzz, we might have sat there half the night without talking.

"I know enough to make somebody nervous," I said. "Somebody found out about my investigation, threatened me, and sent thugs to beat me up. Those guys attacked me on the same day I went to the police department to complain about Sonny selling drugs in the city parks."

Stan couldn't quite see it. "Okay, so assume this Sonny has a connection in the Police Department who tells him what's going on, and you get beat up. It might have everything to do with drugs and nothing to do with Diane."

"Possible," I said. "But I got the warnings on my windshield and my tires slashed before I reported Sonny. Somebody is upset about the investigation, and the fact I got beat up the same day I went to Erikson is hard to ignore. Unless Diane had a prescription for the barbiturate in her bloodstream, the drug was illegal."

"Illegal, but not as illegal as LSD," Stan pointed out.

Buzz piped in. "Clete might be on to something. When we cleaned out Diane's apartment she didn't have any prescription containers—just aspirin and stuff like that. No prescriptions."

"I have a theory," I said. "I think the case has everything to do with drugs, and everything to do with Diane. Somebody I know almost died from a barbiturate overdose. She got the drug from Gabby Khoury and George Rahbani's son, Habi. The barbiturate was Seconal, the same drug in Diane's blood stream—."

"I'll kill him!" Buzz struck his hand with his fist. "So help me God, if Habi Rahbani had anything to do with this, I'll kill him."

Stan got up again and stood in front of Buzz. "Slow down, Buzz. Let Clete finish."

"Remember," I said, "this is only a theory. Stan, sit down, you're making me jumpy." As much as I liked Stan and Buzz, they could get on my nerves.

Stan sat.

I held up my hands. "I need you guys to stay cool and help me think this through."

Buzz looked embarrassed. "Sorry."

I continued. "I hear George Rahbani hates the drug business, so Habi sells on the sly. I found a card for the Rahbani booking agency on the back seat when I used Diane's Falcon to keep tabs on Gordon Kohl. I think Diane went there to try to get bookings for the band."

"Makes sense," said Stan. "Diane worked hard to get the Corn-feds booked."

"Habi Rahbani runs the booking agency," I said.

Stan was starting to get it. "Diane knows this Rahbani, and he sells Seconal. There could be some kind of connection."

Buzz looked as if he were ready to jump out of his seat. Stan still hadn't seen it. Buzz did. "The Rahbani's own the Moonglow and the Ultimate Motel. They're across from K-Mart."

"I think we're getting somewhere," said Stan. I could feel the excitement in his voice.

"Remember, I need you two to help me think this through," I said. "Let's not jump to conclusions. The last person who saw Diane was a K-Mart sales clerk. It was about noon, and the clerk said Diane wanted new makeup because she expected to do more singing. After that, no one sees her again."

Stan nodded. "Because she walks across Sixteenth Avenue to talk to this Rahbani, and he kills her."

"Not so fast," I said. "Diane died from a botched abortion. She might have discussed business with Habi Rahbani and gotten tipsy. After that she could have gone to an abortionist where she was sedated and the procedure failed."

"Bull," said Stan, "Rahbani's in it up to his eyebrows. He's got the Seconal. He's got a motel where you could do abortions. He hangs out with punks and criminals."

Buzz leaped from his chair. "Diane didn't have a boyfriend and wasn't even pregnant! He butchered her."

I stood up. "You don't know that, Buzz. Now, sit down—I'm not finished."

Looking surprised by my outburst, Buzz sat.

I continued. "Even if you think we've got it figured out, we don't know what happened. If we go off half-cocked, we could mess things up so badly no one will ever pay for what happened to Diane. I'd like the two of you to brief Lumir and then take a few days to think things through. We can meet at Lumir's next Wednesday night and talk about where we're at. We can decide then if it's time to move ahead with the police, or the county attorney, or the-newspaper— whatever. Okay?"

Buzz and Stan agreed.

"Okay," I said, "one last piece of information. I didn't bring it up earlier because I don't want you guys going bananas. Habi Rahbani has a reputation for forcing himself on the ladies. There's no evidence he touched Diane, no evidence he does abortions, and no evidence he's a killer. What we have is information that would be helpful for a criminal investigation."

With that, I'd finished what I needed to say. We'd all be short of sleep in the morning, so we agreed to break it up.

As Stan walked through the door, he turned and said, "He killed her, Clete."

"We don't know that," I said.

Buzz followed him out. As he walked by me, he stopped to give me a bear hug. Looking at me with tear-filled eyes, he sobbed, "The bastard killed her, Clete. He killed her."

Randy Roeder

35

Earl Erikson drove onto a quiet lane in Van Vechten Park and pulled up behind the green Camaro. More than anything, he wished he'd stayed an honest cop. Watching his boss prosper as he pulled in those nice big payments from George Rahbani had convinced him he deserved a spot on the gravy train too. Things hadn't worked out. Time to pull the plug.

Earl walked up to the car and looked in the window. Habi Rahbani slumped in the driver's seat smoking a joint. Empty beer cans littered the floor. Earl opened the door, reached inside, pulled the punk out, and slammed him against the rear fender.

"What the hell?" said Habi.

"We're through Rahbani. It's over."

"Huh?"

"Be my eyes and ears you said. Let me know what's happening in the department. Make sure my guys don't get busted. I'll make it worth your while."

Habi's eyes were barely tracking.

"So, I think to myself the boy wants his own business—wants to do something without his Daddy. Sell a little weed, give his friend Earl a little money, what could be wrong with that? Little do I know the guy's as dumb as a jackass, lazy as a dead cat, and crazy as a monkey on moonshine. Be my eyes and ears, my ass."

"Something wrong, Earl?"

Earl couldn't believe he'd gone into business with the sack of stupidity who'd just spoken.

"Do you have any idea of the risks I'm taking? Not just on the police side. Every time I do something for you, I cross your old man. I must be crazy."

"That's your problem," Habi quipped.

Earl grabbed him by the shirt collar and slapped him.

"My problem? My problem is I'm doing business with a guy so dumb that when somebody comes to me to complain about his operation, he has his boys pound on him the same damn night."

"You get paid for your risk."

"Paid for my risk? Listen up Rahbani. This guy—me, your eyes and ears, is through. It was bad enough when you cut up that little stripper. 'Take care of it, Earl,' you said. 'Extra money,' you said. I go pick up the body, and I see where you cut her, and I have nightmares ever since. Let me tell you something. There's not enough money in the world to wash that out of my mind."

"It's okay."

Earl slapped him again. "Okay? You think it's okay? Then that Novacek woman. What were you thinking? Your Daddy fixes it with the boss, and I don't get a penny. You screwed me on that one, but I didn't say a thing because it's the boss's deal."

"Listen. Earl, I've got something to tell you."

"No, you listen to me. What kind of an idiot are you? You have Sonny-boy drive around town selling LSD to kids in parks? Then the guy sets up his portable drug store on First Avenue. First Avenue? Are you *trying* to put us all in prison? I'm through."

"Earl, slow down. It's all okay. I don't need you anymore."

"What?"

"I'm leaving town. Keep it under your hat. I'm getting out of this town before it makes me crazy."

Earl took a step back. Although angry that Habi would dismiss him without a second thought, he couldn't believe his good fortune. If things had gotten worse, he'd have had to kill George Rahbani's boy—a dangerous action that could spell his own doom.

"Habi, you can't leave town soon enough for me. Settle up and we're done."

"Just one problem, Earl. I don't have the money."

With Habi, it was always "just one problem." Earl punched the little punk in the gut. Habi doubled over. Earl grabbed him by the hair, lifted his head, and punched him in the gut again. He let go, and Habi dropped to the ground. The detective grabbed Rahbani's belt, rolled him over, and fished the wallet from his jeans. He pulled a wad of cash out of the Syrian's billfold and headed back to the Oldsmobile. Three hundred bucks—not great, but not bad.

Habi Rahbani didn't know how long he sat on the picnic table. The remnants of the hamburger and fries he'd eaten for supper covered his face, hair, and shirt. Earl Erikson could throw a punch, but at least no bones were broken. He stripped off his shirt, wiped his face with the cleanest part of the garment, and struggled back to his car. He checked his watch. Past ten. The park was closed. He had to get out of the place before the cops made one of their regular park checks.

He made it back to the Moonglow. Judging by the cars in the lot, they were having a good night. Even though his manager would be covering for him, he couldn't go in the front door looking like a sewer rat. He parked and walked around to the rear entrance. Someone had broken out the glass, and it looked as if they'd taken a sledge to the lock. He tried to get in, but the door wouldn't budge. Cursing, he walked around to the main entrance. The plate glass front window was covered over with plywood. He pulled on the door and entered. Fady, the club's bouncer, greeted him.

"Where the hell you been?" Fady demanded.

No 'what happened to you,' or 'are you okay?' Just an accusation. Habi didn't need it. "Nice to see you too," he said.

Fady glared at him. "Somebody broke in last night. They rifled your office, took Bobby's cash box, and made off with your safe. We had to call your old man to get the cash to open. He wants you to call as soon as you get in."

Habi rubbed his face with his hands. He'd been so high for the past day and a half he'd neglected the business. His father would be furious. "This hasn't been a good day, Fady. Bring me a towel and a jacket or something. I need to get back to the office."

Habi waited in the entryway. He could see the reflection of the new dancer, Dixie, in the mirror behind the bar. He watched as she danced to her routine's latest number, "Judy in Disguise," while rubbing her breasts with an oversized pair of glasses. The song was okay, but the glasses sucked. He'd have to tell her to lose them.

Fady returned with a t-shirt that must have been used for a rag. Habi put it on. Threading the tables, stopping to greet no one, he made his way back to the office. The room looked like a cyclone had hit. A hole in the wall appeared in the place where his safe had been, no doubt the work of more than one man. The intruders had ransacked the place—opening drawers and cabinets, tossing the contents on the floor. The papers and mementos from his desktop now lay scattered across the carpet. A single item remained on the flat surface, an empty cigarette box—Benson & Hedges.

He'd been so stoned he'd forgotten about Irv and Herm's next interest payment. The cash from the sale of his house was gone.

36

After finishing my shift at Killian's, I walked over to Bishop's Cafeteria to catch a bite. Sonny's death had left me a walking bundle of guilt. Off my feed, I hoped a piece of chocolate pie would convince my jaws that moving up and down was worth the effort. I hadn't felt this lousy since Myra drowned herself, but this time around was worse. I didn't know if I could stand it much longer. Sonny, Diane, Myra, my kids ... A defeated man doesn't have much to look forward to.

As I reached for the cafeteria door, my stomach gave me the 'no way' signal. About to turn around and go home, I heard a familiar voice behind me.

"Evenin' Cletus."

I knew the voice and suppressed a groan. After opening the door and stepping inside, I turned to greet a smiling Pudge Davis holding the door for his wife.

"Good evening, Florian," I said with all the cheer I could muster.

"Layelle, this is Cletus Efferding. I used to run into him on the job pretty regular. Cletus, this is my wife Layelle, and that little fella there's named Edgar."

"Pleased to meet you, Cletus," said Layelle. She turned to coach her son. "Don't hide Edgar. Smile and say hello to Mr. Efferding."

Edgar smiled, said 'hi,' and disappeared back behind his mother.

At this point, I didn't see any socially acceptable option other than to get into the cafeteria line with the Davis family behind me. After the warm introduction Pudge had given me, the situation seemed to call for at least a bit more conversation.

"How's the new job going, Florian?"

Pudge smiled. "Can't complain. Pay's a lot better, and I'm mostly on day shift."

I could see Pudge reveling in my embarrassment. I deserved it.

"How's your project going?" he asked.

He was tweaking me. I had no intention of telling him anything. "It's going. I can't complain either," I said.

"We're back to visit my ma," Pudge said. "We're heading back after church tomorrow."

We reached the point where it was time for me to move ahead and pick up my pie. "Have a safe trip," I said.

Pudge looked down and busied himself with his tray and tableware. Without looking up he said, "Sometimes the department doesn't follow up like it should. It never hurts to talk to the County Attorney when things get bogged down."

"Thanks for the tip, Florian." Nearly overcome with shame and embarrassment, I made a break for the dessert station.

I doubted I'd ever understand Pudge Davis. The man despised me from the moment we met and went on to humiliate me at every opportunity. Fed up with his abuse, I sank to the level of pond scum and tried to get him off my back by threatening to expose the race of his fiancée. Yet today, the man politely introduced me to his wife and child and gave me a valuable tip on how to bypass the police department if my investigation turned up anything useful.

Though no closer to understanding the puzzle that was Pudge Davis, the exercise had gotten me off my preoccupation with my miserable life. I ate the piece of pie that had once seemed more like a threat than a treat. Wrapped up in my thoughts, I hadn't even tasted it.

Hard as it might be, I needed to quit obsessing about Sonny's death. His demise was the last in a series of interlocking events brought about by his own bad judgment. Yes, I pulled the trigger, but the gun had failed. When I couldn't follow through, Sonny got scared and ran in front of a car.

There was plenty of guilt to go around, and no reason for me to take on all of it. I wouldn't have been on the scene if Sonny hadn't tried to knife my friend. Had the police department done their job, Lumir wouldn't have trashed Sonny's car, and Sonny wouldn't have attacked him. If Sonny hadn't sold LSD to children, he'd still be alive.

Maybe he'd dug his own grave, and maybe all I'd done was give him a little push, but the sound of metal on flesh and the sight of Sonny's broken body doing the herky-jerky between cars haunted me.

I stood at the end of Sam and Helene's driveway surveying the scene. They'd set up a big tent in the front yard and hired Joe Abodeely's jazz quartet to provide music—entertainment to make up for a pool party without a pool. Though the contractor had finished the pool ahead of time, the custom pump Sam had ordered from Florida turned out to be defective. Despite the setback, Sam smiled as he came up to greet me. "There's somebody here who says she knows you, and I'm not supposed to let you get away without talking to her."

Sam led me to a spot a few yards from the band where Helene chatted with a few of the other guests. Zora Rohner, the Czech polka champion, turned to greet us.

"Hello," she said. "I ask Mister Sam to see you meet and talk with me."

Sam excused himself and left to greet other guests.

"My goodness," I said. "I didn't expect to see you back in Cedar Rapids."

"Pavel and I, we defect."

"How on earth did you ever manage that?"

"Our—how you say—our minders, they defect too." She shrugged, "We hear Czech government in trouble with Moscow, and maybe they make invasion. It's no good that happens."

A cheerful looking woman interrupted. "Hi. Zora is staying with me while Pavel takes care of paperwork and hunts for a job in the Twin Cities. She's wondering if you could persuade your friend Lumir to do some dancing with her."

"I'd be happy to speak with him."

"There's someone I'd like Zora to meet. Here's my card. Call me when you've had a chance to talk with your friend."

I took the card, pocketed it, and watched as she deftly put an arm around Zora's shoulder and extracted her from the group. A dominant woman who knew her way around a party, she cut Zora from the herd with the precision of a Pecos River cowboy.

"Toodles," she said, wiggling her fingers and leaving the rest of us in wonder at the suddenness of our foreign guest's departure.

Helene shook her head. "Arlene's a real operator. We have a state senator here tonight, and she wants Zora to meet him. She's doing a lot for Zora and her husband. I just hope they survive the experience."

"I'm sure they will but, to change the subject, Abodeely and the boys are swinging. You guys went first class."

Helene's face lit up like a Christmas tree. "You don't think I'd let Sam cheap out on the entertainment after all that digging."

When the band broke into a torrid version of "Night Train," I got happy feet and invited Helene onto the driveway for a little West Coast swing. When the song ended, she asked if I'd make the rounds and invite the single women to dance. Happy to help make the party a success, I agreed and spent the next hour as dance host.

When the evening began to slow down, I made my way over to Sam to thank him for the invitation. He was speaking to a slender, distinguished-looking gentleman wearing blue blazer, repp tie, and white flannel slacks. The conversation centered on the presidential prospects of Hubert Humphrey.

"Cletus," he said, "this is State Senator John Ely, the man responsible for getting Iowa to abolish the death penalty."

I would have responded, but I never got the chance.

"Why Sam," Ely said, "it's not like that at all. Hundreds of people worked long and hard to put an end to the death penalty. I just introduced the bill."

I remembered the fight over the bill had been a humdinger. Ely had taken a lot of heat, and though the measure passed, it remained unpopular. "You got beat up pretty bad on that one," I said. "With so many good causes, why'd you pick it?"

"It picked me. I witnessed a hanging at the state penitentiary. March 15, 1963, Victor Feguer. He killed a doctor for the drugs in his bag."

"Sounds like a bad guy," I said.

"No doubt about it," said Ely. "The federal government chickened out on the execution and asked Iowa to do it for them. The process was so bizarre I didn't think the State of Iowa should be involved in anything like it again."

"How so?" I asked.

"Do you know they give a man a new suit for his hanging? When it's over, they put another new suit on his corpse before they bury him. You've heard about the last meal, right?"

"Sure," I said.

"What you never hear is most men have trouble eating it. Makes sense when you think about. Who'd be hungry when they're going to the gallows. Know what Feguer wanted for his last meal? A single olive, with the pit in it."

"Strange when you think about it," I said. "Show somebody a few bits of consideration so you don't feel bad about killing him."

Ely looked haunted. "They found the olive pit in his suit pocket when they laid him out him for burial. You're involved in something like that, you don't forget. I'll never forget watching him drop. The rope snapped tight, and as he hung in the air, he suddenly took a deep breath. I saw a human life fighting to preserve itself. I haven't been the same since."

The image of an airborne Sonny bouncing over the top of a car flashed through my mind. I stared vacantly, unable to continue the conversation.

Sam came to my rescue. "Clete lost a good friend this summer."

"You look pale, Clete. Are you okay?" asked Ely.

"Sometimes I wonder if I'll ever be okay again."

Habi Rahbani was feeling good as he cruised First Avenue on his way over to the Blue Moon Tavern. A bruise the size of a dinner plate still decorated his abdomen, but he'd quit passing blood. A couple of white cross amphetamines buzzed through him. Alert and ready for the night ahead, he intended to play pool until the place closed. Going on eleven, his favorite hangout would be ruled by the indefatigable matriarch known to regulars as "Ma" Moon. Ma ruled the roost with an iron hand and kept the place in order by use of the well-timed putdown. When Ma let you have it, you became the butt of the barroom's jokes for the rest of the night. You knew better than to cut up.

As he pulled his Camaro up to the Nineteenth Street stop light, a yellow Mustang pulled into the lane alongside him. The driver began revving the car's engine. A challenge.

Habi looked over to see a hot-looking redhead smiling at him. Since his lightweight Camaro had more power than he could handle and drag racing wouldn't get him a date with her, he shook his head sideways. She stuck her tongue out at him. "Stupid broad," he said to himself, "thinks she's God's gift to men." He shook her off again. With that, the driver of the Mustang smiled sweetly and raised her middle finger.

That did it. No way he'd let the little witch flip him off. Habi revved his engine, the light changed, and he dumped the clutch.

The redhead had the jump on him, so he rapped it out until the Camaro sounded ready to explode and then power-shifted into second. Off like a bullet and feeling the amphetamines, Habi whooped as he buried the accelerator. Smiling, closing the gap, he tasted victory—the babe was going down.

He didn't see the pothole. The steering wheel jerked and slid through his hands. As the Camaro fishtailed to the right, he overcorrected, and the view through his windshield shifted from oncoming traffic to an office building. He recovered enough to keep the back of his car from sliding around to the front and tromped the gas pedal again, hoping to straighten his vehicle. It did, but at an angle to the lane. The Camaro jumped the curb and ate a light pole.

Habi awoke in a private room at St. Luke's Hospital. He felt like Cassius Clay and Sonny Liston had used him for a punching bag. From the top of his head to the nails of his toes, his body throbbed. A masculine voice floated somewhere above him.

"Habi."

He opened his eyes. The light was so intense it burned his brain. He closed his lids.

"Habi."

He recognized the voice. "Baba," he said.

"You are lucky to be alive, Habi. They had to cut you out of the car, but not a single bone is broken. You have a concussion. They are keeping you overnight for observation, and I will drive you home where your mama will look after you. I will be gone for a few days on business. You have so many bruises and cuts you look worse than a dead man. You frightened your mama so much she went hysterical, almost crazy. I had to send her home. She can cry there as well as here, and at home, your sisters can look after her."

Habi groaned.

His father's voice hardened. "Drag racing! What is wrong with you? You are lucky you didn't kill someone. You were awake when they brought you in, raving about some woman. They gave you pain medication that put you to sleep. The police will be coming to talk to you. Do not talk to them unless our lawyer is here. With luck and money, maybe we can save your driver's license."

"Did they catch her?" asked Habi.

"Who?"

"The girl in the other car."

"You wrecked your car drag racing with a woman? Habi, I wait and wait for you to become a man, but it never happens. It is time you married." George Rahbani sighed. "Give me the name of your insurance agent. I will start the paperwork."

"I don't have insurance, Baba."

George Rahbani rubbed his forehead. "Habi, you have disappointed me lately and now this. You realize that not only have you lost your car, but even if we save your license, there will be a fine or bribe to pay. Do you know you broke that light pole, and you must pay for a new one? I will not bother to ask you about hospital insurance, because I don't want to know your answer. I expect you will have to sell your house and motorcycle to get yourself out of this trouble."

Habi let out a groan that dwarfed all his previous efforts. His father returned home and went back to bed.

George Rahbani fidgeted with his pen as he waited for Habi. His business trip had not gone well. His son's blunder with the Novacek woman had set in motion a series of events beyond anything he'd anticipated. For the first time in thirty years, he faced a setback that threatened to destroy his business, ruin his standing in the Lebanese community, and force his family into economizing. He shook his head sadly. He had no alternative but to cut Habi loose. There was a knock on the door. For once Habi was on time.

"Come in, Habi," he called as he steeled himself for a conversation he'd hoped would never take place.

"Good morning, Baba," Habi looked cheerful as he took a seat on the other side of the desk.

"Habi, I have some bad news, and you will not like what I have to tell you."

"Is Mamma okay?" Habi asked.

"Your mamma is fine. This is about business. Your mistake with the Novacek girl has caused no end of trouble. Fixing the problem cost more than I ever expected."

"I am sorry for the trouble I have caused you, Baba."

"You know I didn't have much money in the Golden Key," George continued. "The club was a short-term lease, so when the building was taken for urban renewal, I got nothing. I hoped to invest in a new club, but the money for that operation has gone to keep you out of trouble. Now everything but the fixtures will be sold at auction, and that money, too, must go to the payoff."

Habi looked at him with astonishment.

"I have more bad news. Even with the money from the auction, I do not have enough to get you off the hook. The motel and lounge will have to go. I won't get a good price, because I can't wait for the right buyer. The fixer wants his final payoff in October. After I pay him, there may not be enough left over to see your sisters graduate from Bryn Mawr and Radcliffe."

Habi planned to be long gone by October. Still, if he played his cards right, he might persuade his father to give him a small loan. "But Baba," he said, "without the motel and Moonglow, what will I do? I need money."

His father looked at him with disbelief. Habi watched him turn and walk to a table where he picked up a stack of G & HR Enterprises cards.

"Our business cards," his father said as he threw them up into the air.

Habi watched as they fluttered to the floor.

"What will you do?" his father said softly. "What will you do?"

The words echoing in his head, Habi looked down at the cards scattered on the carpet. He heard a grunt and looked up to see a large green object hurtling toward him. He turned his head, but not soon enough. The lamp from the end table struck him on his forehead.

When Habi's head cleared, he found himself still seated in his chair. He pulled out his handkerchief, and held it to his head. It came away bloody but not soaked. His father threw a box of tissues to him. "Our business cards are no good anymore. I am dissolving the corporation."

"What?"

"I know you are using drugs and can't be trusted. Your mama, your sisters, and I will be the new shareholders. You will work tonight at the hotel and Moonglow as usual. Gus and I will take over tomorrow and begin to wind the business down. You will not fight me on this. I have used your share to save you from prison. You are still my son. Nothing will change that, but I can no longer afford to have you as a partner."

"I need money so I can start something new. Maybe I can get a loan?"

"No loan. You can keep anything left over when you sell your house and motorcycle."

Habi broke into a sweat. The house and motorcycle were gone. "But it won't be enough."

"Then you will need to find a job. I will not hire you. Maybe you can wash dishes. If it was good enough for me, it is good enough for you."

Numb from shock, Habi had no reply. He knew his father. Baba meant every word he said, and all the forces of hell wouldn't be enough to convince the old man to give him a loan.

37

The day of our strategy meeting Stan called and cancelled. I didn't mind; our discussion would keep for a day or two. In fact, I planned to call it quits. I'd tried to kill a man. His death hung over my head every waking minute. I didn't know what the Sedlaks had in mind, but I would advise following up on Pudge's hint and dump what we'd learned into the lap of the county attorney.

I hit the bed a half hour after I got home from the dance studio. One of these nights, my body would give out, and I'd have to sleep. I logged in some pretty good hours until two a.m., when the police arrested me for driving around town with one of Sonny's arms stuck to the roof of the Nova.

"It's the body parts that always give guys like you away," the sergeant said. "They stick to everything."

Not much chance of sleep after a dream like that. I resigned myself to another night of lying on the bed with eyes open, looking at the ceiling. The phone rang at three. Probably a drunk, but happy for the distraction, I answered.

Buzz didn't take time for niceties. "We need you over at grand-pa's right away."

"What's wrong?" I asked. Too late. Buzz was gone.

I tried again. No answer. A minute and a half later, I closed the front door and made for the car. Something had to be terribly wrong.

Lumir's house was dark when I got there. I rushed up and pounded on the front door. I rang the bell. Nothing. I ran back to the car, opened the trunk, grabbed a tire iron, and made for the back of the house. As I rounded the back porch, I noticed a thin shaft of light showing beneath the shop door. There should have been light showing through the window. It must have been completely covered—perhaps even boarded over from the inside. I didn't like the setup one bit.

I rapped three times on the door, stepped to the side, and raised my tire iron. Buzz opened up. If I hadn't known him so well, I don't think I'd have recognized him. The shop was so poorly lit that the corner street light provided better illumination than what was in use inside. My instinct for self-preservation took hold, and I stepped back.

"Get in, quick," said Buzz.

"What's going on?" I asked. "Is everything okay?"

"Just get in. We don't have all night."

I stepped into the shop. As I surveyed the room, I could make out Lumir and Stan leaning against the workbench. An inefficient, battery-powered lantern next to Lumir's coffee pot glowed feebly.

"Nobody messes with a Sedlak," Stan announced as Buzz closed the door and clicked the lock.

Buzz pointed to a hangman's noose dangling from the beam supporting the building's loft. "Time to put things right," he announced.

What did they think I had done? A shot of adrenalin raced through me but wasn't up to the task. Everything went black. A sharp slap on the cheek brought me back to reality. As I came around, somebody cracked my face again. I looked up and saw a face staring down at me from the shadows.

"We got the stinking snake," somebody said. "He's going to talk, or he's going to hang."

I started shaking like a leaf. A hand waved back and forth in front of my face. "How many fingers am I holding up?"

"Three."

"He'll be okay in a minute or two. Then we can get on with it."

"You okay?" somebody asked.

"What?"

"We knew you'd want to be here but didn't know the excitement would get to you like that."

I looked around the room, unable to comprehend. I saw Lumir uncoiling an electric cord. He plugged in a trouble light. Things got brighter.

As Buzz helped me up, Stan pointed to a figure seated in a chair at the edge of the circle of light. I put two-and-two together and finally came up with four. The guy in the chair must be Habi Rahbani. I'd seen him at the Key a few times, but given the state he was in, I doubted even his friends would have recognized him. His matted hair stuck out in all directions. One of his eyes had swollen shut.

The Sedlaks had tied him to one of Lumir's guest chairs and stuffed a rag into his mouth. Although I'm no great shakes as a Christian, I felt as if I should have at least a little pity for the guy. Somehow, I didn't.

"Stan brought his fancy-schmantzy tape recorder over," Lumir explained. "Since the police will not do their job, we will question this Rahbani and put it on a tape. This, they will not be able to ignore."

Habi Rahbani's nose made a snorting sound. Buzz slapped him. Hard.

"How'd you get him here?" I asked.

"We picked him up," said Lumir. "We waited until his bar closed, and when he came out, Stan threw a blanket over him. Buzz had to hit him to quiet him down. They tied him up and put him in the back of the pickup."

"Grandpa drove," Buzz explained. "I rode in the box to make sure Slime-O didn't try to sit up. I had to thump him a few times to keep him quiet. We knew you'd want to be here, but we gotta hurry. It'll be light in a couple of hours."

Lumir looked at me and pointed to a chair. "You better sit down. You took quite a bump on the noggin. You might fall again."

He was right. I sat.

With that, Lumir cleared the table next to his workbench. "Bring him over here."

Stan and Buzz walked over to Rahbani, picked him up chair and all, and deposited him behind the table. Stan handed Buzz a plastic bread bag and began fiddling with the ropes that bound Rahbani to the chair. When he finished, one of the captive's arms was free. The Sedlaks had planned carefully. I felt like a third wheel, horrified, unsure of my role, but wanting to help.

"Anything I can do?" I asked.

"We owe you much," Lumir replied as he snipped the ends of several small tubes and placed them on the table. "You rest for now."

I recognized the tubes—super glue. Buzz put on the bread bag over his hand as Lumir squeezed the contents of the tubes onto the table.

Lumir finished. "Okay, now," he said.

"Cooperate, Slime-O," Buzz said as he forced Rahbani's hand down into the glue.

Lumir seemed concerned the glue might not bond. "Hold it down for a couple of minutes to be sure. I have never tried the glue on skin before."

The Sedlaks waited silently to see if the glue would hold. I looked over at the hangman's noose and counted the perfectly formed coils above the loops—thirteen. "Who did the noose?" I asked.

"I did," said Stan.

"Junior high?"

"Yup. Picked it up in study hall."

"I think the glue's set." Buzz removed his hand from the bag. It stuck to Rahbani's hand. When he ripped it off, a few strips of plastic stuck to the back of the prisoner's hand. "Okay, Grandpa," he said.

Lumir wheeled his captain's chair to a position opposite Rahbani and laid a carpenter's hammer on the table top. He sat down, picked up the hammer, and stared Rahbani in the eye.

"We do not have all night, Mr. Rahbani. We know you killed Diane. You are here to make a confession. My grandson will make a tape recording for the police. If you do not confess, we will hang you from that rope over there. Nod, if you understand."

Rahbani nodded.

Lumir continued. "Before we remove the gag from your mouth, you must understand one thing: you must speak into the microphone we place on this table and you must do so quietly. We will remove the rag from your mouth. You must not call out when we do. Understand?"

Rahbani nodded again, and Lumir reached for the hammer. He held it four or five inches above Rahbani's hand and let it drop. It landed on a fingernail. Rahbani jerked, screamed into his gag, and began shaking.

"Like that Slime-O?" Buzz cackled.

An unhappy Lumir turned to Buzz and spoke in a low, harsh voice. "Enough! We are not animals who enjoy giving pain. We would not be here if the police had done their job. The man must simply understand that if he cries out, the rag will go back in his mouth and the hammer will drop again."

I had trouble coming to grips with the scene I'd just witnessed. I loved the Sedlaks. Seeing what they were prepared to do to Diane's killer shocked me. Not that I wasn't on their side, but it hurt me profoundly to see the people I loved reduced to the level of vigilantes in their search for justice. I couldn't help but see things were going to end badly—whether for Rahbani or the Sedlaks.

Stan removed the gag. Rahbani as much as confessed with the first words out of his mouth.

"She saw the drugs, and she thought she was too good for me," he blurted.

The Sedlaks had done a good job getting to this point, but in their anger and grief, they'd given little thought to what might come afterward. If I kept their attention focused on getting the confession on tape, their captive might live to see the light of day. I cut in.

"My name's Clete, Habi. Let's start at the beginning. When was the first time you saw Diane Novacek that day."

Rahbani looked at me with his good eye. "She just showed up at my office at the Moonglow, just after lunch. She opened the door and walked right in. Didn't knock or anything. I forgot to lock it. I was packaging—had all my stash out—everything. She saw it all."

"Packaging? Stash?" asked Lumir.

"Drugs." I said. "Dividing batches of drugs into smaller lots for resale."

"She couldn't miss what was going on. I had piles of red devils and white crosses all over the top of my desk. There must have been ten bricks of marijuana on the floor. I didn't know what she was thinking, but since she wanted to be a singer, I thought she might not care. She couldn't take her eyes off them."

"Red devils and white crosses?" I asked for Lumir's benefit.

"Seconal and amphetamines. Anyway, she wanted to talk to me about booking her and those dimwit Zmoleks. See, she asked me to come see them at Ernie's. I did, but they stunk up the place bad. I hoped she wouldn't follow up. She didn't know how to sing. On top of that, she had too much to drink and got tangled up in the cord for the mic."

Rahbani started shaking and began to cough. "Water?" he asked.

"I'll give you water, you son of a bitch!" Buzz started for him.

"No!" Lumir's command stopped his grandson in his tracks. "He will have water."

Stan spoke up. "Cool down, Buzz. Now I have to back up the tape and erase what you said."

Lumir went for the bucket and dipper he kept in his shop. When he held the dipper up to Rahbani's mouth, the guy gulped the stuff like a tormented soul suffering the fires of eternal damnation.

I held my questions while Stan fiddled with the recorder. When he gave the signal, I started in again. "Okay, let's get back to your office. What next?"

"She asked me to sign her, and I said 'No.' That's when things got interesting. She says, 'I think you will,' waves her hand at the stuff on my desk, and smiles at me. The stupid slut tried to blackmail me."

Lumir brought his hammer down with a crack. The microphone flew into the air, and the wooden table top split from one side to the other. His fingers just inches away from the point of impact, Rahbani jumped within his bonds. He wasn't the only one—I nearly wet myself.

"I have a hammer," Lumir said, "and we have a new rule. From now on you will call my granddaughter Diane. Do you understand?"

Rahbani nodded.

"Guys," I said, "call of nature. Break?"

"I need to get that off the tape anyway," said Stan. Buzz needed a break as badly as I and joined me outside at the lilac bushes. The wind from the approaching storm had us facing east.

"To Wilson & Company," said Buzz as he let loose a stream. He'd once worked there. Apparently, he enjoyed his tenure as much as I did.

"Ditto, and then some," I added and irrigated the shrubbery. A flash of lightening and clap of thunder answered in agreement.

We re-entered the shop. Lumir had repositioned the trouble light so it shone directly in Rahbani's face. The guy actually looked a little better than he did in the shadows. He had a heck of a shiner, but his nose looked okay. The improved illumination revealed a wet spot on the front of his pants.

"Slime-O! Looks like we should have invited you outside with us," Buzz said by way of a greeting.

Stan had to take that off the recorder too. When he pointed to me, I jumped back in. "Diane pressured you to get a contract. What then?"

"I decided to kill her."

"Just like that?" I asked.

"My old man knows a lot about business. One of his rules is, 'Never pay blackmail. They'll bleed you until they have everything.' On something like that, he's always right."

I wanted to argue—Diane would have pressed an advantage, but a hardcore blackmailer she was not. Still, we had enough on the tape to send the guy away for good. "What happened then?" I asked.

"I agreed to represent her and invited her into the bar for a drink to celebrate. We were closed until six. I knew the b... ah, Diane, liked her booze. She wanted a martini, so I made her a double. Then another. It wasn't long before she asked for the restroom. I broke down some Seconal capsules and started adding them to her drinks. She kept putting 'em right on down. By four o'clock, she was falling out of the booth."

I knew what was coming. The guy took Diane to a room. Not willing to pass on an opportunity, he made a pass at her, and she was conscious enough to reject him. It didn't matter, he'd have killed her anyway.

Rahbani must have known something about abortions—he faked the one that ended her life. I knew his interrogation would become a train wreck in slow motion. By the time he finished, he'd have talked the Sedlaks into killing him. I couldn't let it happen.

I leapt from my chair. "You bastard!" I screamed and tackled the guy so hard I knocked him over. The impact ripped his glued hand from the table. As we hit the floor, I hissed in his ear. "Shut up, stupid. Shut up!"

Buzz pulled me off Rahbani, and Stan tipped the captive and his chair back upright.

Lumir looked at me and spoke. "Clete, you need to calm down. Now we will need to get that off the tape."

"We have enough to get the case reopened anyway," I said.

"No way," said Buzz. "The more the little slime talks, the tighter the case."

Stan, already rewinding the tape, agreed. "We need as many details as possible."

Buzz cracked his knuckles. "Sounds like you're back in the hot seat, Slime-O. Confess your scumbag eyeballs out."

Rahbani's hand looked like raw meat. His good eye flashed with anger. "You guys think you're such a big deal. There's no way any court will take a forced confession. Then you have a little matter of kidnapping and assault to do great bodily harm." He spat. "Bush league."

I buried my face in my hands. The stupidest guy on the face of the earth didn't know when to keep his mouth shut.

Rahbani continued digging his grave. "Do you think anybody in this town is going to lay a finger on George Rahbani's son? My old man owns the police force. Somebody crosses him, he never forgets. When he comes for you, there'll be nobody to protect you, nowhere to hide. By the time he finishes, you'll wish that no-talent drunken whore had never been born."

Habi Rahbani had just called Diane a whore. To top it off, he'd just made the best possible argument for killing him.

"Don't you think we're rushing things a bit?" I'd been silent after my outburst, watching from my chair as my friends prepared for Rahbani's execution. As far as I was concerned, the guy had it coming. But the Sedlaks didn't deserve what it would do to them. They weren't like Rahbani. They'd feel they'd accomplished something for a day or two, but then the guilt would set in. Lumir would handle it best—he'd served in the First World War. Regret would eat the hotheaded Buzz alive. Stan would bottle it up inside and turn into a robot. Their remorse would affect their marriages. Habi Rahbani wasn't worth it.

Apparently, no one thought we were rushing things. My question went unanswered. The Sedlaks removed their captive from the chair, re-tied him, and laid him on the floor under the noose. I watched from my seat, shaking and quietly sobbing. Rahbani would-n't cooperate. He went limp and wouldn't stand up. Stan took a length of two-by-six from Lumir's woodpile and tied the guy to it so his hips and knees wouldn't bend. Lumir put the noose around Rah-bani's neck. Stan and Buzz lifted the guy up on a chair while their grandfather took the slack out of the rope and tied the free end around a post. The operation took place in silence.

"Stop!" I screamed at the top of my lungs.

For the first time in a quarter hour, someone paid attention to me. "What's the problem, Clete?" asked Lumir.

I made up something on the spur of the moment. "You're do-ing it wrong."

"What?" asked Stan.

"Give him time to pray." I was desperate.

Buzz looked at me, his eyes filled with anger. "Like that would do the guy any good."

Lumir held up his hand. "Clete is right, we must give the man time to get right with his God."

I improvised. "There's something important I haven't told you, and I can't say it in front of him. You need to know before we do any-thing. Let's go outside for a minute. After that we can come back in-side and take care of what needs to be done."

Lumir, Stan, and Buzz looked at each other.

"You mean, he didn't do it?" Stan asked.

"Just a minute, outside," I pleaded.

"Make it fast," Buzz muttered as he led us out the door.

Leaving Rahbani on the chair, we exited the shop. Clearly an-noyed, my friends stood opposite me, their arms crossed. I only had one chance, and I'd better make it good.

"I'm not the man you think I am. I killed Sonny Sontag."

Silence.

"I had a shotgun and pulled the trigger. The shell was a dud. He ran out into traffic to get away from me."

Buzz broke the silence. "What the—"

Stan interrupted him. "Buzz, over here," he said gesturing with his head.

They walked to the lilac bushes some forty feet away and began talking in low tones.

Lumir and I stood across from one another. "Why are you telling us this?" he asked.

"There's more. I killed my wife. She committed suicide because I got arrested for visiting a prostitute. Because of that, I have two kids I can never see again. I stole your shotgun and went after Sonny so he'd quit coming after you."

Lumir said nothing.

"I know guilt, Lumir. And I know how it eats away at you until there's nothing left. I've lived with nothing but guilt since I left Bellevue. Now, with Sonny's death on me, the days get so bad I don't think I'll make it to sundown. At night, it's even worse. Don't do it. Think of Buzz and Stan carrying that kind of guilt every day for the rest of their lives. What will it do their marriages? What about children? Their memories of Diane? Think of your own peace of mind."

Stan and Buzz walked back over.

"Nothing's changed. Let's do it," Stan said. "Clete, you can wait outside if you don't want to watch."

Lumir cleared his throat. "Clete and I don't want to kill Rahbani."

The noose around his neck, Habi Rahbani stood on the chair, watching his captors leave the building. They'd brought him to a woodworking shop. If he could get off this damned chair in one piece, there'd be all kinds of tools he could use to free himself from his bonds. Some of them would make good weapons. The first step would be to work one arm loose. He struggled against the ropes. They were secure. He had no chance to free himself before the men came back.

His captors didn't get it, but the dance man seemed to be trying to save his life. The guy was his last chance. Talk about the only piece of luck he'd had lately. To think he'd almost had his guys from Waterloo kill the fool instead of beating him.

The last few weeks had been a living hell. First Gabby got killed. Then Irv and Herman show up at the Moonglow to squeeze him for Gabby's debts and threaten to kill his family. When he needed cash, Elie Abdo screwed him on the sale of his house. After that, Sonny got killed and couldn't pay him the money he owed. Now Baba wanted money, but Irv and Herm had taken it all. Worse yet, they wanted to muscle their way into the Moonglow when his old man expected to sell. He needed to leave town fast. Baba would have to take care of himself.

What a brick. Before he killed the Novacek woman, he had money, a house, and good wheels. He partied with strippers and had access to the best drugs in town. Opportunity beckoned. Now, even if the dance man saved him, he had nothing.

He'd never get out of Iowa.

I knew I'd won when Lumir announced he didn't want to hang Rahbani. His grandsons revered him. They might try to bulldoze their grandpa, but when push came to shove, Lumir was top dog. My problems weren't over. Things had gone so far that releasing Rahbani would be a complicated affair.

"I can't see how we can get away with letting him go," said Stan. "He can go to the police and charge us with kidnapping, or he can have his old man come after us. I don't know which would be worse."

"He deserves to die." Buzz's anger hadn't cooled.

"And you don't deserve a lifetime of guilt," I said to Buzz. "Not you, not Stan, and not Lumir. I'm not so hot on the idea myself."

Buzz doubled his fists. "After what you just told us about yourself, I don't know if we can trust you."

"Buzz!" snapped Lumir. "Hear the man out."

"I can understand," I said. "But I know something you don't. I know what's it's like to spend every day of your life feeling bad about something you've done. I know you Buzz. You're not like Rahbani. In a week or two, it'll start to eat at you. You'll have trouble sleeping, food won't taste like it did. Nothing will be the same."

Stan spoke up. "Nobody ever said justice would be easy."

"I know something else you don't," I continued. "George Rahbani hates drugs. He doesn't want anything to do with them. Suzanne LaRue told me he'd go berserk if he found out his son was involved with them. We have Habi talking about drugs on tape. We have him talking about murder on tape. He can huff and puff all he wants to, but he'd be hard put to go to his old man or the cops."

Buzz's hands had relaxed. "I don't know," he said.

Lumir stepped in, his timing impeccable. "Let's go in and talk to this Rahbani."

I led the way back inside and stopped in my tracks. Habi Rahbani dangled from the rope, swinging back and forth alongside a toppled chair.

"No!" I screamed and ran forward. I put my arms around him and lifted him up.

Stan and Buzz stood frozen in the doorway.

Lumir yelled, "Somebody get a knife. Cut him down."

Stan moved fast. My eyes registered a blur as he rushed to the workbench, grabbed a hunting knife, and righted the chair. He hopped onto it and sawed furiously on the rope while I held Rahbani.

"Buzz," I pleaded, "help me!"

Diane's beefy brother rushed to my side.

"Take him," I said.

Buzz took the weight just as the rope parted. As he eased Rahbani to the floor, I struggled frantically to loosen the noose. The guy wasn't breathing. I started mouth-to-mouth resuscitation as soon as Buzz set him down. Working furiously, I blew in, counted, and repeated.

Lumir touched my shoulder. I ignored him and kept counting and blowing.

"Clete," he said softly, "the man is dead."

Randy Roeder

38

I stretched on the crisp, scented sheets of a luxurious double bed. The smell of coffee drifted in from the kitchen. Eight months had passed since Habi Rahbani had gone to whatever fate awaits murderous punks in the afterlife. My friends and I would never know if he'd fallen off the chair or killed himself.

Though he didn't deserve it, I'd done everything I could to save the man. The Sedlaks would have to find a way to work through the despair and self-doubt that accompany guilt. They'd put themselves into the same position I'd been in when I'd gone after Sonny. They intended to kill Rahbani, pulled back too late, and he died anyway. Their last-minute change of heart couldn't alter the fact he'd still be alive if they hadn't put a rope around his neck.

I didn't know it, but when I worked so hard to save Rahbani, I saved myself. I'd been willing to sacrifice my friendship with the Sedlaks to protect Habi from them, and them from themselves. They'd know guilt, but nothing near what they would have experienced if they'd kicked the chair out from under him. I'm no great thinker, but as far as I was concerned, my attempt to save Rahbani went a long way toward making up for what happened to Sonny. I doubted Diane's church would agree, but that was their problem. I'd take what I could get.

I expected the revelations about my past and my resistance to the hanging would break my friendship with the Sedlaks. It didn't happen. Their reaction to Myra's suicide had been "Why on earth didn't you tell us?" Although Buzz and Stan had a lot to work through, they realized why I'd tried to talk them out of killing Habi. I couldn't get a read on how Lumir felt about the events of the night. A guy who's gone through the horror of a World War is pretty tough. He thanked me for finding Diane's killer and working to save his grandsons' peace of mind.

The clock radio went off. I'd set it for KCRG, in time for the eight o'clock news. The announcer led off with the police report.

A spokesman for Cedar Rapids police confirmed yesterday the department still had no leads in the murder of Habi Rahbani. Police were called to the REA dam south of the city in mid-September after a fisherman reported an object resembling a body bobbing up and down in the circular currents below the spillway.

The badly decomposed remains were sent to the Linn County Medical Examiner where dental records were used for identification. Citing the nature of Rahbani's injuries and the fragments of cord attached to the body, the Examiner's Office reported the cause of death as homicide by a person or persons unknown.

Frustrated by the lack of evidence, the Police Department once again asks anyone with information on the whereabouts of Habi Rahbani on August seventh to contact the Detective Bureau. The Rahbani family has offered a ten-thousand-dollar reward for information leading to the prosecution and conviction of the killer.

Nothing I hadn't heard before. Must have been a slow news day. According to Stan, Habi floated loose because Lumir planned it that way. He'd seen what happened to families when a son went missing in war and couldn't bear the thought of the Rahbanis wondering about Habi for the rest of their lives. Lumir knew quite a bit about how bodies behave in water. During the war, he'd been assigned graves detail and fished more than his share of doughboys and Tommies from muddy, godforsaken French rivers after the big battles. He tied Rahbani with enough weight to keep him underwater long enough to destroy evidence, but he'd attached the weights with thin cotton cord that wouldn't hold up to conditions.

I put the Rahbani mess in a box and shoved it to the back of my mind. It was a new morning and time to think about the day ahead.

I heard approaching footsteps.

"Good morning, Sunshine." Suzanne walked into the room tightening the bow on her satin kimono. "Breakfast out, or in?"

"In," I said and grabbed her around the waist to pull her back into bed.

Lumir and Stan had convinced me to go for counseling. After talking it out until I was blue in the face, I realized I'd messed up royally, but Myra had taken her life because of a serious illness. For the first time since her suicide, I understood that a woman who slept with me might regret the experience, but she'd be unlikely to kill herself afterward.

Suzanne put her arms around me and giggled.

"Oh, Cletus," she said, "you're insatiable."

Acknowledgments

A big thank you goes to Jim and Shirley Theiss and John and Betty Rogers who spent hours giving me a feel for life in 1960s Cedar Rapids. Without their help, I would never have caught the ambience of the place. Every writer needs a muse, and Betty excelled.

Though events in the book have nothing to do with them, I'd like to thank those who served as inspirations for the story's characters. All are good sports. Jim and Shirley Theiss appear in much-altered form as Jim Weiss and his sister-in-law Shirley. International polka champions Pavel and Zora Rohner came to life after an evening on the dance floor with Paul and Zora Ronan. Sue Duffy inspired cabaret singer Suzanne LaRue, a character with whom she has nothing in common. And save for one detail, Sam and Helene Auld are unlike Sam and Helene Olds. Like their fictional counterparts, the Aulds dug their swimming pool by hand.

As state senator, John M. Ely worked tirelessly to abolish capital punishment in Iowa. The information about him is courtesy of Wikipedia and Carey Goldberg's "Federal Executions Have Been Rare but May Increase," in the New York Times, May 6, 2001. The quotes on the Feguer execution are Ely's, paraphrased for the sake of the story. The location of the conversation and the conversation itself are fictitious.

I'd like to thank my editors, Shannon Ryan and Ronda Swolley, for wrangling my prose, and those who commented on the draft: Nancy Kraft, Cuin Ferrin, Bill Hart, Dylan Moonfire, Cassie Moore, Stacie Sugioka, Nick Tharalson, Aime Wichtendahl, and Laura Bosley Whitmore. Bill, especially, went above and beyond the call of duty.

And Jenn, thank you for the wonderful cover design.

Coming in 2018

Cletus Efferding is back!

Seven years older and on his first real vacation in over a decade, Cletus Efferding finds himself entangled in a web of deceit going back nearly a century when a down-and-out fisherman discovers an antique coffin on a sandbar south of his home town.

The fisherman's mysterious discovery and a lucky purchase at an estate auction make for pleasant vacation diversions, but when a pair of semi-retired hitmen show up, Clete's summer holiday turns ugly. Caught up in a network of lies and unable to make sense of a cold-blooded killing, Cletus realizes he just might just need the cemetery plot his parents bought for him.

You won't want to miss Cletus Efferding's next adventure when he comes face to face with his family's ...

Sins of Omission

http://randyroeder.com/

CPSIA information can be obtained
at www.ICGtesting.com
Printed in the USA
FFOW03n1120200917
40057FF